Best Man Falling

a novel by
Patrick Driscoll

Copyright © Patrick Driscoll, 2017
Cover design by Tom Holt

ISBN: 9781520876177

*For Susan and Raymond Driscoll -
for buying me that old, clunky typewriter and never once
complaining about the racket it made.*

1. This Page Intentionally Left Blank

We're sitting at the bar of The Shoemaker's Arms when Dave asks me to be his best man. I'm aware I should be experiencing some gushing sense of pride – this ancient baton of honour passed between men throughout the centuries – but really I'm wondering what exactly the role will require, how much it will set me back gross, and why a more suitable candidate hasn't been selected. There's the speech to consider, the stag do to organise, and all of this before the fact I'm not entirely sure Dave is marrying the right girl at the right time for the right reasons. It brings a certain treachery to proceedings, like how the England boys must have felt giving the Berlin *sieg heil* in '38.

"What about your brother?" I ask. "Won't he be offended?"

"Nah, he wouldn't want to do it anyway. He'll only get pissed."

"Your uncle? Or Simon?"

"Simon? The only time I see Simon these days is when the MOT comes round. Are you seriously suggesting I ask my mechanic to be my best man?"

"I just don't want to be treading on anyone's toes, that's all."

"Eddie, you're my best mate. Makes sense you're my best man as well, don't it? Of course I want you to do it."

"Well, I'm honoured, Dave. God. Really, I am…"

"Good! That's that settled, then. Just don't go mentioning Amsterdam in the speech." He laughs and punches me on the arm. "Reckon this calls for another round, eh?"

And there it is: signed, sealed and delivered.

My head's spinning. I feel hot and itchy beneath my clothes.

"Who'd have thought it, eh?" Dave asks. "A twat like me settling down and getting married."

"Yeah, who'd have thought it?"

Dave laughs again and calls over Vic The Barman. Vic The Barman is a great slab of a man, with a soft, gelatinous face always set on full-beam. He's been serving us drinks here since before we were legally old enough to procure them, so it's fair to say we've got a lot of love for the guy. He's the kind of man you'd like in a father were it not for the questionable hygiene or the borderline alcoholism. Actually, Vic has four kids by two different women and hasn't sent out a child-support cheque in over a decade, so he's probably precisely *not* the kind of man you'd want as a father unless you liked eating fish-fingers for dinner every night. But he does make a good barman. The best.

"Hey, Vic," Dave calls. "Eddie's just agreed to be my best man."

I'm not entirely sure where the agreeing part had come into it.

"Well, now that's sound news, Eddie. Good on yer, son."

He offers a meaty hand across the bar and I shake it. For me, handshakes are for the closure of big business deals, Prime Ministerial victories, the winner of the Formula One Grand Prix Championship. I've achieved precisely nothing and already people are shaking my hand over it. It becomes quickly apparent that this best man thing is going to take some getting used to.

"You alright, Eddie?" Dave asks. "Looking a bit peaky."

"Yeah, fine. Just a bit overwhelmed by it all, I suppose."

"Ha! You soft sod." He clinks his glass against mine.

Dave's been my best mate since we were seven years old, and I suppose in many ways hasn't changed a bit since the day I met him. Dave with his boyish charm and his puppyish need for everything to be okay. And if it's not okay, he makes it okay. I can't ever remember seeing Dave truly upset. I mean, I've seen him *upset*, of course – the death of his grandma springs to mind, closely followed by Northampton Town losing the Division One Playoff Final at Wembley in '98 – but always a temporary, bounce-back kind of upset. You could never say Dave was feeling depressed, or troubled. It just wasn't his style.

"Yup, that's me done now, Eddie. Time to smarten myself up, start taking work more seriously, give the fags up for good. Dave Atkinson: off the market." He turns on his stool to the near-empty pub. "It's official, ladies!"

A couple of the drinkers raise a smile. The last

time a female of the species walked into this place, Vic turned on the Glade *Plug-In* in celebration. The Shoemaker is a pub of the old-fashioned ilk, with tattered upholstery and the kind of gaudy, mottled carpet designed to not show up the stains. On the wall hangs a beaten-up old dartboard. In the corner stands a squat, wooden hood-skittles table. An old Willie Nelson song is playing on the jukebox, one that Willie Nelson himself probably can't remember writing.

"Jesus, Dave," I say. "You make it sound so…final."

"Nah, nothing final about it, mate. A beginning, in fact. Kids next, we're hoping. Let's see…wedding's in June, so all being well there could be a little rug rat on the scene by early next year."

I never thought I'd see the day. Dave scheduling his life like the Christmas telly in the *Radio Times*.

"June?" I ask. "This June?"

"Yup."

"But that's five months away."

"No sense in pissing about, is there? We love each other."

"Of course. Just all a bit of a surprise, I guess."

"A surprise? Ed, Forest losing at home today was a surprise. This is a *celebration*. You should be chuffed for me."

"I am! It's great. Really great."

"You do think I'm doing the right thing, don't you?"

Tread softly, Ed, for you tread on Dave's dreams.
"Well, do *you* think you're doing the right thing?"

I ask slowly.

"Does the Pope shit in the woods? Abso-fucking-lutely."

"Then me too...that's all that matters...you should follow your heart...abso-fucking-lutely."

Dave's frowning at me now, giving me that look he always gives me when I've said something stupid, which is fairly often.

"Ponce," he chuckles, going back to his pint.

♂

The best man.

In centuries past, it was common practice for a man to choose a woman from the same town or village to marry him (her choice in the matter appeared limited at best). But from time to time the women simply ran out, and so it was that the man would have to look further afield, usually to a neighbouring settlement. Now this neighbouring settlement clearly wasn't too keen on the idea of its women running out either, and so would become fiercely suspicious of any outside admirers. So it was that the man had to use all his cunning, wit and guile when deciding how to make the lady in question his. Of course, more often than not, the man possessed very little cunning, wit *or* guile, and so would choose to kidnap her instead. This could be a dangerous mission, so he often took with him–

I peer over the top of my computer screen. All quiet on the desktop front.

This could be a dangerous mission, so he often took with him the best man in the village to clear up any unfortunate mess that might ensue. Providing all went well and they didn't both have their skulls crushed, the guardian would accompany the happy couple back home, warding off any further kidnappers along the way. And then he would secure the ceremony, sword at the ready, awaiting the arrival of the murderously angry in-laws and–

"Ey up, Eddie!"

I shoot a nervous glance over my shoulder.

Arthur.

Arthur's been working the post-room here at Bloom & Co Insurance Services for just about as long as anyone can remember. His eyesight has deteriorated so badly over the past few years that it's no longer possible to predict whose post you're going to get in the mornings, but he's something of a respected institution at the company, so everyone quietly puts up with his mistakes and Arthur himself seems to have no idea he's doing anything wrong.

"Hey, Arthur," I say.

"On that Internet again?" he asks.

"Research," I reply, shrugging. It's not a complete lie.

"Everything alright?" he asks. "You seem a little shaky."

And this coming from Arthur, hunched and wrinkled like a prune, engulfed in a giant woollen cardigan. Endearingly, he still wears a bow-tie to work each day.

"I'm fine," I reply. "Just made me jump, sneaking up on me like that. Finally found some WD40 for those wheels?" I nod to his mail trolley.

"You were in a world of your own. What you looking at, anyway?" Arthur squints and brings his tortoise-like face closer to my computer screen. "Oh, right. Someone gonna be a best man, then?"

"Yeah."

"And that's a bad thing?"

"I didn't say it was a bad thing, did I?"

"Well, you don't look like a bloke that's just received good news."

"It's just that people'll be expecting me to say stuff, won't they? And they'll all be looking at me."

"Aye, people looking at you. Really, that's terrible, Eddie. I feel for you. Well, I'll see you around," he says with a chuckle, pushing his trolley back out into the corridor. "Try not to sweat over it too much, eh?"

"Yeah, see you, Arthur," I say.

I look back to the screen.

Arthur's right. I'm being ridiculous. At least I won't have to kill anyone like these guys, after all.

I loosen my tie. It's hot in here, despite the chilly weather outside. It always amazes me to think how a company that adjusts insurance losses to the tune of millions of pounds each year can't quite seem to adjust its own central-heating system to a satisfactory standard. If it was hot outside, they'd be freezing us to death with the air-con.

I take a client report from my desk and head off down the corridor in search of Helena. Helena's the office assistant around here, came from Poland a year or so back. I don't know what she was expecting when she set off, but I'm guessing her idyllic vision of life in England didn't include a thousand photocopies a day. Still, if the EU brings girls like Helena to a town like Northampton, I say open up the gates and roll out the welcome mat.

I find Helena at her usual station: photocopier 4B. She seems to be having some trouble with the machine, digging about inside its guts with a letter-opener. One of the many alluring things about Helena is her complete disregard for any kind of office dress code. Each day she comes in wearing jeans and brightly-coloured tops and bangles that rattle about whenever she moves. Even her hair is non-conformist: a wonderful shock of auburn swept back from a face so ludicrously pretty it hardly seems real, like it's made of porcelain.

As she's bending into the machine now, I notice her jeans have slipped down a little, leaving an agonising glimpse of her pink thong on display. It sends a sharp jolt of arousal though me, an unexpected bit of colour in the otherwise drab and monotone planet of Bloom & Co.

"You know," I call down to her, "if Sting saw what you did every day I reckon he'd have a heart attack."

"Sorry?" she asks, her head still buried inside the copier.

"You know. Sting? Rainforests?"

"What?"

"Never mind. You need a hand?"

Helena wriggles backwards, sending my

testosterone levels off the scale for a second or two, and then straightens up so her face is close to mine.

"Hi," I stammer, a little schoolboyishly.

"Hi. Sorry, what were you saying?" she asks, her cheeks a little flushed.

I nod down to the copier. "Just wondered if you needed a hand?"

"Oh, yes. It's jammed."

"Right. I'll take a look then, shall I?"

I begin to fiddle about with the various levers and drawers, hoping to God I haven't just bitten off more than I can chew. Having to call IT out now would be a huge admission of defeat. I can just imagine how Pete would love that, coming down from the top floor to take over rescuing the damsel in distress. No, I couldn't allow it. I'd rather be here all day.

"Good weekend?" I ask, trying to draw her attention away from what I'm doing.

Helena shrugs. "Went to a vodka bar with a few friends. Didn't get to bed until six."

I struggle to think of a suitable response. "Oh, I suppose you like that," I say eventually. "Vodka, I mean. Being Polish."

Helena looks at me blankly. "Do you know what the problem is?" she asks.

"Hmm? Oh, yeah. It's a paper jam. Here." I point to the offending piece of paper, screwed up tightly within the machine's intestines, covered in black ink.

"Can you get it out?" she asks.

"I'll give it a go. I'll need that letter-opener."

She hands it across to me and I set about digging

the cursed thing out. "Actually, I had a bit of a crazy one myself," I lie as I work. "Went to Smithy's. You know Smithy's? Anyway, we were in this kebab place. It must have been – oh, I don't know – about five or six in the morning–"

"Don't poke it so hard," Helena says. "You'll tear the paper and we'll never get it out then."

"Don't worry," I say. "I've done this before. So, anyway, we were in this place and–"

The letter-opener suddenly springs towards me, spattering ink onto my shirt and shredding the paper in half, leaving the remainder stuck deep inside its belly with no means of retrieval.

"Shit," I sigh.

"I told you."

"Well, look, perhaps if I just unplug it and get round the other side."

"I'm calling IT," she says.

"No, no! Don't call IT!" I can already see Pete's face, ginning and smirking, smirking and bloody grinning.

"I'm calling them – it'll be quicker." And with that, she turns and heads back down the corridor.

"Okay," I call after her. "Cool. I'll just see what I can do here."

I grimace. *Cool.* Who the fuck do I think I am? Only after talking to Helena am I struck by how much younger she is than me. Somewhere in my head, I'm still nineteen and waiting to take on the world, rather than staring down the barrel of thirty. Somewhere in my head, girls like Helena are just waiting for the right combination of perfectly placed words from me before they fall into my arms. Then I open my mouth and the truth lands a sucker-punch: Helena's a fish in another pond. Quite when I stopped fishing there, I don't know; it seems to have happened entirely without my noticing. It reminds me of an old clock my grandmother used to own. There was no second hand on the thing, so as a child I would stare incessantly at the minute hand, seeing if I could catch it move. I never could, yet still the time somehow went by anyway. And I suppose that's what getting older is: you don't notice it yourself, but the world sure gives you a good kick in the balls to remind you every once in a while.

"You forgot your letter-opener," I sigh quietly to myself, tossing it down on top of the copier.

It is, to some degree, my job to predict the outcome of things in life. Given a portfolio of fifty properties, I can to a reasonable degree of accuracy predict the losses on those properties over, say, a period of five years. I can predict how many will burn, how many will flood, and how many will be vandalised. I know that a lifelong smoker can be expected to live ten years less than a lifelong non-smoker. A smoker who quits at the age of thirty can be expected to live the same a lifelong non-smoker, but after the age of thirty the life expectancy begins to erode, and I can, using a reliable programme, reasonably assess what percentage of those ten years have been chipped away by any one individual. That's not to say I can tell a person exactly when he or she is going to die, of course, but give me a hundred people and I'll have a pretty accurate prediction – give me a thousand and I'll have an even better one.

So it has always been a surprising and mystifying disappointment to me that I can never predict the outcome of any conversation I have with a woman, no matter how many conversations I have. So far as I can determine, the law of large numbers does not apply to women as it does to insurance. Each one is so utterly unique and incomparable to the next that collectively they are illogical. So, invariably, just as it might be tempting to believe that some sort of handle on the situation has been grasped, that some faint pattern is emerging from the chaos, a curveball is thrown, an anomaly discovered. You end up with ink on your shirt and IT Pete laughing in your face.

Once back at my desk, I check my phone for the familiar blinking light, until I remember that Pete disabled the messaging facility for me last week. He's not such a bad bloke, Pete. It makes me wonder why he wasn't asked to be the best man instead. He's Dave's mate too, after all. And he's good with things like this, like sorting out the phone for me, like fixing the photocopier. He'd be much better suited for the role

I consider the feasibility of ringing Dave now and suggesting the idea to him.

Dave, I've been thinking, see.

Whoa, steady on there, mate. You'll do yourself an injury.

Dave, I'm serious. Listen, it's about this best man business. I told Pete the other day, and I probably shouldn't be saying anything, but he's pissed off. I mean, really *pissed off. Wants to know why you didn't*

ask him. He'd never say anything, of course – such a proud man deep down. But I'm thinking I should do the honourable thing. You know, kind of...step aside. Clear the gangway, if you like. I mean, you'd *know you wanted me as your best man. And* I'd *know you wanted me as your best man. I could be like a...a best man in spirit!*

Ed

Yes, Dave.

You really are a big ponce.

I sigh and sit back in my chair, chewing the end of my pen. There has to be something I can do. Men have overcome bigger obstacles than this before. Men have been to the Moon, for Christ's sake. Just needs a little forethought. Neil Armstrong didn't just jump in the rocket and ask where the ignition switch was, after all. No, he had a plan.

A plan of action.

I open the drawer and pull out a notepad, the one I take into the meetings with me when I'm trying to appear interested. I leaf through the first few pages, past all the insane little doodles I seem to have created. They look like the kind of childhood etchings that turn up on the news reports after the capture of a serial killer, the damning evidence proving he was stark raving bonkers all along. I push this to the back of my mind, eventually finding a blank page. On it, I write:

Operation Understudy:

I sit and stare at the two words for five full minutes. Then I write:

1) Injury.

It would have to be pretty serious, of course. No reason why a man with a broken arm or even a broken leg couldn't do the job. Something really debilitating. Or something so horrible to look at they wouldn't want me in the photos.

No, too dangerous.

I think some more, and then I write:

2) Feign injury.

I throw the pad down in despair. Operation Understudy aborted. Perhaps I shouldn't be too surprised. Neil had the whole of frigging NASA behind him, after all. I'm just one man, and what can one man achieve against such insurmountable odds?

Angrily, I pick up the pen again and write:

3) Emigrate.

4) Convert to Judaism - conflict of interest?

5) Set honey-trap for Dave.

"What's cooking, Eddie?"

I look up from the pad. It's Pete, leaning nonchalantly against the office partition, one hand wedged in his pocket. Pete's your standard IT nerd, right off the production line: wire-framed glasses, stripy jumper purchased from Next, dark hair gelled into a tidy little peak at the front.

"Did you just ask me what's *cooking*?" I ask.

"Yup. Anyway, photocopier 4B? It's sorted now."

"Piss off, Pete."

Pete ignores this, pretending to inspect the condition of his nails. "Yeah, she was pretty grateful," he says.

"You work in IT," I sigh. "She wouldn't touch

you with a shitty stick."

"Oh, as opposed to insurance?"

He's got a point. Over the years, I've come to discover there's no exciting or redemptive way to tell a woman you work in insurance, no way that will soften the dull thud or make her want to sleep with you any more. You may as well tell her you spot trains or you're big into the art of stuffing dead animals. My guess is the effect would not be too dissimilar.

"Actually," Pete says, "we had a good old chat."

"No, you didn't."

"Put a good bit of groundwork in there."

"Did you actually talk about anything other than the photocopier?" I ask.

"Of course."

"What then?" I demand.

Pete looks momentarily stumped. "She was telling me all about Poland," he says eventually. "Sound like an interesting place."

"Really? Tell me one thing about Poland."

"Hitler invaded it," he replies.

"That's what she told you about Poland? That Hitler invaded it? You're so full of shit, Pete. Besides, she's too young for you. She's too young for *me*. We need to start considering women…you know…more around our own age."

Pete sniffs dismissively. "There *aren't* any women around our own age. They're all shacked up. We'll have to wait 'til they've come out the other side, all divorced and miserable, and I for one am not hanging around for that. You knock yourself out if you like."

"They can't all be attached," I insist.

"No, the crazy ones aren't. Because *they're crazy.*"

"Speaking of divorce," I say, "Dave asked me to be his best man on Saturday."

"*What?*"

"I know."

Pete pushes his glasses further up the bridge of his nose. "What about me?"

"I know! He's seems to think I'll be good at it."

"No, you won't."

"I know! Look, if you really wanted to do it, it's probably not too late to have a word with him."

Pete chews this over for a time. Then he smiles. "Nah," he says. "I think I'll leave it to you – you've known Dave longer, after all."

"Bastard," I sigh.

Pete gives the top of the partition a satisfied little tap. "Right, I've gotta go. Fancy the pub tonight?"

"No, I've got stuff to do," I reply. "Work stuff."

Pete frowns. "Fair enough. You know you've got ink on your shirt, right?"

"I'm aware of it, thanks."

"Oh, and you forgot your letter-opener."

I reach out and snatch it. "It's Helena's," I say. "I'll take it back to her later."

"You're pathetic."

"I'm aware of it, thanks."

"See you later, Ed."

"Bye, Pete."

♂

Home.

Home is a one-bedroom flat in a converted shoe factory near the centre of town. Bare brick walls, Formica breakfast bar, coloured-plastic bathroom sink. *Modern living,* as the estate agents would have it. I imagine it's supposed to carry an air of New York chic, and if you shut the blinds tight enough you can almost get away with it. Then somebody starts screaming the air blue on the street outside and you remember it's Northampton out there, not Fifth Avenue.

On the menu tonight: chicken stir-fry. My cooking regime is more dependent on the order in which things go off rather than any kind of culinary desire, but I *am* getting better at it. Mum did all the cooking when we were kids, Kate and I, and she died before I learned how to boil an egg. Dad was no Jamie Oliver, so after that we became more of a ready-meal and takeaway kind of family. Dad worked hard on the roads all day, digging – *skull-dragging,* as the old Irish boys called it. Some days I feel like I should be doing it, like my blood isn't cut out for this office life, or like I'm just pretending. But give me a shovel and I'd barely know which end to use, so perhaps somewhere along the line I should be grateful.

Dad earned good money on the roads, and was able to put us both through university. I came out the other side like a dog out of a carwash. Didn't know where to go or what to do with myself. I think Dad had it in mind that a degree might be a golden ticket to somewhere, at least a way of keeping me off the roads myself. Nobody in the family had ever been before, so who was to know? The reality of the thing was that pretty much everyone had a degree in something or other, so all it did was open a lot of doors to a lot of offices, all of them much of a muchness. If a man worked in an office a hundred years ago he was probably doing something pretty important – now he's just afraid and following the crowd.

I eat my stir-fry in front of Standard Liege v Rapid Bucharest on ITV4. It really is a good stir-fry. I found some Delia books of Mum's a few months ago when I was helping Dad clear out the attic. I didn't think Dad could make much use of them, so I dusted them down and took them home with me. I suppose these were the things she might have taught me to cook had she been around, perhaps things she even cooked herself at one time, so I'm working my way through them like a monk through the Holy Scriptures.

Halfway through the meal, the phone rings and I make a passable juggling act of the stir-fry and the water while trying to get to it.

"Hi, Eddie. It's Kate."

"Kate! Good to hear from you. It's been a while."

And it really has. Kate moved to London five or six years ago, and although it's only an hour away she may as well be in another country. London has a way of sucking people up and erasing the memory of any kind of former life they may have had.

"How's Dad?" she asks.

"He's alright. Settled in the flat now."

Dad moved into a new flat two weeks ago, leaving the house he bought with Mum, the house we grew up in.

"Good," Kate says. "Makes more sense, really. Never liked to think of him knocking around that house all on his own."

"He's just installed a heated towel-rail," I say.

There follows a short silence while we both try to work out the relevance of this statement.

"Great. Listen, Eddie. Me and Jess'll be up at the weekend, so we'll pop in and see him. We'll swing by your place, too."

"That'd be good. Dad'll like that."

I smile at the thought of Kate and Jess cooped up with Dad in that little flat. Dad has always doted on Kate, thinks the world of her, but he can't quite get his head around her being a lesbian. In fact, I don't think he can get his head around what exactly a lesbian is altogether, so he has this strange habit of treating Jess like some kind of ever-present female friend whenever they meet. He treats them as a person might treat two single flatmates who may well live together, but certainly don't get up to anything *sexual*, at least not with *each other*, and Kate and Jess duly oblige by playing along. Perhaps one day he'll come round to the idea, but Kate and Jess have been going a good five years now, so nobody's holding their breath. More likely he still thinks her lesbianism is a passing fad that she's picked up in London, like drinking semi-skimmed or recycling her plastics, and one that will soon fizzle out the moment she moves back north of Hemel Hempstead.

"How's life up there anyway?" Kate asks. "Any news?"

"Not much. Dave's getting married."

"What? Really? To a woman?"

"Yep, I'm pretty sure."

"Wait, this isn't something he's found on the Internet? This woman isn't in desperate need of a visa, is she?"

I laugh at this. "Stop being a bitch. It's Alison. You've met before. Anyway, he told me to tell you you're invited. Jess too. That reminds me, what *do* lesbians wear for weddings, dresses or suits?"

"Now *you're* being a bitch," she laughs. "No, that's really good news. Good for Dave. Tell him we'd love to come. And how about you? Anything on the lady front yet?"

"Well, I've been seeing a lot of Badger lately. You know, I really think we're finally starting to bond."

Badger is Dad's curmudgeonly Jack Russell terrier. A family friend bought her for Dad after Mum died, I suppose thinking he could use the company. In truth, I couldn't imagine a dog worse company than Badger. She really doesn't have a lot of time for human beings, and would rather spend the day staring at a blank wall than having to interact with one. Still, a cynical person might conclude her personality compliments Dad's perfectly, and that the two of them were made for each other. I've been walking Badger a lot more since Dad moved into the new place (although Badger likes to walk off ahead, no doubt nurturing the concept that in actual fact she's walking me).

"I keep telling you, get your arse down here," Kate says, an urgency creeping into her voice. "More women than you could shake a stick at. Even a dork like you couldn't fail."

"Well, thanks Kate, that's really touching. And what about Dad?"

"Dad's fine. He'd still be digging holes if his back would let him. He doesn't want you moping around that town on his account."

"I'm not *moping*."

"Yes, you are. I can hear you moping from the other end of this phone."

"God, Kate, you sound more like Mum every day."

This brings about an awkward silence, and I immediately regret saying it.

"Just tell me you'll think about it," she says after a while. "They've got museums here, and theatres, and galleries, and a bit of *bloody culture*. You know, all that stuff you used to be interested in before you became a fucking zombie."

"Well, thanks for calling, Kate. You've really brightened up my evening."

"Eddie," Kate says in her stern motherly voice.

"Okay, okay. I'll think about it."

"Make sure you do. And I'll see you on the weekend, turd-face."

"Whatever, lezza," I say, hanging up quickly and laughing to the empty room. Our phone conversations always end on insults; it's just a matter of who can get the final one in before the line goes dead.

I finish off the rest of my dinner and fall asleep on the couch, the dulcet tones of Steve Rider and Andy Townsend deconstructing the weaknesses of Rapid Bucharest's back four.

"*Well, Andy, what about Ricardo Fernandes? He's having a torrid time of things out there tonight, isn't he? You think they'll bring some changes at half-time?*"

"*I think they'll have to, Steve. They really need to get their act together if they're going to make anything out of this second-half.*"

"*And what do you make of Eddie Corrigan? Just not been on form lately, has he?*"

"*That's right, Steve. Hard to know what to say about Eddie, really. He's been struggling for a while now, and since the announcement of this best man episode, things seem to have just gone from bad to worse for him. It's a shame to see.*"

"*Yes, there seems to be little explanation for it. It just goes to show the importance of the psychological side of the game as well as the physical.*"

"*Very much so, Steve. He hasn't been scoring for a while, and that's when those little doubts start to creep in mentally.*"

"*And can you see any way back for him now, Andy? We've heard murmurings about a possible transfer to London coming from his lesbian sister. Do you see this as an option for him?*"

"Well, it remains to be seen, doesn't it, Steve? Certainly something needs to change, and change pretty fast. He does seem to have got himself into something of a rut just lately, and he's no spring chicken any more, let's remember."

"*Indeed. Well, thanks for your thoughts, Andy, and thanks for tuning in at home. Don't forget there's plenty more action coming up this week with* Eddie's Love Life *and also* Eddie's Job, *where we'll be considering whether Eddie should really be carrying on like this, and analysing in full detail where it all went wrong.*"

I awake with a start on the couch, gasping. My shirt is stuck to my back with perspiration. The hard blue screen of the TV gapes openly back at me.

Sighing, I switch it off and stagger through to the kitchen, where I gulp down three pints of water before collapsing into bed.

2. Spilt Milk

Tuesday night, and I'm in The Awl & The Moon.

The Awl is a little more upmarket than The Shoemaker, a little less spit-and-sawdust, but Tuesday night is quiz night, and so for one evening only the place drops its pretences and you can almost pretend like it's a normal pub. The place fills with a strange, transient crowd: the quiz crawlers – an odd assortment of tweed-clad schoolteachers, retired folk, and middle-aged men who really should have put their big knowledgeable brains to better use. Still, it's a safe-haven, a place where there's no danger of Dave popping in for a swift one.

I need some time alone. I need to get my head straight.

It's five-to-nine and the sheets have been handed out. Ted the quizmaster is fiddling about with his mic. On the table beside him sits a pint glass half-filled with pound coins and raffle tickets. Ted and his quizzes. He tours the county, Ted, a quiz for each day of the week and not one of them the same, always keeping one step ahead of the crawlers. They try to get a hold of him – what papers he reads, what sports interest him most – but Ted's not one to be tied down. He's a man for all seasons, and where his questions come from nobody yet knows. The day they find out is the day he is beaten and worthless.

I order another Guinness and close my eyes. All day I've had Andy and Steve in my head, running me through my working day with painful in-depth analysis. *See how he's leaving that claim to one side there, Steve. Now, that should be bread-and-butter stuff for the lad, but his mind's all over the place. And as for that phone - it beggars belief that he's just going to let it ring like that, it really does.* And not just Andy and Steve either, but Gary Lineker, Alan Hanson, Mark Lawrenson: the whole shebang. Even the BBC boys have muscled in on the broadcasting rights to my consciousness.

"Bleriot."

For a while I think it's just another voice in my head – Gaby Logan, perhaps – but then it dawns on me the voice came from somewhere around me. Somewhere in the real world.

I turn to my right. Somewhere amidst all the static, a woman has taken a seat next to me. She's slightly built, elfishly pretty. Yes, definitely pretty. She's wearing a top that says something across the front. I can't read it properly without staring at her breasts.

"Sorry, did you just say something?"

"Louis Bleriot." She looks across to me. Amazingly pretty eyes. "First man to fly the Channel."

I remember the quiz. "Oh, right. Yeah, I think he was."

"No *think* about it. He was. Bet nobody got that. I'd have got that."

"I think you're a bit late if you wanted to join in." I say. "Ted runs this thing with an iron fist."

"I'm happy just listening."

It occurs to me that she's slightly drunk. It occurs to me that *I'm* slightly drunk.

She runs a hand through her brunette hair, cut short yet feminine, and exhales loudly.

I take this opportunity to give her a proper sizing-up. She's wearing a dark skirt with black tights. The skirt's not short enough to be slutty but short enough to get me thinking. A cardigan hangs loosely around her shoulders, hanging open in the middle, and I'm trying again to read what's written on the t-shirt below when she looks across at me. I avert my gaze over her shoulder, looking about for a husband or a boyfriend or any kind of large male who might wish to punch me for what I'm about to do.

"You here alone?" I ask.

She places her drink down and looks to me sternly. "What, because I'm a woman I can't have a drink alone? Is that the inference?"

"No, I..."

"Or was that just a lame chat-up line?"

"Err..."

"*You're* here alone, aren't you? I don't assume because I see you sitting here alone that there must be something weird about it."

"Well, actually, I *am* going through something of a crisis."

"I don't care! I didn't come here for conversation, or to listen to your woes, and I certainly didn't come here to be *leched upon*. Now, please, can we just sit here...quietly...and drink."

"Fine by me," I huff.

I take another sup of Guinness. I look around the bar, the ceiling, anywhere but at this woman. But there's a mirror behind the bar, and I can't help catching glimpses of her there. She really is pretty; the kind of woman who gets prettier the more you look at her.

"James Cameron," I say.

"What?"

"James Cameron."

"I thought we weren't talking."

"We're not."

"Then why are you telling me your name?"

I turn to her smugly. "James Cameron directed *Terminator II*. I'd have got that."

She looks nonplussed. "It's still talking."

"It's not talking. I'm doing the quiz. *You're* talking to *me*."

"Well, can't you do the quiz silently? As in: in your head."

"Look, what's your problem?" I put down my pint. "I came out for a quiet drink, not to be abused by some crazy woman. You know, that's why they don't let women in pubs on their own. Because they're sanctuaries from people like you in the first place."

"*What* the fuck did you just say? *Who* exactly doesn't let women in pubs on their own? You? The James Cameron Society of Pub Dictators?"

"My name's not James Cameron."

"I don't give a shit what your name is, you misogynistic pig. And just for the record, *that's* my problem. All men are pigs. Pigs and arseholes."

"Ah," I say. "Now we're getting somewhere."

"No, now we are not *getting somewhere*. Don't talk as if you've sussed me out with your big pig-man brain. You don't know the first thing about me. Not the first damn thing."

Fortunately for everyone else, our conversation is being drowned out by Ted's amplified warbling.

"Look," I suggest, "let's just forget either of us opened our mouths, shall we?"

"About the most sensible thing you've said so far."

"That's that settled, then."

"Fine."

"Good."

"Agreed."

We sit in silence, drinking. I start to wish I'd brought out some cigarettes, the post-smoking-ban escape option. But I didn't. I think of the crushed, half-empty packet of Embassy in the bedside-cabinet drawer back at home, nestled somewhere among the coins and the cufflinks and the conspicuously unopened pack of condoms, still in the cellophane. I find myself wondering whether condoms expire or not. I'm pretty sure they do. I wouldn't have a clue as to the average shelf-life, though. I suspect it'd be quite a while. A year? Two? Christ, what a sorry state of affairs when a man gets to wondering when his condoms go off.

"Benjamin Disraeli," she says confidently beside me.

She orders another drink, a Malibu and coke.

What was that thing I had to do for work tomorrow? That thing someone wanted me to do? Ah, couldn't have been that important.

"Lithuania," I half-guess.

She forages around in her purse for coins, checks inside the zipper for notes. "Do you take cards?" she asks the barman.

"Minimum five pounds," the barman says.

"I've got it," I interrupt. "Another Guinness as well, please."

"Well, thank you, James Cameron," she says, without much conviction.

"My name's Eddie."

"Do you smoke, Eddie?"

"I left my cigarettes at home."

"I'm offering you a cigarette."

"Oh. Okay then."

The drinks arrive and we take them unsteadily out to garden, slaloming around an alarming number of patio heaters, steadying ourselves against a wall. She lights a couple of cigarettes and passes one across to me.

"So, just for the sake of my dislike of awkward silences," she says, "what's this crisis of yours, then?"

"Oh, it's nothing. Stupid really. What about you? Who's the arsehole?"

"Boyfriend. *Ex*-boyfriend, I suppose. Joe. I found out tonight he's been shagging someone else. Jesus, what a prick!"

"Was it serious?" I ask.

"No, not really. I don't know. Maybe." She shakes her head quickly and blows a funnel of smoke out into the chilly night air.

"And he knows you know?"

"I threw a pot of paint over his car. Two pots,

actually."

"Yep, that'll give it away."

She laughs. "Sorry, I'm not normally this...*annoyed*." Then she hiccups. "Wait, what did you say your name was?"

"Eddie."

"I'm Marla. Fancy coming back to mine, Eddie? I'm only round the corner."

"Err...I'm not sure. I wouldn't want to be taking advantage."

"You lying bastard."

Six minutes later, we're crashing noisily through Marla's front door. Marla's putting her finger to her lips and going *shhhh* a lot, even though she's the one making most of the noise. She trips over a cardboard box in the hallway and I somehow manage to catch her before she falls.

"Moving out?" I ask, noting the cardboard box is just one of many in the hallway. I'm suddenly struck by the worrying notion that she might live here with her only-very-recently-turned-ex-boyfriend. Perhaps this is a ploy to make him jealous. It does all seem a little too easy, after all.

"Nope," she says, hiccupping again. "Moving in."

Marla leans back against the wall and pulls me towards her. We kiss in that heavy, misguided way that drunken people do. Her lips are warm and taste of coconut. She raises a leg and curls it around my back. I place a hand on her thigh, creeping slowly upwards.

"Wait!" she says, breaking the kiss suddenly as though just remembering she left the oven on.

"You want a coffee or something?"

I pretend to think about it. "Probably rather just move straight on to the sex if it's all the same with you."

She laughs as though it's the funniest thing a man has ever said to her in her life, and I'm reminded again that I *really, really* am taking advantage. "I like you, Eddie," she slurs. "You're funny."

And with that she takes my hand and we go falling up the stairs together.

♂

"Oh, shit."

I awake in a bed that's not mine. Definitely not mine. Something is digging into my forehead. It's the eye of a teddy bear. I've been sleeping on a teddy bear.

"Oh, *shit!*"

I sit up. The room swoons into some kind of focus.

Marla is standing by the window, peering through the blinds. She's in her knickers, topless. If she turned I could see her breasts. Just like that.

"What's wrong?" I croak.

She turns and I can see her breasts. "It's my parents!"

The combination of Marla's breasts and Marla's parents at this time of the morning overloads my mind. I open my mouth to speak but nothing comes out.

Marla sighs and reaches for a t-shirt.

"Why are your parents here?" I finally manage.

"They've come to see the house. They haven't seen it yet. Jesus, why are they always so *early* about everything?"

"What time is it?"

"Ten."

"Oh, shit."

I jump out of bed, stub my toe on one of Marla's cardboard boxes, and hop around the room cursing.

Marla barely seems to notice my pain. "You're going to have to pretend to be my boyfriend," she says, quite matter-of-factly.

"*What?*"

"They're my parents. I don't want them thinking I'm the kind of girl that takes random men home from pubs for one night stands."

I realise that I'm naked. Absurdly naked. "How about I just hide?" I suggest.

"No! They've come to see the house. They'll want to see everywhere."

"I could hide in the cupboard. They won't want to see in there, will they? It's just a bloody cupboard."

"You don't know my mum. Besides I'm not having you hiding in the cupboard. Now *you're* making me feel like a slut."

I consider my options. The back window. The roof. For an insane moment, I imagine myself climbing inside the toilet cistern.

The doorbell rings.

"For God's sake, put some clothes on, will you?

Now, we've been dating for a couple of months. I like Audrey Hepburn movies and salsa dancing. I don't really like salsa dancing but they think I do. My middle name is Jennifer."

"Jennifer," I say a little woozily. "That's nice."

"Get dressed!"

I start fumbling around the room for my boxer shorts. Nowhere to be seen. Christ, what did she do, tear them to shreds? Hazy memories return to me, bringing a smile to my face.

The doorbell rings again.

"I'm going down," Marla says. "I'll stall them for a while. Now, *please* don't fuck this up."

I find the boxers under the bed. "What about Jeff or Jack or…whatever?"

"Joe. They didn't like him anyway. Never said it, but I could tell. They haven't seen him for a while, so as far as they know we've been broken up for months, okay?"

"Look, I'm really not comfortable with all this. Perhaps I should just hide, after all."

"Yeah, you came along and I realised what a great guy you were, so I called it off with Joe and *yadda yadda yadda*. Perfect."

"I swept you off your feet."

"Don't get carried away, Romeo. It's a story. But that's good – keep in character. Right, I'm going down. Don't be long."

"Marla, wait."

But she's already gone, hurrying down the stairs while the doorbell chimes away for a third time.

Fuck.

I spend the next couple of minutes fishing around on the floor for the rest of my clothes. Downstairs, I can hear cheery voices, a mother cooing over this and that.

I check myself out in the mirror. Bedhead. Morning breath. The imprint of a teddy bear's eye deeply set into my forehead. Isn't it obvious that I'm not some kind of Prince Charming? Won't it be horribly apparent that I'm just a bloke who, with a little luck and a lot of Malibu and cokes, managed to fluke a shag out of their beloved daughter?

But I need this over and done with. I'm already late for work. Shit, late for work. On top of everything else. I'll tell them I lost my keys. Or I had car trouble. Yeah, car trouble, and I had to take it into the garage. They know what a heap of crap it is, after all. I moan about it to them all the time.

Two minutes later and I'm tiptoeing down the stairs into the unknown. I should probably stop tiptoeing. Strangers tiptoe. Boyfriends stroll.

I enter the living room, doing my best impression of a strolling boyfriend.

Mum's rooting through one of Marla's unopened boxes; Dad's inspecting the fireplace for structural imperfections. Mum is very mumsy regal: pleated skirt, jacket and brooch, shoulder-length silvery hair styled at no small price, I imagine. Dad is more casual in a polo jacket and chinos.

Marla turns and smiles, hurries over to me all doting girlfriend. She really is frighteningly good at this. "Mum, Dad," she chirps. "This is Eddie."

She flings an arm around me and tiptoes up to

kiss me on the cheek. She still smells incredibly good, which is more than could be said of me, I should think.

Mum stops rooting and Dad gives the fireplace a final methodical tap. They both come towards me. Mum kisses me on the cheek and Dad gives me a curt handshake while we exchange overlapping pleasantries. Mum = Jean, Dad = Robin. Remember or face the wrath of Marla.

"I'm so glad you're meeting at last," Marla chirps.

My head aches. I want to sit down and eat a bacon sandwich and watch awful TV and think about nothing. I certainly don't want to be doing this.

An awkward silence prevails, so Marla pipes up again. "Eddie works in architecture."

My stomach tightens. I feel as if I've actually been punched.

"Well, that's interesting," Jean says.

"Funnily enough, I was just looking at that fireplace," Robin says. "Not too sure about it myself. What do you reckon?"

"Err...well..."

"Darling, don't bother him with work-talk now." Jean to the rescue. "Marla dear, you didn't mention there was a new man in your life."

"Well, we didn't want to make a big deal of it, Mum. Not until we were sure."

"So, the two of you are serious then?"

"Oh, yes. Got the keys cut and everything."

Jean and Robin are looking at me like a curious painting they can't quite fathom. I've been forcedly smiling since entering the room, and I'm becoming increasingly aware of the fact that I must look quite mad – just standing and smiling, smiling and standing. But it seems wrong to stop smiling now, and I wouldn't know what to do otherwise.

"So then, Eddie," Jean says, rubbing a hand lovingly up and down Marla's arm, "where did you meet my wonderful daughter?"

The whole family look to me expectantly, Marla included. Robin is smiling and nodding sagely, awaiting a reply.

From me.

I should probably reply.

"Salsa dancing," I blurt, immediately regretting it.

My stomach rumbles forlornly, the beginnings of a monster hangover. The shock from this train wreck of a morning must have been holding it at bay until now.

"Oh, well," Jean coos. "Our own Fred and Ginger. You'll have to show us what you're made of some time."

"Eddie's a terrific dancer."

I smile a little harder, dying inside.

All of a sudden great waves of nausea are washing over me. I feel like I'm at sea. Christ, how much Guinness did I drink last night? Just the thought of alcohol makes me suddenly retch, which I manage to pass off as a strange little cough.

"Isn't the house wonderful, Eddie?"

Sweat begins beading on my pallid brow. My mouth is producing the saliva of ten men. "Oh yes," I breathe. "Wonderful."

"And you're in the housing side of things yourself?" Robin asks.

"Oh, you know. Some residential, some commercial. A bit of everything, really."

"I suppose this sort of thing may be a little bland for you," he chuckles.

I start reeling off some nonsense about practical architecture being the future, something about merging innovation with common-sense design (which I can only assume I've picked up off the telly), but all I'm really concentrating on is holding down the contents of my gurgling stomach. By the time my little speech is over I feel like I've contracted The Plague.

"And you live locally?" Robin asks.

"Yes. Yes, I do. I'm sorry, could you just excuse me for a moment?"

I walk out of the room, and no sooner am I through the door than I'm sick into my own mouth. There I am in Marla's hallway, my cheeks puffed out like some wretched, demented hamster harvesting his own puke, and the worst news of all is that there's another surge on the way. And I'm clean out of cheek-space.

I'll never make the stairs – that much is clear – so I dart into the kitchen, shut the door, and fall to my knees before the small flip-top bin that appears majestically before me. I slam my palm down on the foot-pedal just in time, and begin filling the bin with a blackened substance that I'm ashamed to call my own. I'm trying to vomit as quietly as possible, which is difficult when your stomach contractions are more violent than Glasgow city centre on a Saturday night. I'm making a strange noise like a muzzled pig.

"Must have gone to the loo," I hear Marla saying in the other room. "Take a look in the kitchen next, Mum."

I quickly pick up the bin, still retching dryly into it, and stagger across the kitchen. The lid is swaying about and repeatedly bashing the top of my head. When I reach the kitchen door I wedge a foot underneath it.

The handle turns a couple of times without success. I hear Jean murmuring on the other side. She tries again.

"This door's a bit sticky, dear. Did you know that? You'll have to get that fixed."

I groan into the bin.

"You're not doing it right," Robin says. "Here, out of the way."

The handle twists a couple more times, and then he's hitting the door with force, actually shoulder-barging it and jamming it firmly over my foot.

The pain is exquisite. It even takes my mind off being sick.

"Some of these new doors are like this." *Bang!* "Just have to wear them in, that's all." *Bang!* "I'll soon have it open."

"Stop!" I yelp.

"Eddie?" Marla says.

"Yeah, it's me, honey."

"What are you doing?"

"It's just...it's Wednesday," I gasp. "You know, bin day. So I was just taking out the bins. I thought I heard the lorry outside."

"No lorry out there," I hear Jean mutter. "Doesn't look like anyone else has put theirs out either."

"Are you sure it's Wednesdays, Eddie?" Robin asks.

"I thought it was. Perhaps I got it wrong, though. They only come every fortnight now, don't they? Bloody council."

"Eddie, stand back from the door," Marla pleads.

"Okay. Just let me just get this sorted."

I remove bin-bag and tie it into a knot, looking around for a suitable place to hide it. There really are few places to hide a big bag full of vomit in a ten-foot-by-ten-foot kitchen, so I decide to keep hold of it instead. I prize my battered foot from beneath the door and it opens immediately. I scamper to the far side of the kitchen like a cornered and wounded animal as Marla, Jean and Robin pile inside.

"Didn't hurt you there, did I, Eddie? Thought the blasted thing was stuck."

"No, not at all," I lie, trying not to wince at the pain. "The bin took the brunt of it."

"That's good."

Jean's looking around the kitchen, her nose twitching like a ferret's. "Have you got a blocked sink in here, dear? There's a funny smell about."

"Yes, we noticed that, didn't we, Marla?" I say. "I'll have to pick up some un-blocker on the way home."

"Might be a rat," Robin suggests, furrowing his brow. "Friend of mine had a rat die behind one of the units once. Lord, it stunk the place to high heaven. He practically had to demolish the whole kitchen before he found out what it was."

"I'm sure it's the sink," I say, conspicuously aware that I'm still holding a bag of my own sick. "Like I say, I'll pick something up. Now, I hope you don't mind me rushing off, but I really am running late."

"Not at all," Jean says. "I'm sure we'll be seeing a lot more of each other now Marla has stopped hiding you away."

"Mum!"

"I'm sure we will, Jean," I say, nervously chuckling. "Now, I really must get going. These buildings won't build themselves."

I head out of the kitchen with the bag, making a wide berth around Marla's parents. I find my shoes by the front door, although I have no recollection of leaving them there.

"You're taking the rubbish with you?" Robin asks.

"Yes. I'll leave it out."

"But I thought we agreed it wasn't today."

"Oh, right. Well, I'll take it to work and bin it there. It's really no bother. Anyway, lovely to meet the pair of you." I feel the need to add a little something more here. "Your daughter, she really is…really is great."

I put on the shoes, which for the left foot is like trying to squeeze a mouldy pear into a matchbox. Jean and Robin are still looking at me oddly. I smile one last time and dart from the house as quickly as possible.

Outside, I gasp in the crisp morning air, and it occurs to me that I've been holding my breath for a very long time indeed. I walk down to the end of the driveway, looking for the car. Then I remember the car's not here, so off I go, bin-bag in hand, limping crookedly down the street like a madman escaping the asylum.

♂

I arrive at work at 11.24, breathless. I have my excuses prepped, something nice and generic about the starter motor, but I arrive find the office empty.

There's a Post-It note stuck to my computer screen:

Call Marla - 06652 654980

My mind runs through how many Marlas I know other than the crazy one I've just slept with. None. Well, one, but I was just a kid and she was the old lady down the road and I'm pretty sure she's dead now. Still, it could be a client, someone whose house has burned down. In the current scheme of things, I'd consider this the lesser disaster.

I call the number.

"Hello?" comes a voice on the other end.

"Hi…Marla?"

"Hello, Eddie."

My mind races. "How did you get my number?"

"It's in your phone. The one you left on my bedside table this morning."

"Oh, shit."

"I'll be in Café Garda around five-thirtyish if you want to pick it up."

I consider the alternatives. Perhaps she could leave it in a discreet but clearly defined location, like a Russian spy with a dossier.

"Okay, I'll come by after work," I sigh.

"Fine. Oh, well done on the parents situation by the way. They seemed to really like you."

"Well, I'm pleased it all worked out for you."

"Lowest form of humour, Eddie."

"Look, this has just been a really bad day for me so far-"

"You weren't moaning last night. Actually, come to think of it…"

I glance sheepishly around the office. "Look, I have to go," I hiss. "I'll see you later."

"Great, I'll dress nice."

"Lowest form of humour, M-"

But she's already gone and I'm talking to a dead tone.

3. Chocco Mocha Latte

Café Garda is the kind of place that divides its coffee into categories and sub-categories, and sells every flavoured tea except tea-flavoured tea. The kind of place you see bewildered OAPs rendered speechless at the till whilst young Eastern European girls repeatedly bark things like *frappe* and *Americano* at them like malfunctioning robots. The machines behind the counter work relentlessly, hissing and chuffing like steam trains. This is the industrial age of coffee, bringing its own languages and customs. But for a smattering of soft-leather sofas near the entrance, the entire place seems to be constructed of differing shades of wood, all of which has been varnished to within an inch of its life.

I spot Marla and join her at the table.

"Hi," I say, deciding that some rudimentary attempt at conversation should probably be made before I start demanding the phone back.

"Hello, Eddie. How was your day, darling?"

I offer a pained smile. "Oh, wonderful. Yours?"

She's still wearing her coat, a patterned scarf wrapped around her neck. A knitted cream-coloured hat sits crookedly on her head. "Well, let's see now. I finally got rid of the parents around midday. Went to this new exhibition at The Fishmarket. Mostly just blokes with their cocks out from what I could see, but interesting enough I suppose. Took a call from the ex: all *rah-rah-rah-*

you-threw-paint-all-over-my-car and then *boo-hoo-hoo-I'm-so-sorry-honey-I-love-you*. It was pretty embarrassing, frankly. So, yeah, my day's been wonderful, too."

I feign a look of surprise. "There were blokes with their cocks out in the fish market?"

Marla laughs, almost begrudgingly. "You're pretty funny, Eddie. In a dorky kind of way, I mean. I was assuming it must have been the drink."

"Touching. Now, come on. Hand over the goods."

She starts fumbling about inside her handbag.

A waitress comes to the table and Marla quickly orders two coffees before I'm able to refuse. She finds the phone and hands it across to me. "You got a text," she says. "From Dave. Wants you to come over to his place or something."

"You read my text?"

"The stupid thing kept beeping at me. Can't you change the setting on it or something?"

"I don't know. Anyway, that's not the point! You could have put it on silent."

"I don't have time to be working out how your phone works."

"But you have time to read my texts?"

"*Text*, Eddie. Singular. Besides, what's the fuss all about? Dave wants to meet you. Hardly scandal of the century." She leans forward across the table. "You know, some girls might think you left the phone on purpose, just so you had an excuse to buy me a coffee today."

"Some girls need clinical assistance. As we've so

very clearly established from this whole episode."

The waitress returns with two trough-sized cups of coffee. She's a youngish girl, eighteen perhaps, her hair blonde and wispy and set back in a ponytail. Marla places a hand on her forearm as she sets down the drinks.

"Let me ask you something, honey," she says. "This man sitting here: do you find him attractive?"

The waitress gives me a quick once-over, bored and unenthusiastic. "No," she says in a heavy accent, "not really. He's okay, I suppose."

"If I were to tell you that last night I had sex with this man, what would be your reaction?"

"Marla!" I gasp. "Are you *actually* insane?"

"Shush, Eddie, let the girl answer. This is important."

The waitress shrugs listlessly. "That he's lucky."

"Thank you, dear," Marla says, sending the waitress on her way. "So, there you have it, Eddie. The fact is you got *lucky* last night. You should be grateful. So less of the pithiness, please."

"Yeah, I'm eternally grateful. And as for *this morning* – well, I never wanted it to end. Which reminds me, why did you tell your parents I was a bloody architect?"

"Well, I had to tell them something. I don't even know what you do."

"I work in insurance."

She frowns. "Well, I could hardly tell them that."

"How about not telling them *anything*?"

"How about not doing whatever the hell it was

you did in my *bin*? I was merely expressing an interest in your life as my wonderful, doting boyfriend."

"Great. And what exactly are you going to tell them became of this wonderful, doting boyfriend? That I joined the Foreign Legion? That I died in a freak boating accident?"

"Both good suggestions, but we haven't crossed that bridge yet."

I nearly choke on my coffee at this. "*We* have crossed every bridge we're ever going to cross, Marla. How you get out of this nice little hole you've dug for yourself is quite your own business."

"Actually, they've invited us to dinner. This Saturday. I've said yes."

"Oh my God. You *are* actually crazy. I was kidding at first, but it's true."

Marla sighs. "Look, don't get your knickers in a twist. We'll work a way out of this. We just need to do it right."

"No way. Absolutely no way am I being a part of this anymore. This is your problem. You fix it."

"Relax. You're so uptight all the time. This thing will work itself out. But I will need you to come on Saturday. Look, at the worst you'll get a free meal. At Benedict's – which, by the way, is a pretty bloody nice restaurant."

"I don't care if it's at The Ivy! I'm not doing it."

"Now you're just being childish."

"I'm being childish? Marla, I'm not the one who can't admit to my parents that I've had sex with somebody without practically being married to them first."

I look around to check nobody's listening in. Fortunately, the place has become busy with the after-work rush, so our words are camouflaged under a constant din of activity: conversation and laughter, cutlery chinking against porcelain, the low hum of generic jazz playing through the café's sound system.

"I'll pay you," Marla says suddenly, as though in a flash of inspiration.

"How much?" I ask.

"Actually, you weren't supposed to agree to that."

"Well, I guess I'm not such a fabulous guy, after all. Three hundred and I'll do it."

"*Three hundred quid?*"

"No, three hundred Chocolate Buttons. Yes, three hundred quid, Marla. And for that you get a virtuoso performance. I'll have the olds eating out of my hand."

Marla swirls a spoon around in her coffee, as though fishing there for an answer. "Deal," she says after a while. "Three hundred it is."

"Fine. But this is the last time. You better get your excuses all worked out, because after this I'm gone."

"Fair enough. But you'd better be impressive."

"Oh, don't you worry, Marla Jennifer. I'll have them ordering the wedding papers *for you*."

I sit back in my chair, half-annoyed and – actually – half-flattered. This must be how gigolos feel, I suppose: used and a little delighted. To think that anybody, even crazy Marla, would be prepared to pay three hundred pounds for just one evening of my escorting services does actually come as something of a compliment. I feel like going home and doing upside-down sit-ups in my pants. "You realise the sex will be extra, of course," I caution.

"Oh no, Eddie. Just the sparkling wit should suffice."

I reach across the table and pluck one of the napkins from its silver holder. "Well, I suppose for this kind of money I should do a little research," I say, taking a pen from my jacket pocket. "Like, for starters, what the hell is your last name?"

"Dimitri."

"Are you Italian?" I ask, scribbling on the napkin.

"No. Are you dyslexic?"

"What?"

"It's spelt with an *i*, not an *e*. And there's no *y* in it."

I scribble it out and write it again, though I'm pretty sure it's still wrong.

"How old are you?" I ask next.

"Twenty-eight."

"And...err...no, that should do it actually."

"Really? Wow, such probing insights. I feel like you've read my diary."

"Are you always such a sarcy cow?"

For a split-second she seems genuinely taken aback. Then her expression softens. "Only around such highly attractive men," she replies, reverting back to form. "Defence mechanism, they say."

I push the napkin into my jacket pocket and

stand from the table, feeling a little James Bondy about the manoeuvre. "Oh, and it was only sick, by the way."

"I'm sorry?"

"In your bin. I was sick."

"Well, that's nice to know. Thank you for telling me, Eddie. For a moment there I thought you'd done something really embarrassing."

I think about saying something to counter this, but soon realise there really is nothing to say, and so I toss down change for the coffee and leave without saying goodbye.

♂

I'm standing in Dad's kitchen, which is about the size of an A4 piece of paper. The units are plush and modern-looking enough, but all crammed in like the bunched fingers of a perfectly manicured hand. It makes me wonder what Dad's done with all of Mum's crockery. While the kettle boils, I rummage through the fridge: microwave lasagne, microwave chicken korma, microwave spag bol. Thursday, Friday, Saturday.

"You really should start learning to cook for yourself, Dad," I say, as I take the teas through to the living room. "It's not like you haven't got the time."

"Ah, you know me and food, son. All goes down the same hole, dunnit?"

The living room is sparse, minimalist. It all seems a little too modern for Dad, a little too much like *my* flat, come to think of it. There's something disconcerting about having your dad living in a place like this. Dads should live in houses cluttered with garden equipment and boxed-up vinyls and books from the 1970s with "50p" written in pencil on the first page. My dad apparently now lives in a bachelor pad. I half-expect to see a show guitar propped up in the corner.

I take a seat on the black leather sofa beside Dad. "What inch is that?" I ask, nodding to the new TV.

"Thirty-six. Didn't look thirty-six in Curry's. I even got the lad there to fetch a tape-measure to prove it."

"Bet he loved you."

"I suppose it's because Curry's is pretty big in itself. Takes the perspective out of everything. Looks massive in here though."

"The picture okay?"

"Yup."

"Everything tuned in alright?"

"Tune themselves these days, don't they?"

"So you don't need me to do anything with it?"

"Nah. Thanks, son. Everything's done."

"Good."

We sit in silence for a time, slurping at our teas. My tongue still feels a little burnt from the hurried cup of coffee I drank with Marla earlier.

I look around the room, wondering if there's one bit of furniture that hasn't come with the property, right down to the faux-Persian rug and the large arty photograph of a flower on the wall, which I'm amazed Dad hasn't taken down.

"Dave's getting married," I say.

"Oh aye? To Alison?"

I can't help but laugh a little. "Yeah," I reply. "To Alison."

"Well, that'll be good for him, won't it?"

"You've never met her," I remind him.

"No," Dad agrees, blowing across the surface of his tea. "But I'm sure she's fine."

"Wow," I say. "Maybe we should get you to do the speech."

Dad looks across to me, stony-faced, ignoring my sarcasm as usual. "When's the wedding?" he asks.

"June."

"This June?"

"That's what *I* said. Too soon, isn't it?"

Dad shrugs, takes another sip of tea. "I'm sure Dave knows what he's doing. He's a sensible sort of bloke. That reminds me, I wanted you to ask him to come and look at that kitchen door. It's still not closing right. Might need sanding down a bit."

Dave's a carpenter by trade, like his father. Or like Jesus, as he prefers to say.

I nod and look over the back of the sofa at the door. "Yeah, I'll ask him. You're invited to the wedding, by the way."

"Really?" Dad appears to think about this for a while. Then he nods. "Okay."

"Kate's coming too."

"Okay."

"I'm the best man."

"That's good."

I look over to Dad, at his balding, liver-spotted head, and I wonder if one day I'll have a balding, liver-spotted head. Wouldn't catch me in that stripy cardigan though, not if I was a hundred. Why *does* he wear that cardigan? It's like a knitted declaration of celibacy.

So far as I'm aware, Dad hasn't had another woman in his life since Mum died, almost twenty years ago now. Shit, twenty years. It doesn't seem like yesterday since the funeral. In fact, I remember it a lot more clearly than I remember yesterday. Funny how the days seep into one another once you get into life's routine, days without detail. But that one I remember with absolute clarity, the dustiness of the church, the way it made people cough and feel bad about disrupting the service, the stark winter sunlight out in the graveyard, how it bleached the trees of their colour until they matched greys of the headstones – only Mum's was black marble with gold lettering. Reading the name on the thing, it somehow didn't seem to connect with anything in the real world.

"Freeview, is it?" I ask Dad after a time.

"Yeah."

"You'll get all your channels there, then. You'll get your documentaries on that."

"Yeah?"

"And your cowboys. There's one channel that just shows old films all day. Plenty of cowboys on that."

"That's good."

I think of Dad in the churchyard, standing silently by, and Kate squeezing my hand a little too hard, crying softly until I'm struck with the notion that perhaps I should be doing the same. But I'm just wincing in that blunt light, and probably looking as though I'm crying, which isn't the same thing no matter how you consider it. And Uncle Mick nearby, smelling of Rothman's. And the priest's lilting Irish voice swirling all around us, until the words themselves become less important than the manner in which they are spoken.

Then we're tossing in the dirt, one after the other, and once everyone's done all the men go to work on the earth, still suited and booted and muddying their shoes, the old-fashioned Irish way. Uncle Mick giving me a go on his spade, making me feel grown-up and involved, but really I'm not much use (the spade alone is so heavy that I'm only picking up tiny amounts of earth each time). And there's Dad next to me, ploughing on like a machine, heaving great mounds of the earth, grunting each time his spade slices into it. I stop to watch him, and Uncle Mick goes to take the spade back, but he's changing his mind, and one by one the men are dropping away until it's just Dad digging on his own, and all we can hear throughout the churchyard is his rhythmic grunting and exhaling, slicing and heaving. He's working feverishly, head bowed, but I manage to catch a look at his face just once, and I don't know if it's the light of the day or the sweat in his eyes or the fact that he's crying for the woman he's putting to the earth. So I turn away, feeling the moment should be his alone, and see Kate standing a way off, watching us, clutching herself tightly, her body juddering with grief as the first spots of rain come down.

Badger comes padding in from the hallway, her nails *click-click-clicking* on the hardwood flooring and shaking me from my thoughts, bringing me back to the present. She watches us for a few moments without interest. I notice how grey she's looking these days. It started with just a patch on the crown of her head, but now her entire coat has this strange grey-brownish tint, like she's been left out in the rain too long to rust.

"How's the back?" I ask Dad.

"Oh, you know, son. Comes and goes."

"Did Kate ring you?"

"Yeah. Coming down on Saturday. Taking me to The Boathouse."

"That's good. Do a nice steak in The Boathouse."

"Yeah."

"You'll get a nice pint in there."

"Yeah."

Badger comes over and sits on my foot, making a point about the unimportance of my foot and therefore by association the unimportance of me. It's her way of saying she wants her walk without seeming needy.

"Right, better take this one out, then" I say, standing.

"Righty-oh, then. Wrap up warm, won't you? Weather's bad out there."

"Yeah, I will."

We begin making our way over to the front door.

"What about the Town, eh?" I ask as we walk. "Two wins on the bounce. Can't grumble with that."

"No, son, you can't. Not in this league."

"We'll have to get ourselves down there one Saturday."

"Aye, when it's a bit warmer, son. You know how the cold plays my back up."

"Yeah, when it's a bit warmer. Right, I'll be back with the little scamp soon."

"I'll be off to bed in a bit," Dad says. "Just let her back in with your key, will you?"

It's barely past nine o'clock, but Dad's always been one for the early nights. A lifetime of getting up before the sun rises will do that to a person. There's no need for him to be up so early anymore, but I've no doubt he still does, like those people who lose a limb and spend the rest of their lives trying to scratch it.

"Alright then, Dad," I say. "I'll do that."

"Righty-oh. Night then, son."

"Yeah, night Dad."

He closes the door and I'm left standing in the hallway alone, Badger sniffing around my ankles.

And I feel inexorably sad.

4. Any Button to Continue

"Mate! Anyone would think you've been avoiding me."

Friday, and I'm standing on Dave's doorstep in the cold.

"Course I haven't been avoiding you. I lost my phone. Then I found it again."

"I rang you, like, six times last night."

"I know. I got your voicemails."

"Then why didn't you call me back?" Dave asks.

It's a fair question. Truth is, I'd been avoiding his calls deliberately. I just didn't have the will to pick up the phone.

"I meant to. I've just been busy. You know, with work and Dad moving and…whatnot. Look, aren't you going to let me in? It's freezing out here."

Dave screws his face up, like he does when he's thinking, working out the probability of what's been said. Then his expression brightens in a flash, and it's all been tossed aside, filed under 'Too Complicated'. "Yeah, come on in," he chuckles.

I step into the hallway.

Dave's rubbing a towel through his scraggly blond hair. He's wearing a t-shirt that's stuck to his body in damp patches. The t-shirt says 'Save Trees, Eat Beaver' on it.

"Bear with me, Ed," Dave says. "Just got out the shower. Go on through to the living room. Allie'll keep you company."

Dave goes running up the stairs and I'm left

standing in the hallway. For a childish moment, I consider just waiting here for him.

"Eddie," calls a voice from the living room. "Is that you? Come on through."

I walk through to the living room.

Alison's sitting on the sofa in her dressing gown, her feet propped up on the coffee table. She has tiny pieces of cotton wool stuck between her toes and the caustic odour of nail-polish remover fills the air. Her dressing gown has slipped a little too far down her leg, although she seems not to have noticed.

"Hi, Alison," I say, turning my attention to the figurines on the mantelpiece so not to stare. I pick up the first one to hand and pretend to inspect it. Turning it about, I realise it's a wooden carving of an African tribal woman, complete with ludicrously exaggerated curves and humongous breasts.

"Dave's choice, not mine," Alison explains.

"Doesn't surprise me," I say, conscious of where my fingers are on the thing.

I quickly set it back down and look around the room. It's one of these knocked-through jobs where the living room and the dining room combine into one big space. I haven't visited much since Dave and Alison moved in together, and every time I'm back I'm amazed at how much has changed. They bought the place as a doer-upper, but from what I can see now it looks like an actual fully-fledged home where proper grown-up couples live. Dave's changed the windows and varnished the floor and hung new doors. The walls and ceilings are freshly painted, and it looks as though they've bought up half of IKEA to deck the place out.

"Like what we've done?" asks Alison.

"It's great. I'm amazed at how you can afford it all what with the wedding coming up."

"Oh, it hasn't been too bad," she says. "You can pick up a lot of this stuff cheap these days. And Dave can do a lot of the work, of course."

Much to my relief, Alison switches to painting the other foot and I can finally look at her. It's plain to see what attracted Dave to Alison; she's a remarkably good-looking woman, good-looking in the traditional sense that everything is in order and nothing is out of place. Her features are pretty and sharply defined. Her blonde hair, which is usually flowing about her shoulders, is for now tied up so to be out of the way.

I've only known Alison for a little over year – as long as Dave's been going out with her – and for the most part of that year they've been tucked away in this house. I could probably count the amount of times I've met Alison on the fingers of both hands, and the amount of times I've had an actual proper conversation with her on the fingers of just one.

"Speaking of the wedding," she says, "I hear you've been asked to do the honourable thing."

"Huh? Oh, yeah. Well, some poor bugger's got to give him away, I suppose."

Alison laughs. "Good for you. Has he given you any of the details?"

"No, not really."

She sighs and rolls her eyeballs in that *typical Dave* kind of way. Then she gets up and hops over to the dining-room table. She picks up a magazine and passes it across to me. "This is where it's going to be. Felston. In the Cotswolds. Lovely place."

I start leafing through the pages. So far as I can see, Felston is a picture-postcard village. Going by the photos, it's a lot of little limestone bridges and babbling brooks and winding lanes, all set snugly within a patchwork of green and brown fields. There's a handful of cottages and a Post Office and, at the heart of it all, an impressively ancient-looking church, its proud spire punctuating an impossibly blue and cloudless sky.

I quickly pass the magazine back. "Looks great!" I say.

Before I know it, another leaflet is thrust upon me.

"And this is The Bull. Beautiful old pub in the village. Function room at the back. We'll be staying the night here: you, me, Dave, and the maid of honour. There's not enough room for the others so we've put them up in a guesthouse just down the road. It's wonderful, Eddie. Like something out of a film."

My head's spinning a little from all the information. "Well, you seem to have it all worked out," I say.

"God, that's not even the half of it. We've got the menu, the flowers, the dresses. That reminds me, Eddie, we'll have to get you measured up for the suit."

"Of course."

"I'm thinking mauve."

"A mauve suit?"

"No, silly. Mauve waistcoats. To match the bridesmaids' dresses."

"Oh, right. I see."

"Mauve suit," she laughs, returning to the sofa.

Dave comes thundering down the stairs and bundles himself into the living room. "Alright then, Eddie?" he booms.

His t-shirt is still sticking to him where he hasn't dried himself properly, revealing a softness around his chest and midriff. It's the softness of male contentment. He's always been a big lug of a guy, but big in the naturally thickset sort of way, and now he's acquired a new kind of shape, the kind brought on by eating too much good food. In his younger days, Dave chased more women than I'd care to remember – having his fair share of success, too – and now I'm inclined to think it's the loss of this chase that's slackened him up a little. Still, having said this, I don't think I've ever seen him looking so happy.

"Allie's just been showing me the wedding stuff," I tell him.

"Yeah? Looks good, right?"

"Looks great."

"I was just telling Eddie about getting him measured up," Alison says.

"Feel like I'm going to my own funeral," I chuckle.

Dave turns to me. "Why would you feel like you're going to your own funeral?"

"Oh, you know. I just mean about getting

measured up. You know…"

And the words are out before I can control them.

"…like for my coffin."

Dave's giving me that look again. "Well, I'm glad our wedding makes you feel that way, mate."

"Oh, I didn't mean…"

But I'm not exactly sure what I did mean, so I trail off.

Dave goes over to where Alison is sitting and playfully clambers over her.

"Dave!" she squeals. "My nails!"

"Your nails will be fine. Your lips, I can't vouch for. Not after I kiss 'em off."

And then he's actually on top of her, pinning her down. Alison's giggling away girlishly and Dave's making groaning noises – proper sex-groan noises. His hand is slipping inside her dressing gown, and I find myself staring at the ceiling whilst he tickles shrill little yelps out of her.

"New light fittings, Dave?" I ask, just in case he's forgotten I'm here.

"What's that, Ed? Oh yeah, they're new."

"I like them. They seem to…emit a lot of light."

"Well, yeah, that is kind of the idea of 'em." He climbs off Alison and comes over to me. "Now, it's time for me to show you something," he says. "Something pretty amazing. But I need you to close your eyes first."

"Why?"

"Just stop being a knob and close 'em."

I close my eyes.

"Prepare yourself, Ed. You're about to experience something the likes of which you've never experienced before – something beyond your wildest dreams."

For a terrifying moment, I think Dave's going to suggest a threesome. I'll just pop my eyes open and there will be Alison, unsheathed of her dressing gown and writhing on the sofa. "Okay," I mutter nervously.

Dave goes to stand behind me, laying a hand on each of my shoulders.

Shit, it's really happening. For once in my life, my sick little brain is right on the money.

"Keep those eyes closed, Ed," he says, leading me forward.

I sense we're not heading for the couch, thank God, but leaving the room instead, through the kitchen and then down a flight of stairs. I put my hands out to steady myself, and touch bare bricks on both sides.

We're going down into the cellar.

The sex dungeon.

"Now, open 'em up, Ed," Dave announces when we're at the bottom.

I open my eyes. Darkness. "I can't see anything, Dave."

"That's 'cause I haven't got the lights on yet. Gimme a tick."

"Well, what was the point of me closing my eyes? Could've broken my bloody neck coming down h–"

Dave turns on the lights and I'm stunned into silence. A kind of hushed reverence befalls us, like pilgrims arriving at the Promised Land. Sprawled out before us is a sea of chrome and shiny plastic, a techno-nerd's wet dream: electronics stacked three, four storeys high.

"You've got a PlayStation 4," I say dreamily.

"Oh no, Ed. Pete's got a PlayStation 4. *I* have a home-entertainment system." He spreads his hands out as he says this. "System-linked. Surround Sound. Look at those woofers. Blow your bloody head off, just one of those could. Of course, I'm pretty much soundproofed down here now. And for the *piece-de-resistance.*" He walks over to the far-side wall and pulls down a projector screen, perhaps six-foot wide. When it's fully drawn, he stands before it with folded arms, like an army general standing before the map of a great land he has conquered.

"This is…," I search for the appropriate word, "*incredible.*"

"If you build it," Dave says, strolling up to me manfully and clapping his hands on the sides of my arms, "they will come. This is what I've been ringing you for, man. I wanted you to be here when I first fired her up."

"Oh, you didn't have to wait for me," I mumble apologetically.

"It just felt like you should have been here. Remember the Spectrum, with the rubber keys. The Commodore 64. The Amiga. Shit, we had some times on that. Think we nearly burned the thing out in the end." He laughs. "And the PS1. Ha, we barely knew where to put the disk in."

"The Dreamcast," I remind him.

"An underrated beast," Dave adds wistfully. "See, this is what I mean. We can plot our lives out with these things. Like markers in the sand. This latest one – what with the house and Allie – you know, it just felt like kind of a big deal. A new chapter. And I wanted you to be there when I opened that first page."

I consider pointing out that perhaps a married man shouldn't be playing video games at all, but I don't want to ruin the moment, as much for myself as for Dave.

"So, you've had a go on it already, then?"

"Of course I've had a go on it. I couldn't wait for you forever. You got some catching up to do, my friend." He passes across a control pad, like he's giving me the keys to the mansion.

"What are the graphics like?" I ask.

"Eye-watering," he sighs. "Why don't you see for yourself?"

I move towards one of the leather armchairs that Dave has placed strategically in the centre of the room. "Wait a minute. Are these La-Z-Boys?"

"Oh yeah. Ordered them in from the States. Just give us a shout if you want the massager switched on."

I sit down, kicking the leg-rest forward and falling into a state of near-horizontal bliss.

"Fancy a cold one before we start?"

"Yeah, I'll just fetch a couple, shall I?" I say, attempting to stand again.

"No, Ed. You shall *not* just fetch a couple." He looks across to me, holding my gaze until the penny drops.

"Oh, you are shitting me!"

"I shit you not, Private Corrigan."

"You are *shitting* me."

"Why don't you see if I'm shitting you?"

I reach down the arm of the La-Z-Boy and open the door of a small hatch. Cold steam rises from it as though I'm opening some kind of alien portal, and there inside stands two rows of icy cold lagers.

"Oh, God," I gasp.

Dave laughs raucously, banging a hand repeatedly on the arm of his chair.

"Dave, this room is your greatest achievement," I sigh, cracking open one of the beers.

"You know what, Eddie? I think it just might be."

And for the next three hours we sit there, bathed in the soothing glow of the projector screen, barely conversing but for the odd *'good shot, Dave'* or *'flank 'em, Eddie'*. It *is* just like old times, back with the Spectrum and the Amiga, and by the end of it all I half-expect to hear Mum's voice calling from somewhere upstairs, saying that we'll turn our eyes square or that it's time for Dave to go home.

♂

I'm sitting on my bed, feet hanging over the edge. There's still some mud on the ends of my trouser-legs. A little of it has gotten on the floor and on my Transformers bedspread, although most of it on the Decepticons. Dad won't mind, probably won't even notice.

I'm on the Atari ST. Operation Wolf. *My finger punching like mad on the joystick button.*

The door slowly creaks open, and Dave pops his head inside.

"Alright, Eddie."

"Alright, Dave."

"Your dad let me in."

Tap-tap-tap-tap-tap.

"Mind if I come in, mate?"

"No," I say.

"I brought the new Galvatron. He turns into a gun."

"Rad." Tap-tap-tap-tap.

Dave walks to the centre of the room, standing about awkwardly. "What you playing?" *he asks.*

"Operation Wolf."

"What level?"

"Ammunition Dump."

Dave nods as though impressed and comes to sit beside me on the bed. "I brought Galvatron," *he says, holding up the plastic action-figure.* "He turns into a gun."

"You already said that."

"Oh, right."

On the screen, I'm shooting strange, pixelated blobs that loosely resemble members of a guerrilla terrorist organisation.

"Sorry about your mum, mate." *It's the first and possibly only time in my life that Dave will apologise to me.*

"Why? Didn't kill her, did you?

"No, mate! Of course I didn't!"

"It was a joke, Dave."

"Oh, right."

A tank comes into view on the screen, and I concentrate all my firepower on it until it explodes. A horrible screeching noise erupts from the monitor.

"What was it like?" he asks.
"Bit weird."
"Is that mud from...?"
"Yeah."
"You've got some on your bed."
"Only on the Decepticons."
"No, look. There's a bit here on Optimus Prime."
"Dave!"
"Sorry."

The door opens again and Kate wanders in. Her eyes are still red and swollen, but I guess she's done all the crying she's going to do for the time being.

Dave sits up a little straighter and brushes his hair with his hand. He's always doing this around Kate.

"Hi, Dave."

"Alright, Kate. Sorry about your mum."

"Thanks. Listen, Eddie, I'm going out for a bit. You going to be alright?"

I shrug, not taking my eyes from the screen, still tapping away like crazy.

"Don't worry, Kate. I'll look after him."

"Thanks, Dave. You're a good friend."

I don't look at Dave, but I know his freckled cheeks must be blushing like mad.

"I'll be back soon," she says. "Dad says we can have pizza tonight."

"Mega," I say, without much conviction.

Kate drifts out of the room like a ghost.

"Reckon your dad will let me have some?" Dave asks when she's gone. "Some pizza, I mean?"

Dave's always on the take for food. Mum used to call him "The Human Dustbin".

I shrug. "Reckon so."

"Or I could just have a slice of yours. Don't wanna

upset anybody."

"Whatever."

Dave starts playing with Galvatron, clicking away at his arms and legs, trying to work out how to transform him properly. When he's done, he points the gun at me and pulls the trigger. The end of the barrel flashes and it emits a shrieking sound effect. It all seems pretty cheap.

"You know what, Ed? I don't think I like Transformers much anymore."

"Me neither," I say.

The TV screen turns red, indicating that I've died, and the words '**You Have Sustained a Lethal Injury – Continue Yes/No**' flash before me.

And Dave, who'd normally be fighting me like a jackal for the joystick about now, just quietly puts his arm around my shoulders and lets me play again.

5. Dancing Indiscrete

6) Skip Town

I sit looking at what I've written, playing the scenario over. I couldn't just disappear, of course. That would be awful. But I could book a holiday somewhere and throw my passport into the sea, tell Dave I lost it. By the time they repatriated me it could all be over and done with. Not Europe, mind. You can fly Europe on a library card these days. They'd have me back in no time. But nowhere too dangerous, either. I saw a documentary on Channel Five about Thai prisons the other night and it was enough to put a person off for life (which is, I suppose, the whole point). Or was it Malaysia? Probably best just to leave out Southeast Asia altogether, play it safe.

America, perhaps. Good old Uncle Sam. They speak English over there, at least. Fewer complications with the officials. Although don't they still execute people in some states? I should probably find out which states execute people and which ones don't before setting off. But then, why would they execute me for losing my passport? Seems a bit harsh.

Christ, I'm a selfish bastard. A horrible, selfish bastard.

I'm lying on my sofa in my favourite slouch clothes, my cotton sweatpants and hoodie. I don't wear the hoodie out and about these days. People tend to think you're going to steal something. But it's probably the most comfortable piece of clothing I've ever owned, so I saved it for my Saturday afternoon doss-abouts. The Cobblers match is playing in the background: Carlisle away. The internet connection isn't so great here, and the radio-feed keeps interrupting, but I've learned that if I put the laptop on top of the fridge I catch about fifty seconds of every minute, which is about as good as it gets. IT Pete nearly shat a baby when I told him I thought it might be the fridge keeping the laptop cool. I'll never hear the end of that one.

I check my watch. Three-thirty. Four and a half hours until I meet Marla and her parents. I spent this morning sifting through my wardrobe, considering what I should wear. What do people wear for dates these days, anyway? I almost opted for a shirt-and-tie combo, until I decided it made me look too much like I was going for a job interview, which in actual fact is exactly what it's starting to feel like, albeit a job interview with a guaranteed pay cheque.

I must have been crazy, agreeing to this.

The intercom chimes and I go to answer it. It's Kate, presumably with Jess and Dad in tow, so I buzz them up. Whilst I wait for them to come up the stairs, I give the place a quick once-over, check there's nothing embarrassing lying about.

"Hellooo," Kate coos cheerily as she comes through the door. She hurries over and hugs me, rubs her knuckles gently against my head.

I give Jess a hug too, but decide to draw the line at hugging Dad. Bit too weird.

Kate's looking pretty as usual, wrapped in a

grey winter coat and scarf. She has these great tumbling curls of hair, chocolate-coloured, and she's forever throwing them about, tucking them behind her ears, an infectious kind of liveliness always buzzing around her. It's fair to say that most of my mates fancied Kate growing up, with Dave fronting the queue. Of course, Kate didn't have the slightest of interest in any of them, although at the time I put this down to the fact that they were all knobs rather than the fact they all *had* knobs.

I suppose Jess is the guy of the two, if that's really the way it works. She's certainly the most tomboyish of the pair, although oddly she wears a lot of pink. Her hair is kept in a neat little bob, and she looks quite short and squat when standing next to Kate. If it were a straight relationship you'd probably say Kate was out of Jess' league, although perhaps the leagues work differently for lesbians – like in rugby union, or cricket.

"Good to see you, Eddie," Jess says, in her light Edinburgh brogue.

"You too, Jess. How's London?"

"Yep, still there."

I always ask Jess how London is, and she always tells me it's still there – a pretty stupid habit on the part of both of us, I suppose, but a little ritual we've come to enjoy over the years.

"What's the score, son?" Dad asks, noticing the commentary coming from the kitchen.

Dad's not wearing his cardigan today, I notice. Maybe Kate made him take it off before coming out. Today he's wearing a white shirt and a pair of reasonably new-looking jeans with his favourite pair of John Lobb's (which he's even gone to the trouble of giving a good polish by the looks of things). He's left the shirt un-tucked and it covers up his beer-belly quite nicely. Kate and Jess probably did a hurried makeover on him before leaving the flat.

"Nil-nil," I tell Dad, and he gives a *no-news-is-good-news* kind of nod.

Kate starts to walk about the flat, picking things up – a plate, a fork, a cup of tea that I hadn't quite finished, actually – before taking them through to the kitchen. I like to think of myself as pretty house-proud these days, but clearly not quite house-proud enough for Kate. If the place was immaculate she'd still find something to pick up. She's been playing mother for so many years now that I suppose it's hard to let such a thing go.

"How was The Boathouse?" I ask Dad.

"Pretty busy."

"Saturday afternoon," I say. "Gotta expect it."

"Yeah."

"Food alright?"

"Yeah, nice steak. Cooked it just right."

"Good." I don't really know what else to add to this, except to perhaps tell Dad not to bother applying for the *Sunday Times* food-critic position any time soon.

"Listen, Eddie," Kate says, coming back in from the kitchen. "We've got some news." She looks to Jess, grinning wildly and clapping her hands together. "We're having a baby!"

"*Adopting* a baby," Jess adds quickly, before I

can make some wisecrack about it.

Although really I'm too stunned to be wisecracking. Kate having a *baby*? I didn't see that one coming.

"Really?" I say. "Well, that is some news."

"I didn't want to tell you over the phone. But we've been so excited about it."

"And they...let you do that these days, do they?" I ask.

"Yes, Eddie," Kate sighs. "They let us have bank accounts now and everything."

"I mean, I just wasn't sure...you know, where the law stands, I mean. Not really been keeping abreast of the news lately."

"It should all be fine," Kate says. "Not to say there won't be some obstacles in our way, but as long as we can prove we're decent people I don't see what should hold us back."

"And if all else fails," I suggest, "you could always adopt a child from one of these third-world countries like the movie-stars do. Scotland, say."

"Oh, fucking hilarious, Eddie," Jess sighs, but she's smiling.

"No, well, that's good news," I say. "*Great news.* I'm really pleased for you. Hey, I could be like the father figure!"

Kate and Jess are looking to one another dubiously. "Well, they do say that's important," Kate murmurs. "And, of course, there'll be Dad, too."

I look to Dad, who appears mystified by the whole thing. He's wearing the kind of expression you see on soldiers of the Great War in those old, grainy newsreels. He's got trench-face. I can only imagine how he took the news the first time around.

"Good news, eh, Dad?" I ask.

"Yeah," he replies. "If you say so, son."

Kate rolls her eyes. "Of course, Dad would rather see me physically inseminated, but what can you do?"

Dad actually winces.

"He spent most of the afternoon talking about Callum bloody O'Connor."

"I was just saying he's got his own firm now," Dad protests. "Tarmacing. Ten vehicles. Lot of money involved. And I remembered he always had a shine for you in school."

I look to Jess and shrug apologetically. She smiles back.

"So, when do you get it then?" I ask.

"Oh, it's a long process we have to go through," Jess replies. "And we're still only at the beginning. It'll be ages yet."

"But we thought you should both know from the outset," Kate says.

"Well, yeah," I say. "You know, good luck with it all and everything."

"Thanks, Eddie," she says. "I knew you'd be pleased for us."

Kate and Jess both hug me so that I'm sandwiched between them.

Dad makes his way unsteadily over to the sofa and sits down. He's probably had a few bitters in The Boathouse to calm his nerves.

"Tea?" I ask, once I've been released.

I receive an order of two teas and a coffee and go through to the kitchen. Kate follows behind me.

"So, Dave's getting married, eh?" she asks. "Has he asked you to be the best man?"

"Yep," I say, flicking on the kettle.

"That's great. You must be excited about it."

"Yeah, it's...pretty exciting."

"You out tonight celebrating?"

"No, I've got this thing. A dinner thing."

"Like a dinner *date* thing?"

"No, not really a date. More of a...well, I'm not sure what you'd call it, actually."

"But with a woman?" Kate asks.

"And her parents."

"Her parents! Sounds pretty serious."

"Oh, yeah," I say over the roaring of the kettle. "It's pretty damn serious alright."

♂

Marla was right; Benedict's *is* a bloody nice restaurant. So nice, in fact, that it's not altogether apparent what style of cuisine it provided, just something vaguely European and served with an element of disdain. I'm glad I put the shirt on now – my proper going-out shirt. Yet still I feel broadly inadequate.

The restaurant itself is traditional fare: small, low-roofed and heavily shadowed, with orangey orbs of candlelight emanating from the ten or so tables dotted about. Intimate, you might call it. Too intimate, if you happen to be dining with the

Dimitris. The windows are draped with thick, ornately patterned curtains that belong to another century. Decorating the walls are curious instruments from a lost age, the kind you can only hazard a guess as to what purpose they ever served all those years ago. The one above my head looks disconcertingly like a Victorian bedpan. I mean, who puts bedpans where people are eating? I couldn't care if it came off the bloody Ark; it's still a place where a people used to crap.

"Nice, isn't it, Eddie?" Marla says, rubbing my knee.

"Yeah, it's lovely."

"Would you believe you can actually get frogs' legs here?" Jean asks, flipping through the menu. "Have you ever had frogs' legs before, Eddie?"

"Can't say I have, Jean."

"I've heard they taste like chicken," she remarks.

"Really? They're always saying human beings taste like chicken, aren't they?" It's supposed to be a quirky little conversation starter, but it just comes out sounding deranged.

Jean peers over the top of her spectacles at me. "Is that so?"

"So they say," I mutter, floundering under her glare. "Cannibals, I mean."

"Like those rugby chaps in the Andes," Robin chuckles, grinning mischievously. "Ate the buttocks first, you know. Makes sense, I suppose."

"Robin, really!" Jean gasps. "Hardly talk for the dinner table, dear."

I share a little conspiratorial glance with Robin,

and we smile at one another. Getting in with the old man.

Robin's dressed smartly in a jacket and tie. It makes me wonder whether I should have worn one after all, but it's too late to worry about such things now. Hopefully he'll understand that it's a generational thing and no reflection on my level of devotion to his daughter. I'll just have to be extra charming, lay it on a little thicker.

The place seems remarkably quiet for a Saturday night. On the table next to ours is a young loved-up couple, leaning into one another and whispering sweet nothings back and forth. Two middle-aged men are stationed tightly in the corner, one playing a keyboard and the other an acoustic guitar. They look bored and actually in pain, as though each note they play is another death-knell for any dreams of a real career in music they may have been falsely harbouring. I guess they never figured it would turn out this way.

The guy next to me is flirting and giggling, like he's fallen out of the love-tree and caught every ounce of sap on the way down. He's staring deeply into his girlfriend's eyes, playing footsie, and generally making me feel like I should be doing things a little more boyfriend-ish rather than just sitting here like a spare part. But I'm hoping to warm to the role as the evening progresses. I owe it to Marla, after all, what with the price I'm coming at tonight.

"So, Eddie, what is it your parents do?" Jean asks.

Jean's made quite the effort tonight, too. She

wearing her hair up, a silk satin scarf wrapped around her neck, making her look, quite appropriately, a little French.

"My dad's in the construction business," I reply. "Although he's semi-retired now." I feel like the biggest arsehole for lying, but out it comes anyway.

"I suppose that's where you picked up the bug yourself."

"I suppose it is," I agree. "Dad's always saying he couldn't keep me off the Lego bricks as a kid."

Jean and Robin laugh graciously at this. It might be bullshit, but it feels good. Feels like I'm finally getting into my flow. Anyway, what does it matter? This whole situation is bullshit, after all. What harm will sprinkling a little more on top do?

"And your mother?"

"My mum, she...err...passed away." *Passed away*. Like I'm a bloody priest or something.

"Oh, gosh, I *am* sorry, Eddie," says Jean, and she seems quite genuine about it. "Was it recently?"

"No, no. I was nine."

Marla's looking at me strangely now. I guess she's trying not to look shocked, because it really is something she should already know. She reaches across and squeezes my hand, and this seems perfectly genuine too. I squeeze back and give her a little smile.

Marla's looking incredibly good tonight. She's put on a little black sparkly number – for whose benefit exactly, I don't know, but I had to refrain from appearing knocked back when I first set eyes on her.

"That must have been hard," Jean says.

Trying not to look knocked back at the sight of your pain-in-the-arse daughter, Jean? Yes, I suppose it was.

"Oh, you know, I was young," I reply. "I think it was harder on my sister, really."

"Your sister's the eldest?"

"Yes. By three years. She lives in London these days, so I don't see so much of her. I saw her today, though. She told me she's having a baby, in fact."

"*Really?* Oh, that's fabulous news. When is she due?"

I consider this one. "I'm not really sure. Not for a while yet."

"Saw this documentary on TV the other night," Robin pipes up. "This *man* was allegedly having a baby. Of course, it all turned out to be this enormous whopper. But he had the lot of them going! Reporters from all over the world had come to see him. Ha, what a wheeze!"

This pretty much kills off any further conversation of Kate's baby, and we get on with the business of ordering our food. I pluck for some kind of chicken dish cooked in a mystery sauce. From the prices on the menu, I see how they can afford to be so empty. A meal for four should just about cover the month's rent on the place. Then Robin orders up a bottle of champagne and I decide not to worry about the cost anymore.

An hour or so later, and things are going swimmingly. Everyone enjoyed the food, and the second bottle of champagne is well on its way down. Even Jean is getting a little light-headed and giggly.

I've been finding out a lot more about Marla. It's odd doing things this way around, like taking a crash-course in Girlfriend.

Marla's something of a budding artist, it seems. She's been painting since she was a child, and she once spilt a pot of acrylic on the Dimitris' brand new cream carpet. Robin seems to be in full support of her artistic tendencies, although I get the impression that Jean, without fully coming out and saying so, would rather she put her efforts into something more practical. She's sold a few of her paintings locally – a long time ago, from what I can gather – although not anything like what she'd need to sell to make a career out of it. I haven't been able to glean what it is she actually does for a living. Perhaps nothing. Maybe Robin and Jean still help her out. I get the impression they're pretty well-to-do, after all. I really should have investigated these matters a little more intently back at the coffee shop. It'd be a fine set of circumstances if Robin and Jean cottoned onto the fact I had no idea what Marla went out and did every day.

As well as the painting, Marla also had a pony when she was a child. The only time I've even *seen* a pony in Northampton is when the Gypsies come to town. Maybe she didn't grow up around here. Again, I should've asked. Her pony was called Twinkle, but one day she fell off Twinkle and after that developed a pretty insidious fear of anything hoofed. Twinkle had to go, and so he was sold back to the pony club. This is all told with great relish by Jean while Marla squirms away with embarrassment.

"Do you do any sports yourself, Eddie?" Robin asks.

"Oh, I play a little football." *Playing a little football* actually amounts to a Sunday afternoon kick-about I had down the park with Dave and the boys maybe six months ago now.

"Enjoy a spot of the old tennis myself. We'll have to have a game sometime."

I look to Marla uncertainly. "Err, yeah, that sounds good, Robin. Look forward to it."

Besides from the painting and the pony, I also manage to determine the following: Marla is an only child, she once played Mary in the school nativity play, she once dated a Welshman called Gavin who played for Northampton Town Rugby Club (and might have gone on to play for Wales were it not for an unfortunate calf injury), she nearly died scuba-diving off the Egyptian coast in 1998, and she went through something of a 'grunge phase' in her teens, wearing her hair in dreadlocks until finally she grew sick of not being able to wash it anymore, much to Jean's overwhelming relief. By the time the drinks are finished, my head is so full of Marla's formative years I feel as though I've read a triple-decker biography of her life in one sitting. It's just a shame I'm learning so much about her at the time when I'm going to need it least.

Just as the evening seems like it's drawing to a pretty satisfactory close, lover-boy on the table beside us, who has by this time done just about everything to his girlfriend short of impregnate her, stands from his chair and goes over to talk to the musicians in the corner. After a short discussion, they bring the manager of the restaurant – a short, Gallic-looking man – into the conversation. The manager is shrugging extravagantly and looking about the restaurant. Then he comes over to our table.

"Excuse me, ladies and gentlemen," he says in a heavy French accent. "The couple 'ere are on their anniversary. They wonder if they will be able to dance before they leave, and I wanted to check that this would not be disturbing you. They 'ave been practicing their salsa dancing since their 'oneymoon, you see."

The blood drains from me.

"Ooooh," Jean coos. "My daughter and her boyfriend here do salsa dancing. Of course it wouldn't be a problem. Why don't the two of you join them?"

"Ah, no," I protest. "I'm a little-"

But the damn Frenchman is already scuttling excitedly over to the couple to explain. The boyfriend breaks into a smile and approaches us.

"You guys do salsa?" he asks.

He's a bronzed thing, tall and statuesque. He looks like he may actually come from the place where salsa dancing originated, wherever the hell that might be. Probably the same place as the dip.

"They *met* at salsa class," Jean cheers. The woman's half-bloody-pissed

"Really?" the bronzed statue asks. "I haven't seen either of you around. Where do you go?"

"Daventry," Marla quickly replies.

Daventry?

"Daventry?" Jean asks.

"They were oversubscribed here," Marla quickly explains. "Couldn't get in."

The bronzed statue looks confused for a while, but then waves it aside. "Anyway, come on over, guys. We'd love for you to dance with us. It's always more fun with a group."

"Happy anniversary!" Robin cheers, raising his champagne glass.

Marla cautiously stands from her chair.

I try to think of any way I could just not move, just stay here and not move. Perhaps if I shut my eyes for long enough it will all just go away.

Marla takes my hand, squeezing it in that same way she squeezed it after finding out my mother was deceased, and I realise then I have no choice but to join her. She leads the way over to the musicians and I follow with heavy steps, slouching like a man on his way to the gallows. Before I'm even there the guitarist is counting us in and then we're off, like horses out of the traps. In my case, I'm actually dancing like a horse, one that's stuck in the middle of an ice-rink. I'm trying to watch what the bronzed statue is doing, but it's hard because my limbs are flailing and getting in the way. He's gyrating his snake-hips around his girlfriend, so I'm trying to do the same to Marla, but somehow my version seems far more lecherous and uncoordinated, rather more like a public assault than a dance. The hideous charade goes on for five or six minutes, and rather than improve I seem to be getting worse. I'm praying for the band to stop, but on they go, endlessly round and round with the same maddening chorus.

The bronzed statue's girlfriend is looking at Marla sympathetically, as if she's wondering how it's possible for a woman to be with an abomination like me. *I can free you*, her eyes seem to be saying. *There are many more men out there, men who can dance the salsa like lions! It doesn't have to be this way*. But Marla, God love her, is not even looking at the woman; she's looking at me. She's watching me dancing like a freak and she actually seems to be having fun – or, at least, she's displaying no outward signs of humiliation.

When finally and mercifully the music comes to an end, I turn to the bronzed statue and his girlfriend, sweating and breathless. I feel like I've been through hell, and I'm pretty sure I've got the look to match. My squashed foot is throbbing with pain. The heat from my body has turned my shirt into a crinkled mess and, catching a glimpse of myself in a nearby mirror, I see my face has come to resemble a boiled ham.

"Thanks, guys," I say to the couple, as though addressing fellow professionals. "Appreciate that."

I take Marla by the hand, determined to salvage one small iota of masculine pride from the wreckage of what has just happened, and storm back to the table.

"Well, that was very good," Jean says on our return. She says it in the tone of a primary-school teacher addressing the class dunce. *At least you tried*, she might just as well have added.

"Mexican variation of the dance," I mutter. "Probably a little different from what you're used to seeing."

"We've ordered the bill," Robin explains, as though sensing I might want to make a sharp exit.

"Eddie'll get this," Marla offers, slipping a hand up the back of my shirt and rubbing my sweaty back.

My heart lurches up into my throat.

"Oh, no, no, no," Jean says. "Don't be silly. We can't let Eddie pay."

"Mum, calm down. It's alright. We agreed before we came out. Honestly, it's our treat."

"Oh, well, really Eddie. That *is* kind. Of course, we must take the two of you out soon. *Our treat*."

"Bu-"

Marla looks at me imploringly, a quiet murderousness in her eyes. "Just pop it on the card, Eddie," she says steadily. "It'll be alright."

Whatever fight was left in me has gone. I just want to get out of the place. I just want it over with. But I make a mental note to add the cost of the bill to the three hundred pounds she already owes me.

"Of course," I say, barely able to conceal my disappointment. "No problem."

I walk over to the bar in a daze to square up the bill. There's a slightly worrying moment when the card-reader seems to be creaking and groaning forever without spitting out the receipt, and I'm thinking the account just won't take it, but it eventually relents and the card is handed back to me still hot from the punishment.

We order a taxi for Jean and Robin while putting on our coats and I try to avoid the puzzled glares of the bronzed statue and his girlfriend as we shuffle out into the street. Even the mournful expressions of the musicians seem to deepen as I pass.

"Are you sure you don't want to share our taxi?" Jean asks outside, a little wobbly on her feet.

"No, Mum, we'll walk. We're not far from here, and you're going a different way."

"We'll have to swap numbers, Eddie," Robin says. "About that tennis match."

We exchange numbers awkwardly in the cold, and just as we're done the taxi pulls up beside us.

Before getting in, Jean totters over to me and gives me a big motherly hug, rubbing my back vigorously. "Oh, I'm so glad Marla has finally found one she's sticking with for once," she whispers into my ear. "You seem nice." She kisses me wetly on the cheek.

Sticking with? For once?

We say our goodbyes and wave them off, and then it's just the two of us.

Alone.

"What the fuck was *that*?" I ask.

"What the fuck was what?"

"With the bill."

"Well, I don't want them thinking I'm going out with a stingy bastard, do I?"

"You owe me, like...I don't even know *how* much you owe me now."

"Well, I don't just walk around with that kind of money on me, Eddie."

"There's a cash-point over there. I'll happily escort you."

"Look, give me your bank details and I'll transfer whatever I owe you tomorrow. Honesty, anyone would think I asked you to re-mortgage your house. It's only money."

"Yeah, it's only…"

I fumble around in my pocket and find the receipt

"…*two hundred and ninety-six pounds and thirty-eight pence*, Marla. That's all!"

"Now you're just being a prat, Eddie," she says, turning and walking away.

I limp after her as quickly as I can. "You had this planned all along, didn't you? *Have a dessert, Mum. Just order another bottle, Dad.* Jesus, I should've seen it coming. You've taken me for a right royal ride here, haven't you?"

"Well, you weren't complaining when you thought my parents were paying. Couldn't get it down you bloody quick enough."

"That was the *deal*."

"Yeah, well, maybe I'm not so hot on the idea of my parents thinking I'm going out with you anymore."

"Oh no, Marla. No way. You're not turning that one on me."

"I mean, what was all that talk about *eating people*, for God's sake? You were supposed to be making an impression."

"Well, your mum seemed more than impressed."

"My mum was three sheets to the wind."

"And that's my fault now?"

"What I mean is I could have brought Mr. Bean along tonight for all the difference it would have made. He might have salsaed a little better, too."

"Ow! Wait!" I cry. "Stop walking so fast."

We're passing a bus shelter, so I hop over to the bench and sit down to catch my breath.

Marla stops and turns. "What's wrong with you?"

"My foot. It's killing me."

"Why?"

"Because your bloody dad used it for a door-wedge the other day, that's why."

"Don't talk about Dad that way," she says, walking back and hunkering down before me. Then she's actually taking my shoe off and rolling down my sock.

"Ow! What are you doing?"

"What do you think? Trying to get a look at it."

"Why? Are you a nurse now?"

"I work part-time at the vet's."

"You're a vet?"

"Receptionist."

"Oh, a vet's receptionist!" I gasp. "Thank God you're here. And what does a vet's receptionist know about the human foot?"

"A damn sight more than an insurance…whatever the hell you are! Now stop being a baby."

She yanks off the sock. The pain causes me to convulse and bash my against the Perspex glass of the shelter. Whoever said you can't feel pain in two places at the same time hasn't met Marla Dimitri.

"Ow! Fuck!"

"Christ, your toenail's black," Marla gasps.

"I think it might be falling off."

Suddenly, inexplicably, Marla is laughing – actual proper belly-laughter.

"What the hell are you laughing at?" I ask, incredulous. But then it catches hold of me too, and I'm laughing along with her. I don't really know what we're cackling at, but there's just something intrinsically funny about the pair of us at this bus stop, me with my bare foot out and Marla staring at my blackened toenail, which may or may not be falling off.

Right on cue, a bus pulls into the stop and its doors open with a hiss. The driver peers out at the pair of us, craning his neck to get a better view of what's going on. It occurs to me that from where he's sitting it must look as though there's something pretty untoward occurring with Marla down there.

I wave a hand in the air. "I think we're okay," I manage between the laughter.

The driver shakes his head in disgust and pulls away from the stop.

Marla's still laughing hard, her head practically in my lap now. She puts her hands on my thighs and hoists herself up, sitting down on the bench beside me. We sit there just chuckling away for a while, encased in our fogged-up Perspex cocoon.

"You're a fucking idiot, Eddie. You know that, right?"

"Funny," I say. "I was just thinking the same about you."

And before I know it, we're kissing in the bus shelter like a couple of teenagers, kissing for a good ten minutes until our lips go numb with the cold. It's as much catfight as canoodle, with Marla pushing me back against the shelter one minute and me pushing her back the next. She alternates between domineering and submissive as though some kind of psychiatric condition may be involved, but it doesn't bother me because I feel the same; sometimes it's nice to have Marla clambering all over me and other times it's nice to throw her back and let her know I won't be bossed about.

When it's over we sit for a while in silence, both a little embarrassed and confused. And then we take a slow and breathless walk home to Marla's place, where I kiss her goodnight at the front door and don't even try to come in for sex. It's probably the most gentlemanly thing I've achieved in my life so far, and on the hobble home I don't know what surprises me more, the fact I forgot to give Marla my bank details or the fact I'm fairly sure I actually had a pretty good time tonight.

6. Life Passing By

"It's like all this *The Lord of the Rings* bollocks," Dave says, twirling a beer-mat around on the table. "I mean, I'm a grown man, right? What do I wanna watch a load of puppets fucking about for?"

"And where exactly are the puppets in *The Lord of the Rings*?" Pete argues. He pushes his glasses further up the bridge of his nose, which means he's getting pretty huffy about it. "Have you actually seen *The Lord of the Rings*, Dave?"

We're sat in The Shoemaker: me, Dave, Pete and Brian.

"I've seen the adverts. Fucking puppets. Load of old bollocks, if you ask me. And don't even get me started on Harry-fucking-Potter."

"They're well-written books," Pete sighs.

"They're the degradation of society, is what they are."

This takes us all back a bit. We're all used to Dave getting vociferous about things after a few pints, but he doesn't usually come out with things like *the degradation of society*.

"Okay, fair enough," Dave concedes. "Let's say they're well-written books. *For kids*. They're kids' books. And all you see is these knob-heads reading them on trains. Grown-arse adults! I mean, where's it all gonna end? We'll all be sitting around watching *Rainbow* in ten years' time if we're not careful."

"Fucking loved *Rainbow*," Brian says.

"More of a *Button Moon* kind of kid myself," I say, pleased that Brian is trying to lighten the mood.

"No, you're missing the point, lads. Fair enough, we all loved *Rainbow*; we all loved *Button Moon*. But you wouldn't sit around watching them on a Saturday night now, would you?"

Brian shrugs.

"Alright, Bri might, but he's a dick. I'm talking about normal people."

We all burst out laughing and Brian chucks a beer-mat at Dave. Only Pete's not laughing; he's still got a cob on.

"Have you actually read *The Lord of the Rings*, Dave?" he persists.

God, Pete. He can be like a dog with a bone once he gets hold of these things.

"No, Pete. I haven't read *The Lord of the Rings*. I bow down to thee, o' holy geekmaster."

"I tried to read *The Lord of the Rings* once," Brian says. "Fuck me, it was boring."

Brian doesn't like much unless it's got guitars, hot women or explosions in it. In many ways he's the most honest man I know.

Brian plays rhythm and vocals in Disorder of Conformity, Northampton's foremost thrash/electro/glam-rock fusion band. He doesn't look very glam-rock though. He looks pretty bargain-basement-rock in a faded denim jacket with patches sewn onto the arms and an equally faded Lynyrd Skynyrd t-shirt. For all the years of known him, he's had shoulder-length, dirty-blond hair, but in the last few weeks he's tried to creep a little way into the twenty-first century by getting a few inches trimmed off it and greasing it back with hair putty. He's still got a fair way to go if he wants to catch up to present day, but it's an improvement.

"Look," Dave says, "the point I am *trying* to make is-"

"We all get the point you're trying to make, Dave," I interrupt. "People are watching too much kids' stuff. We get it."

"I'm just trying to conclude my point, Ed."

Conclude his point? Jesus, what's he done, fallen asleep in front of The History Channel or something?

"You're just trying to wind Pete up, more like," I say. "You know how he gets about this stuff."

"I'm just trying to pull him back from the brink, Ed. He should be thanking me. It starts with *The Lord of the Rings*, and before you know it, you're playing *World of Warcraft* eight hours a day and wanking over imaginary cartoon girlfriends in *Second Life*. It's a slippery slope. And what kind of friend would I be if I just sat by and watched?"

"Watched Pete wanking over imaginary cartoon girlfriends in *Second Life*?" Brian asks. "A pretty shitty friend, if you ask me."

Everyone's laughing now, even Pete.

"You can be such a bell-end sometimes, Dave," Pete shouts over the laughter.

"Ah, I'm sorry, mate. You know I'm only pulling your leg, right?"

In fairness, Pete's always been a bit of a nerd. When Dave and I were messing about on the ZX

Spectrum in the old days, Pete was actually taking his apart and rearranging the chipboards inside. Nine times out of ten he would bugger the thing up completely and it would never work again, but I remember once he did actually build his own games console. It was terrible, of course, but pretty impressive that he'd managed it at all.

It feels good to be out again, amidst all the laughter. These nights have been becoming increasingly infrequent over the past year or so, and I didn't quite realise just how much I've missed them. Maybe it's Dave settling down or simply the fact we're getting older. I don't know. All I know is that it feels good to be around them again. They might be a motley crew of no-hopers to the outside world, but they're the closest thing to brothers I've ever had.

The Shoemaker is pretty busy tonight. The skittles team has a home game on, and every now and then we're interrupted by a huge thunder-crash of tumbling pins, wood on wood. The Shoemaker is renowned for having the poorest skittles team in the county league: fifteen played, fifteen lost for the season so far. And judging by the amount of cursing coming from the regulars, they're about to chalk up another defeat tonight.

We've got ourselves a decent table by the fire and the air is tinged with the pleasant odour of wood-smoke. Our table is strewn with empty pint glasses and folded-up packets of crisps. Shadows are flickering in the firelight. Vic likes to say he keeps the lights low for ambience, but really it's because he's a tight-arse and doesn't like going above forty-watt bulbs. Just like he'd tell anyone the log-fire is for effect, when really it's because the central heating has been on the blink since the late-Nineties.

"To my left, Scottish rivers," Dave says, out of the blue.

Pass The Buck: the stupidest drinking game in town. It works a little like *Wipeout*, only with less Paul Daniels and lot more beer. Pretty much the only rule is that when a player is thinking they must be continuously drinking.

"Forth," I say.

As the next player, Pete brings his pint to his lips and begins to drink. I can see his eyes moving about the room, deep in thought. After a time, he puts his pint down with a gasp. "Clyde?" he ventures.

"Confirmed," Dave says.

Now we're looking at Brian, who's trying to play it cool. "Tyne," he mutters nonchalantly, not even raising his glass.

"*Scottish* rivers, knobber," Dave says. "Drink! Four fingers."

The only other real rule is that an incorrect answer incurs a drinking penalty, four fingers' width of beer.

Brian shakes his head. "Shit game, anyway," he sighs, taking a huge slug of his pint.

"Your category," Dave tells him when he's finished.

"Nah, I can't be arsed."

"Come on, Bri," Dave insists. "Your category."

"*The Lord of the Rings* characters."

"Oh, fuck off."

It's a clever tactic though, and Dave gives up trying to initiate another round.

It's Thursday night. That's one, two, three, four, *five* nights in which Marla hasn't phoned or texted me. I don't know what that means. I'm not versed enough in these things to know. Maybe it means she didn't take my number. I've got her number on a screwed up Post-It note inside my pocket. But I'm damned if I'm calling it. Not if she isn't calling me. But then, how could she if she didn't have my number? She was sifting through my texts craftily enough, though – I would have thought she might have had the common decency to take my number whilst she was at it. And I suppose there's a chance she may have written down my work number before she called me that morning. Or maybe it showed up on *her* phone when I called her back. Although I'm pretty sure work numbers are withheld.

Besides which, maybe I don't want her calling me anyway.

I'm free. Liberated.

Christ, what a head-fuck.

"Your round, Bri," Dave says.

Brian grumbles, rummaging around in his pockets for coins before going over to the bar. We usually end up feeling pretty guilty about Brian's rounds. Technically, he hasn't had a job for two and a half years, and it's something of a mystery as to how he manages secure funds. The band (or D.O.C., as he's taken to calling it lately) certainly isn't good enough to sustain a full-time income for him. Yet he never seems to struggle too much. No doubt he's fleecing the British taxpayer in one cynical way or another, so we never question him too heavily over it for the sake of saving an argument.

Brian comes back carrying all four pints at once and lays them down sloppily on the table.

"Take some empties back, Bri," Dave says.

Brian sighs and takes the empties over to the bar. "You know, technically, I shouldn't be buying *any* drinks tonight," he huffs on his return.

"Why's that then?" Dave asks.

"'Cause it's my bloody birthday, isn't it?"

A silence falls over us. We exchange glances – Dave, Pete and I – summing the thing up quietly, apportioning blame. Somewhere along the line, it occurs to us we're probably all equally to blame.

"Has your birthday always been in January, Bri?" I ask.

"No, Eddie. It used to be in the summer but it clashed with everyone's holidays so they moved it. Course it's always been in January, you div."

"Shit," Dave sighs. "Sorry, mate. I'll get you a power-shandy next round."

A power-shandy is half a lager and a bottle of Smirnoff Ice in a pint glass. It's a pretty pricey drink in the general scheme of things, but I'm not sure it constitutes a worthy gift under the circumstances.

"I'll get you one, too," Pete offers.

Brian brightens up a little. It seems two power-shandies might just make amends, after all. He looks to me, waiting.

"Yeah, I'll get you a power-shandy as well, Bri," I say

"Aw, cheers, lads." He's bright as a button now. "Fuck it, anyway. Doesn't matter. I almost forgot myself this time. Can't believe I'll be thirty next year. What a pisser!"

"Yep, it's creeping up on us, boys," Dave says, clapping his hands together.

When I was a kid, thirty would have seemed pretty old. The kid-version of me probably would have testified that a thirty-year-old man should have a wife, a mortgage and kids of his own. Savings in the bank and a half-decent pension plan. Of the four of us sitting here, only Dave is anything like close to having those things. Pete was seeing a girl in the Communications Department a while back – meek little thing, hardly saw anything of her – but he hasn't spoken about her for months now, so I guess she must have dumped him somewhere along the line. You wouldn't always know with Pete; he keeps those kinds of things to himself.

And if playing the guitar is supposed to get you the ladies, then I don't quite know where Brian has gone wrong. He *talks* about women a lot, and he's got a porn collection to make Hugh Hefner's eyes water, but he never seems to have much joy with actual living women of the real world. Probably it's a communication issue.

I'm struck with the sudden and sharp image of me, Pete, and Brian sitting around this same table ten years from now, forty years old, not moved on an inch in our lives, just doing the same things, bemoaning the same old problems, working in the same fucking office and listening to the same shit every day. It knocks the wind right out me, literally leaves me breathless.

And then it's over in a flash and I'm back in the present. Brian has downed his pint and is balancing the empty glass upside-down on his head – some kind of birthday ritual that I've missed, I presume. Dave is roaring with laughter at Brian and pointing at the glass on his head.

And it's then I realise that after this I'm going round to Marla's place because I miss her.

♂

At chucking-out time, we get chucked out. Even Vic The Barman has limits to his hospitality, it seems.

Outside the pub, we all hug goodbye, declaring our love for one another in ways we would never dream of doing sober. When sober, our goodbyes would never stretch beyond a slight, courteous nod of the head, but drunk we're all ardent humanitarians and so quite an emotional scene ensues. When it's over, we each go our separate ways.

As I walk, the pavement scrolls before me distortedly, like the wobbly walkway of a Funhouse. But it's the wobbly walkway of destiny, pushing me forward on my noble quest. *God, why am I so pissed?* It's a Thursday night, for crying out loud. Still, it's Friday tomorrow, which is sort of like the weekend. I'll just have to drink lots of coffee and avoid the phones. Besides, tomorrow's another world away, and there are more pressing matters at hand right now.

It takes me half-an-hour or so to get to Marla's front door, which is actually only a fifteen-minute walk from The Shoemaker. I'm aware that it must be quite late, as nobody else seems to be about. Still, I haven't spotted any milk floats yet, so it can't be too bad.

I spend some time considering which of the three doorbells might be Marla's, not wanting to disturb her neighbours. Then I realise there's actually only one doorbell there, so I hold a finger out carefully and push the one in the middle. Nothing happens for a while so I press it again.

At last there's a little commotion from inside, and the door opens.

Standing before me is a large man. He's not wearing any clothes, but luckily has a towel wrapped around his waist. His dripping torso is like the trunk of a giant oak tree, thick-set and toned. Great bulging muscles.

I check the house number.

"Hullo, mate," the man says.

"Hello," I say, quite absurdly.

"Don't tell me." He grins and points a finger at me, his thumb cocked like the hammer of a gun. "Eddie, right?"

For a second I consider telling him I'm from the double-glazing company, working a little overtime. But I probably smell a little too much of lager to get away with that. "Right," I say instead.

"Thought so. Come on in. Marl's told me all about you."

Marl? Bloody toss-pot. And I'm not sure about *Marl* telling this gorilla *all about me* either. Makes me sound like an annoying relative. Or a stalker.

"Thanks," I say, stepping into the hallway.

I'm trying to keep calm, not jump to any conclusions. Okay, this guy sounds pretty Welsh and looks like he might play rugby, but that doesn't mean a thing. There are three million people in Wales, and one and a half million of them happen to be male. And rugby happens to be a very popular pastime for the Welsh.

"I'm Gavin," he says, holding out his hand.

Fuck.

I shake the hand. The hand is approximately three times the size of mine.

Gavin goes to the foot of the stairs. "Marl!" he roars. "Someone here to see you, luv."

Marla appears at the top of the stairs, wrapped in a duvet. "Oh – Eddie. What are you doing here?"

I must admit, it does seem a pretty valid question now. "Oh, you know," I reply with a shrug. "I was just passing by."

"It's one o'clock in the morning."

"Is it? Well, I wouldn't have guessed it was that late. Probably best be off then."

"No – no. Look, stay there. I'll come down. Just give me a minute."

She disappears out of sight and I'm left standing there with Gavin.

"You want a coffee?" he asks. "Or a glass of

water?"

"Coffee would be good."

Gavin walks through to the kitchen, his back muscles rippling like the shifting continents. I follow after him.

"So," I say, "Marla tells me you played for the Saints."

"Aye, used to. Picked up a nasty injury, though."

"Oh, that's…that's a shame."

"Aye. What happened, right, was this bloke was bearing down on me. Big Maori bugger. So I gets him like this, right?"

And he actually grabs either side of my head in demonstration.

"I says, *no way Jose, you ain't coming through here, boyo.* So he goes *bosh* – right in my ribs like this, right? And I goes *no way am I having that*, so I gets him like this."

Gavin demonstrates a headlock on me, and my neck is crushed against his wet, lavender-scented bicep.

"Ha, he didn't like that too much. So, down we go together."

Gavin makes a suddenly downward jerking motion, and the towel slips free of his waist. He doesn't even flinch, just keeps me there in the headlock with my eye-line forced down towards his pendulous member, which is swinging about his muscled thighs like a separate living being.

"But as soon as I go down, I feel something in me leg just tear. Just like that. Couldn't move afterwards. Bloody agony, it was. And you know what that Maori says as he gets up? *Serves you right.* Can you believe that? *Serves you right*, he says. Well, I'm ballsed if I'm ever setting foot in New Zealand after that. Not even on holiday."

Marla comes walking into the kitchen. "Jesus Christ!" she cries. "Let go of him, Gavin – you'll kill him."

Gavin releases his grip and I can breathe again.

"Eh? Oh no, we were only messing about, Marl. I was just showing Eddie here how I got my injury."

Marla looks to me.

"Yeah, it's fine," I gasp. "No sweat."

Marla breathes a sigh of relief. "God, I thought the two of you were fighting. Wouldn't have fancied scraping you off the floor after that, Eddie."

"Well, I don't know about that," I rasp, through my throttled windpipe.

"Gavin, could you give us a couple of minutes, please?" Marla asks.

"Sure thing, babes. I'll catch you back upstairs." Only now does he pick up his towel, throwing it over his shoulder and giving Marla a little wink. Then he and his dick saunter out of the kitchen, leaving the two of us alone.

I'm still in shock over what has just occurred. I don't think the reality of it will sink in for a few days yet.

Marla moves over to the kitchen counter and continues making the coffee.

"Sorry about Gavin," she says. "He's like a big kid sometimes. Doesn't know his own strength."

"So…still seeing him then, are you?" Considering he was standing bollock-naked in her kitchen only seconds ago, it does seem a slightly redundant question.

"I'm not *seeing* him, Eddie, no. He passes through town every now and then. It's just a casual thing."

"But like a casual *sex* thing?" Visions of that appendage are still haunting my mind, and I wince at the word *sex*, as though I'm the one on the receiving end of it.

Marla sighs and passes the coffee over to me. "If that's what you want to call it, then yes."

"Right. No, that's fine. Just so long I know…you know…the lie of the land."

"The lie of the land? This isn't the Battle of Waterloo, Eddie. Look, I don't want you getting all funny about this."

"I'm not getting *funny* about anything."

"Good. Because you and me – you know that's just a pretence, right?"

"Right."

"And I'm not one for getting tied down in these things."

"Of course."

"What happened on Saturday happened. I can't deny that. Maybe it was the champagne, I don't know. But after all that crap with Joe I'm not about to go diving into anything again. At least not for a while."

"Absolutely."

"And us being together? I mean, *Jesus*. We'd end up tearing each other's throats out."

"God, it would be mental."

"I mean, I'm just not sure I could handle being with someone like you," she says.

"Well, y – wait a minute, what does that mean?"

"Oh, you know. The negativity. The constant need for attention. It would drive me nuts." She chuckles at this. Actually fucking chuckles.

"*My* need for attention? Oh, that's rich coming from you. Why do you think you've got *him* lying up there in your bed right now? Right after Joe. And right after me. I don't know, I mean maybe mummy didn't buy you enough ponies as a child or something?"

"What?"

"I mean, it may come as a surprise to you, but this isn't normal behaviour, Marla. None of the things you do could be classed as *normal behaviour.*"

"Oh, don't try psycho-analysing me, Eddie. You'll only embarrass yourself. And if you want to talk about normal behaviour, then here's a tip: it's common bloody courtesy to call a girl after a night out. You know, let her know you're actually still on the planet."

"Well, I didn't hear *my* phone ringing."

"I don't have your number!"

"Then you should have bloody stolen it."

"I should have stolen your number. That's the basis of your argument?"

"Yes."

"God, Eddie. Look, it's late. Perhaps we sh–"

"Or what about your dad? Your dad's got my number, but you haven't. That's just about how fucked-up this whole situation is."

"What, I should have called him and asked him for my own boyfriend's number? That would've been clever, wouldn't it?"

"Well, you could've done something. Something other than going and shagging...*him!*"

"See, I knew it. I *knew* it. You *are* getting funny. *He* has got nothing to do with you. Look, you're drunk. Let's talk about this another time."

I put the coffee down firmly, slopping it over the work surface. "No. Let's not talk about this another time. Let's never talk again. How about that?"

"You're upset. I understand."

"I've heard enough of this crap," I huff, making for the front door.

"I don't want this to cause problems, Eddie."

"Piss off!"

And now *I'm* pissed off because she thinks I actually care about any of this, when she was the one practically holding me to ransom in the first place. Now all of a sudden I'm the one acting irrationally.

Which is just bollocks.

I open the front door and walk out onto the driveway. Then I remember something, so I turn and walk back towards the house. "You owe me five hundred and ninety-six pounds and–"

Marla slams the door in my face.

I bend down to open the letterbox. "And *thirty-eight pence*," I yell through it, before storming off into the night.

7. Mum's The Word

"What's up with you, Ed? You've had a face like a slapped arse all day."

Dave's fixing his bow tie in the mirror. I'm standing next to him, struggling with my own. It's becoming embarrassingly apparent that we are men truly unaccustomed to bow ties.

We're in Handley's Gentlemen's Outfitters. It's a musty, high-end kind of establishment, the type that wouldn't normally dream of letting guys like us within a mile's radius of it were it not for the fact one of us happened to be getting married. The proprietor – an angular, thin-lipped, prissy character – is standing over by the till, keeping a steady eye on us.

I fight with the bow tie one last time until the thing falls apart, lolling impotently around my collar. "Ah, fuck it! Can't we just get clip-on ones?"

"No, we can't just get *clip-on* ones, Ed. This is supposed to be a classy wedding, not a sixth-form ball. You're not dressing up in the hope of getting a hand up Sticky Vicky's prom dress here. This has to be done right. We have to look co-ordinated. And I don't think Allie would be very pleased if we all turned up in *clip-on ties*."

"Yeah, well, she doesn't have to wear one of the bastard things, does she?"

In the mirror, I see Brian emerging from the cubicle behind us. "Do I look like a dickhead in this waistcoat?" he asks, pulling at it awkwardly.

"Bri, you've looked like a dickhead for the last twenty-nine years," Dave says. "That waistcoat isn't going to make any difference now."

"I just don't see why it has to be *purple*," he sighs.

"It's not purple. It's mauve. Allie wants mauve."

"Well, I guess we can't have everything now, can we?" I sneer.

"Right, that's it," Dave snaps. He takes me by the arm and pulls me into one of the cubicles, drawing the curtain closed and plonking me down onto the chair. "Just what the hell is wrong with you? Spit it out, Ed."

Brian comes into the cubicle, still pawing at the waistcoat. "What's happening?" he asks.

"I'm trying to find out what's wrong with Eddie."

"Nothing's wrong!"

Everything's wrong. It's been three weeks since my late night drop-in at Marla's. Three weeks of stewing over it. Three weeks of no contact. Three weeks of nothing.

"Bollocks," Dave says. "You've had the arse on all day. Hasn't he, Bri?"

"Well, you have been pretty moody to be honest, Ed. More so than usual, even."

The curtain rustles about a little, and then Pete steps inside. There really isn't room enough for four people in here.

"These trousers are too short," Pete says.

"It's because of your legs," Dave explains.

"What's wrong with my legs?"

"They're too long."

"What do you mean they're too long?"

"For the rest of your body. You've got a short body and long legs. You look like a fucking crane. We'll have to get Jeeves out there to give you a proper measuring."

Pete inspects himself in the mirror behind me, considering the crane theory. "Anyway, what's going on in here?" he asks.

"I don't know," says Dave. "There's something wrong with Eddie."

"There's *nothing* wrong with Eddie," I sigh.

"Well, you have been a bit of a misery-guts, Ed," Pete says. "You mean like a mechanical crane or an insect crane?"

"I need to get out of here," I say, standing from the seat.

Dave pushes me back down. "No way. You're not leaving here until you tell us what's wrong."

"It's a woman," Brian says knowingly. "Gotta be a woman."

"Don't be stupid, Bri. This is Ed we're talking about here."

"Well, in actual fact, Dave, it *is* a woman. So why don't you just piss off?"

"Ah, nice one, Ed," Brian coos. "Is she fit?"

"I don't want to talk about this."

"Wait a minute," Dave chuckles, "does this mean you've actually been getting yourself screwed?"

"Yes!" I bark. "Royally!"

"Well, I must say, that comes as a relief to hear,

Ed. Because, just between me and you – and these two clowns here – you know, we were kind of starting to wonder."

"What's that supposed to mean?" I ask.

Brian lays a hand on my shoulder. "Thought you might have gone over to the other side, mate."

"Oh, great. Just great. Love-life advice from Clark Bent and Twat Sabbath here."

Pete and Brian put on a big show of being offended.

"Well, there's no need to be like that about it, mate," Brian huffs.

"We were just concerned for your well-being," Pete adds.

"So, does this mean you're not a nonce after all, Ed?" Brian asks. "Because if not, Pete owes me a fiver."

"Oh, sod off, Bri," I sigh. "Besides, a nonce is a sex offender, not a gay person. Try sticking your head in a dictionary every once in a while."

"As if nonce will be in the dictionary," he scoffs.

"Double-or-quits says it is," Pete offers.

A terse little cough comes from the other side of the curtain. Jeeves. "Are you gentleman…okay in there?" he asks.

"Yep, fine thanks," Dave calls back.

"If you require any assistance, please don't hesitate to ask, will you?"

"Okay, thanks."

We all wait for a few moments in silence until we hear him walking away.

"Now listen, Ed," Dave says. "I don't know what's wrong with you and, to be perfectly honest, at the moment I don't particularly care. I'm not having you ballsing this up for me. This is important. You're my best man and I need you here with me now. Okay?"

"I'm here, aren't I?" I protest.

"I mean *here* here," he says, tapping at his forehead. "I need you on board. *Compos mentis.*"

"Fine."

"So, Ed, just sort it out. And Pete, sort those trousers out. And Bri, the colour scheme is mauve, so you'll be wearing fucking *mauve*. Okay?"

We all grumble and nod.

"Anybody else got any problems they'd like to share with the group?" Dave asks.

We all grumble a little more and shake our heads.

"Good. Then let's crack on with it, shall we? Jesus, if picking out the suits is this hard, I dread to think what the wedding itself is going to be like."

"I'm sorry, Dave," I say. "This is your day. We should all be with you on this."

"Good man."

"Sorry, Dave," Brian says.

"Sorry, Dave," Pete echoes.

"Forget it."

Dave holds out his hand, palm down.

Pete slaps his hand on top of Dave's.

Brian slaps his hand on top of Pete's.

And now they're looking to me.

"Come on, Ed," Dave urges. "Fucking *Thundercats*, right?"

I can't help laughing now. "You know that's

pretty lame, don't you?"

"Eddie," Dave says, sternly.

I give a roll of the eyes, letting them all know I still think it's pretty lame, but I slap my hand on top of theirs anyway. "Fucking *Thundercats*," I agree.

♂

I bend down and pick up a good-sized stick, toss it high into the air. It arches impressively across a sky the colour of dishwater, landing about a hundred yards away.

Badger doesn't move a muscle, just casts me a look of overwhelming pity.

"Something wrong with that dog," I tell Dad. "What kind of dog doesn't chase a stick?"

"An intelligent one?"

"An ignorant one, more like."

"Besides, you're not supposed to throw sticks for dogs," Dad says. "They can impale themselves on 'em."

"Well, you're a bundle of joy today."

We're in Abington Park. It's a cold, bleak Sunday morning in mid-March. The trees are stripped bare, their knuckled branches clawing at the pale sky. The lake is covered sporadically with thin patches of frost. The air remains pregnant with the memory of rain, or snow, but for now it has held out. It's eerily quiet: no bird chatter, no *anything* chatter. Usually on a Sunday, the park would be full of squealing toddlers, football players yelling instructions, lovers in conversation. If it was warm they'd be out, and if it snowed they'd be out in equal measure, but it's that kind of chilly intermediary period where nobody knows quite what to do with themselves, and so they stay inside.

We arrive at the bandstand, a deserted and sad-looking thing in itself at this time of year. It's an octagonal structure, with stone steps leading up to its stage and a pretty peaked roof for a shelter. The cold has got into the paintwork, peeling it away in places. It'll be summer before another coat is applied.

Dad climbs up the steps and walks across the stage, which seems rather an odd thing for Dad to be doing. I follow him up, leaving Badger down below making strange grunting noises. She won't want to put herself out by coming up here.

"You know something, Ed?" Dad asks, burying his hands deep in his coat pockets and turning to face me. "This is where I asked your mum to marry me. Right here."

"Really?"

"Yup."

"Wow. I never knew that."

I look around the bandstand. It seems to have taken on new meaning in light of this revelation. Before, it was just place we used to kick a ball about as kids, and years later as teenagers where we used to bring bottles of cheap, high-percentage cider for the evening. I spent a fair few nights up here in those days, misty-eyed with drunkenness and staring up at the stars, talking crap with the boys, smoking roll-ups made from the tobacco we stole from Brian's dad (luckily, Brian's dad smoked like a chimney, so he never noticed the dents we used to make in his supply). You could really see the stars out here, away from all the streetlights. I remember that. There was one formation that to my mind looked just like a tennis racket, and in the most sentimental moments of my intoxication I used to image they were in some way connected with Mum.

Ursa Minor. The Little Bear.

"How old were you?" I ask Dad. "When you asked her to marry you, I mean?"

"How old was I?" Dad looks surprised by the question. "Oh, I don't know. Thirty, perhaps. Thirty-one. Why?"

"No reason."

I walk over to the railings of the bandstand and lean against them, looking out over the park. Dad comes over and stands beside me.

"I don't suppose you remember much of her, do you?" he asks.

"Dad, I was nine, not two."

"Remember the time she brought home that hamster for you? And it escaped from its cage the next day?"

"Yeah."

"We couldn't find it for a week. Then it turned up one night, right out of the blue. Just ran right across the living room like it had never been away. Christ, your mum screamed the place down. She thought it was a rat." Dad lets out a choked little laugh, the warmth of his breath casting steam into the air.

"Yeah, I remember," I say.

"Ah, she thought the world of you, son. If you ever did something wrong, it was always me who had to give you the bollocking. She just couldn't do it."

"I thought that was just you being an arsehole."

"Ha! No, she was proud of you. Always was. Sometimes talking to you, it was just like talking to a little man, you know? All these ideas floating around in your head. She liked that. It's like she thought you'd grow up to change the world or something."

I snort a little. "Yeah? Well, she was a little off the mark there, then."

Badger comes trotting into view around the perimeter of the bandstand. She's looking up at us, as if annoyed that we've interrupted her walk for this moment of human insignificance.

"Well," Dad says, "there're a million ways to change the world, son. And most of 'em aren't the ways you're expecting."

It might just be the single most profound thing Dad has ever said to me. I'm stunned into a few moments of silence whilst I chew it over.

"So, anyway," Dad says brightly, completely changing tact, "Kate's gone and put me on one of these dating website things."

It takes a moment to register what Dad's saying, so wild is the tangent.

"Really?" I ask. "Like, internet dating?"

"Yup. I suppose you might think that's sad."

"No! I mean, no – of course not. I just didn't

realise you knew how to switch a computer on, let alone go online."

"I'm taking night classes. At the college. And Kate's sorted me out with this broadband crack. Ten pounds a month."

"Yeah? Well…that's a good deal!" I say.

"Yeah?"

"Absolutely. And computer classes? Wow. That's great."

"I'm enjoying it. Sometimes I feel a bit like the class dunce, but you have to start somewhere, right?"

"And what would they know about laying a gas main, eh?"

"Fuck all, son," Dad says, giving me a mischievous wink.

"Fuck all," I agree.

Badger turns her back to us and sits down. Reverse psychology, Jack Russell-style.

"How's Dave doing?" Dad asks.

"Fine," I say. "Busy. We've bought our suits now."

Dad nods. "I've been there before, by the way. Being the best man."

"Really?"

"Aye. We used to say it was like shagging the Queen."

"A great honour but no-one wants to do it," I say, smiling.

"Oh," Dad says. "Heard that one already, eh?"

"How did you find it?" I ask.

"Nervy. You know me, son – not really one for speeches and all that. But you've just got to get on with it. You'll be fine."

"Yeah," I say, nodding.

"Your Mum actually told me to imagine everyone naked. Christ, imagine your Aunt Sylvie naked! Don't think that would've helped very much."

I laugh. "Mum was there?"

"Oh yeah, of course she was."

"What else did she say?"

"Nothing much that I can think of. Probably just told me to make sure my flies weren't hanging open or something."

"She didn't offer you any other advice?"

Dad smiles. "Don't worry, son. Everyone gets a little worried about it. It's fine."

"What about *your* wedding?" I ask. "Who was the best man there?"

"Uncle Mick."

"And how did he do?"

"He got drop-down pissed before the speeches," Dad replies, laughing. "Could barely finish a sentence. I don't think your mum ever properly forgave him for that."

I laugh too. Uncle Mick was Dad's younger brother. He lived his life like he knew he wasn't staying very long, and he was right, too. Too much drink and bad food; too many cigarettes and mad women. He was dead at forty-five, choked on a chicken-bone outside a local takeaway one night. I reckon St. Peter probably took one sniff of his breath and turned him away at the gates.

"Ed?" Dad says.

"Yeah," I reply.

"Is that woman waving at us?"

I look out across the park. There's a man and a woman out there a few hundred yards away. It's hard to say for sure due to the faint mist hanging in the air, but Dad's right; it does look like the woman's waving at us. They're heading in our direction, the woman more quickly than the man; he's hanging back a little. But she's hurrying on regardless, still waving a hand high in the air, and–

Jesus wept.

"Dad, this might seem a little strange."

"What might?" he asks.

"What's about to happen. But I need you to play along with whatever I do. I need you to just follow my lead and go with whatever I say, okay?"

"Ed, what are you tal–"

"You work in construction. No, you *did* work in construction. You're semi-retired."

"Eh?"

"And I'm probably going to say some stuff about architecture that won't make a lot of sense."

"Ed, are you feeling alright?"

"Christ, the woman must have eyes like a *hawk*."

"Who is she?"

I sigh. "She's my...kind of girlfriend's mum."

"You've got a girlfriend?"

"No, not really. Not at all, in fact. But she thinks I'm her daughter's boyfriend."

"Why on Earth would she think that?"

"Because...well...look, it's a long story. Just trust me on this, will you?"

It suddenly occurs to me that there's no real reason for me to be doing this anymore. I have seen or heard from Marla for weeks. Where's the sense in dragging Dad into it all? I'd be well within my rights to tell Jean and Robin the truth, just come right out and tell them that Marla was playing a game all along, only now she's found a better offer in the arms of Gavin the nearly-man of Wales so I probably won't be seeing much of them anymore, thanks all the same. It's not like I owe anyone anything, after all. In fact, the only person owed anything out of this entire bloody mess of a situation is me: five hundred and ninety-six pounds and thirty-eight pence, to be precise. So why should I care?

But as Jean nears and I see her expectant face beaming up at us, I just know I'm going to keep up the lie, even if I don't quite understand why. Perhaps it's because the truth reflects pretty badly on me, too. Or perhaps there's a twisted little part of me that thinks giving up on the lie and giving up on Marla are one and the same thing. And maybe I'm not quite ready for that yet. Not whilst she still owes me money, at least.

Jean reaches the bandstand, looking uncharacteristically flustered from the exertion of hurrying over here. She's wearing a pristine white coat and an expensive-looking handbag is hanging over her shoulder.

"Ahoy there," I call down to her. Fuck me, I can be a prick sometimes – it's a bandstand, not the HMS Belfast.

"Eddie!" she gasps. "What a surprise!"

Robin catches up behind her. His cheeks are reddened from the cold and his hair, usually set neatly into a side parting, is a little ruffled.

"Hello there, Eddie!" he shouts up to me.

Badger sidles up alongside Jean, rubbing the side of her face against her leg. She's picked a fine time to start caring for humanity.

"So, Marla tells us you've been working away," Jean says. "On a big project in London."

"Yes, that's right. It's a sports facility. You know, for the Olympics. We're kind of on a tight schedule with it all."

"Oh. Marla told us it was a cinema," Jean says, frowning.

"Yeah, a cinema as well. It's a...big...you know...complex."

"Oh, I see. Well, it all sounds terribly important," she says, chuckling a little.

"Well, it's been pretty stressful," I say. "More than just a bricks and mortar job, anyway. It's a lot of added pressure to think that the hopes and dreams of the entire nation are resting on our shoulders, but I think we're doing okay."

Dad's looking at me like I've gone off my rocker.

"Oh, excuse my manners," I say, slapping Dad a little too fiercely on the back. "Jean, Robin – this is my dad, Geoff."

"Lovely to meet you, Geoff."

"Err...likewise," Dad says, nodding like he has a spring for a neck.

"Yours?" Jean asks, bending down to pat Badger's grizzled head.

"What, Dad?" I ask. "Yeah, I've had him for ages."

"Oh, Eddie," Jean titters. "You are a one."

"She's Dad's," I tell her. "Mind you don't touch her ears now."

"Oh, nonsense." Jean's actually tickling her under the chin and ruffling her ears up and Badger doesn't mind one bit – she actually seems to be enjoying it, the creep.

"Anyway, how about we all go and get a coffee?" Jean suggests, rising to her feet again. "Get properly acquainted." She smiles at Dad. "And get out of this awful cold for a bit, too."

Dad's frowning deeply, as though he's just been asked to name the capital of Mozambique.

"Yeah, that sounds great, Jean," I say quickly. "We're on our way down."

♂

The Chestnut Tree is a cobbled together teashop-cum-ice-cream-parlour situated slap-bang in the middle of the park. It doesn't have to try too hard, as once here you're marooned, and where else is a person going to go? It really only specialises in two lines of produce: teas and coffees when it's cold, ice creams and cans of soft drinks when it's hot. In the corner sits an automated monkey called Bananas, who for the princely sum of one pound will dispense a cheap plastic toy worth half that. I'm willing to bet no child has invested in Bananas' wares since the turn of the century, yet still he jumps to life every five minutes or so inside his Perspex box, raucously touting for business. I can see where Bananas got his name; it must drive the workers here half-mad listening to his crap all day.

"You must be very proud of Eddie, Geoff," Jean says.

We're seated in the middle of place, too close to Bananas for my liking. Robin has just returned from the counter with a tray of cups and saucers. Dad's pushing the teabags around in the pot with a spoon, stoking it up to maximum strength. I wish he'd stop doing it.

"Huh?" Dad asks, looking up from the pot. "Oh yeah, of course. Very proud."

Clearly deciding he's squeezed as much life as possible out of the bags, he begins to pour out the tea. I try not to wince at the blackness of it.

"Ah, builder's tea!" Robin cheers, taking a cup from the tray.

Full of surprises, is Robin.

"And did you always want Eddie to follow in your footsteps?" Jean asks.

"Oh no, not at all. I always wanted him to get an education." Dad looks to me quickly, like he knows he might have just said something wrong.

"Dad went more of a self-taught way about it," I say, trying to repair the damage.

"Don't blame you, Geoff," Robin says. "A lot of this university stuff is all Daffy Duck these days, if you ask me."

Dad smiles politely, although he clearly hasn't a clue what Robin is saying.

"And have you met Marla?" Jean persists.

I step on Dad's foot.

"Oh, yeah," Dad pipes up. "Of course. Lovely

girl."

"We couldn't believe she kept it all hush-hush like that. Not like her at all."

"Well," Dad says, actually squinting in concentration from the effort of thinking what to say, "it came as something of a surprise to me, too."

"We'll all have to go out for dinner some time. Eddie treated us to a lovely meal a few weeks ago."

"And don't forget you still owe me that game of tennis, Eddie," Robin adds.

"You just pick the date, Robin. I'll be there." I make a jokey little forehand-drive motion with my teaspoon. Like a prat.

"*Eddie fucking Corrigan!*" booms a voice out of nowhere.

I nearly drop the spoon with the shock of it. For a while I think it may have come from inside my head, the big booming voice of God calling me out for being a pillock. But then I look around the table and see that everyone else is looking pretty shocked, too. If Jean's eyebrows arch up any higher they'll be crawling off her face.

I turn around on my seat. The guy behind the counter is looking at me and grinning wildly. He's wearing a black-and-white chequered apron with a matching chef's hat. I search his face and there's something familiar there, but I can't quite grab hold of it.

Then it hits me: Danny Kilbride, from school.

From what I recall, Danny spent most of his school days committing random acts of vandalism and crushing people's heads against the wall. I haven't seen him in years. I don't think he even stayed on for the sixth-form. But then I guess Danny never really was one for higher education, not unless they've started handing out diplomas in elbow-drops and full-nelsons.

"Danny, right?" I say, wishing we'd chosen any other café on Planet Earth.

"Fucking yeah, man." He pulls off his hat and throws it down on the counter. "Fancy seeing you here, you old cunt."

From the corner of my eye, I see Jean physically flinch at the word.

There's a strange noise in my ears, which I soon realise is from my teeth crunching together.

Danny walks around the counter and approaches the table. The sleeves of his work smock are rolled up, revealing his tattooed forearms. His face has fattened out a little in the intervening years, but there's no mistaking him: those mean little eyes, that oversized forehead just perfect for butting things.

"Been a while, Danny," I say

"Fucking-A, it's been a while. Hey, remember Lucy Wainwright? Christ, what a goer. Still, you don't mind so much when they look like that, do you?" he chuckles. "Had a few good rides on her, I did."

"Look, Danny, can we–"

"Having said that, mind, I saw her on Facebook the other day. Pretty rough these days, to be honest. Put on a shit-load of timber, if you get what I'm saying. Couple of sprogs on the go, too. Makes me think I had a lucky escape, y'know."

"Danny, I'm kind of in the middle of som–"

"You still hanging about with that weasely little fucker? What was his name? Pete something. Pete Pritchard. Ha! Fucking Pete Prichard, man. Remember that time I hung him from a tree by his feet?"

Actually, I don't remember this, but I make a mental note to remind Pete the next time I see him.

"Anyway, where you drinking these days?" Danny asks.

"I'm in London quite a lot, actually."

"Yeah? What you doing down there, then?"

"Err…architecture, mostly."

"What, buildings and shit? Never had you down for that sort of thing."

I stand from my seat, unable to bear it any longer. I put a hand on Danny's elbow, hoping it doesn't rile him into a fit of bullish aggression, and lead him away from the table back over to the counter.

"Danny, mate," I say quietly. "It's really good to see you again, but I'm in the middle of something, see."

Danny looks over my shoulder at the table. "Oh yeah? What's that, then?"

"It's the missus' old dear, see." I hate myself for talking his language, but I'd do anything to have him out of the way right now. "We're just trying to give her a nice day out, you know. And she gets a bit nervous around strangers."

"Ah, I see," Danny says, nodding knowingly. "I get ya. Keeping in with the missus, eh? Good move, Eddie. You always were a clever fucker.

Always need something to fall back on, don't you?"

"You know it, Danny." I'm practically pushing him back behind the counter now.

"But you watch out for yourself, yeah?" Danny says. "Just remember, Ed, you only get one life, and you've only got one dick."

"Right. Thanks for the advice, Danny," I say, nodding.

"And there's plenty of fanny out there, chief."

"Thanks again."

"Just get yourself down Bridge Street one Saturday night. Place is teeming with it. Can't beat it."

I pull a stupid face, making a cutting motion with my hand across my neck.

"Oh, right. I get you, Eddie. No problem, mate. Mum's the word, eh?"

I give Danny a wink and turn away, hoping it's the last time I'll ever have to encounter him in my life.

"Sorry about that," I whisper when I get back to the table.

"Someone you know, Eddie?" Jean asks.

"We renovated a secure unit down here a few years ago," I tell her. "Danny was in residence there. Somehow he got it into his head that we went to school together." I laugh at the absurdity of such a notion. "Still, it's good to see they've reintroduced him into the community."

"Oh, I see," Jean says, nodding and trying to look sympathetic. "Is it safe for him to be out like this?"

I look over to the counter, where Danny is giving me a couple of thumbs-up and making an exaggerated mime of zipping his mouth shut.

"Oh, I'm sure he's been risk-assessed," I reply. "Still, probably best that we drink up all the same, eh?"

8. Small Steps & Giant Leaps

Mum died on 13th April 1989, and two days later ninety-four people died just going to a football match.

I watched the thing unfold on *Grandstand*, on an old Toshiba TV with bad reception. The fuzziness of it all seemed to fit the confusion of what was happening. It didn't seem like people were dying. It just seemed like everything was happening in slow motion. It was like forty-eight hours later the world was joining me in a slowed down state of bewilderment, and we all stayed like that for some time afterwards. But strangely enough, this isn't the tragedy I associate with Mum dying. That dubious accolade goes to something that happened three years before.

Right from the time I could talk, I was crazy for anything Space-related. I'd look at the Moon at night, hardly being able to fathom that a man had been up there, even though it had all happened before I was born, even though I'd never lived in a world where men *hadn't* been up there. I think perhaps had I lived in such a time I would have killed myself wondering about it.

I used to hound Mum and Dad relentlessly for a telescope, although they couldn't afford the kind I wanted, so I ended up with a cheap little knock-off from Argos. It was more like looking through a pair of binoculars than a telescope. Its only feature appeared to be that it made the Moon look ever-so-slightly larger. But it wasn't enough to deter me. I had all the books, knew the planets and the constellations back to front. I used to stay up way past my bedtime to watch *The Sky at Night*, and on 28th January 1986, I hurried home from school to watch as Christa McAuliffe and six other crewmembers were launched up into the air and blown into oblivion.

Christa McAuliffe was a pretty normal school teacher from a place called Concord, New Hampshire – like the plane only without the *e*. She'd always wanted to be an astronaut but she never became one, I suppose for the same kind of reasons as everybody else never becomes one. But in 1984, NASA ran a competition to send a teacher into Space, and Christa won that competition. She was to be the first civilian to go, and I became quite taken with the idea that if they carried on taking civilians into space they might one day take me, conveniently overlooking the fact I wasn't American and I was at the time not much taller than the vacuum cleaner.

So Christa went up there with all my aspirations, and came down with a good deal of them, too. She had a son, Scott, who was nine years old at the time she died, and an Irish father called Edward Corrigan, which I remember thinking was strange as that was my name, too.

And now, abstractly, when I think of Mum dying, I can't help thinking of that forked plume of burnt jet-fuel set against the blue Floridian sky, and of the day I stopped caring about Space.

♂

"I just want to tell you guys something. Something pretty important."

Brian's on stage at O'Grady's. The stage is actually just a slightly raised seating area with the chairs cleared away. He's swaying about a little, but using the mic stand to keep his balance. Even by Brian's standards, he's drunk a considerable amount of alcohol – probably more alcohol than a musician should consume should he wish to maintain an air of professionalism.

"I want everyone here to listen up 'cause this is important," he slurs into the mic.

Nobody is listening in particular. Once upon a time, O'Grady's would have been heaving with the town's Irish. There would have been music most nights of the week, singing and shouting and laughing. The Irish have diluted over the years though, in number and in blood. What's left is rag-tag army of second, even third generation Irish, watered down and carrying around only loose, mythologized ideas of Ireland itself. The old pubs could never have survived without change, so they've opened themselves out to the younger crowd one by one, to kids who want to play rock music rather than the old songs – kids like Brian, I suppose, and kids like me.

A few twenty-somethings are dotted about on the seats, and a handful of old-timers are hunched over the bar, like ancient rocks forged into a riverbank. Brian will usually throw in heavier, faster versions of *The Black Velvet Band* or *The Fields of Athenry* just to keep them on side, but tonight he doesn't seem to have much of a plan at all.

"I just wanna give a shout out," he warbles, "to my main man out there, my *amigo* – Dave Atkinson. Where are you, Dave? There he is, ladies and gentlemen."

"What time did he start drinking?" I ask Dave.

"God knows. But I'm guessing early." Dave waves to Brian, forcing a smile. "Said he was *jamming* earlier, which usually means he's getting pissed."

"We have to get this man a job," I say.

Brian stumbles, almost falls over, and the crowd starts paying attention now, hoping to witness a *You've Been Framed* moment.

"I second *that* motion," Dave agrees.

"Anyway," Brian goes on, "Dave here is biting the bullet soon. He's getting married, folks. How about that, now?"

An unenthused scatter of applause goes round.

"Yep, he's finally leaving us, and he's walking down that aisle…that aisle of life…that aisle of love."

Brian's losing his audience now.

"So, I just wanna dedicate this next one to you, my friend. It's about losing someone you love, but wishing that person all the happiness in the world."

Brian tries to coolly turn from the crowd for the intro, but turns too quickly and goes lurching forward, clattering into the cymbals and falling over. There's an awkward delay whilst he gets back to his feet and the drummer has to rearrange the cymbals to their original position. Brian appears to be pretending the whole thing never happened, or perhaps he's already genuinely forgotten.

He raises the mic to his lips and counts the band in. There's quite a lengthy and overblown intro, so it takes us a while to realise that Brian, quite astonishingly, is singing *Always* by Bon Jovi (although maybe 'singing' isn't quite the right verb).

"What the fuck?" Dave chuckles, as Brian warbles on about how *this Romeo is bleeding*.

"This is just creepy," I say, digging into my pocket for my phone. Having video evidence of this could prove invaluable at a later date.

The crowd are getting into it now, laughing and clapping along. It's the kind of ironic applause that people like to offer when witnessing somebody make a complete arse of themselves, but Brian is too drunk to notice. He seems to think it's genuinely going down a storm and, encouraged, he's drawing the air in with his hand and pumping his fist at the crowd. Even the drummer looks a little unsure of what he's got himself into.

"What time is it?" Dave asks.

"Five minutes later than the last time you asked," I reply.

"Eddie."

I tut and look at my watch. "Half-nine."

"I better get off after this. You should probably think about doing the same. I want you on form tomorrow."

"I'll be fine. Relax."

Tomorrow is rehearsal day. We're going up to the Cotswolds, to Felston. Dave insisted on a dummy run of the wedding. Correction: Alison insisted that Dave insisted on a dummy run of the wedding. I'm imagining a day of being pushed about and told where to stand.

"Just make sure you get Piss-Head up there home at a reasonable hour," Dave warns.

On stage, Brian's letting Dave know that he'll be there 'til the sun don't shine, 'til the heavens burst and the words don't rhyme.

"Listen, Ed," Dave says. "I just want to put it on record that I'm really glad you're my best man. It really means a lot to me."

"Really?"

"Of course. And I didn't mean to have a go at you the other day. It's just I've been under a lot of stress lately, what with all the wedding arrangements and everything."

"Ah, forget it," I say.

"But that doesn't mean I don't appreciate what a good mate you've been to me over the years. And I shouldn't let the wedding take over everything. I know you've got your own life to lead. Like with this mystery woman – who, by the way, you still haven't told us anything about."

"Oh, it's nothing serious."

"Looker?"

I think about Marla for a moment or two, and a strange melancholy descends on me. "Yeah," I reply a little sadly. "Yeah, she is."

"Good," Dave says. "You deserve it." He chinks

his glass against mine.

Brian's building up to a crescendo now, so he mounts a table in the front of the stage. The legs of the table are as wobbly as Brian's, and he rocks from side to side, extending his arms either side for balance. The crowd *ohhs* and *ahhs* in anticipation of its collapse. Then, just as the guitarist hits his final note, Brian throws himself forward with all the grace of a startled wildebeest. I'm sure in his mind's eye it was to be a majestic arching leap, the perfect finale to the perfect performance. In reality, the table flips over behind him and Brian goes tumbling forward, his legs peddling ten-to-the-dozen through the air.

There's a sickening *snap* when he lands, and the audience gasps in unison.

Brian lies crumpled in a heap, not moving. The fact that he's not crying out in pain is probably the most worrying thing. The seriously injured hardly ever cry out; they just lie silently in disbelieving shock, wishing life had a Rewind button.

The crowd has had their *You've Been Framed* moment, only suddenly it's not particularly funny anymore. They're just sitting around shaking their heads, confused at what to do next.

Dave takes control of the situation, rushing over to Brian and kneeling down beside him. I follow behind.

"You alright, Bri?" I ask.

Dave rolls Brian over onto his back. His eyes are circling around in his head, unable to focus. "Was it beautiful?" he asks, in a dazed whisper.

"Yeah, Bri," Dave replies. "It was beautiful,

mate. Really touching." He rubs Brian's shoulder soothingly.

"We should probably get him to the hospital," I suggest.

"You think?" Dave asks. "How do you feel, Bri? Reckon you can walk it off?"

Brian's muttering away nonsensically, something about turning up the heating.

"He needs to go to hospital, Dave" I persist.

"We don't know that for sure, Ed."

"You heard that crack as well as I did."

"It may have been the table. Let's wait till he comes around."

"I don't think that'll happen any time soon."

Dave starts rubbing at his forehead, and I can tell he's frantically considering the alternatives. DIY surgery, perhaps.

"Okay, okay," he sighs at last. "We'll take my car. But this better not take long."

♂

There's probably never a good time to visit the Accident & Emergency ward of Northampton General Hospital, but ten-past-midnight on a Friday night is perhaps one of the worst.

Everything is bathed in white; a stark and unforgiving brightness hammers the senses. There are no hiding places here. The price for getting repaired is to display your sins under the cold, artificial lighting like a slab of cold meat at a deli-counter. Dozens of posters are tacked to the walls

– sexual health advice, the perils of high alcohol consumption, and so on. Somewhere along the line, the NHS has overtaken the Catholic Church as market leaders of the guilt-peddling industry – because a society needs guilt as much as it needs a legal system or a financial currency. It brings a certain structure to things to know who the wrongdoers are and where they most prevalently lurk.

There's an odd array of characters dotted about the waiting area, sitting or lolling or hanging over the plastic chairs. There's a guy in his late teens sitting on his own, casually holding a tea towel against the side of his face. The tea towel appears to be saturated with blood.

Another group of lads sit over the way. One of them has a full size bath towel strapped to head with a belt, and his legs are shaking, presumably through some kind of post-traumatic shock. A chubby girl in an ill-fitting skirt and boob-tube is sitting slightly away from the group. Two police officers are trying to interview her, but she's just wailing uncontrollably, saying over and over that *he was just minding his own*. Sitting across from the blubbering girl is a strangely normal-looking middle-aged man in a wax jacket and chequered flat-cap. There doesn't appear to be anything outwardly wrong with him.

"What you reckon he's in for?" I ask Dave.

"Dunno. Probably got a golf ball stuck up his arse or something."

"Or maybe he's just waiting for someone."

Dave sighs impatiently and folds his arms.

"How long is this gonna take? We've been here for hours. It's alright for Sleeping-fucking-Beauty over there."

Brian's sitting on the other side of me. He's been asleep for the whole time, snoring loudly with his head dangling awkwardly over the back of the chair.

"I'll go and see what's happening," I say. "You want a coffee or anything?"

"No. I just wanna get the fuck out of here. We've got the rehearsal at midday tomorrow. And the place is a good two-hour drive away. I was only supposed to be out for a quick drink."

"Don't worry, Dave. We'll get you back soon. We must be near the front of the queue now."

"What queue?" he asks, exasperated. "That bloke who just went through was here ages after us."

"Well, he did seem to be losing a lot of blood," I point out.

"Not as much as I'll be losing if I don't get a decent night's kip. Christ, Allie's gonna kill me."

"I'll go and see what I can do," I say in a reassuring tone, patting Dave on the shoulder.

I rise from the chair and walk over to the reception desk. The receptionist is a huge, West Indian lady with a formidable temper. When we first arrived, I thought she might put us over her knee and spank us for our stupidity.

"Hi, err…" I say, looking around her uniform for a nametag. She's not wearing one. "Hi," I say again.

The receptionist folds her arms defensively and

casts me a loaded smile. "Hello," she says slowly, in a heavy accent.

"My friends and I back there were just wondering how close we were to being seen."

"You will be *seen* when the system calls you, sir. I will let you know. As I have already informed you."

"It's just we've been here for a couple of hours now, see. And we've noticed people...you know...kind of jumping ahead."

"Sir, there is a system of priority."

"Of course. Absolutely. And that makes sense. I can understand that. It's just, my friend – he's in a lot of pain right now."

The receptionist looks over at Brian, still fast asleep and snoring away.

I cough to get her attention back. "And he needs to keep that foot elevated. We can't ensure that happens whilst he's slipping in and out of consciousness like this."

"Sir, your friend will be called when the system says it is time. Go and sit down."

"Oh, right," I sneer. "And when exactly does the *system say it's time*?"

"Sir!"

"Never," I sigh under my breath.

"Sir, I do not have to take that kind of *racial abuse*," she says, elevating her voice.

"What? No, I didn't–"

"Everything okay here, ma'am?"

I turn around. One of the police officers has stopped interviewing the girl and has come over to the reception desk.

"This man just called me the N-word," the receptionist says, her face folding in disgust.

"Now, wait a minute. That's not–"

"Sir!" the policeman barks. "What I need you to do now is settle down and step away from the desk."

"This is ridiculous. I was jus–"

"Sir, that's a direct order." He lowers his hand by his side.

"What is that?" I ask. "A Taser gun? You gonna Taser me now? It's just I didn't realise this was Nazi Germany. Look, I'm tired. My friends are tired. We just want him looked at."

Dave steps up behind me. "Ed, what's going on?"

The policeman puffs out his chest and strengthens his stance. "Sir, I need you to back away. There's no need for you to get involved here."

"Ed, I thought you were sorting this out."

"I am, Dave. I can handle this. Just leave it to me."

"Sir, I will *not* ask you again."

"Let me show you something," I say, reaching into my pocket for my mobile phone.

My intention is to show them the video footage of Brian stage-diving. Then I can argue my point about him being genuinely injured and in need of medical assistance. Sadly, my intentions are cut short by a searing pain that seems to shoot around my entire body and charges up into my skull. My brain feels like it's been set on fire.

I double up immediately, crumpling to the floor

like a rag-doll. Every muscle in my body has been disabled. I'm vaguely aware that I'm making a low, steady groaning noise, but there's nothing I can do about it. It's as though somebody else is controlling my vocal chords. From the corner of my eye, I can see some sort of double-pronged dart sticking into my arm, a tangled wire trailing from it.

"Hey," I hear Dave yell.

Another searing bout of pain tears through me.

"Sir!" the police officer roars. "Every time I pull this trigger it sends twenty-five thousand volts into your friend here. I suggest you back away and start complying."

The pain subsides a little. I want speak. I want to tell Dave to back away and start complying. But I can't. Nothing will leave my mouth but this low, constant groan.

"You hold the fort here, Mel," the officer says.

The voice sounds far away, as though I'm at the bottom of a deep well. The last part I barely hear at all:

"I'm taking these clowns in."

♂

We're sat on a bench, halfway down a long, dimly lit corridor, my feet only just touching the floor – Dad to one side of me, Kate to the other. Nobody has spoken for the best part of an hour. The air is still, almost soundless. All that can be heard is the soft brush of a mop on the floor, a caretaker's idle whistling. From time to time, a distant coffee-machine whirs to life, the clank of a plastic cup dispensing. When the soft tread of plimsolls sound on the floor, Dad looks up – every time – and then hangs his head back down again. Mostly they're nowhere near us, just a trick of acoustics created by the emptiness of this labyrinthine building. Even when a nurse does pass by, she either just smiles at us or ignores our presence entirely.

My belly grumbles, although I feel no hunger. The Wimpy I had three hours ago will be the last thing I'll eat for a long time that isn't either forced down or brought back up, or both. I try to hide the noise from Dad, guiltily.

"Either of you want a drink?" Dad asks. "A hot chocolate?"

Kate shakes her head. She looks pale. Her hair is clumped together in the places where her fingers have been.

"Eddie?"

I try to sink into the bench, make myself small. Make myself invisible.

"Eddie?"

I want Dad to stop talking, to stop asking me if I want anything. I feel as though I'll never want anything ever again.

"Eddie?"

"No," I reply sharply.

"A cold drink, then?"

"I don't want anything."

"But you should prob–"

A door clicks open further down the corridor and a doctor appears, silhouetted against the light from a window behind him. He starts walking towards us, looking down at his feet too much, like he's not just *doing it to see where he's treading.*

He scratches the back of his head.

Dad stands as he approaches. I hear the breath leaving his body.

And the doctor, nearly with us now, scratches the back of his head again.

♂

"I don't believe this. I mean, I just don't *fucking* believe this."

Dave's sitting on the bed, holding his head in his hands. I'm standing in the corner feeling pretty sheepish about things. The cell is small and claustrophobic, with padded walls. A florescent light buzzes away above our heads.

"Funny how they only used to keep nutters in padded cells," I say, looking about the room. "Now everyone gets one. I guess it's a health-and-safety thing. Probably saw a lot of claims."

"Do *not* talk to me, Ed," Dave cries into his hands. "Please, just don't talk to me. I can't handle that right now."

"Well, I didn't know he was going to bloody shoot me, did I? I should be the one who's pissed off. I've been the victim of police brutality here."

"You got Tasered for twatting about. Hardly Rodney King, is it?"

"Well, you wouldn't be saying that if they Tasered you. I mean, is this what it's going to be like from now on? Police Tasering anyone they think is a twat?"

Dave looks at his watch. "Nine o'clock we have to leave. Nine o'clock at the latest. That's five hours away."

This jolts a sense of urgency into me. I need to do something, anything, rather than just sitting here listening to light buzzing and going slowly mad.

I head over to the door. "Guard!" I shout through the hatch. "Guard!" It feels weird saying it, like I'm a character in one of Dad's cowboy movies.

The hatch slides open, revealing an officer's face on the other side. Thankfully, it's not the one who brought us in. This officer is a younger guy, perhaps no older than us.

"What?" he asks.

"I need a piss," I tell him. "And a fag."

"Well, you want the Moon on a stick, don't you?"

"I'm entitled to both of those," I say haughtily. "It's a breach of my human rights to deny me either."

"Alright, alright," the officer says, looking down the corridor. "No need to be a dick about it."

He unlocks the door and escorts both of us down the corridor to the toilets. We all go inside, the officer included, and he points us in the direction of a couple of urinals. When we're done, he takes us further down the corridor to a small, enclosed outdoor smoking-area. I'm amazed at how relaxed it all seems to be; he hasn't even cuffed us.

Dave and I light up, and I offer a cigarette to the

officer. He looks around warily, scratching at his acne-scarred cheeks before taking one.

Dave wanders off on his own, running his hands through his hair and muttering to himself.

"How long you been a policeman, then?" I ask the officer.

"About eighteen months," he replies.

"You like it?"

"Yeah, it's alright. Something different every day, I suppose. I was in the building trade before this. It's all fallen to shit, though. Good job security here. I guess there'll always be crime, right?"

I shrug. "Right."

"What did they bring you lads in for, anyway?"

"Drunk and disorderly. It was just a misunderstanding, though."

"Did Jonesy Taser you?" he asks.

"Yeah."

The officer laughs. "Bloody Jonesy. We only got the Tasers last Tuesday. He's been like a dog with two dicks ever since."

"Jesus," I gasp. "Don't ever give him a real gun, will you?"

"Not likely. What's up with your mate?"

I look across to Dave, pacing up and down the perimeter of the smoking area like a panther in a zoo. "It's his wedding rehearsal tomorrow," I explain.

The officer laughs again. "Oh, shit."

"Oh, shit," I agree. "By the way, did those other officers say anything about a third guy when they brought us in?"

"Third guy?" the officer asks, frowning. "No.

Why?"

"We left a friend at the hospital. Asleep."

"What was wrong with him?"

"Dunno. Broken ankle, we think."

"Yeah?" The officer looks over to Dave, who is still pacing back and forth in a state of agitation. He throws down his cigarette and crushes it under his shoe. "Ah, look, you guys don't seem too pissed to me. I'm going off-shift in ten minutes. I'll drop you back at the hospital, if you like. Just don't go making a song and dance about getting Tasered, alright?"

I hold my hands up in the air, palms out, smiling benignly. "Already forgotten," I promise.

♂

"Not much of a copper, was he?" Dave says, as we walk along the ambulance bays. "Just letting us go like that, I mean."

"I think he's fairly new to it all," I say. "Hope it doesn't get him into trouble."

"Nah, he'll be alright."

As we reach the entrance, the automatic doors slide open and Brian comes hobbling out on crutches, his right foot strapped in a blue cast.

"Rock and roll, boys!" he cheers. "Check this shit out."

"Is it broken?" I ask.

"Fractured," he replies, with a hint of disappointment. "Where did you two go? I woke up and you were gone."

"Long story," Dave replies, glaring at me. "Now, come on, let's just get home. We've got a big day ahead of us."

We turn and start heading back to Dave's car. Brian's struggling with the crutches, splaying them out too widely like the legs of a newborn fawn. I slow my own pace to accommodate for this, but Dave's rushing off ahead, turning back every few moments and barking orders for us to hurry up.

"Seems like he's losing it," Brian says to me.

"He's just under a lot of stress," I point out. "He'll be alright."

"What about you?" Brian asks. "Hardly the picture of tranquility yourself these days."

"Me? I'm fine."

"This best man stuff getting on top of you?"

"What? No. Of course not."

"Or maybe it's this new woman of yours, eh?"

"Well, that's not going to be a problem anymore."

Brian arches his eyebrows. "Bloody hell, that was quick. Even by your standards."

"Thanks."

"You wanna talk about it?"

"Not really."

"Thank fuck for that."

We reach the car and I help Brian into the back seat. Then I climb into the passenger seat and Dave, impatient as ever now, is pulling away before I've even managed to get the door shut.

"She's shagging someone else," I say, as we course through the hospital car park.

Dave, who up until now hasn't been privy to any of the conversation, turns to me. "Eh?"

"The woman I mentioned before. She's shagging someone else."

Dave's clearly still a little too wound-up to convey sympathy with any real level of conviction. "Oh," he says.

"Some Welsh bloke. Used to play for the Saints."

"Gavin Roberts?" he asks.

I turn to him, aghast. "You *know* him?"

"Well, I know *of* him," Dave replies. "Good player, actually."

"Great. That makes me feel a lot better."

"What's the problem?" Dave asks. "She's shagging someone else. Just fuck her off and forget about it."

"Well, actually, I have," I reply. "Sort of."

Dave sighs and shakes his head. "That's your problem, Eddie. You're too soft."

"It's just at first I didn't want anything," I explain. "Then I kind of did. I don't know, I just thought we might have had something, I suppose."

"I think I'm going to be sick," Brian sighs in the back.

"You know, it's not a crime for me to discuss my feelings, Bri," I say.

"No, I mean I *really* think I'm going to be sick."

"Shit," Dave sighs, slamming on the brakes.

I hear the back door open, followed by the sound of Brian retching. I turn around to see him lying on his stomach across the seat, his head hanging out the open door.

"This is the worst night ever," Dave sighs.

"Worse than the night Bri got his hand stuck in that drain cover?" I ask, over the sounds of gagging.

"Yeah. Absolutely. I didn't have a wedding rehearsal the next day then."

"Oh, just so you know," Brian says, gasping for breath. "I'm being sick metaphorically, too."

"Shut up and get on with it!" Dave barks.

Dave and I sit silently for a time, wincing at the sounds from Brian behind us. Above us, a hint of deep marine blue has crept into the sky, the first signs of the impending morning.

"Look," Dave says, "whoever this girl is, you should forget about her. She sounds like a piece of work."

"It's not like that," I say.

"Well, either way, you've got bigger fish to fry at the moment. Consider the wedding a welcome distraction."

Try *giant pain in the arse*, Dave.

"Focus on this," Dave goes on, "and I guarantee you that once it's all over, this woman will seem like nothing more than a distant memory."

In the back seat, Brian hoists himself up into a sitting position. "Okay," he groans. "Okay, I think I'm good."

"I'm serious, Ed," Dave says. "Wash this woman out of your mind – for my sake, if nothing else."

I nod. "No, you're right. You're absolutely right. She's gone, I promise. Tomorrow's a new day, eh?"

"Yeah," Dave agrees. "Tomorrow's a new day."

Brian groans again, lying down across the back seat. "Have you two boys finished jerking each other off?" he asks. "Because I think I'm pretty much ready to go home now."

9. The Ecclesiophobia Blues

I'm sat in the back of Pete's Ford *Mondeo*, staring out across the rolling green fields, occasionally catching glimpses of my reflection in the window. Funny how we only look at this kind of England from motorways and railway lines these days, through reflections of ourselves. I'm counting the pylons as we pass them, as I did when I was a kid. Pete's driving and Brian's up in the passenger seat – *riding shotgun*, as he insists on calling it. I don't mind. I prefer to be back here anyway, with room to stretch out and sleep (at least, there would be room to stretch out if it wasn't for Brian's crutches getting in the way; there seems to be no way of positioning them so they're not leaning against my head or poking me in the ribs).

From the sat-nav, Yoda orders us to bear right onto the A40.

"Can't you change the voice on that thing?" Brian asks.

"I downloaded it specially," Pete explains.

"I don't care. It's shit. Doesn't even sound like Yoda."

"Well, I'm not buggering about with it now."

"I'll do it, then."

"No. You'll cause an accident."

Brian sighs and sinks back into his seat.

The foot-well below me is littered with empty boxes of computer equipment. We didn't have much choice but to take Pete's car up here. I wouldn't have trusted my heap of junk to make the journey, and Brian can't drive for another six weeks. Dave's driving Alison up in his work van. We lost him on the A43 about an hour ago. Pete's taking it slow and steady. Still, given the choice between Pete's cautiousness and Brian's dragster racing, I reckon things have worked out pretty well.

Brian starts to forage around inside the glove compartment. "Have you got *anything* in here that's not utter shit?" he sighs, pulling out a CD and hanging it between his thumb and forefinger, as though he might catch something from it. "Lionel Ritchie? Is this some kind of wind-up?"

"He's earlier stuff's good," Pete says.

"No, Pete. His earlier stuff is shit. Just like his later stuff and his middle stuff. Haven't you got any Led Zeppelin? I just fancy a bit of Zep now."

"No."

Brian rummages about some more until he finds something that will suffice. "Ha! Remember this, Ed?" He's holding up *Use Your Illusion II* by Guns N' Roses. "Bought this the day it came out. They released 'em both on the same day, but I could only afford one."

Brian opens the case and slides the disk into the player.

"Why didn't you buy the first one, then?" Pete asks.

"Everyone was buying the first one. So I bought the second one." He attempts to head-bang when the heavy part of *Civil War* kicks in, but grabs the back of his neck with a sharp intake of breath.

"Jesus, my neck ain't half aching today," he groans.

"I'm not surprised," I say. "I've never known anybody to sleep through so much."

"I can't believe you got Tasered and I fucking missed it," he sighs. "How gutting is that? I'd love to see someone get Tasered in real life. Especially you."

Pete's laughing now.

"Hey, Pete," I say. "Guess who I saw the other day? Danny Kilbride. You remember him, don't you?"

Pete quickly shuts up and starts fiddling about with the sat-nav.

"What's the point of a *practice* wedding, anyway?" Brian asks a little huffily, more to himself than anybody else.

"They're quite popular these days," Pete explains.

"Bloody stupid if you ask me. When are we stopping for petrol? I feel a bit car-sick."

"Nothing to do with the ten pints you drank last night, then?" I ask. For Brian, not having a hangover is a matter of pride.

"I've always been prone to car-sickness," he says, ignoring the question. "I once puked up in the back of Dad's Capri on the way to Devon. Plus, I'm pretty juiced up on co-codamol right now."

"Don't you dare puke in here," Pete warns.

"Right you are, Pete," Brian says. "I wouldn't want to ruin this lovely interior." He winds down the window a little and puts his mouth against the gap, taking in large gulps of air.

"Some services coming up at the next junction," Pete says, looking warily across to Brian. "We'll stop off there."

♂

A zombie comes lumbering towards Pete, moaning almost pornographically. It looks a little porno too, dressed in a torn-up police uniform, suggesting a life respectable public service before the infection took hold. It's the George Michael of the zombie world.

Pete raises his gun, biting his lower lip thoughtfully, waiting for his moment. The zombie keeps stumbling forward regardless, thinking of nothing but Pete's brain and how tasty it might be. Pete continues to wait. I look to him, puzzled, questioning his judgement now. The zombie's hands are almost upon its prize, and it lets out a final groan of anticipation. Pete pulls the trigger, point-blank. The zombie's head shatters into pieces, its contents showering the scene. It stumbles a few steps forward, headless, blood jetting from its sorry stump of a neck, and then sinks down to its knees off-screen.

"Good call," I say.

"Head shots are more effective close up," Pete explains with a scholarly nod.

Over the next three or four minutes, Pete befriends a beautiful woman, speedboats his way through Venice, and uncovers some bewilderingly confusing conspiracy plot involving the US

President and, so far as I can make out, Joe Mangle from *Neighbours*. Then, finally, he is overcome by a hoard of zombies in an overcrowded alleyway and they dutifully set about devouring his flesh.

"Tough break," I sigh. "Now you're one of them, dude."

Pete sets the pink plastic gun back in its pink plastic holster. On the screen, the scoreboard flashes up.

"You know you chose the pink gun over the blue gun, right?" I ask. "Could be some psychology to that."

"Fuck off, Corrigan."

Brian hobbles up behind us. He's made an effort to dress smartly for the day, although his idea of dressing smartly involves throwing an old, well-worn dinner jacket over an AC/DC t-shirt. "Alright, losers?" he asks. "What do you say we grab some munch before setting off again? I've cleared a bit of room now."

"Charming," Pete says, checking his watch. "Alright, but we better make it quick. What do you fancy?"

"Something stodgy," Brian replies. "Need a bit of stodge to keep me going."

We leave the arcade and walk through the main shopping area. The place is like an airport lounge: a vast, glass-roofed terminal with endless streams of coffee shops and bookstores and fast-food outlets. We pass a clothes shop, a Thai noodle restaurant, a pharmacy, all set alongside avenues of exotic-looking palm trees. I wonder momentarily why it should be that in England palm trees only seem to grow inside shopping centres. It also occurs to me that, should a zombie invasion really strike, this would be a pretty decent place to hole up. A person could survive for months in here without ever having to leave. Of course, there would be a problem with quite a bit of the food. The Thai noodles would last more than a few days, and the same goes for the pre-packed sarnies. But there'd be tinned goods and preserves, and I guess they'd have quite a bit of stuff in frozen storage behind the scenes in a place like this – presuming the electricity supply wasn't down, of course. And then there's the security issues to consider, what with there being so many access points and-

"Eddie," Pete says. "You still with us, mate? What you having?"

I look up to the board. Burger options shine down on me, impossibly juicy and fat-looking things, backlit and flaunting it like parading Las Vegas strippers. These are the hot, unattainable sisters of the burger you actually end up getting – some disappointing and slippery back-room squib of a thing, limply spilling its mysterious contents around your chin like a cold, overeager tongue.

"Skyscraper Meal," I say, without enthusiasm.

Our food arrives in a worryingly quick timeframe and we take it over to one of the undersized tables, jostling for space.

"I'm a cripple," Brian says, pulling the tray across and inspecting each of the burgers manually until he finds his own. "Cripples deserve more space. It's the law."

"What law?" I ask.

"You know, Blue Badges and shit."

We finally agree a share of the table and set about eating our food. Midway through the meal, Brian pulls out a tub of prescription pills, struggling with the childproof cap for a while. He finally gets it open and swallows two of the tablets down with a huge slurp of coke.

"You sure you're not taking too many of those things?" I ask, through a mouthful of burger.

"Nah, it'll be alright. Just keeps the pain off. Still itches like a bastard, though."

Pete checks his watch for the umpteenth time. "They may even be there by now," he says absently.

"Stop worrying," Brian sighs. "Everything's fine. You're such a bloody worrier. Hey, you know what I was thinking about today?"

"World peace?" I ask.

"No, Corrigan. You tosser. I was thinking about asking Dave if he wants C.O.D as the wedding band. We wouldn't even ask for any money or anything. Unless he insisted, of course."

I exchange awkward glances with Pete.

"Not really wedding music, is it, Bri?" I say.

"We can do covers. Tone it down a little."

My mind drifts back to last night's rendition of *Always*.

"He's probably already got something lined up," Pete tries.

"Well, I'll ask him anyway," Brian says, shrugging. "No harm in asking."

In the sense that there's no actual harm in

merely *contemplating* genocide proving you do actually go ahead and do it, I suppose he's right.

"So, what do you guys reckon to all this wedding business, anyway?" I ask, as casually as possible.

"Mmm?"

"I mean, you reckon Dave's doing the right thing?"

Brian thinks about it for a while, taking another noisy slurp of coke, and shrugs. "Seems happy enough to me."

"Well, he might be happy now. But this is the rest of his life we're talking about. You don't think he's rushing in a little too quickly?"

Brian shrugs again. "Haven't really thought about it. As long as he's happy."

"What about you, Pete? You don't think he's a little young to be getting married?"

"Ed, he's twenty-nine. I hate to be the one to break this to you," he says, looking around conspiratorially and lowering his voice in mock-scandal, "but we're not that young anymore."

"Yeah, I suppose you're right."

"Why?" Pete asks. "Don't you think he's doing the right thing?"

"Oh, no. I mean, yeah. I mean, I'm sure Dave knows what he's doing."

"Well, there's a resounding display of approval," Pete says.

"Hey, Ed," Brian chuckles, "remind me not ask you to be *my* best man. You're just ever so slightly too much of a cunt."

"Don't worry, Bri. By the time you find a

woman that'd be prepared to marry you, I'll be cold in my grave."

Brian pops a chip into his mouth. "Here's hoping," he says cheerily.

Pete laughs. "That's fucking funny. He got you there, Ed."

I take a bite of my burger and the meat slides out the other side, landing on the table with a wet slap.

♂

We arrive at Felston shortly before noon. Coming into the place, a person could be forgiven for thinking that the last century hadn't occurred. We pass a cluster of pretty, stonewalled cottages, one of which has been converted into a teashop, its quaint little sign creaking stiffly in the breeze. Crossing over a little humped bridge in the road, the cottages give way to larger houses, set tightly together in neat plots of land, each with different coloured doors and windows, each fronted with tiny but immaculately kept gardens. From the window of one of the houses, a ginger tomcat eyes us with suspicion, as though our arrival is far and away the most interesting thing to have occurred in Felston this decade.

"Looks like something out of *Postman Pat*," Brian remarks.

"His was black and white," I remind him.

"I'm talking about the place, you div."

As the houses recede, we enter the commercial

hub of the village – a post office, a newsagent's, and a good-sized pub. The Bull. The post office and the newsagent's both have posters stuck to the windows screaming "SAVE OUR POST OFFICE", suggesting that Felston's commercial centre could well be cut by a third in the not-too-distant future if the powers that be have their way.

We soon arrive at the church. A number of cars are parked outside, cluttering the narrow road, Dave's work van among them. It's a white Citroen Berlingo, the side-panels stencilled with *R. Atkinson & Son* in black lettering. I told him it was a stupid name when he first signed up with his dad. He didn't seem to care.

"This must be it," Pete says, quite unnecessarily.

He parks the car and I clamber out of the back, fighting the crutches and the empty boxes all the way.

Once outside, I look up at the church. It's a dizzyingly tall structure with high, arched windows, its soaring spire decorated with gargoyles and other Gothic figures. It seems ludicrously grandiose for a village of this size.

Standing by the gates, I can feel my breath becoming shallower and my heart rate quickening. I instantly know what's happening, so I close my eyes and take deep, purposeful gulps of air. It doesn't seem to help much, like a recurring nightmare made no less frightening through its familiarity.

"Come on, fudge-packer," Brian says a little woozily, hobbling into the churchyard.

We pass through the gates and set off down the

path, though the graves of the ancient dead. Skeletal yew trees line the way.

My breath quickens as we walk. I try not to look either side of me.

I try not to look at the dead.

The temperature seems to drop a few degrees and a deep chill courses though me. I pull my jacket closer to my body, although I'm perspiring despite the cold. My throat suddenly feels bone dry. I swallow and quicken my pace.

We clatter noisily into the church, drawing a collective creak from the pews as everyone turns to face us.

Brian waves a crutch in the air. "I object!" he calls out, his voice echoing sharply off the walls and the high, stained-glass windows.

Nobody seems to find it funny.

Dave's standing amongst a small group of people clustered around the altar – the main players, I guess. They all seem too casually dressed for church, like it's some kind of make-believe playground wedding. Alison's wearing an informal party-dress in place of a wedding gown; Dave's dressed in a smart pair of jeans with a crisp, white shirt, unbuttoned at the collar.

I wave to him a little oafishly

Dave breaks away from the group and comes storming down the aisle towards us. I can see by his face that he's pretty pissed off.

A familiar smell hits me: dust and wood and some other indefinable scent that only churches seem to produce. It's the smell of sorrow and grief. It's the smell of the dead. Suddenly, I'm nine years old again, standing awkwardly in an oversized suit. A kicked-in-the-balls kind of sickness rises up inside me – an actual physical ache.

"Where the hell have you been?" Dave hisses as he approaches.

"Not late, are we, Dave?" Brian asks. He tries to look at his watch, jabbing Pete in the gut with the end of his crutch in the same motion. Pete lets out a girlish little yelp of surprise.

"Yes," Dave says, through gritted teeth. "Yes, you bloody well are. Have you two let him get pissed again?"

"It's the meds," Pete explains, slapping the offending crutch out of the way. "They've spaced him out a bit. Probably best to stick him somewhere at the back out of the way."

Dave turns to me. "And what's wrong with you? You look like shit. Are you sure you haven't been in the pub?"

"It's nothing. I'm fine. Just a little car-sickness, I guess."

Dave looks mindfully at each of us, and then quickly shakes his head. "Look, there's no time for this now. We've already got things underway. You two go and sit down – *quietly*. And Ed, you come with me."

All four of us set off down the aisle, the sharp ding of Brian's crutches resounding throughout the church.

And then I see something that stops me in my tracks.

The others plough on ahead, until Dave notices my absence and comes to a halt. He turns back, waiting for me to catch up, only I'm rooted to the spot. Dave gives an exasperated shrug, imploring me to move through the sheer desperation in his eyes. But I can't move. Nothing seems to matter anymore. Not Dave. Not the wedding. Not even the gigantic stained-glass Jesus staring mournfully down at me from behind the altar.

Because there amongst the group, nestled snugly alongside Dave's bride-to-increasingly-soon-be, stands Marla Dimitri.

♂

I'm back outside, leaning against Pete's *Mondeo* and gasping for air, both hands placed on the bonnet as though awaiting arrest for the second time in as many days. The sickness receded the moment I passed back though the churchyard gates, but my head is still spinning with the confusion of it. *What is she doing here? Is this another twisted game of hers? Has she, somehow knowing I was the best man, managed to wangle her way into the wedding just to make things more difficult for me?* I don't remember telling her about it – at least, not specifically.

Dave emerges from the churchyard and crosses the road to join me. I stay bent over, looking down at the tarmac, awaiting a barrage of verbal abuse. When it doesn't arrive, I straighten up and look him in the eye as best I can.

He's frowning, giving me that familiar look, only this time it's tinged with something else, something I can't quite translate. He remains silent, takes out a pack of cigarettes and lights one up. Then he moves around to the front of the car and sits on the bonnet, resting his heels on the front bumper.

"Aren't you going to say anything?" I ask. "Aren't you going to call me a twat?"

Dave takes a long, thoughtful draw on the cigarette, exhaling slowly. "You're a twat," he says.

"I'm sorry, Dave."

"Don't be sorry," he says quickly. "Just tell me what the fuck's going on. And I want it told before this cigarette is finished."

I sigh and shrug my shoulders, unsure where to begin. "What is *she* doing here?" I ask.

"She?" He draws impatiently on the cigarette.

"Marla."

"You know Marla?"

The question leaves me baffled. "*You* know Marla?" I ask back.

"I should hope I bloody well know her, Ed. She's only the maid of honour, after all."

Dave's words drain the last grain of hope left in the egg-timer of my soul, the last hint of possibility that this might all just be some terrible misunderstanding. "Why?" I ask. "I mean...*how?*"

"How is Marla the maid of honour? Is this seriously what you're asking me now?"

"Yes."

"Well, many years ago a fifteen-year-old Alison went to school with a fifteen-year-old Marla. I won't bore you with details of the intervening years, but some time later a decidedly handsome and charming man called Dave asked Alison to marry him. Naturally she said yes, so Alison asked her good friend of many years, Marla, to be the maid of honour, just like I asked some berk called Ed to be my best man. That's generally the way these things work, you know."

"Man, this is *so* fucked up."

Dave rubs at his temple. "Shall I assume from the commendable way you're handling this that Marla also happens to be the woman you've been losing brain-cells over these past few weeks?"

I kick the car tyre in frustration.

"I'll take that as a yes," he sighs.

"Dave, you don't know this woman. Trust me. You might think you do, but you don't. Not like I do, anyway. She's crazy. I mean, literally certifiable. She's neurotic. She's heartless. And she'll stop and nothing – and I mean *nothing* – to get her own way."

Dave rolls the cigarette butt between his thumb and index finger and flicks it out into the road. It lands with a spark.

He stands from the bonnet. "Well, I tell you one thing she is for sure, Ed. She's in there right now, standing next to her friend and supporting her through this. And here *we* are out here." He shrugs. "Now, I sympathise with you – I really do. It's not an easy situation for anyone to be in. But this is my *wedding* we're talking about here, not some playground fling. Whatever's going on between you and Marla sure as hell isn't as important as that, okay? So, I'm going back inside now. And you're going to follow me. And you're going to go through all the motions. And, most of all, you're going to do it all with a great big fucking smile on your face. Understand?"

"Yeah. Just give me a few moments. It's all a bit overwhelming."

Dave moves closer to me. "I've seen you comatose, man – fucking *comatose*. Not eating or sleeping or leaving the house. Remember that. And I came round your house every day – every fucking day without fail – just to try and pull you out of that shit. I didn't have to come round. Don't you think I had better things to do? I could have been out there playing footy and pissing about, just like everyone else. But I came round because you were my friend, and I wanted to be there for you. Remember those times now, Ed. That's all I'm asking of you."

I want to tell Dave that I don't need reminding about any of that. I want to tell Dave that if he knew what I was feeling just five fucking minutes ago he wouldn't think I needed reminding. I want to tell him that every day is *still* every day for me, especially days like today when I have to smell and see and feel just about everything I don't want to all at the same time. But I don't. I just stand there with this coiled spring inside my guts.

"Look," Dave sighs, "I didn't mean to bring that up. I shouldn't have said that – it was out of order. But you *are* coming back in there with me, like it or lump it."

And I already know that I will go back. It was never my intention to be out here in the first place, more of an uncontrollable reaction to seeing Marla, like sneezing at pepper.

"Okay," I say. "Just promise that you'll try to…I don't know…keep her off me a little."

Dave laughs incredulously. "Keep her off you? Jesus, Ed, I know Marla's a bit of a livewire, but don't you think you're going a little overboard with this?"

"Just…please, Dave."

"Okay, okay. I'll make sure you're distanced. Christ, anyone would think it's you pair getting married in there. Now, come on, shake a leg."

Dave slaps me on the arm and makes his way back into the church.

I follow behind. "One more thing, Dave," I say as we walk. "If you notice me with my eyes closed at any point when we're in there, don't go taking it the wrong way or anything. It's no reflection on the marriage."

Dave stops walking and turns, shaking his head in disbelief. "And why in God's name would you be closing your eyes in there?"

"It's churches," I say, looking gloomily over his shoulder. "I don't know. They just kind of…freak me out."

"Churches freak you out?"

"Yeah."

"Ed, churches don't freak people out."

"Well, they freak *me* out."

"And you only thought to mention this now? Standing outside the church?"

"I was sort of hoping it might have gone away."

"You're one big fuck-up lately, Ed. You know

that? Look, close your eyes if you want. Chant Hari Krishna in your head for all I care. I just need you to stand in place and do what they tell you. It'll be over before you know it. Then we can all go and have a pint in The Bull, okay?"

I nod weakly, raise a smile from the grimace.

"Cool," Dave says. "Now, come on, soldier. Front and centre."

10. Cold Cuts

Reverend Hall seems young for a vicar: mid-thirties, perhaps, but still boyish in appearance, with his hair neatly combed into a side parting and doughy cheeks that look as though they only require shaving every third day or so. He's casually dressed like everybody else – still wearing his dog collar, of course, only with a green woollen jumper over his shirt and cream-coloured chinos in place of formal trousers. I'm trying hard to concentrate on these little details; this way, I can still look at him and appear interested without having to think too much about the bigger picture. Still, it's hard to follow the gist of what he's saying; it's just a lot of *and then I'll ask you* and *you'll be standing here* and *repeat after me* all merging into one big tangled mesh of words.

Once I've finished analysing his appearance to the smallest of details, I find myself wondering about his personal life. Is he married? If not, how does he cope with the celibacy? Is it vicars who can't have sex before marriage or is that something else? And does masturbation count?

Reverend Hall stops talking and turns to face me.

My heart leaps. I wonder if I may have been speaking my thoughts out loud, or whether he has read my mind with some kind of divine superpower. Something's up, anyway, for him to be looking at me that way.

I smile back pleasantly and nod, encouraging him to proceed.

Now Dave's looking over his shoulder at me, too. I redirect the smile towards him and give a little wink, as if to say everything's fine, *I'm* fine, don't you worry about me, Dave. He nods his head tersely. I nod back. He nods again. I begin to think that perhaps he didn't see my initial wink, so I wink once more.

"Eddie," he barks.

I'm surprised he's breaking up the ceremony like this. I look to Reverend Hall and back to Dave.

"What?" I ask tentatively.

"The ring."

A sudden fear rises in me. Nobody said anything about the ring. I worry that perhaps I've overlooked something, that this is going to mess everything up, that Dave is going to hate me for the rest of our lives.

"I don't have the ring, mate," I explain.

Dave sighs and rubs his forehead. "*Pretend* to give us the ring, Ed," he says.

Laughter trickles around the church.

"Oh, right. Yeah." I reach into my pocket and take out an imaginary ring box. I open the imaginary lid and feign a look of awe at the sight of the imaginary treasure inside. I pass it across to Dave, who pretends to snatch it from my hand with a stern glare.

The mock ceremony continues and I look away from the altar, feeling a little dizzy. I glance across to Marla. She frowns in exaggerated confusion and mouths something at me. It may be *why didn't you tell me?* To my surprise, there's a sick little part of me that actually pleased to see her again. Maybe it's just the incredible amount of stress my brain is under, but there's something comforting about seeing her here. She's grown her hair a little since we last met, and now it's tucked neatly behind her ears. She looks summery in a floral gypsy-skirt and blouse. Every common-sense particle of my brain is trying to deny the fact that I'm finding her incredibly beautiful standing there.

The background behind her starts to lose focus, like the colours running on a canvas. I quickly look down to my feet, my hands, my twiddling thumbs. Anywhere. It feels like someone has pulled a belt tight around my chest, and everything about this place pulls it one notch tighter: the sounds and the smells, the scuff and squeak of shoes on marble, the blunt coughs from the pews.

I just need to stop thinking about these things. I just need to forget where I am.

I close my eyes, like I promised myself I wouldn't, and try to imagine I'm in a pleasant place: a tropical beach, a cooling breeze from the sea, a cocktail served to me in a hollowed-out pineapple. But the illusion won't hold. It's too ludicrous, too far removed. The beach fades away and suddenly I can smell freshly cut grass. I can hear the faint buzzing of insects. A garden emerges around me: the brightly coloured flowerbeds first, then a neat little lawn, a plastic garden chair, a blue pedal-car with white racing stripes, the number "86" stencilled on its bonnet. Difficult to pedal on the grass, I remember - better off sticking to the pathway.

I look up to the sky, hard blue and cloudless. An aeroplane inches its way along, leaving a fluffy white trail in its wake. I hold up my thumb, the way a painter does when checking for scale, and cover up the plane, uncover it, cover it up again.

I can feel someone behind me, sense her there, and I hear the faint trickle of her laughter, as warm as the day.

"You and that sky, Eddie," she says.

I don't turn, still covering and uncovering the plane with my thumb. But I allow myself a smile.

"You'd probably be happy just living up there, wouldn't you?" she says. "Yeah, I think you probably would."

I don't reply, sensing it's not really a question.

A clatter comes from the garden shed, Dad clumsily putting back the mower.

She sighs gently, laughs again. Laughter echoing down the years.

More sounds of disarray come from the shed, a tumbling down of tools, Dad cursing. I laugh myself now, the hot scandal of words I'm not supposed to hear. It makes me wonder why my ears aren't being covered, or why Dad isn't being chided for the looseness of his tongue.

I sense a vacancy behind me, displaced air where once a person was. I turn around and she's gone, the back door gently closing to.

I open my eyes and gasp quietly, as though resurfacing from a deep lake. Marla is still watching me, her head tilted slightly in curiosity. When she sees my eyes are open, she frowns and shrugs a *what's up?*

I look up to the stained-glass Jesus staring down on us. He's covered in a red shawl, his head haloed with light. He's carrying that familiar expression: sympathetic forgiveness, a little pity perhaps, all underlined by something more menacing, some latent accusation.

I look away, back to the congregation in the pews. Nobody but Marla seems to be picking up on my state of mind, thankfully. Dave's mum is sitting attentively, proudly watching the bride and groom to be. His dad, quite frankly, looks bored, slouching and admiring something up in the rafters. It seems to be a pattern with much of Dave's family – the women watching with great interest, the men appearing uncomfortable in their seats and thinking other things, most likely the pub. An enduring attention span is not a trait easily found within the male branch of the Atkinson gene pool.

On the other side of the pews – Alison's family – things are a little different. They all appear immaculately turned out even for the test run, many of the men in suits or at least shirts and ties, most of the women sporting nice dresses, although not so nice as to outdo themselves for the real occasion. The men all look like doctors or solicitors. I wonder for the first time what they think of Alison marrying a chippie.

The congregation starts to blur, causing me to rock unsteadily on my feet.

I close my eyes quickly, trying to steady my breath. *Neil Armstrong, Buzz Aldrin, Pete Conrad,*

Alan Bean, Alan Shepard, Edgar Mitchell, David Scott, James Irwin, John Young, Charles Duke, Eugene Cernan, Harrison Schmitt. Twelve men who landed on the Moon and came back home. Twelve men who made it.

I look up once again to the giant-sized Jesus, overcome by the sense that out of everyone here he is focusing specifically, and suspiciously, on me.

♂

The church is full. Family members I barely know, Dad's friends from the pub or from the road gangs.

Jim McBride, who taught me to play dominoes six months previously, and who I can never look at directly on account of his glass-eye.

Sean Garraty, who insists so often on lecturing me about a struggle, even though I have no idea who or what he's talking about. I'm just left with a vague sense there's somebody I should be disliking, until Dad, if he's around, leads me away cursing Sean's name, saying we're away from all that now and to stop filling my head with such nonsense, and Sean, if he's drunk enough, saying you're never away from it, wherever you go.

Tony and Dermot O'Hanley: brothers who haven't spoken to one another for coming up fifteen years, but both here now on Dad's behalf. Nobody can remember what the argument was ever about in the first place, not even Tony or Dermot themselves, but it's beyond that now; the thing has become bigger than the both of them, like a tumour left untreated. "The only place they'll ever talk again will be up there," it was often said, "and by then neither eejit will know what to say."

Uncle Mick's alongside me, holding the hand of his latest girlfriend, a heavily made-up bottle-blonde in a too-short skirt, the wet smack of her chewing gum sounding.

And Mum's friends from work a couple of rows back. It looks as though half the Weston Favell branch of Tesco have turned out. She was popular there, liked the job. It was why she didn't go back to the accountancy firm after her maternity leave as planned, even though the pay was better there. She didn't like the phones, the computer, the taking of minutes. She preferred real people, she said, real-life people, and that's what she got at the supermarket. It seems strange to look at them sitting there – people of all colours, shapes and sizes – all these lives she's touched and affected and I don't even know a single one of their names.

Mum's out in front of the isle. The coffin seems too small or too plain or too something to be in any way associated with her. I can hardly believe she's in there; a part of me still thinks it might all be part of some cruel and elaborate trick, that she'll just pop up out of there and we'll all go home laughing over how they got me good this time.

Kate's up on the altar, reading her eulogy. The priest wasn't keen on the idea, wanting to stick to a traditional homily read by himself, but Kate was adamant, and given the choice between bowing to his god or to a bereaved twelve-year-old girl on the warpath, he opted for the latter.

She looks like a woman up there in her neatly pleated funeral dress, no longer like my sister at all – my sister who played with dolls and platted hair and wanted a kitten more than anything else in the world – but a fully grown adult. I know right there in that moment I'll *never see her with those dolls again, never have to fight her off from platting my hair, never hear another word breathed about that kitten. I know that standing up there she's just as much saying goodbye to a part of herself as she is to Mum.*

She's speaking carefully, her voice measured and unfaltering. I know most of the speech, anyway, because I heard it being practiced over and over through the bedroom wall last night. She cried a lot at first, but she read it again and again and again, until they became just words like any other words, like a shopping list or a nursery rhyme, like how if you say a word over and over enough times it loses all its meaning and becomes faintly ridiculous. I guess it was the only way she could have got herself through it, to strip the thing of its meaning like that.

In the speech, she tells a story of how we went to Dunstable Downs one day – me, Kate, Mum and Dad – and how we strayed off the beaten track, with Dad carrying me on his shoulders. It was a good two hours before Dad finally admitted that we were lost, and right there and then the heavens opened. We were stuck out in the open, about to get the worst drenching of our lives, until Mum fashioned a shelter using everything she had in the picnic hamper – a blanket, a newspaper, even the wicker from the hamper itself – and we all huddled together under there, keeping perfectly dry. Half an hour later, the rain stopped and the sun appeared, so we packed up all our stuff and went off to find the car.

I suppose the story stands for an example of Mum's industriousness, or perhaps it's a metaphor for something, but sitting there in the church listening to it being told, I'm just left with the cold realisation I don't remember any of that happening at all.

♂

"And you're not a bloody French mime artist, Ed. Just pass me the ring normally next time."

"I thought it would make it more realistic," I explain.

"It looked like you were taking the piss."

We're walking en masse from the church into the heart of Felston. Dave has hung back with me a little to give me a rundown of exactly where I went wrong, which would appear to be just about everywhere. The sun has broken out while we were in the church, and Felston is looking its best, with pockets of colour blooming from its hanging baskets, the cottage windows glinting in the late afternoon light.

"And you need to sort out this fear of churches crap," he adds. "We can't have that happening on the day itself."

"It's not a problem. Honestly, Dave."

"I can't believe you know Marla," he says, shaking his head.

"I can't believe *you* know Marla," I echo.

"So, she's the one who's been cheating on you?"

"I'm not sure you could call it that."

"I can't believe it," Dave repeats. "She doesn't seem like the type."

"Well, like I said, it's not like that. I think we just got our wires crossed or something."

"This isn't going to cause problems, is it?"

"No," I reply. "Really."

"Because what I said before still stands. You need to forget about it. I need you here, remember? *Compos mentis.*"

"Yeah, I know. I'll be alright."

We reach The Bull and everyone begins to filter inside. It's an old country pub, built in the Tudor style of whitewashed plaster with blackened oak timbers. The roof is thatched, its windows small and leaded.

Dave stops me before entering. "Look, just try to relax a little, will you? It's a wedding. It's supposed to be fun. Ever since this whole thing started you've been like a completely different bloke."

"I know. And I'm sorry. It just took a little adjustment on my part, that's all. But everything's fine now. Let's get in there and mingle. Start enjoying ourselves, eh?"

"You're sure you're alright?"

"Absolutely," I say.

"Because you can always talk to me about these things, you know? I'm getting married, not castrated. It's still the same old Dave here, Ed." He punches me playfully on the arm. "You know that, right?"

"Yeah, I know. Fucking *Thundercats*, right?"

"Yeah. Now, I better get in there and show my face. Keep an eye on Bri for me, will you?"

"Will do."

Dave starts to make his way into the pub, stopping in the doorway. "Oh, and by the way, Ed," he says. "That *Thundercats* thing. Just so you know...it's a little bit lame, mate."

"But you-"

Dave disappears inside before I can go any further. I sigh and follow after him.

The front bar of The Bull is the kind of small, low-ceilinged space typical of country pubs. The décor is still a little Seventies: striped wallpaper, old black-and-white photographs of the village as it used to be – strikingly similar to the village as it is now, as it happens. A bottleneck has formed at the bar, with the Atkinsons in pole-position and Brian not far behind, putting on his helpless-lowly-cripple act in the hope of preferential service. Clearly the landlord has been overwhelmed by the sudden surge of customers, and he and a young female assistant are frantically working the pumps.

By the time I get to the bar things have cleared out a little. I order a Guinness from the young assistant, who meets my eye for a fraction longer than necessary whilst taking my request. She's attractive in a hippy-ish, free-spirited kind of way. Her interest catches my attention, and as she pours the drink and waits for it to settle, I look at her for longer than I probably should.

Dave's dad spots me at the bar and makes his way over.

"I'll get that, love," he calls to the barmaid.

I consider protesting but decide against it. Protesting against Dave's dad paying for your drink is like protesting against airport expansion – admirable in a loose, ideological kind of a way, but ultimately pointless.

"Thanks, Clive," I say instead.

"No worries. Bit young for you, ain't she?" he whispers, nudging me with his elbow and winking at the bargirl.

"Oh, no," I say quietly. "I was just…looking. I mean, daydreaming. You know, looking into space."

"Oh, right," Clive says. "Looking into space."

He's a formidable man, Clive: thickset, sturdy like a solid oak table. He's dressed in a checked short-sleeved shirt, revealing heavily tattooed forearms, the colour now gone from most of them so that they merge into a nondescript bluey wash – relics from his younger, more reckless days. He's developed a gut in later life, but it's a hard, stoical kind of gut, and only adds to the impression of Clive's immovability. Legend has it that Clive was a bit of a fighter in his day, and even now at sixty-odd years of age, I still wouldn't want to get on the wrong side of him.

"Nice day for it, eh?" he says.

"Yeah. Nice day."

"Get down here alright?"

"Yeah, no problem. Pete's got sat-nav."

"Don't trust those things myself," he says. "Rather trust what I got up here." He taps the side of his temple. "Which way did it send you?"

I explain our route and then Clive's off, blurting out a baffling number of b-roads we should have taken and turnings we missed. He's not lying; he doesn't need sat-nav. Somewhere in Clive's head is a fully interactive road map of the entire British Isles, just waiting to be interrogated at a moment's notice.

Dave's mum, Denise, appears at Clive's side. Denise is pure Essex – bolshy and opinionated, with laugh that just comes at you like a steam-train. But she's one of a kind. She was great to us after Mum died, forever checking up on us and bringing food to the house in freezable plastic tubs. She's in another of her overly revealing designer-label dresses today. Over the years, Clive must have spent the annual GDP of a small European country keeping Denise in labels, but clearly he feels it an investment well spent.

Denise fusses over me for a time, kissing me on the cheek and ruffling my hair, making me feel like a kid again. I chat with the pair of them for a couple of minutes until the barman announces that the function room has opened and the buffet is available. This causes a second surge from the crowd, as most people haven't eaten since breakfast. I still have the service-station burger sitting heavily in my gut and my memory, so I'm not as keen as others.

I hang back and allow the more eager to pile through, waiting alone by the bar. It gives me time to mull over what I said to Dave outside, whether I actually believe any of it myself. In truth, the whole thing had been much harder than I expected. I hadn't anticipated that my reaction to being inside a church again would be quite so severe. I had secretly hoped it might be a case of the fear of the thing being worse than the thing itself. As it had turned out, the thing itself was pretty horrific in its own right – and this was only the test-run. Add the news of Marla's involvement into the mix and that's one big shit-cake sitting on my plate.

The barmaid approaches. "Cheer up," she sighs. "Might never happen." She pulls a comical face as if disgusted with her own cliché.

"I reckon it already has," I tell her, smiling faintly.

I finish my drink and make my way through to the buffet. Things are far more comfortable here in the large, high-ceilinged function room. The crowd no longer seems so overbearing, and the light is flooding in from the high windows. Towards the rear, there's a good-sized dance floor and a stage. The stage is empty for now, but a handful of children are trying to climb up onto it. A young boy is attempting cartwheels on the dance floor to impress one of the girls. Sadly for him, it seems cartwheeling isn't his forte, and she looks on unimpressed. Watching them, I'm struck by the realisation of just how early in life a male of the species will do something idiotic in order to garner the interest of a female.

I join the buffet queue, scanning the room for Marla as surreptitiously as possible. She's nowhere to be seen, and after a while my eyes start to hurt from the overuse of their corners.

"Hi, Eddie."

I start a little, turning round to see her standing behind me. "Oh…hi."

"Well, this is a turn up for the books, isn't it?"

"Yeah," I say, digging my hands awkwardly into my pockets. "Yeah, you could say that."

"I had no idea. I mean, the text from Dave, of course. But I didn't know it was *Dave* Dave."

"Lot of Daves in the world," I say with a shrug.

She snorts, as though picking up on some double meaning. "Yeah, there sure are. How are you, anyway?"

"Oh, you know. Fine. Great. Cool. You? How's Gavin?"

Marla gives a little roll of her eyes. "I wouldn't know. I haven't seen him since…well, you know. I told you, it was never anything serious. In fact, I don't think we'll be seeing each other again."

"Oh?" I ask, a poor attempt at causal. "Why's that, then?"

"I don't know. We're just different. I guess he's a little too…*simple* for me."

"Well, yeah, I could've told you that."

"I meant simple as in uncomplicated, Eddie."

"Yeah, of course. So did I." My mind scrambles for a change of subject. "I saw your parents a while back. In the park."

"Yeah, they said."

"You do realise they still think we're…you know?"

"I just haven't got round to telling them," Marla says. "Not properly, anyway."

"They think I'm working in London. On some big project for the Olympics."

Marla bursts out laughing, turning a few heads. "Well, I can't be blamed for that one."

"I open my mouth and these things just come out. I swear, it's like a disease. And your dad won't stop texting me about playing tennis. I don't know how much longer I can hold him off."

"Just play. It's only tennis. You'll be making an old man happy. And I'll tell them we broke up. Brownie's Honour."

"I don't believe you were ever a Brownie."

Marla shrugs in submission. "Got me. But I'll tell them."

"Well, just try not to make me look like too much of a bastard, eh?"

"Edward Corrigan. Are you developing a soft spot for my parents?"

"I just don't want them getting the wrong idea."

"Well, they've kind of been getting the wrong idea since the day you met them."

"I know. But...I just...oh, I don't know. Just think of something good to say."

We reach the front of the queue and I take a paper plate from the pile.

"God, I'm starving," Marla says at the sight of food. "I hope nobody heard my stomach rumbling in the church."

"Oh, I was wondering what that was."

"Hilarious, Eddie."

"Not particularly hungry myself," I say, popping a greasy chipolata in my mouth straight from the communal dish. "We stopped off for a burger on the way up here."

"At a service station?" Marla asks, wrinkling her nose.

"And?"

"Nothing."

"No, come on," I insist. "Spit it out."

Marla sighs and readies herself, as though she's

about to give an important lecture. "Well, think about it. Why do people stop at service stations? To pee, right?"

"Or to get petrol," I suggest.

"To get petrol and to pee."

I think back to our little unscheduled stop this morning and consider telling Marla that, with friends like mine, there are many more functions of human biology that call for the use of the Great British service station. But I don't want to put her off her food.

"So?" I ask.

"So, would you ever in your life eat in a restaurant where the primary function of the place is to take a pee? Couple this with the fact that high proportion of British men don't even bother to wash their hands after using the toilet, and you've got yourself a breeding ground for germs, my friend." She prods her index finger against my chest. "Probably got a whole load of the little buggers crawling around in your belly right now."

"Great. Thanks."

"Well, you asked."

With our plates filled we move away from the buffet, heading for a quiet corner. Dave notices us and looks as though he may be about to intervene, but I discourage him with a quick shake of my head.

"So, what was all that about back there, anyway?" Marla asks

"What was all what about?"

"Back in the church. You looked like you were about to pass out."

"Oh, it's nothing. Just not a big fan of churches."

"You're scared of churches?" Her face lights up at this revelation.

"I didn't say I was scared of them. I said I wasn't a fan."

"I don't think I've ever met anyone who's scared of churches. Doctors, dentists. I even had a boyfriend who was scared of sponges once. But churches? That's a new one on me."

"Like I said, it's not so much being scared of them. I'd just rather not be around them."

"Maybe you're a vampire," she says, smirking.

"Maybe you're an idiot," I suggest, picking the olives off my pizza slice.

"Come on, Eddie. It's nothing to be embarrassed about. Everyone's scared of something."

"I'm not embarrassed. I'm not scared. Look, can we talk about something else?"

Thankfully, saviour comes in the unlikely form of Brian, bounding towards us on his crutches. His hair looks a little wild, and I'm guessing he slept through most of the service.

"Have you *seen* Alison's mum?" he asks excitedly. "I'm talking *proper milf.*"

"Err...Marla, this is a friend of mine. Brian." I desperately want to use the word acquaintance instead.

Brian looks to Marla, noticing her for the first time. He gives her a horribly obvious head-to-toe inspection. "Well, it's a pleasure to meet you, Marla," he says, lingering a little too long over the *pleasure.*

Marla smiles a little mockingly. I have to give her credit; she knows a fool when she sees one. "Nice to meet you too, Brian," she says.

"So, how do you know this loser?" He nods dismissively towards me. "Because I should probably tell you right off the bat, he's nowhere near as interesting as me."

"Really?" Marla asks. "Well, I guess it's lucky he makes up for it with his huge penis then, isn't it?"

I could kiss her right now.

Brian holds Marla's eye for a good while, trying to figure her out. Then, thankfully, he gives up the ghost and changes tact. "Where's Pete?" he asks, looking around. "That gyppo's supposed to be getting my food. I bet he's fucked off somewhere."

"He's at the buffet," I say.

"Oh, yeah. Hey, Pete! Pete!" He's actually roaring across the room, oblivious to anybody else. "Get me some of them Wotsits, will you? And a couple of sarnies. Beef and mustard, if they've got 'em. And grab a couple of those cheese-on-stick things, too." He looks to Marla and raises his crutches in explanation. "Can't carry the plate, see."

"Right," Marla says. "I'm sure it must be a terrible burden for you. Dare I ask what happened?"

Brian arches his eyebrows. "Injured in the line of duty," he purrs.

"And what duty is that?"

"The duty of entertainment, sweetheart." He reaches into his jacket pocket and pulls out a card, handing it across to Marla.

"Disorder of Conformity?" she asks incuriously.

"We're a little, y'know, *out there* for some people. But, hey, who cares about all that mainstream bullshit anyway, right?"

"And is it normal for rock stars to carry business cards?" she asks.

Brian looks hurt momentarily. He snaps the card back. "Well, like I said, I don't really care for what's normal."

Marla smirks. "Clearly."

Pete arrives from the buffet, carrying two fully loaded plates. Instead of taking one, Brian simply starts picking at the food, seemingly oblivious to the fact it means Pete still has both hands full and can't eat any of his own.

"Where's my pint?" Brian asks.

"I'll get you one after we've eaten," Pete replies. "Christ, I can't carry everything."

Brian sighs and shakes his head, as if to suggest that Pete *could* carry everything if only he tried a little harder.

"Are you sure you should be drinking on all this medication, anyway?" I ask.

Brian frowns. "Who died and made you Quincy?" he asks.

"That doesn't even make any sense," I say, taking a plate from Pete so he's able to start on his own food.

Brian, perhaps through wilful callousness but more likely out of sheer blind ignorance, continues to eat from the plate left in Pete's hand.

"So, did you ask Dave about playing at the wedding, Bri?" I ask.

"Yeah. He says the entertainment is all tied in with the events company. He has to go with that they say. Can't get out of it."

"Ah, right. Shame that."

Pete looks to me, smiling.

My phone begins to judder around inside my pocket. I put it on silent for the ceremony and had forgotten about it. Nobody else is aware the phone's going off, of course, so Pete looks surprised and a little hurt when I quickly push the plate back into his free hand.

Digging the phone out of my pocket, I see Dad's name flashing on the display, which strikes me as a little odd. Dad's not really one for phones. He's forever complaining that the buttons are too small and he can't see the screen. Certainly a call like this is out of the ordinary.

"Dad," I say into the phone.

"Hello?"

"Dad."

"Hello?"

"Dad. Can you hear me?"

"Ah, I can hear you now, son. Think I had the wrong bit to my ear."

It makes me wonder exactly how many *bits* of a mobile phone there can possibly be.

"What's wrong, Dad?"

"Oh, nothing. Well, yes, something actually. It's Badger. She doesn't seem right at all."

"What do you mean *doesn't seem right*?"

"Well, she's not her usual self. She's just lying on her bed and not moving very much. Doesn't seem right at all."

Marla's looking to me with concern.

"Well, okay. Listen, Dad, I think we're pretty much finishing up here now, so I'll come back, okay?"

"Righty-oh, son."

"If she gets any worse, you call me, okay?"

"Righty-oh. Will do."

"I'll be there as quick as I can."

I hang up the phone.

"What is it?" Marla asks.

"It's my dad's dog. She's poorly."

"Poorly how? Is she eating alright?"

"I don't know. I didn't ask."

Marla rolls her eyes and shakes her head. "How's her breathing?"

"I didn't ask. I think I should just get back as soon as possible."

"I'll come with you," she says quickly.

I look to Marla in surprise.

She shrugs. "I work in a vet's, remember?"

"Did you drive here?"

"No. I can't drive."

I look over to Pete, recalling the slow journey up here. No chance.

Breaking away from the group, I head across the room to where Dave's standing. He's chatting to Alison's parents, talking in an oddly adjusted accent, which I assume he thinks makes him sound more refined. Spotting me, he introduces me to the Gardeners and I make a hurried job of greeting them, trying to remain as polite as possible without getting caught up in conversation.

"Dave, I need your van," I say, once the

formalities are out of the way.

"What?"

"I need your van. Badger's not well."

"Is this a joke?"

"No."

"Well…will you be insured on it?"

"I'm insured on all vehicles."

"How are you insured on all vehicles? Is that even possible?"

"I'm fully comp."

"Ed, that's not what fully comp means." He looks to the Gardeners, smiling awkwardly, trying to maintain his cool façade.

"Look, I work in insurance, Dave. I know more about this than you. Just trust me, will you?"

"Well, how am *I* supposed to get back?"

"Someone here can give you a lift, can't they? There's space in Pete's car."

"Or you could come back with us," Alison's dad suggests. "It's not a problem."

Dave smiles falsely again, realising now that he really hasn't been left with much of a choice in the matter. He digs into his pocket, fishing out his keys. "Just make sure you lock it up, okay? I've got all my tools in the back."

"Yeah, I will."

"And mind that third gear. She's a little stiff. And drive slowly!"

"Thanks, Dave."

I hurry back over to Marla.

"Come on. Let's get going," I say, holding up the keys. "Dave's lent me his van."

"Will you be insured?" she asks.

"Not exactly, no."

We make our way across the function room, smiling and nodding politely to the people we pass until we're back out into the warm street. The afternoon is slipping away now, shadows stretching themselves out across the pavement like lazing cats. As we're making our way back up the hill towards the church, Marla holds out a hand to stop me walking.

"Look, Eddie," she says. "I know this can't be easy for you."

"Nothing about any of this is easy for me," I say. It's about the most conciliatory thing I can think of right now.

"You know, given the choice, I probably wouldn't have wanted you as the best man, either."

"Well, I'm sorry to have disappointed you."

"I didn't mean that," she sighs, shaking her head. "What I mean is this isn't easy for either of us."

"Well, I wasn't the one shagging the Welshman, was I?" I turn on my heels and continue walking up the hill.

"Don't be like that," Marla says, hurrying after me.

"I'm not being *like* anything. Why do you always talk like that? Like I'm acting just as you're expecting me to act? You hardly even know me. My life was just fine before you decided to have a drink in The Awl that night."

"No, it wasn't."

"There you go again," I gasp. "Talking like you

know me better than myself. Well, you don't, Marla. In fact, going by recent events, I'd say that overall you're a pretty crappy judge of character, okay?"

"Look, if it helps, I'm sorry."

I shrug. "Is that supposed to be an apology?"

"Yeah, well, maybe I *am* a crappy judge of character. Because I had no idea you'd take it this way. To be honest, I'm surprised you even cared."

I stop walking. *"What?"*

"All you ever seemed to care about was the money."

"Bollocks."

"Or schmoozing my parents."

"Wasn't that exactly what I was being paid to do?" I remind her.

"What about *me* in all of this? Didn't you ever think about that? I mean, why the hell didn't you pick up the phone and call me?"

"Because…I was… look, can we not talk about this?"

"That'd suit you, wouldn't it? Not talking about it?"

"And what does that mean?"

"You know, maybe if you talked about things a little more, it wouldn't have quite turned out this way?"

"So it's my fault now?"

"No," Marla sighs. "I'm not saying that."

"Well, just what the fuck are you saying? Because all I've done so far is listen to you go on and on, and do every stupid little thing you've asked me to do. And look where that's got me."

"I'm saying I was confused. I didn't know what you were thinking."

"You know what, Marla? You're right. It *would* suit me to not talk about this. So if you're going to insist on coming along with me, I'd appreciate it if you could do it quietly."

I turn once again and carry on up the hill.

"Please, let's be mature about this," Marla says behind me.

"What was that, five seconds?"

"Okay, okay," she sighs. "No talking."

"Good."

"Fine."

"Agreed."

11. Strange Creatures

"Did you hear them calling her Badger Corrigan?" Dad asks. "Like she's a real person?"

"It's just for the system," Marla explains. "Plus, some people like it. You know, part of the family and all that."

We're sitting in the waiting room of the veterinary surgery. The air smells faintly of rabbit hutches and antiseptic. Two dogs are sat with their respective owners, eyeing one other warily across the room. On the seats opposite, a young girl sits with her mother, holding a pet-carrier. Inside the carrier, a shuddering bunny peers out from the gloom.

Badger was sent through on an emergency basis as soon as we arrived. I got the discomforting impression that the emergency basis wasn't merely because Marla worked here. In any event, I'm not sure veterinary practices have employee incentive schemes: twenty percent off your next cat worming, two-for-one on dog neutering.

Badger went through forty-five minutes ago and we've heard nothing since. We'd arrived at Dad's earlier to find her lying on her bed, her breathing shallow and laboured. It hit me then how much I'd been neglecting my Badger duties lately – how much I'd been neglecting Dad, more truthfully. I hadn't been visiting or taking her for walks as often as usual. Only my mind had been so preoccupied with other things.

Dad had told us how she'd been lethargic for some time, refusing her walks. But she was still eating normally – wolfishly, in fact – so Dad had thought it was probably just old age kicking in. Only in the last few hours had her condition declined to such a point that he decided to call me.

Marla had taken control then, ordering me to get Badger into the van. I'd scooped her up like a baby – probably the only time in her life she's ever allowed me to hold her – and the three of us had hurried here, with Badger making these odd little whimpering noises all the way. It was worrying to hear such pitiful sounds from a dog usually so proud.

"Well, it's nice to finally meet you at last anyway, Mr. Corrigan," Marla says. She's sitting in between us, hunched over with her legs folded, kicking her leading foot back and forth. "Just a shame it couldn't have been under better circumstances."

"Geoff, please," Dad says, smiling a little sadly. "Eddie's told me all about you. Forgot to mention how pretty you are, though."

I look to Dad incredulously. Is he actually *flirting*? And when did he start wearing his shirts like that, unbuttoned with a t-shirt underneath, a t-shirt with an actual proper logo on it?

The surgery door opens and a vet enters the waiting room. He's a middle-aged, officious-looking man, with wire-framed glasses perched upon a hard, beaked nose. He's dressed in loose-fitting scrubs, a paper facemask hanging around his neck. Laying a clipboard down on the reception desk, he mutters something to the two ladies behind it. From the instant respect they afford him, it's clear he's somebody pretty important, probably the owner of the practice.

The man sighs deeply and scans the waiting room, peering over the top of his glasses at the people waiting. Singling us out as the only clients not already in possession of an animal, he makes his way over.

"Mr. Corrigan, would you like to come through?" he asks.

Dad and I both stand.

"Shall I come?" Marla asks.

The vet looks confused as to why Marla is here, or at least why she's not behind the reception desk where she jolly well belongs.

"It's okay," I explain. "She's with us."

We're led away from the waiting area into a small, private room. The vet closes the door behind him. He looks mildly anxious, and I quickly get the impression he's not entirely comfortable with this part of the job. He strikes me a hard, clinical man of science, and hardly a people person at all.

"It's not good news unfortunately," he says sharply. "I'm afraid the animal has passed." *The animal.* Badger's gone from having a surname to being *the animal* in just under an hour. But seeing as she has apparently also gone from this mortal coil to the next in the same time, I guess that's the least of her worries.

"She's dead?" Dad asks, astounded.

"I'm afraid so, yes. She didn't suffer."

"How?" I ask. "I mean, why?"

"Well," the vet says, drawing in his breath, "she was pregnant."

"Pregnant?" Dad just stands there, mouth agape. "How could she be pregnant?"

The vet looks confused momentarily, as though considering whether he really needs to explain the concept of the birds and the bees to a man in his sixties. Then the penny drops. "Some dogs hide their pregnancy well," he explains. "Particularly smaller breeds such as…"

He looks about for his clipboard, searching for a name, and then realises he left it on the reception desk.

"Such as Jack Russell terriers," he says instead.

"I mean, I suppose I noticed she was a little fatter," Dad murmurs. "I thought she was just getting old."

"Well, she was certainly old to be carrying pups," the vet advises. "Had we been aware of her pregnancy earlier, we would have strongly recommended termination."

"You would have put Badger down?" I ask.

The vet looks to me. "Termination of the pups," he explains, furrowing his brow.

"Oh."

"I can't believe she was pregnant," Dad sighs.

"Wasn't she spayed?" I ask.

"I thought all of that was done before she came to me."

"It would appear not," the vet interrupts. "In fact, under the circumstances, I'm amazed she hasn't been pregnant before."

"Oh, you don't know Badger," I explain. "She's

isn't – *wasn't* – exactly what you'd call sociable."

The vet again gives me that dull look, as if to suggest that an animal's character trait affecting its chances of pregnancy is the most patently stupid thing he's ever heard. "On the bright side," he goes on, "we did manage to save all the pups."

"Pups?" Dad mutters, still in a state of bewilderment.

"Yes. Five, in fact. We had to perform an emergency C-section. It's miraculous they all pulled through."

"Five," I gasp. "Is that normal?"

The vet gives me one final look to suggest that I am, in his considered and professional opinion, a complete idiot. "Perfectly," he says flatly. "About average, I would say."

Dad moves slowly across the room, sitting on a plastic chair in the corner. He exhales heavily and runs a hand over the soft tortoise-shell of his scalp. Marla walks over to him and strokes his shoulder. It's a small gesture, but one that blindsides me. She didn't even know him an hour ago.

"I understand this must come as a shock to you," the vet says coolly.

"What happens now?" I ask. "To Badger, I mean."

"We can make arrangements here, if you wish."

"Arrangements?"

"Most people opt for cremation these days. We can return the ashes to you. Or alternatively you could take her away for burial."

I look over to Dad, seeking his opinion. Clearly, he's in no state of mind to give one. And I'm not entirely sure what the Catholic line is on animal disposal.

"We'll take her," I tell the vet.

"Very well. Now, we'll need to keep the pups in for observation. They're still in a fragile state at the moment."

"Of course."

"I suggest we keep them for a week at least – perhaps even more, depending on how they progress. After this, they will need constant attention for some time. Are you able to provide this?"

"Yes," I reply. "Dad's at home all day."

The vet looks over to Dad. "Mmm. Very well."

"That's alright, isn't it, Dad?" I ask. "Just until they're on their feet."

Dad nods his head slowly. "Yes. I suppose so, son."

"And I can help out," I say, hoping this will garner the vet's approval.

The vet nods and pushes his glasses further up his nose. It's actually quite apparent he's not overly concerned what happens to them providing it's nothing he can be sued or prosecuted for. "Then that's taken care of," he says. "Are you ready to take the remains immediately?"

The remains. Jesus.

A sudden realisation hits me. "Where are we going to bury her?" I ask.

The vet looks bemused, as if the question is being asked of him.

"Neither of us have a garden," I explain.

"I have a garden," Marla offers. "You're

welcome to bury her there."

"Are you sure?" I ask. "That's not a bit weird or anything?"

"No, of course not. She has to be buried somewhere."

"And fairly urgently," the vet chips in. He nods over to the window. "Considering the hot weather."

I can't help but grimace at this. Did the man actually have *any* coaching with this sort of thing in vet school? I suppose it's just a small mercy he didn't become an actual real people doctor, cautioning people on the decomposition of their grandmothers.

"Okay," I say. "We'll bury her there."

"Very well," the vet agrees. "Wait here, please." He makes for the door and then turns, as if remembering something. "Oh, and I *am* sorry for your loss. Please rest assured we did everything we could for her, Mr. Corrigan." The sentiment seems more born out of the wariness of litigation rather than any kind of genuine sympathy. He offers a forced smile and leaves the room.

I look to Dad and Marla. She's still doing her best to comfort him, still stroking his shoulder. Dad suddenly straightens up, as if noticing his own weakness for the first time.

"Well, okay," he says quietly. "I suppose that's that, then."

♂

We pull up outside Marla's house in Dave's van. Switching off the engine, I turn to face Dad, sat in the back cradling a bundle of blankets in his arms. Nobody has even looked at Badger yet. We just took her like that, all bundled up and out of sight. For all we know, the vet sent us away with a faulty toaster wrapped up in a blanket. Although, why would he do that?

"This is it, Dad," I say.

He's pretty squashed back there amongst Dave's carpentry tools, his head so perilously close to the roof that I did less than thirty all the way here for fear of hitting a bump in the road and knocking him unconscious. Still, it didn't seem right asking Marla to go back there either.

"Righty-oh. Grab the shovel, will you, son? I don't want to go dropping her."

I reach over into the back seat and take the shovel. Marla insisted that she had her own perfectly serviceable spade that we were free to use, but Dad's funny about his tools and insisted on needing his own shovel for the job. I was a little too embarrassed to admit I wasn't entirely sure of the different between a spade and a shovel, so I held my silence. Besides, with two tools at our disposal, I can at least make some arbitrary attempt at helping.

We climb out of the van and, remembering Dave's words, I make sure to lock up properly. As we walk in silence to the house, Marla smiles reassuringly at me.

Once Marla has unlocked the front door, we pass through the hallway and into the kitchen. I try to erase the memory of the last time I was here – or the first time, for that matter. It's a kitchen, just like any other.

"Tea?" Marla offers.

"That'd be nice," Dad replies. "We should probably get right to it, Eddie."

I look out the back window. It's a pleasant, fair-sized garden of good width, with flowers on each side and a small shed at the end, standing in the shade of an apple tree. Beneath the window is a neat little patio area with a table and chairs. I'm surprised. I never would have put Marla down as the green-fingered type. Perhaps she inherited it this way from the previous owners.

"Anywhere in particular?" I ask her.

"How about down the end there?" she suggests. "By the tree. She'd probably like it down there."

"By the tree it is, then. Think that'll be alright, Dad?"

"As long as we keep a little way off the trunk. Don't want to get in the way of the roots, do we?"

He's good with the logistics of holes, Dad, having spent most his life digging them.

Marla unlocks the back door and we walk out into the garden.

"Better leave her down here, eh?" Dad says. "In the shade."

He settles Badger down gently within the shade of the house and removes his shirt. I pass the shovel across to him and we set off down the garden, stopping when we come to the tree.

"Yeah, it's a good spot," Dad says, patting the trunk. "Reckon this'll do us, don't you?"

"I'll go and look for the spade," I say.

I head off for the shed, finding it unlocked. Inside, I discover a cluttered mess of gardening tools and half-used paint pots. I manage to find the spade and by the time I return, Dad has already set about digging the hole. There really is an art to the way Dad digs. It like watching a creature do the one thing it was born to do, the one thing it does without question or forethought. A lion chases down an antelope, a frog catches a fly, and my dad digs a hole.

I stand there watching him for a minute or two, oblivious to the world around him. I watch him throwing the mud in clean, steady swings, watch him bring the heel of his boot down on the broad edge of the blade, digging for the good earth below. There's such fluidity to his motions that he makes it all seem effortless. After a time, I join in, trying to imitate his actions. I find to my surprise that I'm getting into the swing of things, too. By the time Marla comes out carrying two cups of tea, we've made pretty decent progress.

"I'll leave them on the table here," she shouts down the garden.

"Okay," I yell back, waving.

She moves one of the patio-chairs out into the sun and sits down, lighting up a cigarette.

"So, that's Marla?" Dad says quietly, going back to his digging.

"Yep, that's Marla."

"Quite a looker, eh?" he says, smiling.

It surprises me. I can't remember ever hearing Dad talk about women this way before. I'd always felt he retired his libido for good the day Mum died.

"Yeah, I did notice you mention that," I say, frowning.

I go back to work, digging in tandem with Dad so that together we become like a double-armed excavating machine. After a while, Marla calls down to us that our teas will be getting cold, so we down tools and head over to the table.

Marla has put her feet up on another chair and shimmied up her skirt so her legs will catch the sun. She's put on a pair of sunglasses and brought out a paperback to read.

"That's good digging, son," Dad says, slurping at his tea.

"Yeah?"

"Yeah. Should be done in no time."

A feeling of pride swells up inside me. Strange I should get such a sense of vindication from something as basic as digging a hole. It's a feeling that outweighs anything I ever took away from, say, getting a reasonable grade at university. As I stand drinking the rest of the tepid tea, crazy fantasies drift into my mind, firstly surrounding giving up the office job and working on the roads like Dad, but soon expanding with alarming momentum until I'm imagining myself as some sort of travelling, self-sufficient gypsy-type (only a nice, olden-times gypsy with a horse and a red-painted wagon and a floppy straw hat.). I'd sell trinkets to people, do a bit of tinkering on the side.

No, ridiculous. Nobody lives like that anymore.

Dad swigs down the last of his tea and gasps

extravagantly, like he's starring in a television commercial for the tea-makers. "Righty-oh, son," he chirps. "Better get back to it, eh?"

Marla closes her book and peeks over her sunglasses at us. "Don't you boys be overdoing it. I don't want to be carrying you out of here."

"Actually, Dad, she does have a point," I say. "You should be minding your back."

Dad waves a hand dismissively. "Ah, no bother. I told you, it's only the cold weather that plays her up. I'm right as rain. But *you* might want to be watching yourself. You're not used to all this physical work, after all."

It makes me hope Marla has gone back to her book and zoned out of our conversation. "Don't be daft, I'm fine," I say, offhandedly. I put my cup down on the table, more eager than ever to prove my willingness now. "Let's get back to it, shall we?" I practically cheer, already heading back up the garden.

Once Badger is settled into her eternal resting place, we find it takes less than half the time to refill the hole than it took to dig it. Before long, Dad is patting down the last of the replanted earth with the back of his shovel. I feel physically shattered, but I do my best to conceal this as Marla approaches to inspect our handiwork.

"Should just about do her, I reckon," Dad says happily. "I'll pop round another time and get this re-turfed, Marla. Be like we were never here."

This last statement brings an odd sense of melancholy over me. "Should we perhaps say something?" I ask.

Dad looks at me a little peculiarly. "If you reckon so, son," he says.

"No, well, I just thought perhaps we should. Anyway, she had a good innings."

"Yeah, she did."

"And she'll be with Mum now."

"Yeah," he agrees, a little more cautiously this time. "Yeah, I suppose she will."

I look up to the sky. "Mum, if you're listening," I shout. "Whatever you do, don't touch her ears."

Dad furrows his brow, looking at me incredulously. Then his face softens and he breaks into laughter. I'm laughing as well, and it feels good, standing in the sunshine after a good bit of honest work, making Dad laugh like this.

"Do you know, she used to sleep under my bed every night," Dad says, once the laughter has faded. "Badger, I mean, not Mum. I always kept her bed in the kitchen, but without fail she'd always find her way under my bed at some point during the night."

"Well, what do you know?" I say. "Never had Badger down for the needy type."

"I suppose it was only when she thought nobody was looking. She just saved all that stubbornness up for when people were around."

"Strange creature," I say, shaking my head.

"Yeah, strange creature," Dad agrees. "Anyway, I suppose I better be getting myself back to the flat. Get myself cleaned up, like."

"Going somewhere?" I ask.

"Well, I've got what you might call a date. I suppose I should have thought about cancelling it, but I reckon I could do with a bit of cheering up after all this."

"You've got a date?" I ask. "Someone you met online?"

"Not exactly, no. I met her at the computer class. Her name's Barbara." He laughs. "Looks like all this Internet stuff's paying off already, eh?"

"Looks that way," I say. "You should definitely go. It'll help take your mind off things. I'll drop you back. I should probably be getting Dave's van back, in any case. He'll be giving himself a hernia worrying about it by now."

"Okay," Dad says. "Thanks for today, Marla. I mean that. She'll be happy here. It's a nice spot."

Marla smiles. "Yeah," she agrees, "it is."

"Righty-oh, then. I'll see you in the van, shall I, Eddie?" Dad smiles and makes his way up the garden, clearly sensing we need some time alone.

"Listen, thanks for letting us do this today," I say to her as we head towards the house. "I mean, burying a dog in someone else's garden – that's a pretty big deal. A lot of people would have freaked out over something like that."

"It's fine, Eddie," she says. "I'm happy to help."

I prop the spade up against the house and take off my muddy shoes, carrying them into the kitchen and giving my hands a good wash at the sink. The last thing I need is Dave giving me any more grief for dirtying up his steering wheel.

"And sorry for having a go at you earlier," I say over the rushing water. "I'm just tired. Didn't get much sleep last night."

"Forget it," Marla says. "I probably deserved

it."

"No. You didn't." A sudden thought hits me. "Hey, why don't you let me buy you dinner tonight?" It comes out sounding a little too much like an advance for my liking. "As a thank you for today," I add quickly.

Marla wrinkles her nose. "Can't, I'm afraid. It's the hen-do tonight."

"Really? Busy day. Well, another night, perhaps."

"You won't add it to my tab?" Marla asks, smiling.

I dry my hands on one of Marla's tea towels. "I won't add it to your tab. You know, you can pay me back in instalments, if you like."

"Such a gent," she says, snatching the towel from me.

I pick up my shoes and head through to the hallway. The living-room door has been left slightly ajar. Inside, I spot a large canvas painting hanging above the fireplace.

"Hey, is that one of yours?" I ask.

Marla seems confused for a moment. She follows my line of sight into the living room. "Oh, yeah," she says. "One of mine."

I push the door back and walk into the living room, despite the fact I get the impression Marla would rather I didn't.

The room feels a lot more spacious than the last time I was here, free from the clutter of Marla's moving-in boxes. It's decorated in neutral colours, so everything appears fresh and new.

I walk over to the fireplace. The painting depicts

a large human face, only painted abstractly so you really have to look at the thing before it becomes clear. It's painted in varying shades of green, so that the visage seems like a silhouette, or like it's half-shrouded in darkness.

"This is really good," I say, genuinely impressed.

Marla twists a little shyly on her feet. "You think?"

"Yeah. Absolutely. I mean, I'm no expert, but I really like it. I'd buy it, anyway."

"Careful, Eddie," Marla says. "I might hold you to that one day."

"I'm serious. You should do more to get your stuff out there."

"Oh, I don't know. I can't see too many people wanting to buy anything."

"Well, they can't buy anything unless they can see it, can they?"

"No," she agrees, "I suppose not."

I turn away from the painting to make my way from the living room, jumping a little when I see Dad at the window, his nose pressed to the glass, peering inside. He begins to make strange hand gestures and after a time I realise he wants us to open the window. Marla does so, fighting with the stiff handle until the window jars open suddenly.

"What is it, Dad?" I ask.

"You should probably get out here, son," he says. "I don't think you're going to like this very much."

♂

I'm sitting in the "86" racer, which really is getting too small for me these days. I can only pedal it by bending my legs to such a degree that my knees are up by my ears. I'm trying to crash into Dave, who's sitting in a large bucket we found in the shed. The point of the game is to see if I can upturn Dave, but it's hard to gather momentum when it's so hard to pedal. I just keep bashing into the bucket and Dave, the big lug, barely moves.

"My turn now," Dave says. "Let's see if I can knock you over."

"One more go," I protest, already pedalling back around.

Just as I'm about to take another run-up, the sound of a chiming nursery rhyme comes drifting across the garden: London Bridge is Falling Down.

The weather is unseasonably warm, and the ice-cream vans have come out early.

"Ice-cream van," Dave cheers, jigging about excitedly inside the bucket so that it topples over without any intervention from me at all.

Laughing at Dave as he rolls about helplessly, I climb out of the car. "Wait here," I say, even though he's in no position to go anywhere.

"Ask if I'm allowed one, too," Dave calls after me. "Otherwise, I could just have some of yours."

I roll my eyes as I walk up the garden. Same old trick. "Okay, I'll ask," I yell back.

I open the door and step inside the house, my bare feet instantly cooling on the kitchen tiles.

"Mum, the ice-cream van's here," I say.

Mum's washing up, her back turned against me. "Well, that's nice, dear," she says absently.

I consider this for a while, and then opt for a different angle. "Can I have an ice cream?" I ask.

"You don't need an ice cream, Eddie," Mum says.

Dad took us to the Wimpy Bar earlier, after it emerged that the chicken for tonight's dinner had been left in the freezer. To my mind, Wimpy and ice cream are hardly connected at all, about as far removed as needing an ice cream and wanting *an ice cream.*

"Aw, Mum," I whine.

"Eddie, I'm busy. You can see that, can't you?"

"But the van'll be gone soon."

"You'll have missed it by now, anyway," she says.

"Not if we hurry."

"Eddie, no!" she barks.

"Please."

"Eddie!"

I stamp my foot on the tiles, as childish as I've ever been, and hurry from the kitchen.

Back out in the garden, Dave has freed himself from the bucket and is sitting on the bonnet of the pedal car. "Well?" he asks.

"We're not allowed."

Dave sighs and rests his chin in his hands. "Bollocks," he sighs.

I pick up the bucket, furious now, and squeeze myself inside it. "Come on, then," I say. "Knock me over."

Dave moves into the seat of the pedal car. He looks even more uncomfortable in there than I was.

The chimes from the departing ice-cream van ring out, and Dave looks wistfully into space, as though contemplating the ice cream that never was.

"Knock me over," I demand.

This shakes Dave from his thoughts, and he smiles devilishly as a new thought alleviates his melancholy, the thought of smashing into a bucket with me inside it. He tracks back down the garden in the car, setting himself up for a good approach. Turning, he begins pedalling furiously, building up quite a speed. I begin to have second thoughts about my offer, but it's too late now; Dave's bearing down fast and, in any event, I'm still stewing over the ice cream. I want the impact. The release.

Dave hits the bucket and I go falling backwards, hitting the grass hard. It knocks the breath from my lungs.

"Ha!" *Dave cries in victory.*

I stay lying on the ground, half-winded, looking up to the sky. There's an airplane trail up there, blue on white, like Mr. Whippy fresh from the machine. The sky starts to blur, and I realise tears are welling up in my eyes, spilling down my cheeks. I don't move until Mum's face looms fuzzily above me, cutting out the sun.

"Eddie," *she says softly,* "sorry for snapping. I'll get you an ice cream now. From the shop instead."

I quickly wipe my eyes, determined not to let Mum see I was so upset over anything as trivial as an ice cream. "Dave wants one, too," *I say croakily.*

"Only if it's not too much bother," *I hear Dave say.* "A Twister, if they've got one."

I rest up on my elbows, shaking my head at Dave.

Dave shrugs. "Or a Screwball, if not," *he says, as though offering a second choice might redeem him somehow.*

"Two Twisters, then," *Mum says.* "And you boys stop being so boisterous out here. You'll hurt yourselves."

Mum heads back up the garden.

"Why did you ask for a Twister?" I ask Dave. "I wanted a Funny Foot." Funny Foots are my favourite. Dave knows that. Everyone knows that.

Dave shrugs.

I look up the garden but Mum's gone, the back door closing gently to.

12. Hit & Run

"Do you think anyone saw anything?" I ask.

Dave's rear bumper is hanging off. One side of it has completely broken away from the vehicle and is resting on the tarmac; the other side appears to be clinging on by a single remaining screw. Unfortunately, the bumper didn't take all of the impact, and one of the rear light has been smashed. Tiny shards of red glass are scattered on the road. Something must have hit it with a fair amount of force to do this, something that would have made a lot of noise.

Marla looks to me. "If they had," she says, "you would have thought they'd have left a note."

"Yup," Dad agrees, looking up and down the road as though searching for a culprit there. "Would've left a note."

"Well, you'd like to think whoever *did it* would have left a note," I say.

Dad tuts and shakes his head, resting his hands on his hips. "Dunno what the world's coming to, son," he sighs. "People crashing into things and not leaving notes. When did people stop leaving notes?"

I walk around to the front of the car, checking under the windscreen wipers. "I don't think it was an agreed thing, Dad," I say. "I don't think they had a committee."

"Well," he sighs, "people just don't give a shit these days, do they?"

I pop the wipers back into place and walk back around to re-inspect the damage, as though looking at it enough times might make it go away. "Dave's gonna to go ape when he sees this," I sigh.

"You can pick another bumper up easily enough," Dad says encouragingly. "And those lights just pop out. New one won't cost much." He checks his watch. "Scrap yard'll be closing now, mind."

Dad takes the van keys from me and unlocks the back doors. He disappears inside the vehicle, emerging moments later holding a screwdriver. "Can't drive her anywhere like this," he says. "Have to take the whole thing off for now."

I watch forlornly as Dad sets about removing the few remaining screws. Once done, he pulls the entire bumper free. It comes away with a horrible cracking sound, and he gets to his feet with a groan, holding the bumper out. "Here you go, son," he says.

I stand looking at the bumper, wanting nothing in the world to do with it. I sigh and take it while Dad opens the back doors again. I slide the bumper into the van, but soon realise the vehicle isn't long enough to accommodate the whole thing properly, so I have to rest one end of it up between the front seats.

I thank Marla one last time and kiss her on the cheek. It seems a little formal after everything that's happened, but I'm not entirely sure where we are in the kissing goodbye stakes these days.

"I'll see you soon, then," I tell her, climbing into the driver's seat.

Although the day is cooling, the van has been sitting in the sun for hours, and it's stiflingly hot inside.

Dad rolls down his window as we pull away, waving to Marla.

"I've got the air-con on," I tell him.

"Righty-oh, son."

"I mean it won't work with the window down."

Dad thinks about this for a while. "Well, why do we need the air-con on if the window's down, anyway?"

"Because it's not the same," I explain.

Dad shrugs. "It's all air, isn't it?"

I sigh and roll my own window down. Dad's suspicious about air-con in the same way he's suspicious about alternative medicine. His GP once prescribed a course of acupuncture to help with his back, but Dad left before getting halfway through the first session, grumbling about how it was all just a load of *hippy mumbo-jumbo*. No doubt he feels using an internal air-conditioning system when there's a perfectly serviceable window available amounts to something equally as modern and daft.

"See your mirrors alright with this thing here, son?" Dad asks, nodding at the bumper.

"Not really. What time's your date, anyway?"

"Not until seven. Plenty of time yet."

I check my watch. Ten past five. "So, you heard any more from Kate?" I ask. "About the baby, I mean?"

"No. You?"

"Nope."

"Maybe she's changed her mind," Dad suggests.

"I don't know. She seemed pretty determined to me."

"Well, there aren't many things in this world Kate isn't determined about. Doesn't always make them right."

I look over the bumper to Dad. "You don't think she's doing the right thing?"

"I didn't say that, did I? I've just always thought Kate should have more of a...*male influence* in her life. I mean, who's gonna work when they're looking after the baby?"

"I expect one will work and the other will stay at home."

"But which one?"

"I don't know. I suppose it'll depend on who's bringing the most money in."

"And she'll have to give the job up completely," Dad goes on. "I mean, they won't just let her have the time off. They'll know she's not actually *pregnant*."

Kate has a pretty high-flying marketing career down in London. Dad's always been pretty vocally proud about that, and I suppose the prospect of her having to give it up is just another reason for him to be blowing cold over the whole idea.

"I'm sure there must be laws," I suggest.

"What laws?" Dad asks.

"Adoption laws. I don't know. Kate must know what she's doing."

"I'm not so sure this time, son," Dad says, shaking his head. "Really, I'm not."

"Well, it doesn't look like you're going to have much say in it, does it? So I suppose you'll just have to get used to the idea. Either that or drive her away again."

Dad turns to me quickly. "What do you mean *again*?"

"Why do you think she shot off to London as soon as she could?" I ask.

"It's not my fault if there's nothing around here for…"

"Lesbians, Dad?"

"Well, yeah."

"That wasn't the only reason she left."

"It was nothing to do with me," he huffs. "I didn't say a bloody word about it at the time. I kept my beak well out of it."

"Yeah, well, maybe that was part of the problem."

Dad folds his arms defensively. "Look, this town. It's just not the sort of place where she could have lived that kind of life very easily. It was nothing to do with me. Can we talk about something else, please? I just buried my dog, for God's sake."

"Oh, come on," I sigh. "The world's moved on, Dad. You should try moving on with it someday."

I switch on the radio to prevent the conversation from descending into a full-blown argument. It comes on pre-set to Classical FM, some thunderous Wagner-esque number that makes us both jump. Just what the hell is going on with Dave lately? I remind myself to ridicule him later (perhaps much later, once he's had a chance to calm down about the van) before switching the station over to Five Live.

"And Rochdale are getting pulled further down towards the bottom three there, aren't they?"

"They'll have to be careful, Simon."

"Whereas it's another win for Kettering Town today. They're going great guns at the moment."

"Very much so. They've got good strength in depth these days, and no doubt towards the end of the season they'll be there or thereabouts."

"And Eddie Corrigan?"

"Well, we were saying earlier in the season, weren't we, Simon, that it looked all but over for Eddie? We all thought he was a certainty for the drop. So let's give credit where credit's due. He's somehow managed to keep his head above water down there."

"Some pretty murky waters though, Alan."

"Indeed they are, Simon. It's all pressure down there for Eddie at the moment, and Marla seems to be giving out some very confusing signals."

"Just what is going on with her?"

"It's hard to say, Alan. She's a wildcard, I'll give you that."

"And this latest episode with Dave's van?"

"Well, it does make you wonder, doesn't it, Alan? Surely we must be asking ourselves now if this is the kind of person Dave wants for his best man in the first place."

"So what we're really saying is: this is one that could go either way."

"Absolutely. And we all saw how he went to pieces in the church back there. I mean, that really is unforgivable. At this level, to just capitulate like that – it's completely unaccep-"

I switch off the radio.

"Hey, we didn't hear the Cobblers result," Dad whines, turning to me with a wounded expression.

"Red button it," I reply.

♂

There's a banging on the front door, so loud we can hear it from the garden. Probably Mum forgetting her key, as she's prone to doing. With the promise of ice cream still foremost in my mind, I make for the house, leaving Dave behind, jammed into the racing car like a bottled cork.

Inside the house, I pad across the kitchen, taking care to step only on the black tiles so not to fall into the imaginary burning chasm below. From upstairs, I hear the sudden suction of water: Dad emerging from the bath.

The banging comes again, frantic, like somebody with bigger concerns than a melting ice cream.

"Hang on," I shout.

I fiddle around with the Yale lock for a while before getting the door open.

It's Manish from the corner shop: a stout, chubby man with a cheerful, round face. He's sold me a million penny sweets over the years, enough liquorice laces to tie a bow around the world. Only he doesn't look so cheery today. He looks strange.

I notice the sweat glistening on his bald, mahogany crown.

"Eddie," he says in that sudden patter of his, a machine-gun fire of syllables. "Is your father home?"

I look over my shoulder, up the stairs. "Dad," I yell.

A sudden thought hits me. If Manish is here, how will Mum be able to buy the ice cream? I'm not sure I could take the disappointment all over again. On the plus side, at least I could explain to Manish about wanting a Funny Foot instead of a Twister. He could explain to Mum at the counter, and Mum would laugh.

Dad comes down the stairs, stopping mid-descent. He's thrown on a pair of jeans and a t-shirt. His dark, thinning hair still twinkles with bathwater.

He sees Manish and frowns – Manish just standing there all out of context like that.

Manish looks up the stairs. "Mr. Geoffrey, quickly," he says breathlessly. "You must come quickly."

"Manish, what is it?" Dad asks.

"Mr. Geoffrey, please," he says, turning behind him to the street outside. "Your wife. You must come."

The mention of Mum seems to kick start Dad into action, and he hurries down the stairs.

"Wait here," he barks as he barges past, almost sending me crashing into the hallway wall.

And then I'm alone.

I look to the open door. It suddenly feels cold and dark in the hallway, and the skin of my forearms starts to tingle – the phantom prickling of hairs yet to be grown.

Before I really know what I'm doing, I'm heading for the door.

Outside, the world seems brighter than before. Perhaps it's just my eyes adjusting after the darkness of the hallway, but the great, bleaching light seems to envelop me, seep inside me. It's as though I left a different world back in the garden and here on the other side of the house is a new one, one to which I'm not yet acclimatised, one from which I might never return. I think of Borman, Lovell and Anders on the Apollo 8, going a thousand times further than anyone had ever been before, going to the far side of the Moon. Did they worry in that moment, during the darkness and the radio silence, about the likelihood of them ever making it back?

I push through the garden gate and I'm out into the street barefooted. The paving slabs are scorching hot, forcing me to hop from foot to foot.

Further down the road, I see Dad running, with Manish alongside him. It seems strange to see grown men run. It makes me wonder at what age people usually stop running.

I look back to the house, our old house, safe and secure.

And then I'm running too, running after Dad and Manish. Seeing them disappear around the corner, I quicken my pace, my feet hammering painfully on the concrete.

I reach the end of the road, still unable to spot them, but keep on.

As I draw closer to the shops, I notice the commotion. Groups of people are gathered outside the shop-fronts, looking on curiously. A man stands outside the barber's, still wearing his bib, his hair only half cut. On another day, it might have been funny. People are talking and pointing and shaking their heads. On the other side of the road, an ambulance is parked crookedly. Two men in bright green overalls are hunched over something lying in the road. Ahead of me on the pavement is a torn shopping bag, its contents scattered, milk blotched like a white sun. And to either side of the milky splodge, like two orbiting satellites, are two unopened ice-cream lollies: one Twister and one Funny Foot.

♂

Dave's looking at me oddly, looking at the bumper in my hand. Clearly he's trying to piece the two things together in his mind.

"Oh, you're fucking kidding me," he says flatly.

I look sheepishly down to my shoes, letting him know that, no, I'm not fucking kidding him and, yes, the bumper does belong to him.

"What happened?" he asks.

"I don't know. I just found it like this. Somebody must have gone into the back of it."

"Weren't you in it?"

"No."

"Well, where the hell were you?"

"Burying Badger. She died."

"Badger died? What? Look, get in here."

I take off my shoes and step into the hallway. Dave's changed out of the shirt he was wearing earlier, back into his more familiar jeans and t-shirt combo. The t-shirt of the day says 'Silicon Valley' on it, with a landscaped depiction of a pair of breasts beneath. It really does make me wonder how long he's going to continue wearing such items; surely a married man shouldn't be walking around with these kinds of things emblazoned across his chest, after all.

"Badger's dead?" Dave asks again. "How?"

"She was pregnant."

Dave exhales, puffing out his cheeks. "Wow, man," he sighs. "That's heavy."

"Yeah," I say, "heavy."

"You realise you look like shit, right?" he asks.

"I've been digging. Badger's grave. Guess it's not really the weather for it."

Dave studies me for a while longer. Clearly he's a little annoyed by the fact that news of Badger's demise means he can't berate me as much as he would like to about the van.

"Go on through," he says.

I walk through to the living room. Alison is standing in front of a mirror above the fireplace, adjusting her hairclips. She's still wearing the party dress from earlier, revealing a good deal of leg to me again.

"Hi, Eddie," she says breezily, turning to face me.

"Hi, Alison. You look great, by the way. I don't think I had the chance to say earlier."

"Ah, thanks." She kisses me lightly on the cheek, brushing away a spot of freshly applied lipstick that she leaves behind. "Is your stomach better?" she asks.

"My stomach?" I ask.

"Yes. Dave said you had diarrhoea earlier. Back in the church."

I look behind me, intent on expressing my dissatisfaction at his choice of alibi, but he's not there. I guess he's outside inspecting the full extent of the damage.

"Yeah," I say, turning back to Alison. "Yeah, I'm fine now, thanks."

"Ah, that's good." Alison looks to the bumper in my hand, frowning. "What's that?" she asks.

"Oh, it's a van bumper," I explain. "Belongs to Dave."

On cue, Dave comes walking into the room from behind me. "Bloody light's a goner, too," he grumbles.

"I know. I'll pay for the repairs, of course."

"Bloody right, you will."

"Oh, don't be such a grumpy-bum, Dave," Alison says. "I'm sure it wasn't Eddie's fault."

I shrug helplessly. "I wasn't even there," I explain.

"See, Dave," Alison says. "He wasn't even there."

She's growing on me, Alison – a little more each time we meet.

"Fancy a cup of tea, Eddie?" she asks.

"That'd be nice."

"Dave, fetch Eddie a cup of tea, will you?"

I see Dave physically stiffen, his jaw tightening. "I don't see why Eddie should wreck my van and I have to make him a cup of tea," he says.

"Dave, stop being a baby," she says. "I always say *you can fix cars but you can't fix people*. Isn't that right, Eddie?"

"Absolutely," I reply, smiling at a now defenceless Dave, feeling some small sense of retribution for the diarrhoea story. "No sugar in mine, please."

Dave turns silently away and heads for the kitchen. I hear him crashing about in there, noisily opening and closing drawers, rattling the utensils inside.

"So, you ready for your big night out, then?" I ask Alison, who has gone back to preening herself in the mirror.

"Hmm? Oh yeah, should be a good one. Just a meal at Giacomo's, then out for a few drinks around town."

"No wild strippers planned?" I ask

Alison smiles at me in the mirror. "Well, you never know with Marla doing the organising, I suppose."

"How is Marla, anyway?" I ask, as casually as possible. I wonder briefly how much Alison knows about my relationship with Marla, if relationship is what it could be called. I suppose it's plausible that Dave spilled the beans to her at some point today.

"Oh, she's fine," she says. "At least, she will be if this prick of an ex-boyfriend would stop harassing her. At least tonight should be a chance for her to let her hair down, I suppose."

This grabs my attention, although I try to keep my expression from rising anywhere above mild curiosity. "You mean Gavin?" I ask. I thought she told me the over-inflated twerp was out of her life. Maybe he's just not taking no for an answer. Maybe I'll have to clash with him in some sort of duel for Marla's honour. Just the thought of it makes me long for the old days, when such things were settled with guns at twenty paces. At least then it would be a level playing field.

Alison frowns. "What? No? Who's Gavin?"

"Oh, I...err...I just thought I heard the name Gavin mentioned before."

Alison thinks about this for a while. "Oh, you mean *Big* Gavin."

I don't really know how to respond to this. In all honesty, I'm too busy trying to untwine the knot in my guts to say anything at all. *Big Gavin?* Is that how he's known? *Collectively?* I let my stomach settle with the thought that it's possibly just a reference to his physical stature.

"No, no," Alison goes on. "It's Joe. Bloody idiot just can't seem to accept it's over. He just won't let things go."

Well, this one catches me unawares. *Joe?* Do I really have to compete with him as well now? I begin to feel like I've been thrown into some sort of gladiatorial arena, only nobody's told me exactly what the rules are or where the exit points are situated. "Oh, I didn't realise that," I say faintly.

Alison finishes applying the last of her makeup and presses her lips together, in that way women do for reasons I've never fully understood. "Well, why would you? Anyway, on the subject of Marla, you two seemed to be getting on well earlier." She smiles wickedly.

"Yeah, she's...she's quite a character."

"She's a forgetful little so-and-so, is what she is. Shot off without even saying goodbye."

"Oh, I'm sure she had her reasons."

"Mmm. Anyway, I'll have to interrogate her about you later."

I shrug, trying on casual indifference for size. "I'm not sure there's really much to say. So, what's this about her ex? How do you mean, *he won't let things go?"*

"Oh, just a lot of texting. Turning up on her doorstep unannounced. Same old crap, really."

Dave comes back in from the kitchen carrying a cup of tea. He hands it across to me ungracefully, so that a little of it splashes over the rim and burns my hand. Dave either doesn't notice or doesn't care.

"So everything went okay today, yeah?" I ask, wincing a little from the pain.

"I think so," Alison says. "No major hiccups, at least."

"Apart from the latecomers," Dave adds, glaring at me.

"Yeah, sorry about that, mate. Won't happen on the day itself, of course."

"Bloody right, it won't," Dave says. "You'll be coming with me then anyway, so I'll make sure of it."

"Hey, isn't it my job to get *you* to the altar on time?" I ask, chuckling.

"Well, call me an old cynic, Ed," he says, "but I'd rather not take my chances."

"Dave," Alison says sternly.

From outside, a car's horn sounds.

"Right, that'll be the taxi," she says. "You boys play nicely now. How do I look?"

Dave steps over and kisses her on the forehead. "Like a million bucks. Try not to go too crazy tonight, eh?"

Alison laughs and rolls her eyes. "Says you after your boys' night out yesterday. Half-four he got in last night, Eddie. Half-four! What on earth were you lot up to?"

"I told you," Dave blurts. "We went back to Eddie's and just lost track of the time." He smiles at me encouragingly.

"Yeah," I say. "Yeah, it was my fault, really."

"Well, I still reckon you've got a mistress," she says jokily.

"We're not married yet, sweetie, so technically she wouldn't be a mistress, would she?"

She kisses Dave on the lips. "Cheeky bugger," she says, heading for the front door. "Right, I'll see you later on."

She leaves the house and we watch her through the window as she gets into the taxi. "Ah, she's a fine woman, Eddie," Dave says.

"Yeah, she is," I say. "I reckon you've struck lucky there."

"I reckon I've hit the *jackpot*, more like." He turns from the window. "Anyway, how are you feeling?"

"I just spent the last three hours digging a hole after being electrocuted-"

"Twice," Dave interrupts, smiling.

"After being electrocuted *twice* and I'm running on about two hours' sleep. How do you think I'm feeling?"

Dave nods. "It *was* pretty funny, though."

"You weren't saying that last night."

"But it's one of those things you can look back on and laugh at, hey?"

"Well, I'm glad *you* think so. Look at this." I roll up my shirtsleeve and show Dave the burn marks on my arm: two distinct reddish-brown areas where the prongs entered.

"Nice," Dave coos, which was hardly the reaction I was expecting. "Anyway, guess who bought the new *Call of Duty* last week?"

"I'm going to guess you," I say, rolling my sleeve back down.

"Correctemundo, amigo! Shall I fire her up?"

"I really need a shower, Dave," I sigh. "I really need *sleep*."

"You'll be alright. Just have a couple of beers."

"Not really the same thing, is it?"

"Come on, Eddie. Looks like we've got the place to ourselves for the night."

I sigh and shrug my shoulders, knowing that resistance is futile. "Okay, just for a bit. Then I really do have to get going."

"Good man!" he cheers, slapping me on the arm, causing me to recoil in pain. "By the way, I thought it might be an idea if we kept the whole Marla situation on the down-low from Allie for the time being."

"Really?"

"Yeah. You know, I thought it might be an idea if you two could just sort of…steer clear of one another. Just until the wedding's over."

"Why?" I ask.

"Because I know what you're like, Ed. No woman can put up with your crap for more than a few weeks."

"Thanks."

"Which means you'll be on course to be ripping each other's throats out by the time the wedding day arrives. It'll be a fucking disaster."

"Well, I don't know about that," I say. "We seem to be doing okay at the moment."

"Yeah? And for how long? You're just too volatile a person to risk it, Ed. Both of you are, in fact. I think if you just cool things down for a few weeks – you know, put it all on the backburner – then we'll be avoiding a lot of unnecessary complications further down the line."

"You can't ask me to do that, Dave. It's not fair."

"No, but I can ask you do a favour. For me. On the biggest day of my life. I don't think that's asking too much, is it, Ed?"

I sigh. "Well, it doesn't look like you're leaving me much choice in the matter, does it?"

Dave slaps me on the shoulder again. "That's the spirit! Now, come on, soldier," he says, winking. "Let's lock and load."

13. Good & Bad Things

"Thirty-love!" cries Robin, as another of his perfectly placed forehand drives goes whizzing past my ear.

I'm getting a little annoyed at him calling out the score after every point, particularly as he's doing it so loudly, and particularly as there's an attractive young lady playing on the adjacent court. As if looking so out-of-place in my garish beach shorts and mismatching football jersey wasn't embarrassment enough, now I'm getting emphatically thrashed by a man twice my age who seems determined to give the rest of the Dallington Tennis Club a running commentary of my ineptitude. Actually, he's not calling *every* point. I won one about twenty minutes ago, the ball hitting the outside of my racquet with a resounding thunk and limping fortuitously over the net. He didn't have much to say about that one. No, siree. Since that bit of luck I've been sticking to net play, and have been under heavy artillery fire ever since, the ball so far hitting me in the shoulder, the ribcage, the neck and, most painfully of all, the lumber of my spine.

I retreat gloomily back to the baseline and await another of Robin's gargantuan serves. The day is a hot one, only adding to my pains. I'm drenched in sweat. Everything on the other side of the court seems out of focus through my reddened, stinging eyes.

Robin tosses the ball up into the air and sends it thundering over the net at breakneck speed (the broken neck in question presumably being mine had I not ducked my head out of its path at the last millisecond).

"Forty-love!" he yells. "Match point!"

It actually looked a little out to me, but I don't have the strength to mount an appeal. Instead, I trudge over to the other side of the court to receive my final humiliation. I do manage to at least get my racquet to his winning serve, but there's nothing behind it at all, and the ball goes pea-rolling into the net.

"Game!" Robin punches the air with his fist and comes jogging over to my side of the court. He's dressed impeccably in regulation whites. Hardly broken a sweat.

"Well played," I say.

"Unlucky," he offers in return.

"Not really on my game today."

"Not to worry, Eddie. Bigger things on your mind, I suppose – what with all this Olympics business, I mean."

I shrug. "Perhaps. Hey, lucky they don't have tennis in the Olympics, eh?"

Robin frowns. "I'm pretty sure they do."

I pretend to not have heard this as we make our way over to the kit-bags. I'm trying to walk as normally as possible so not to let on the fact my calf muscles are ablaze.

Back at the rest area, Robin sheathes his racquet and slips it into his specially designed carry-case. I wedge mine awkwardly into my rucksack. It's not big enough to accommodate the whole thing, so the handle pokes out through a hole in the zip. I borrowed the racquet from Brian at the last minute. After much frantic ringing around, it turned out that he was the only person I know who owned one – albeit a mid-Nineties relic from his schooldays, one which has done nothing but gather dust ever since.

"You should invest in a better racquet," Robin advises, as though reading my thoughts. "That's half your problem right there."

I don't dare ask what the other half might be. "Yeah, I'll look into that," I say.

Robin sits down on the bench, sipping a blue-coloured isotonic drink. I'm dying of thirst myself, but I don't want to worsen matters by getting my drink out in front of him. It's a used bottle of *R. White's* Lemonade that I filled with tap water before leaving the flat.

"And if we're going to play again, we'll have to see about getting you some proper kit," he says. "I'm not sure I could sneak you past the dress-code gestapo a second time."

The thought of playing again right now makes me feel physically ill, although I can't help feeling a little touched that Robin would even consider it. "Yeah, I'll see to that, too. Like I said, everything's still down in London at the minute."

Robin pops the lid back on his drink and tosses it into his bag. "So, how is everything between you and Marla?" he asks. "The distance not causing any problems?"

"Oh, no. Not really. I manage to get back most

weekends, and-"

And something in my brain clicks. Something just doesn't want to keep this up anymore. Some deep down part of me is just sick to the back teeth of lying.

I sigh and sit down next to Robin. "Look, you seem like a really good guy. A good father to Marla and everything. And Jean, too - good mother, I mean, of course. I don't want to lie to you anymore. Fact is, I never *did* want to lie to you. I just kind of got caught up in it all. You see...Marla and me...we're not really an item. Not in the way we've been leading you to believe, anyway."

Robin slowly looks across to me.

"That morning when you came round her place - well, that was the first time I'd even met Marla. And she wanted to put up this big story - so she wouldn't be embarrassed, I guess. And I just sort of went along with it. Because it was the easy thing to do."

I look across the courts to the attractive girl. Each time she hits the ball she's throwing everything into it, her skirt swinging to and fro.

"But it's not Marla's fault," I say quickly. "I wouldn't want you taking that idea away. She just didn't want to hurt Jean, I suppose. And somehow it all just got out of hand. If anything, it's my fault. I should have said no to it all. I shouldn't have even gone home with her that night. She was drunk. I...I guess I took advantage of her or something. Anyway, the thing I'm trying to say here is that I'm sorry. To you and to Jean. You seem like good people. And I never thought it would go this far."

I let out a sigh of relief, slumping back against the bench. After an awkward few moments of silence, I glance across to Robin. He's looking at me curiously, the side of his mouth curved upwards into a strange smile.

"Eddie," he says at last, "I know you probably look at me and see an old fuddy-duddy who knows nothing about the modern world, but I was a young man as well once, you know. Even had what you might call the odd...*fling*, I suppose. Not too many, but enough. So don't think I can't recognise a case of the morning-after-the-night-before when I see it with my own eyes." He laughs steadily. "I knew you weren't what you professed to be the moment you came creeping down those stairs. Or I should say what *Marla* professed you to be. Just thought I'd have a little fun with it, asking you about the fireplace and what have you. Ha, should've seen your face – what a picture!"

I'm stunned by this. "You knew? Why didn't you say anything?"

Robin shrugs. "Didn't really think it was my place. These things usually sort themselves out one way or another. Besides, I like to consider myself a pretty good judge of character and you seemed like a decent chap, all told. As for taking advantage of Marla, I think we both know Marla's hardly the sort for that. Although, I must say it was honourable what you tried to do just then – take the blame like that. The more we meet, the more I'm convinced I was right in my opinion of you, Eddie. You're a good man; don't let anyone tell you otherwise. And God knows Marla could use one of them in her life after all these years. Not that she'd ever admit to *that*, of course – to herself or anybody else, for that matter."

I run a hand through my sweat-encrusted hair, exasperated. I can't help but laugh at the incredulity of it. "So, in the restaurant – you knew then?"

"Of course. Salsa dancing! Now, that was a hoot. Couldn't make it up." He frowns. "Except you *did* make it up, of course."

"Does Jean know?"

"Good Lord, no. And she never will, either. The thing's too far gone for that now. Whatever happens between you and Marla, I think this is best kept between us, don't you?"

I nod my head. "There's something else, too," I add, deciding to get it all out of the way at once. "Alison Gardner."

"Good Christ! You didn't have your way with her, too?"

"No, of course not. She's marrying my friend. I'm the best man."

"And Marla's the maid of honour," Robin says slowly.

"And Marla's the maid of honour."

"Ah. Well, that does pose a few obstacles, doesn't it? You know we're invited to the wedding?"

"Yes."

"And we wouldn't want Jean to get any nasty surprises on a day like that?"

"No."

"Well then, I suppose what this whole thing

comes down to, Eddie, is how you feel about Marla. And how she feels about you. Of course, if you ever hurt her, I'll have to hunt you down and kill you."

I look to Robin, startled.

Robin shrugs. "I think I'm supposed to say something like that."

I smile and fetch the bottle of water from my bag, supposing it hardly matters what Robin thinks now. I take a good swig from it, gasping with relief. "To be honest, Robin, I don't know how I feel about her. I know it drives me mad not to be around her. But then she drives me mad when I *am* around her."

Robin laughs. "She's not the easiest of people, my daughter. Never was, even as a child. Always wanted something more than what she had. It's just the nature of the girl, I suppose."

"I don't know how this whole thing got so complicated," I sigh.

"Well, that's the way it is."

"The way what is?"

Robin smiles and stands from the bench. "In any case, looks like you'll have the chance to discuss things yourself." He nods across the courts to the clubhouse, where Marla is making her way toward us.

"How did she know we were here?" I ask.

"Oh, I suspect Jean had some say in it," Robin chuckles. "Anyway, I'll leave the two of you to it." He slings his kit-bag over his shoulder. "Just remember, Eddie – it's only life, and it's meant to be enjoyed." He shrugs and looks up to the sky, bathing his face in the sun for a few seconds before looking back down to me. "So enjoy it," he says, with a wink.

On this odd little philosophical tit-bit, Robin turns and heads off the court, leaving me to digest all I've heard. But it's rather too much to digest. I'm like an overly greedy python with a baby hippo in its gut, unable to move.

Robin greets Marla on the perimeter of the courts. They exchange a few brief words and he kisses her on the cheek before going on to the clubhouse. Marla continues walking towards me. She's wearing a loose-fitting white blouse that ripples in the breeze, with jeans and strappy high-heeled shoes. Her face is half-concealed by a pair of oversized sunglasses. In her right hand she's carrying a book.

"Ecclesiophobia," she says loudly, as she draws closer.

"What?" I stand to greet her.

"That's what you have. Ecclesiophobia." She says the word slowly, emphasising all the syllables as though proud of each one. She presses the book against my chest. "Fear of churches."

I take the book and turn it over to the cover. *The Harrington Anthology of Phobias.* "Bedtime reading?" I ask.

"You can borrow it, if you like. But I'll need it back. It's from the library."

"I don't want to borrow it."

"I've marked the page."

"I don't care. Here."

I hold out the book but she walks away, heading

over to the bench and sitting down. She slides the sunglasses on top her head and looks to me, wincing in the light. "So, did you manage to beat Dad?"

"Oh, well, you know...it was pretty close. Actually, I can't remember who won in the end."

"So Dad won?"

"Yeah."

Marla laughs. "He's been playing most of his life. Did he tell you he was once semi-professional?"

"No. No, I guess he forgot to mention that."

"Years ago now, of course. Before I was even born. Still, you never lose it, do you?"

I frown. "Apparently not."

"How was Dave? About the van, I mean?"

"Oh, well, I seem to still be the best man. For the time being, at least."

Marla grimaces and sucks the air in through her teeth. "Not good, eh?"

"I think he might have calmed down by now. Fortunately, I had Alison there to use as a shield." I sit down next to Marla. "How was the hen night?"

"Good. I think we gave her a suitable send off."

"You realise Alison doesn't know anything?" I ask. "About...you know...us?"

"Yes," she replies flatly. "And I'd prefer to keep it that way."

I can't help but feel mildly offended at this. While I hardly want to make a song and dance over the whole thing myself, the strength of Marla's desire for secrecy is a little troubling. Is she *embarrassed* about me?

"What makes you say that?" I ask.

"I just think Alison has enough to worry about at the moment without us making it worse."

It's about as good a response as I could have hoped for, I suppose. "Yeah," I agree. "You're probably right."

"And it's not like we're in a relationship or anything, anyway," she adds.

"No. Of course not."

"So, it's not like there's anything to really tell."

It's difficult to tell where this self-justification is coming from. Perhaps she feels bad about keeping things from Alison. Or perhaps there's more to it than that. Perhaps she's testing me.

"No," I say. "Not really."

Marla hops up from the bench. "Anyway, go and get showered. I'll meet you outside in ten."

"Why?" I ask.

"Because I've got a little something lined up for us today."

"I'm not sure I like the sound of that."

Marla smiles. "Outside. Ten minutes." With this, she turns and heads back for the clubhouse.

And when she's safely turned away from me, I smile back.

♂

"Is this yours?" Marla asks, looking at my P-Reg Ford *Ka* with the kind of expression most people reserve for looking at puddles of sick.

"At least I have a car," I say, immediately on the defensive.

"That's a lifestyle choice. *This* is a lifestyle disaster."

"Well, I happen to like it. It's efficient."

"Efficient like cholera," she grumbles, climbing into the passenger seat.

I pull a silly face at her, out of sight, and get into the driver's seat. "Where are we going, anyway?" I ask, starting the engine.

"You'll find that out when we get there, won't you? Left out of the exit here."

I course through the tennis club car park, doing my best to avoid looking at all the Mercedes, BMWs and Porches lining the way, making my car look like the poor kid on Mufti Day.

"You know, I'm not really big on surprises," I say, as we get on the road.

Marla folds her arms and holds her silence, smiling wryly.

"You're just going to sit there like that?" I ask.

Marla shrugs. "Right at the traffic lights," she says.

"I *could* just stop the car and ask you to get out, you know? I could quite easily just do that."

"Yep," Marla says, "you could."

She takes off her shoes and puts her feet up on the dashboard, levering the seat back a couple of notches. Before long, she starts humming a tune, wiggling her toes with synchronicity in a kind of miniature, digit-based Mexican wave. She seems fascinated with her little trick, staring intently at her own performing toes.

"Can you do that?" she asks after a while.

I look to her toes again. "I expect so," I reply. "Can't say I've ever tried."

"Well, how do you know if you've never tried?"

I shrug. "I don't, I suppose. Not exactly the four-minute mile though, is it?"

"Most people can't do it, actually," she says, a little haughtily. "In school, I was the only person in my class who could."

I smile. "Well, that's...that's quite something. Your teacher must have been very proud."

"Now, now," Marla says. "No need to get all Eddie-ish about it."

I consider asking her what exactly *Eddie-ish* is supposed to mean, only I'm not sure I want to know, so I remain silent.

And we drive in relative silence for the rest of the journey, the only words spoken being Marla's occasional directions, which I am by now blindly following. All I know for sure is that we seem to be heading towards the town centre and the car seat is playing havoc with my bruised and battered back.

"Pull over anywhere here," Marla announces, once we have apparently reached our destination.

I duly park up in the first available space, thankful to be able to exit the vehicle and stretch out my wounded vertebrae.

We're in Bradshaw Street, a dour and grubby looking part of town that even the sunshine can't rejuvenate. The pavement is littered with takeaway boxes and chip papers, remnants from last night's queue for the taxi rank. I briefly consider the wisdom of leaving the car here, although it does have its own inbuilt security system in the sense that no respectable car thief would want to be seen dead in it.

Marla leads me down the street, past a takeaway restaurant from where the smells of kebab-meat emanate. A radio is squawking in a foreign language somewhere. A group of English lads are sitting on a wall on the other side of the road: hoodies and baseball caps, tracksuit bottoms tucked into their socks. A couple of them are attempting to bunny-hop on undersized BMXs, although other than this an air of utter malaise seems to hang over them. It makes me think about the car again, although I try not to be judgemental. No doubt if Dad was here, he'd be muttering about how they needed a good kick up the arse before being put to work on the roads.

We cross over The Drapery, heading down into the Market Square. For almost a thousand years people have traded here, although these days the mainstay stalls seem to be the ones selling discount items and suspiciously packaged DVDs, or the ones that can unlock your mobile phone for under a tenner. It's a fair-sized, cobblestoned square, surrounded on three of its sides by shop fronts. Narrow, arterial alleyways run between them, lending to the impression of this place being the very heart of the town, albeit the very neglected and cholesterol-ridden heart. The smell of burger fat and fried onions only solidifies this image in my mind.

"Hey, you didn't tell me about Joe," I say,

struggling to keep up with Marla.

She slows her pace. "What about him?"

"About him harassing you and everything."

Marla stops walking. "Who told you that?" she asks tersely.

"Alison."

Marla rolls her eyes and sighs and sets off across the Square at full pelt again. "Well, that's private. And it's not a problem."

"Sounds like a problem to me," I say, chasing behind her.

"Well, it's not!"

"Fair enough. But you know you can always come to me with any problems, right?"

"What are you now?" Marla asks. "My protector?"

"No. I'm just saying."

"Well, don't *just say*."

"Fine."

We pass the fruit and veg stalls, where the vendors are calling out their offers of the day in heavy local accents. Heading away from the Square, we pass the bank, the butcher's. It's a Saturday, so most of the shops are busy and thick with gossip, bringing to mind a long series of chicken coops.

"Look, I'm sorry," I say. "I didn't mean anything by it."

"Forget it."

"It's just-"

"I said forget it, Eddie. Anyway, we're nearly here."

"Nearly where? Are you going to tell me what

we're actually doing here?"

"We're going to do a test-run."

We encounter a queue streaming out the door of the bakery and have to push our way through it, ruffling the feathers of those in line.

"A test-run for what?" I ask, once we're safely out the other side.

"Of the church. To help with the ecclesiophobia."

"Will you stop saying *ecclesiophobia*? Twenty-four hours ago you never even knew that word existed."

"And neither did you. Now that I've carried out a diagnosis, we can work on the cure."

"Dia – wha – oh, great."

"Anyway, here we are." She turns to me and nods over her shoulder, towards All Saints Church.

The church is a tall, self-aware building, standing on a busy island around which the traffic hazardously swirls. At its front is a grandiose, high-columned portico, with a paved courtyard area before it. Above the portico is a stout and sturdy-looking bell tower.

"This is ridiculous," I say.

"No, Eddie, being scared of churches is ridiculous."

"For the last time, I'm not scared of churches!"

"You look like you're about to puke."

I sigh and throw my hands up in an overly dramatic display of despair. "Fine! Fine! If I go in there, then can we stop all this nonsense and go home?"

"Absolutely."

"Right then," I say determinedly.

I march off across the road. Marla waits a while and follows on a few feet behind me. I pace across the courtyard and up the steps of the portico, where the sun can't reach. The light is swallowed up in an instant, and the cool stone seems to chill the air even further.

I think of Jim Lovell again, only this time on the Apollo 13. Being up there again. Being told he can't land. Waiting in the dark and the cold on the lunar far side.

Marla catches up but stops short of standing alongside me. "Well, what are you waiting for?" she asks. Her voice echoes around the portico, adding extra weight to the question.

I point to one of the small alcoves cut into the front of the church. "John Clare used to sit there," I say, quite ridiculously.

"What?"

"The poet. He used to sit there. He'd write poems to passers-by for beer money."

"Eddie, you're stalling," Marla says flatly.

"No, I'm not. I just thought you might be interested. You know, a bit of local history and whatnot. It's interesting." I turn to face Marla, who seems distinctly unimpressed. "Okay, okay," I sigh.

Steadying myself with a deep breath, I head through the huge, arched door into a large, sparsely furnished foyer area. I hear Marla following behind me, the heels of her shoes clacking on stone floor.

"See," I say, pointing out a bronze bust to one side. "John Clare."

Marla waves me on, fanning her hands impatiently.

I head through the foyer and into the church proper, finding myself at the beginning of long, barrel-vaulted nave that arches high above me. Four huge pillars line the way down to the intricately decorated altar. Midway down the nave is a low-hanging chandelier, and my eye-line is drawn up the full length of its chain to the interior of a large, perfectly symmetrical dome in the ceiling. Behind me, stretching high above, are dozens of gold-coloured organ pipes of all shapes and sizes, looming like proud trees standing guard at the threshold of some ancient forest into which I have trespassed.

The air seems dry and stilted here, like it hasn't been moved for years, and my mouth quickly loses its moisture. The scale of everything on offer overwhelms my senses, making me feel dizzy and slightly nauseas, so I decide to concentrate on the blank stone flooring for a time until the feeling subsides.

I sense Marla standing behind me, but I don't look around.

Instead I set off down the aisle, slowly at first, feeling as though each step is taking me into some progressively darker place, as though I'm walking down into the dank, spider-ridden cellar of my consciousness.

I push on toward the altar, scanning my eyes across the pews as I walk. The place seems to be empty, and I can't fully determine whether this is a good or bad thing.

I pass the gold-encrusted pulpit and look up to the altar, up to a large painting of Christ on the cross, Mary to one side of him, St. John to the other. Mary's face is turned downward from her son, and folded a hundred different ways through her grief. There's something fascinating about her expression, something raw and human, something beyond the religious.

The dryness of the room makes me cough, and the cough resonates around the church. Perhaps it's the emptiness of these places I dislike so much, the void and the lack of distraction. Perhaps it's that there's just so much time to think. That's all people do in churches, after all. Just think and think until they've thought up gods for themselves.

My legs start to feel shaky, as though they may give way beneath me, so I back away from the altar and sit down on the front pew.

After a time, I hear the slow click-clack of Marla's heels coming up the aisle, and she appears beside me.

"Can I ask you a question without you going off on one?" she whispers, sitting down.

I shrug, although secretly I'd be happy for any kind of distraction right now. "Depends what it is, I suppose."

Marla turns to face me. "How did she die?" she asks quickly.

It surprises me sometimes, to realise just how much awareness is going on inside people without it being acknowledged. "She was run over," I reply.

Marla's hand creeps across, folds itself over the back of mine. "And?"

I exhale heavily. "They never found it, though. The car. They said it just carried on. Didn't even stop to *think* about stopping. Just carried on like nothing had happened."

"There were witnesses?"

I look up to the painting of Jesus on the cross, forcing myself to study the contours of his flayed and naked body. "She was coming out of the shops. People heard the bang. A few made it outside to see the car driving off." The words seem to tumble out uncontrollably. I blink and feel something spill down my cheeks. At first, it shocks me, the way a nosebleed might. "Anyway, one said it was a Renault, someone else said a Ford. Couldn't even agree on a fucking colour," I splutter. "All they could say for sure is that it was going fast. I mean, it must have been, right? To not know grey from red in broad fucking daylight?"

I feel Marla draw a few inches closer, feel her hand move away from mine and up to the back of my neck. She gently strokes my hair, and it's like water on the fire. I push my head backwards into her fingers.

"I'm sorry, Eddie," she whispers into my ear.

"Didn't kill her, did you?" I ask, laughing a little sadly at a twenty-year-old joke that wasn't particularly funny in the first time round.

Marla looks at me, frowning with confusion.

"Sorry," I say. "Yeah, so anyway, that's how she

died." I wipe at my cheeks with the palm of my hand.

"You think this church thing has anything to do with it?" she asks.

"I don't know. I went to a baptism a few years ago. A cousin of mine. And it was like I couldn't even breathe. I suppose that was the first time I really noticed it."

Marla shifts a little on the hard pew, rests her head on my shoulder, still stroking at my hair. "What was your mum's funeral like?" she asks.

"Okay," I reply. "I mean, so far as funerals go, I suppose. Traditional. Kate gave a nice eulogy." I take a deep breath. "I suppose I just remember sitting there feeling useless…helpless. I couldn't even fill the grave properly."

"You filled the grave?"

"All the men do. It's like an honour thing, I guess."

"Eddie, you were nine years old. I wouldn't beat yourself up over it."

"Ah, it wasn't just that. It was like the whole fucking thing. Just sitting there. Not being able to do anything. Not being able to *reverse* anything. Like being trapped."

"Like a claustrophobia thing?" Marla asks.

"I don't know. I guess so. Like I'm drowning or something."

I sigh and stand from the pew, feeling stronger on my legs now for talking about it. I walk back over to the altar, leaning against its wooden railing. I must admit, it does feel a little better to face things like this, to face them dead on and look them square in the eye.

Marla comes up behind me and lays a hand on my back. "It's just a church, Eddie. Like any other church. Maybe it's time to start thinking about letting these things go. Like it said in that book I gave you, these things are usually associated with some negative attachment."

"She went to the shop because of me," I blurt quickly, staring up intently at the altar and feeling the warm prickling in my eyes once again.

"What do you mean?" Marla asks quietly.

"I wanted an ice cream. I wanted an ice cream so fucking badly that I threw this big temper tantrum. And she agreed. She went to the shop."

Marla moves her hands around my waist, so she's hugging me from behind, her cheek pressed against my back.

"I sent her to the shop," I whisper, before the enormity of the statement rushes over me. "I fucking *sent* her to the shop," I say, more loudly.

I don't know how long I stay like this for, possibly only a minute or two, but it feels like longer, crying quietly until my chest muscles ache, until I become like a sponge that's had everything it can have squeezed out of it. And when it's over I stand there, breathing hard, with Marla's arms still around me.

"You know, I thought about what you said," she says, after a time. "About making more of my paintings."

It takes me a while to register this properly. "Huh?"

"You were right. I think I just needed somebody

to say it. Anyway, I've managed to get myself an exhibition. At The Fishmarket Gallery."

"Yeah?"

I feel Marla nodding against my back.

"Next Thursday," she says. "I had to move mountains to get in there. But they had a cancellation, so they've given me a spot. Only a small one. And, of course, now it's going ahead I'm worrying it will all just be this big disaster."

"You'll be fine," I say. "That's good news."

"Will you come along? I might still hold you to buying something."

"Of course," I say, more brightly. "Of course I will. Next Thursday. I'll be there."

I turn to face Marla, who is smiling and looking just about as beautiful as she has ever looked to me. She kisses me just once, a short but sweet kiss on the lips that is over long before I want it to be. Then she pats me encouragingly on the chest.

"Now," she suggests, "what do you say we go and pick a present for Dave and Allie together? Seeing as we're in town, I mean. You'll only going choosing something crap, otherwise."

I laugh hollowly. "Actually, I had a couple of great things in mind. Toaster...cutlery set."

"Come on, dork," she says lightly, taking me by the hand and leading me down the aisle.

14. The Ex Factor

*7) **B**uy a present so hideous as to be barred from the wedding.*

I peek over the shelf at Marla in the adjacent aisle. "Cocktail-making set?" I suggest, holding up the box.

"No."

I quickly scan the shelf below me again. "Salt and pepper shakers? Everyone needs those, right?"

"Eddie, you're the best man. Do you seriously think salt and pepper shakers would make a suitable present?"

"They're shaped like telephone boxes," I add hopefully.

"Still no. In fact, particularly no"

I put my hands on my hips and sigh, scanning the shelves half-heartedly one last time. "Well, I don't know, do I? I've never done this sort of thing before."

"Just think about it for a bit. What kind of things do you normally get him? For his birthday, say."

I mull it over for a while, chuckling in recollection. "This one year we all clubbed together and got him a rocket. You fired it up into the air and it took a photograph on the way down."

Marla creases her brow. "Perhaps we should just leave the choosing to me," she suggests.

It seems May is a bad time of year to be buying gifts. With Christmas done and dusted, and the leftovers long since guzzled up by the monster that is the January sales, the gift section has been reduced to two paltry aisles selling largely useless products.

"Something that means something," Marla says. "Something they'll remember for a long time."

"I'm not sure we'll find anything like that in Boots," I caution.

"Mmm. Maybe you're right. Come on, let's try somewhere else."

We make our way from the gift section and through the automatic doors, back out into the shopping centre. If there's a modern interpretation of Hell on Earth, this place might just be it. A seemingly endless convoy of oversized baby buggies teems back and forward throughout the complex. Most of the women pushing them look barely a decade out of the pram themselves. It's enough to make me wonder whether some sort of social-engineering experiment has been taking place without my knowing.

Coursing along with the buggies are usual flotsam and jetsam of the town: loud, shaven-headed boys, screaming toddlers, strutting tattooed men, mean-looking and steely-eyed. Sometimes I'm left with the belief that aggression passes through this town like a communicable disease, until just about everybody is all pent-up and angry about something or other – or rather, nothing at all. It's as though everyone's expecting that at any given second a team of men in suits might drop down from the sky and start handing out prizes to the nastiest-looking bastards in sight.

Maybe Kate's right. Maybe London is the only answer to all of this now.

We reach the escalators and begin descending.

The Tannoy system is bleating out some aimless, meandering tune, probably only ever produced for the sole reason that it can be played over and over again throughout the course of an entire day without anyone realising it's the same CD on repeat.

Being here, I'm reminded of the time Mum took me shopping to find my own birthday present. Most years it would be a surprise, but this particular year she decided I was old enough to choose whatever I wanted for myself, within reason. And the odd thing was that, after she had said this, I couldn't think of a single thing I wanted. The day before I could have told her a thousand things, and after Christmas, no doubt, a thousand more. But faced with the reality of being able to have anything, I could honestly think of nothing. My mind had simply blanked.

And so we came here to look for inspiration. We went from shop to shop, hour after hour, but the present I wanted seemed forever beyond my reach. What if I chose something, anything, out of desperation, and then the perfect present turned up in the next shop, staring me mockingly in the face? And why couldn't I find anything I actually, *really* wanted? I imagined that this must be how billionaires felt, able to buy up anything their hearts desired: bridges, buildings, boats, planes, mansions, forests, islands. What was the point of anything after this? Surely it only left a heart without desire, which even at such a young age I realised could never be a good thing. And so I could think of nothing that didn't make me feel selfish and empty, even as Mum's impatience at my indecision grew and she began to snipe that I should just chose something, *anything*, as long as we could go home.

Then, as we walked back to the car feeling defeated, we came across a pet shop. In the window was a caged hamster, the same hamster that would a year or so later vanish off the face of the Earth for an entire week, frightening the life out of Mum with his eventual reappearance.

It was the perfect present. It was something I could look after and keep. Something I didn't have to feel guilty or wasteful about.

It was something that meant something.

"Hey, what about one of Badger's pups?" I suggest to Marla, as we step off the escalator.

Marla raises her eyebrows for a thoughtful moment or two. "Not bad, Eddie. Not bad at all."

"Dave could build a kennel," I say. "He'd like that."

"Well, we better check with them first, anyway. They might not even want a dog. It's a big commitment."

"So is getting married," I joke, looking to Marla for a reaction.

But Marla's expression has changed, and she hardly seems to have noted what I said at all, her eyes wide with consternation, her jaw set firm in a thunderous display of anger.

"You okay?" I ask.

"I don't believe it," she growls.

I follow her line of sight across the shopping centre. She's looking over to a jewellery shop, where a man appears to be admiring the watches in the window.

"What is it?" I ask.

But she's already storming off toward the shop, now apparently entirely oblivious to my existence. I wait for a few seconds, momentarily at a loss as to what I should do. Then I follow on, deliberately slowly so to keep a respectful distance.

When she reaches the shop, she heads directly over to the man. He turns to her, starting as if in surprise, only the whole gesture appears far too forced and overblown to be anything but rehearsed. The man looks to be in his early-thirties, dressed quite smartly in jeans with a white shirt and a neat summer jacket. He appears fairly tall from here, only slightly built, as if his body mass has been spread too thinly to account for his height. Already my mind is working overtime, and I'm assessing him, computer-like, for handsomeness, physical condition and potential fighting ability. I would place him no higher than average in the looks department (he has thin, slightly overlong face with a particularly prominent chin, and his dark hair is already receding a little). His lanky frame makes it look as though a strong wind might blow him down. But I suppose from a female perspective, he might be considered handsome in some abstract kind of way, for his tallness and his neat, almost feminine features.

As I draw closer, Marla's heated words become more audible.

"So, what, are you following me now, Joe? Is that it? Are you actually stalking me?"

"No," Joe protests, raising his hands. "No, I'm not stalking you. How can you say things like that, Marla? After all we've been through? How can you even think to use the word *stalking*?"

"It's been weeks," Marla sighs. "It's been *months*. Move on."

Joe looks over Marla's shoulder at me as I approach. "Well, I see *you* certainly have. Don't waste any time, do you?"

"Joe," Marla pleads.

"Where did you find this twat, then?" he asks.

I open my mouth to retaliate but can't think of anything useful to say. It's probably the shortest amount of time ever to have elapsed between somebody meeting me and calling me a twat. In all honesty, it's caught me a little off-guard.

"I'm serious, Joe," Marla says. "You need to stop texting me, you need to stop coming round my house, and you need to stop following me around the streets like a little lost sheep. Okay?"

"You still have a CD of mine," he says.

"I always seem to *still have a CD of yours*. What are you doing, taking them back one at a time?"

"Look," I interrupt, "why don't you write down whatever you think is yours and we'll send it on?" The *we'll* seems to reverberate around the entire shopping centre.

"Here's a better idea," Joe says, jabbing a bony forefinger in my direction. "Why don't you fuck off?"

"Why don't *you* fuck off?" I say. And the award for The World's Most Ridiculous Retort goes to…

"Please, please," Marla says, raising her hands in the air. "Let's not start a pissing-up-the-wall competition, shall we?"

Joe dismissively waves his hand in my direction, as though to suggest I'm not worthy of his time. "Look, Marla, can we go somewhere?" he asks. "Without him around? I think we need to talk."

"No," Marla sighs, exasperated. "No, we can't, Joe. We've done all the talking we're ever going to do. And he's not *him*. He's Eddie. My boyfriend."

My Adam's apple suddenly wants to investigate the inside of my mouth. I fight off the urge to break down into a coughing fit.

"So that's it, then?" Joe asks. "Just like that?"

"Yes. That's it."

"Well, don't you think that's a little unreasonable?"

"You know what I'd say is unreasonable, Joe? Sticking your cock into just about every girl who possibly let you. Wouldn't you agree that's a little unreasonable?"

Now even *I'm* starting to wonder about the appropriateness of my being here.

"I mean, wouldn't you agree that's a little unreasonable, Eddie?" Marla asks, turning to me.

It takes me a while to work out she's actually addressing me. Why is she bringing me into this whole bloody mess? Perhaps she's expecting me to be a little more pro-active. Perhaps I should be grabbing Joe by the collar and hauling him outside, or at least remonstrating with him. Shit, this stuff can be so confusing sometimes. Somebody should write a standardised rulebook stating clearly and concisely what is expected of the male of the species at times like these; at least that way we'd all know.

I clear my throat. "Err...well, it does seem a little insensitive."

Joe's face turns the colour of beetroot. Perhaps it's just my imagination, but I swear I can actually hear his teeth grinding. It's a little disconcerting, being looked at this way. It brings to mind those wild-eyed Vietnam veterans, fed on a never-ending cycle of drugs to keep them perpetually angry and hateful of the enemy.

Marla frowns. She's frowning a lot lately. I'm not being supportive enough, I suppose.

Joe starts breathing slowly and heavily, like a restless bull, before turning his attention back to Marla. "You're twisting this into something it's not, Marla," he protests. "You've never given me a chance to explain."

"I don't want you to explain. There's nothing to explain. It's over. Can't you get that through your thick head?"

"Fine!" he barks, making a cluster of passers-by jump. "Fine! If that's the way you want it." He turns to me. "I just hope you know what you're letting yourself in for, mate. You just watch this one. She'll rip your fucking heart out and stamp all over it. You just see." He sneers at Marla. "Oh, and by the way – I shagged her in *our* bed!" With this, he turns and storms away, shoulder-barging through the crowd.

"So, that's Joe," I say, once he's gone. "Well, he seems nice."

"Don't try to be funny, Eddie," Marla says. "Not now."

"Sorry. Do you want to go home?"

"No! No way. I'm not letting him spoil things." She shakes her head quickly, as though physically shaking the thoughts of him away like water. "So, something for the puppy, then."

"But not a kennel."

"Not a kennel. Let's find a pet shop. Hey, we could tie a little bow around him. That would be *so* cute." She seems brighter already now, alleviating the dark thoughts of Joe with happy thoughts of puppies with bows around them.

I consider how savagely Badger would disapprove of having a bow tied around one of her offspring. She'd probably consider it to be objectifying.

"You don't even know it *will* be a him," I say.

"Yes, I do," she insists. "We'll give them Boris. He'll be perfect."

"Boris? You've given them names?"

"Only temporary ones. The girls at work can't stop fussing over them. There's one that just sits in the corner sulking all day. I've called that one Eddie."

"Nice. Did the vet say how much longer they'll have to stay?"

"A couple more weeks, at least. Until after the wedding, I should think. That's why we need something else. Something to give them on the day as a little clue."

"Well, let's see what we can do then, shall we?" I offer my arm to Marla, as a Victorian gentleman might.

She smirks, ridiculing my high-dorkery, but nonetheless loops her arm around mine and we head off for the pet shop.

♂

We're in Nando's chicken restaurant. The place can't seem to work out whether it's a fast-food joint or a serious eatery, and in reality it's probably somewhere in between. It's decorated pleasantly enough, with dark wood furnishings and giant ceramic pots dotted about, illuminated by the soft glow of uplighters. Abstract paintings hang from the bare brick walls – dark reds, chocolatey swirls – giving the place a general sense of warmth, although I'm not altogether certain if I'm supposed to be in Africa or the Mediterranean.

We've found a quiet little booth in the corner, and Marla is finishing off her lightly spiced chicken-breast wrap. It turns out she's not one for hot food. I've opted for the peri-peri half-chicken with spicy rice, and I'm already regretting selecting extra hot on the 'peri-ometer'. I can feel the heat building up inside my head, and I'm starting to feel self-conscious about sweating so much in front of Marla, sitting there with her decidedly sensible chicken wrap.

I put down my knife and fork, opting for a breather. "So, did you mean what you said back there?" I ask. "With the boyfriend thing?"

Marla shrugs. "Oh, I don't know. I just said that to get rid of him."

"So you didn't mean it?"

"I said I don't know, didn't I? We're not seriously going to have this conversation here, are we? In Nando's?"

"We don't have to."

Marla frowns, perhaps realising she has been in some way trapped, and that *we don't have to* means *I'd very much like to*.

She scoops up a forkful of coleslaw. "Look, let's just say I like being around you. I don't know why because you're kind of a big dweeb, but, yes, I like it when we're together. You make me laugh. And you like being around me too, right?"

I nod.

"There. So we like being around each other. Let's just leave it at that for now, shall we? I can't stand all these *labels* for everything. Like life is a fucking supermarket and you just pick out what you want. Well, it doesn't work like that – not for me, at least."

Seeing how this is getting her somewhat worked up, I decide to change tact. "So, what did you ever see in him, anyway?" I ask. "Joe, I mean."

Marla looks to the ceiling thoughtfully as she chews. "Oh, I don't know. He's wasn't such a bad guy, I suppose, when he wasn't doing his wounded puppy act or focusing on…other distractions. Plus, I suppose his money didn't hurt, if I'm being honest."

Wasn't. Didn't. Past tense. Like he's dead already. Great.

I start to feel a little better. "He's rich?" I ask.

She nods. "*Mega* rich. You remember that car I threw paint on?"

"Yeah."

"It was an Aston Martin."

"Ouch. Well, I never had you down for the materialistic type."

Marla shakes her head and sighs. She leans in a little closer, as though about to give a small child a lesson in basic arithmetic. "Eddie, all women are materialistic, not matter what they say. I mean, perhaps not always to the point of sports cars and fancy hotels, but the bottom line is that no woman likes the idea of being stuck in a caravan in Margate or buying the value brand at the supermarket."

"But it's the Twenty-First Century," I argue. "Most women don't need to be looked after any more."

"No, they don't. But here's the secret." She leans in closer. "Most want to be," she whispers.

I find it hard to believe Marla is saying this, *Marla* of all people. "So you just went out with him for his money?" I ask.

She baulks at this. "No! Of course not! I didn't even know he had money at first. It was just kind of a bonus, like – I don't know – if he was a pilot and could fly me anywhere in the world."

"I don't think pilots are allowed to just do that."

"Pilots with their own planes are."

"Did Joe have his own plane?"

Marla smiles. "No," she says. "Anyway, I don't know why you're getting all funny about it. I'm only talking hypothetically."

I know exactly why I'm getting all funny about it. I had no idea Marla felt like this, and there's nothing hypothetical about my sorry excuse of a bank balance. I suddenly feel acutely embarrassed about harassing Marla over the few hundred quid she owes me, which must seem like chicken-feed to her after being with Joe Mega Bucks, not to mention Gavin the almost-international rugby star. It makes me wonder what on Earth she sees in me. In all honesty, it makes me wonder what she's even doing sitting here with me now – in bloody Nando's, for God's sake. Still, I can't deny that I'm incalculably glad she is. She looks amazing. Even when she's annoyed she looks amazing, or perhaps especially when she's annoyed she looks amazing.

Marla scoots down under the table and comes back up holding the bag from the pet shop. She lays it on the table and starts picking out the contents: a packaged ball, a rubber-chew in the shape of a bone, a Pedigree Chum starter-pack. She takes out the extendable lead last and begins to fiddle about with it. "I think we should wrap this up for the wedding," she says. "They won't get it at first, of course, but that'll be part of the fun. Oh, you should see Boris, Eddie. They'll love him. He's beautiful."

A space seems to open up in the air between us. A weighted silence. Fuck it. "You're beautiful," I say suddenly.

Marla stop fiddling with the lead, looks to me incredulously through the tops of her eyes.

"You are," I say, trying to be all masculine and unabashed about it, like how they are in the movies.

Marla seems to be suffering a moment of uncharacteristic coyness. She blushes a little and looks off to one side. "Are you trying to get into my knickers again, Eddie?" she says. "Because I should warn you, I'm not even pissed this time."

"There's a pub over there," I say, nodding out of the window.

She laughs. "You're such a dork," she says. "You're like…the *king* of dorks."

I reach across the table to brush a stray hair away from her eyes. She braces herself, and seems to consider chastising me for such a clichéd manoeuvre. But then she appears to change her mind and, not knowing what to do, just holds her face still, blinking at me. I'm reminded of the first night I saw her, in The Awl. It was her eyes I noticed then – her mysterious and indefinable eyes that seem to change colour with the days, today a kind of autumnal hazel flecked with a little black, like two perfect chocolates. *Two perfect chocolates*. God, she's right. I am a fucking dork.

I lean across the table and kiss her slowly. Thankfully, she doesn't fight it, or try to pull away, but just lets our lips linger on one another's for a time, until she kisses me back, an unreserved and hungry kind of kiss. Then, as if remembering where we are, she breaks away and leans back in her seat, exhaling heavily. "Well," she says, "that was unannounced."

"Spontaneity is my middle name," I say, attempting a Sean Connery accent.

"Well, the next time you go for spontaneity, Eddie, can I suggest you steer clear of the chillies? Otherwise I might *spontaneously* combust." She reaches for her glass of water and puffs out her cheeks. "And why are you talking like that?"

"It was Sean Connery," I explain, a little wounded.

"Sounded more like a Dutch porn star to me," she says. "Come on, let's get out of here."

♂

I pull up outside Marla's house, scanning the darkened suburbs like a private investigator in a bad, made-for-television movie. "Want me to come in?" I ask. "Make sure he's not hanging around."

"What are you going to do?" Marla asks. "Beat him up?"

"Well, I probably could."

Marla lets out a throaty laugh. I'm not sure if she's laughing at my over-protectiveness or the idea of me winning a fight. Either way, I'm pretty offended.

"Look, you can come in," she says. "If you want."

"Do you want me to?"

"Do you want to?"

"If you want me to."

Marla sighs and steps out of the car. "Come on, then," she calls.

I get out of the car and we walk over to the house. "Do you want to go in first?" she whispers, sliding her key into the door. "In case he's waiting?"

"Probably a good idea," I say, nodding thoughtfully.

"Eddie, I was taking the piss."

"Oh."

"He's not going to be here. And, besides, even if he was, I think I can handle him, thanks very much."

"Of course," I say. "Just trying to be helpful."

"Well, if you want to be helpful, grab these bags and put them in the kitchen. I'm bursting for a pee."

I take the bags off the front step and head through to the kitchen as instructed – the kitchen where I've vomited into a bin, carried a dead dog and wrestled a naked man. I'm starting to think of this place as the kitchen of first-and-hopefully-last experiences.

I rest the bags down on the table and switch on the kettle. While it boils, I can't resist a little nose around Marla's cupboards, all done under the guise of looking for cups (which I actually found in the first cupboard I tried). Besides from the usual things a person would expect to find in a solely female kitchen (flavourless yet healthy breakfast cereals, wholemeal bead, innumerable yoghurts promising transit improvements), I manage to detect a few more telling clues about Marla's life: three copies of Empire magazine in phonebook drawer (a film buff?), non-bio washing powder and long-life light bulbs under the sink (a half-hearted eco-warrior?), a couple of Greek cookery books (a Greek?).

"Looking for something?" Marla asks, walking into the kitchen.

"Cups," I say, rising a little too quickly and bashing my head against the work surface.

"Top-left. Hope you weren't sneaking through my drawers, Mr. Corrigan."

I let out a funny little snort, rubbing the back of my head vigorously. "Please."

I finish making the teas and we sit at the table.

"So, what's the plan for the stag-do?" Marla asks. "Alison tells me it's on Saturday."

"Oh, I've got something lined up."

"Don't tell me." She hold a finger in the air, thinking. "Paintballing followed by O'Connell's."

"Smithy's, actually." I grimace with embarrassment. "You think that's clichéd?"

"I wouldn't worry, Eddie. Stag-dos are supposed to be clichéd, aren't they?"

"Well, I did consider the ballet, but didn't think it would exactly be Brian's cup of tea."

Marla laughs. "Well, you men seem to like predictable things. Women twirling around poles and all that crap. I'm sure you'll have a good time."

"I hope so."

I stand from the table and head over to the window. It's too dark to see Badger's burial patch, but it still seems strange and unreal to think of her out there, somewhere underground. Strange to think how one minute there's an animated, breathing, thinking, living thing and the next there's nothing.

"We'll have to get that patch sorted some time," I say to Marla.

I hear Marla's chair scraping on the kitchen floor and see her reflection appear in the windowpane behind me. She rests her chin on my shoulder.

"Let's not talk about that now, shall we, Eddie? It's late. Maybe we should go to bed."

I smile at her in the window. Strange, also, how such a small cluster of words, perfectly placed, can have such an enormous effect on a person.

"Yeah," I agree, "maybe we should."

15. War & Pete

"Eddie! Eddie, is that you?"

I'm lying flat on my belly in the undergrowth. Inching my head carefully above the thickets, I see a figure a few feet ahead, cowering behind a sheet of corrugated iron. With everyone kitted out in camouflaged suits and headgear, it's getting hard to tell who's who. We were scattered like dead leaves in a heavy gust after the enemy's initial assault.

"Dave?" I yell back.

"Yeah, it's me."

"What are you doing up there? I thought you were supposed to be flanking them."

The iron sheet is being continuous pummelled by enemy fire, making it difficult for us to hear one other.

"Yeah, about that," Dave cries. "Turns out, not such a good idea!"

"Wait there. I'm coming up."

I get to my feet, crouching low, and scuttle crab-like towards Dave's cover. The gun is heavy and awkward to run with, constantly bashing against my knee.

I arrive at the cover breathless and shaky, falling to the ground alongside Dave. The noise of the assault isn't helping matters, the incessant *thwack-thwack-thwack* of paintballs exploding just inches from our heads on the other side of the metal.

"Jesus," Dave breathes. "Getting like

Passchendaele around here."

"Bit of an exaggeration," I say.

"They've got us penned in. How the fuck are we going to get out of this?"

Ten minutes of recreational warfare and already Dave is becoming hysterical. I suppose it's just fortunate that our experience of genuine war has never had to extend any further than the Playstation.

I look off to the right, where I spot somebody slowly crawling along the ground toward us.

"They're trying to flank us," I hiss.

"No, they can't flank us," Dave says, as though personally affronted by the idea. "We're supposed to be flanking them."

"Look, you stay here and create a diversion," I suggest. "I'll sneak around and surprise attack him when he gets closer."

"Okay," Dave agrees. "Don't be long."

I retreat back from the cover while Dave fires off a few stray rounds. Once I'm far enough back to be out of sight, I make my way around the assailant's path so I can sneak up behind him. The plan works perfectly, and I arrive at a small cluster of trees just behind the attacker. He's still crawling on his belly, inching his way towards Dave's cover.

I fire off three rounds, each hitting him square in the buttocks. He yelps in pain and rolls over onto his back.

"What the hell are you playing at?" he cries.

"Bri?"

"I'm on your team, you muppet."

"Sorry. You were lying on your gun. I couldn't

see what colour you were."

"I can't believe you shot me in the arse. I mean, who does that? That'll definitely bruise."

"Sorry. I'm still getting the hang of this thing," I say, nodding to my gun. "Anyway, why were you sneaking up on us like that?"

"I wasn't sneaking up on anyone. I was trying not to get shot. In case you haven't noticed, we appear to be up against the SAS."

"Yeah, it does seem a little one-sided," I agree. "Probably should've mixed up the teams a bit."

As if on cue, I hear the popping of gunfire, and a searing pain cuts into my chest and shoulder. I drop down onto the floor next to Brian.

"Shit," I cry helplessly. "These things really hurt. Nobody said it'd hurt this much."

"Stop talking to me," Brian whispers. "You'll give me away."

"But I'm serious!"

"Shut up!"

Paint splashes across Brian's visor. He lets out a girlish squeal as paintballs thump into his back. More of them splatter across my own visor, obscuring my vision.

"I'm already dead!" I yell pathetically, hoping it might end the onslaught.

"Great," Brian huffs. "Now you've got *me* killed. Nice one, Eddie."

"Sorry, Bri."

Brian stands up and puts the bright yellow safety cap into the barrel of his gun, holding it aloft to indicate he's a dead player as the instructor had advised. I stand and do the same and we head back for base.

"Imagine being shot in the balls with one of these things," Brian muses as we walk.

"I'd rather not."

"I reckon it'd do some serious damage."

"Well, all I know is this isn't as much fun as I thought it was going to be."

"I reckon I'm going to sit out of the next game, anyway," he says. "My ankle's killing me."

We breast a small hill in the forest's terrain and almost walk straight into Dave, crouching on the other side of it. In his panic, Dave clutches for his gun and raises it in our direction. A brief chaotic scene ensues while we both start yelling at Dave, waving our hands frantically in the air, trying to persuade him we're not the enemy.

Dave sighs with relief and lowers his gun. "Jesus," he gasps. "What are you two up to?"

"We're dead," I explain. "On our way back to base."

"Oh, great. What am I supposed to do now?"

"Well, you're *supposed* to capture the flag, Dave," Brian says, "not just spend the whole time hiding."

"I'm not hiding. I was providing cover."

Brian snorts. "Yeah, for yourself."

"Piss off, Bri. Anyway, judging by the state of you pair, it'd be a suicide mission."

"Anyone seen Pete?" I ask.

"Not since we got split up," Brian says. "Probably got shot right away."

We bid good luck to Dave and continue on to the base.

The base is a large, netted-off area, with a few plastic chairs scattered around its perimeter. It's safe to remove the headgear in here, so once inside, we both take off our helmets. Brian's face is reddened and sweaty, his hair a tangled mesh. I daresay I'm not looking any better myself.

A handful of other dead players are dotted around the base, but we can't find Pete among them.

Brian sits down on one of the chairs and rests his foot up on another, wincing in pain.

"You probably shouldn't have played at all," I advise him. "Just because you've had the cast off, doesn't mean you can go running around on it like a madman."

"I was actually wincing at the pain in my arse," he says, glaring at me contemptuously.

Over the course of the next fifteen minutes, players begin to trickle back to the base, one at a time. Somewhere among the arrivals appears Dave, bedraggled and haggard, his torso is covered in paint.

"How did you do?" I ask.

"I got ambushed. Three of the fuckers. Must have hit me about twenty times. God, these things actually hurt. I'm amazed this is even legal."

"Tell me about it," I agree.

"What happens if we get shot in the balls?"

"That's what *I* said," Brian interrupts. "They should give us cricket boxes or something. Fucking sadists."

"Where's Pete?" Dave asks.

"He must still be out there," I reply.

"What? He beat all of us?"

"Looks that way."

"I thought he'd be rubbish at this."

I shrug. "Guess not."

Dave slumps down onto one of the seats next to Brian. "How much longer of this do we have?"

"We're booked in until half-four," I say.

Dave checks his watch. "That's almost three hours away. I'll be dead by then."

A whistle is blown somewhere out in the forest and over the course of the next few minutes the rest of the players return. Pete tails in last, victoriously holding the enemy's flag aloft. A smatter of applause goes around the base as he makes his way towards us.

"How the hell did you manage that?" Dave asks.

"Can't shoot what you can't see," he says with a wink. Clearly he's immensely proud of his achievement, although he's blushing a little from all the attention. "Stealth is the key," he explains.

Brian laughs. "Ninja Pete!" he cheers.

The man organising today's proceedings gathers us around in a circle. He's the stocky, tattooed, ex-soldier type – the kind of man that makes other men butch-up just by being in his presence. I can just imagine him off in some foreign land, committing unspeakable crimes.

He declares our team the winner, thanks solely to Pete's heroics, and the other team offers its reluctant congratulations, like school-kids forced to shake hands after a playground fight. It seems to renew our enthusiasm for the game, this zero-to-hero triumphalism, and we head off for the second match with a newfound vigour. This soon subsides, however, as the next couple of hours are spent rolling through stinging nettles or heavily entrenched in muddy bunkers. As if in punishment for our earlier piece of good fortune, the enemy becomes even more merciless, pounding us with suppressing fire at every given opportunity. As the variations on the games roll by – capture the enemy bomb, storm the enemy fort – our resolve steadily dissipates, until our time is finally up and we trudge back to base like the last broken-spirited besiegers of Stalingrad.

We find Brian back at the base, sitting with his feet up. He's smoking a cigarette and drinking a can of Strongbow. "Alright, wankers?" he cheers on our arrival. "How d'ya get on?"

"Bloody carnage," I sigh, sitting beside him. "Where did you get that?" I ask, nodding to his can.

"There's an offie not far from the entrance down there," he replies. "Thought I'd go on a little recce."

"Got any more?" Dave asks breathlessly.

Brian leans to one side and rummages through a plastic bag beneath his chair. "Nope," he says after a while. "Last one."

"How many did you buy?" Dave asks.

"Four or five," he says with a shrug.

"You've sat here and drank five beers while we were out there getting killed?"

"Well, I had bugger all else to do, didn't I? It's not my fault I'm injured."

"You jumped off a pub table," I remind him. "It's precisely your fault you're injured."

Dave stands. "You know, maybe if you didn't get so pissed all the time you wouldn't even *be* injured," he says. "And talking of getting pissed, haven't we got a stag night to be getting on with? Come on, let's find Pete and get out of this hellhole."

Just as we decide to leave, the instructor gathers us around once more and declares it's time to end proceedings with the traditional "Shoot the Stag" ceremony.

I look to Brian and can't resist a little smile.

"So," the instructor yells, "if we can just have the stag and the best man step forward, then we'll get on with it."

"And the best man?" I query, my voice emerging a little too high-pitched.

"Yep," the instructor replies, grinning.

"Is that traditional?"

"Yep."

"Are you sure?"

"Well, I work here every day, mate. I think I'd know, don't you? Stag and best man go into The Hole, everyone else gets to finish off the last of their bullets."

Brian looks to me and returns my earlier smile. "I'm going to find Pete," he says cheerily. "He won't want to miss this."

♂

I take some small comfort from the fact that The Hole isn't actually a hole. It's more of a small, squared-off arena, with a couple of iron sheets in place for cover. Encircling the arena is a rope, around which the other players are allowed to run a full three-hundred-and-sixty degrees, ensuring there's no real place for Dave and I to safely hide. I'd estimate there are fifteen players or so out there, Brian and Pete among them, undoubtedly smiling like jackasses. Fifteen players. That's a lot of ammo to be expended, I realise with a heavy heart.

"Can I tell you something, Dave?" I ask.

"Sure." Dave's looking pretty nervous himself, his eyes peering out wide and alert through his visor.

"I never really wanted to be your best man anyway."

He looks across to me, holding my glare. He studies my face, and I can almost hear the cogs of his mind at work. Then he laughs, his eyes brightening. He punches me on the arm. "Come on, Ed," he says. "It won't be that bad. Just a bit of paint, after all. Bulldog spirit and all that, eh?"

"Yeah," I say. "Bulldog spirit."

The instructor yells out a call of five seconds.

"Hey," I say, "ever see that film, *Butch Cassidy and the Sundance Kid*?"

Dave thinks about it for a while. "Nah," he replies. "Why?"

"Never mind," I say.

And then all hell breaks loose.

♂

It's fair to say Smithy's nightclub has seen better days, and that those would have been long before any of us were born. The place hasn't undergone a refurb in years, and still carries the air of a mid-Nineties, house-music club. Hard shards of strobe lighting cut back and forth across the room, so overblown that if you look towards the DJ booth at the wrong moment you're liable to have your retinas burnt out. The seating is at a scarce premium, and upholstered with sticky black leather. Behind the bar, the fridges are stocked to bursting-point with brightly coloured bottles of alchopops.

I order four bottles of hideously overpriced lager and pass them down the bar.

"Don't they do pints?" Brian asks.

"What, since the last time you asked twenty minutes ago?" I say. "No."

He tuts. "Money for old rope," he sighs.

Brian's been saying *money for old rope* a fair bit lately. I guess he's only just recently discovered the phrase, although I'm not altogether sure he knows exactly what it means; he only seems to be contextually right about fifty percent of the time. He's been in a pretty off mood this evening, moaning about the beer every five minutes and making a big show about how it hurts every time he sits down. I keep telling him that Dave or I would happily trade places with him (when we changed out of our paintball gear earlier, we discovered our bodies were covered in countless discoloured whelks, to the point where we looked as though we were suffering from some kind of horrendous medieval skin disorder), but Brian is having none of it, and is certain he is the worst afflicted.

There's a strange crowd in Smithy's tonight. Clusters of pimple-faced teens are dotted around. They've sweated outside with their dubious IDs, and no doubt consider gaining access to this dump one of the crowning achievements of their young lives so far. Alongside these are those folks at the other end of the spectrum, men and women who have been through divorces, house sales, custody battles, and come out the other side uncertain of what they should be doing next. So, they end up back in the clubs of their youth, only as hideous carnival-mirror reflections of their former selves, leering over prospects far too young for them and finishing the night off drunk and horny and sad.

There are even a few people within our own age-range, the age-range that shouldn't really be here at all, that should be at home painting nursery walls or snuggling up with DVDs or some bullshit like that. In fact, I suppose when it's considered this way, by society's expectations, there's not a single person in this place tonight who should actually be here.

We turn and lean up against the bar, inspecting the clientele. We're in that awkward too-sober-to-dance phase of the evening, so we just stand and observe.

Across from the bar, a group of women are

seated in one of the booths. They appear to be around our own age, although it's hard to tell with the lighting so low. I'm sure many an awkward and possibly illegal mistake has been made due to the poor lighting here, although I doubt any judge in the land would accept the lighting of Smithy's nightclub as any kind of viable defence. The women are being quite raucous, and bunches of helium balloons float above their heads, so I'm guessing it must be some kind of private party.

"Pretty fit," Brian comments, listlessly.

This draws nothing but a couple of idle nods from Dave and Pete.

One of the women, a pretty brunette, breaks away from the party and heads over to the bar. She's dressed as casually as the club will allow, in a pair of jeans and a black Lycra top. I once heard it said that it takes a man six seconds to determine whether or not – hypothetically, at least – he would sleep with a woman, and I'd say it took about three for this woman to get four yeses from this impromptu panel of judges propping up the bar.

The woman sidles up next to Brian, waiting for service. Brian is staring fixedly ahead, as though utterly unaware of her being there. He takes a nervous little sip at his beer.

"God, don't you just hate this kind of thing?" the woman asks.

Brian turns, as though noticing her for the first time. "Yeah," he says, clearly having no idea what he's agreeing with. "Hate it."

"So, what are you guys doing here?" she asks.

"We're on a stag night," Brian replies. "Dave

here's getting married."

"Yeah? Congratulations."

Dave raises his bottle towards the woman. "Thanks."

"Some stag night," she says.

"Yeah," Brian agrees with a tentative little laugh. "Eddie arranged it all," he adds suddenly, as though to exonerate himself of any blame.

I smile at her and give a *what-can-you-do* kind of a shrug.

"I'm Jo. You guys want to join us?" she asks. "I swear if I have one more conversation about colour schemes, I'll scream."

We look to each other, shrugging our shoulders, trying to reach some kind of wordless consensus. Then we agree and, once Jo has ordered her drink, we follow her over to the table.

Our arrival causes a strange kind of excitement among the ladies, some of them actually shrieking with ear-piercing tenacity. Anyone would think a boy band had just arrived.

I sit alongside Dave in the booth, as though to announce my staunch unavailability. I almost want one of them to make a pass just so I can explain how I'm fairly sure I'm in some kind of a relationship these days.

Most of Jo's friends are dressed pretty revealingly, in short skirts and strappy tops. They appear so uniform in this way that it's hard to differentiate between them, and the names wash right over me when Jo does the introductions.

"Doesn't seem fair, does it?" Dave whispers to me. "A year ago I would have killed to be sitting at this table."

"Yeah, tell me about it," I say.

Dave looks to me, frowning. "What does that mean?" he asks.

Then I remember my pledge to him, about steering clear of Marla until the wedding is over. "Oh, nothing. I just mean I remember what you were like a year ago."

Dave laughs and punches me lightly on the arm. "Just remember to keep that out of the speech," he reminds me.

The speech. Christ, I hadn't even thought about that. I'll have to have a look on the Internet. Perhaps there's some sort of template to download.

Across the table, I'm picking up the odd stray word from Brian and Jo's conversation. He seems to be telling her that he's a musician. She's presumably asked about the kind of stuff he plays, so he's off on his favourite subject, describing how he melds various genres together with great expressive hand gestures. And I'll be damned if she doesn't actually appear to be interested. Her eyes are not glazing over or rolling in their sockets, the usual female reaction to this kind of thing. She's listening intently, even throwing in the odd laugh. Brian himself appears to be shocked by this turn of events, but he's on a roll now, gabbling on and on like I've never seen before. And when it's her turn to talk, he seems to be actually properly listening, not just doing that smiling and nodding thing he does while clearly thinking about the best way into the poor victim's knickers. I've never known Brian to care much about anything that occurs outside his own existence, so it seems strange to see him listening with genuine interest like this.

The night rolls along quite successfully, the only downside being that none of the ladies appear interested in making a move on me, after all. Dave seems to be having a good time: dancing to embarrassingly cheesy music, throwing back mysterious, syrupy shots, and introducing the girls to the innumerable amount of drinking games we have either learned or devised ourselves in The Shoemaker over the years. Brian and Jo are getting along swimmingly (I'm pretty sure I even saw him sneak a kiss from her while we were all dancing), Pete seems to be enjoying himself, and me – well, truth be known, I've been on Cloud Nine ever since events with Marla took a turn for the better.

My mind drifts back to the other night round her place, and it brings a smile to my face. The smile stays for approximately thirty seconds, until a dark shadow descends across our table and I look up to see Danny Kilbride standing there. He looks a little different from the last time I saw him back in The Chestnut Tree. He almost looks smart, without his chequered work apron and hat, now wearing a white, long-sleeved shirt that covers his tattooed forearms. Still, there's no hiding that thuggish visage of his, that craggy forehead looming like a cliff face, that big square chin jutting out like the Iberian Peninsula. The top buttons of his shirt are unfastened, revealing a cheap-looking gold chain. A couple of his fingers are adorned with tackily oversized sovereign rings.

"Alright, fellas?" he cheers, opening his arms out wide.

Typical. You can avoid a person for the best part of fifteen years and then bump into them twice in as many months.

A horribly awkward silence follows, so I decide I'd better pipe up. "Alright, Danny?" I ask.

Dave's face changes, his expression darkening. My guess is he's just realised who Danny is.

"Well, fuck me," Danny roars. "We've got the whole crowd in, ain't we? Dave, right? And Billy?"

"Brian," he corrects.

"Brian. Yeah, that's it. Well, looks like you've all done alright for yourselves." He winks towards the ladies. "And…oi, oi! Pete fucking Pritchard!"

Pete shifts uncomfortably in his seat.

"Ha!" Danny goes on. "You were a right little fucktard in school. Remember?"

Pete's face reddens. He pushes his glasses further up his nose.

"Mind if I sit down for a bit?" Danny asks.

We all remain silent while Danny looks around the table, awaiting a response. Then he laughs quietly to himself and makes a move to sit down regardless.

Pete suddenly stands, stopping Danny in his tracks. "You were a twat in school and you're a twat now, Danny. Nobody liked you. Nobody. Sure, people may have been scared of you, but that's not the same thing, and look where that got you in the end. Here. Alone. In a shitty club. With nobody to talk to. Well, what goes around comes around, Danny, and you brought that life on yourself. So don't you fucking dare ask to come and sit down at this table now. Because you don't deserve to, and nobody wants you here." He takes a deep breath and straightens himself out. "Now," he says, more calmly, "I'd like you to go away, please."

Danny face contorts throughout Pete's little speech, as various emotions seem to course through him: first confusion, then disbelief, then pain, then annoyance, then outright anger. He's breathing through his nose slowly, trying to quell his rage, until he appears to arrive at something close to sadness. "This how you all feel?" he asks, not looking at any one of us now but staring ashamedly down at the centre of the table.

"Yes, Danny," I say after a time. "That's how we all feel."

"It's how we all feel," Dave chips in.

"Yeah," Brian agrees, his arm still lolling around Jo's shoulders. "How we all feel."

"Right," he says, regarding each of us steadily one last time. "Right, well you only had to say so." With this, he turns from the table and leaves.

"Shit!" Brian gasps, laughing and clapping his hands. "Pete, you were fucking brilliant, man. Did you see that? He was *shitting it*."

We all congratulate Pete for the second time today, and he sits down again, not looking embarrassed this time but rather at peace, smiling contentedly, as though a great weight has been lifted from him.

"Wow," I say. "It seemed to really affect him. I

almost felt sorry for him. You know, maybe he learned something there. Maybe he'll change his ways. I mean, stranger things have happened, right? Hey Pete, you may just have had an effect on the rest of that man's life today. That's something to think about, right?"

"Err, boys," Dave interrupts warily, "I'd hold back on the hippy love-in for just one minute, if I were you." He nods over to the corner.

Danny's standing over by the staff entrance to the bar. The head barman is talking with him, and together they seem to be recruiting a posse of doormen. It starts with one, then second, then a third – three great, hulking men in heavy, black coats. There's a lot of gesticulation towards our table, and then the bouncers turn their attention to us.

"Right, might be about time to drink up," I suggest.

"Good idea," Dave seconds, swilling down the last of his beer.

"Well, it was nice to meet you, ladies," Pete says, standing.

"Hey, but I'm having a good time here," Brian groans.

Danny starts to head over to our table, the three bouncers following behind him. He's leaning forward as he walks, his shoulder hunched like a bull, his enraged, square face bobbing up a down.

"Run!" Dave yells.

This seems to spark the rest of us into life, and we go leaping over the sides of the booth like frogs escaping a jam jar. Danny and his goons are already halfway towards us by the time we remember how to operate our legs and go bounding across the dance-floor, casting a few revellers aside. In my mind's eye, I can see our pursuers drawing ever closer, like the T-Rex in *Jurassic Park*. This only heightens my sense of urgency as I go hurtling down the stairs – three or four at a time – praying none of us takes a fall now.

We all make it down to the bottom and go dashing past the cloakroom, startling the woman behind the counter.

Once outside in the street, we stop and turn to face the nightclub entrance.

We're all breathing hard, doubled over with our hands on our knees.

"You think they've given up?" Pete asks.

Just at that moment, Danny and his bouncers burst through the door, shaking their fists in the air and collectively yelling in a kind of guttural war cry.

"Shit!" Brian gasps. "Run!"

We turn from the marauding barbarians and flee down the street.

"The alleyway!" Dave cries, spotting a narrow turnoff.

We all bustle down the alleyway and continue on, feet scuffing against the loose stones.

"I don't think I can run much more," Brian shouts to us. "My ankle."

Looking over my shoulder, I see the bouncers have given up chase, clearly not wanting to leave the club unattended, but Danny still persists.

"Hey, it's just Danny," I gasp, my lungs now

close to bursting.

"So?" Brian says.

"Well, there's four of us and only one of him."

We carry on running, considering the mathematics of situation, the equation of the fight.

"Hey, he's right," Dave says. "On three, everyone turn and run the other way, okay?"

"You sure?" Pete asks.

"I'm sure, Pete," Dave replies. "Come on, we can do this."

We all agree and, once Dave has counted us in, turn on our heels, running back towards Danny.

Danny skids to a halt. His face betrays his surprise; clearly he wasn't expecting such a dramatic switcheroo. He looks at a loss momentarily, glancing over his shoulder for his absent henchmen.

"Shout," Pete gasps. "Do your war cry."

We all start yelling at the top of our lungs, shaking our fists and bearing down on Danny quickly now.

Danny's expression turns from one of surprise to one of confusion, then fear. "I'm gonna tear your fucking hole out, Pritchard!" he yells, before turning and running back down the alley and out of sight.

We gradually slow down our pace until we come to a halt.

Brian's cackling breathlessly. "That was crazy! I can't believe we just did that."

"*I'm gonna tear your fucking hole out,*" Dave mimics, laughing. "What kind of a shit thing is that to say?"

"He was panicking," I say. "We had him scared."

"Good call with the war cry there, Pete," Dave says.

"It's like animal behaviour," Pete explains. "Making a lot of noise to scare off a rival."

"So much for being a ninja," Brian laughs, shaking his leg about as if to kick off the ache.

"Hey, what would you have done if he'd have stood his ground?" I ask.

"Christ knows," Pete chuckles. "I've never hit anyone in my life."

"I'd have battered him," Brian offers.

"Course you would, Brian," Dave says, patting a hand on his back. "Hey, sorry about having to run out like that."

"No worries," he says, reaching into his pocket and pulling out a scrap of paper. "Got her number, anyway. She's amazing, right? She's the best girl you've ever seen in your life?"

"Yeah," Dave agrees. "Best girl I've ever seen in my life."

We all turn and start the slow walk up the alley, away from the club.

"So, I guess we're barred from ever going back there again," I say.

Dave shrugs. "No big loss, eh?"

"Sorry if the stag do was a bit of a washout, mate."

"You're joking, aren't you?" he chirps. "Best night I've had in ages."

"Really?"

"Yeah. I haven't run like that since those

Peterborough fans chased us to the station that time."

"Oh, right," I say. "Well, I'm glad you had a good time."

"Look, all that matters to me is that you guys are around to see me off. The next time we're all together it'll be my wedding day. So it's good to get a bit of craziness out of my system."

"The last crazy night of the gang," I say wistfully.

Brian pats at his pockets. "Ah, shit," he sighs. "I left my fags in there."

"Yeah? Wanna go back and get them?" I joke, throwing my own packet of cigarettes across to him.

"Nah," he says, catching them. "I'll leave them for Jo. She might think that's romantic."

Dave laughs. "Fucking Romeo over here."

"So what do you reckon, then?" I ask. "Shall we try another bar or something?"

Dave checks his watch. "It's nearly three," he says.

"Is it? Probably best just getting off home, then."

We take the short walk to the taxi rank, by the church I visited with Marla. And whilst we wait in the queue I think about her, wondering whether I'm a little too drunk to give her a call when I get back, or whether three in the morning is a little too late to be doing such things. Probably best leaving it till tomorrow. But there's a warm glow in my belly that goes above and beyond the alcohol. It's the sense that I'm here tonight among friends, standing by a church that no longer looks so scary at all. It's the sense that Marla might just be thinking about me tonight. It's the sense that Dave's about to marry the woman he loves, that Brian's luck seems to be on the up, that Pete just did something life-changing tonight.

It's the sense that everything might just be alright.

16. To Have & Have Not

I remember coming to The Fishmarket with Mum back when it really was a fish market, and a huge, stinking palace of wonder for any boy under the age of ten. The mongers' yells would echo throughout the vast, glass-roofed complex, row after row of goggle-eyed fish glaring out from the displays at passers-by. A fish would be picked up, tossed on the counter, and decapitated in an instant before my startled eyes. Live crabs would writhe in buckets. Eels would lay agog in beds of packed ice. It was a noisy, bewildering place, alien to anything I had known before, and I always viewed a childhood visit there rather like an expedition to another world, as opposed to the pretty mundane thing it actually was: picking up fish for that night's dinner.

Today, it seems an oddly quiet place, hushed by that strange reverence people seem to unquestioningly afford artistic venues. The stalls and counters have gone, torn out long ago, most of the space now left open but for a few instillations at the centre of the rooms: sculptures and dress displays. The walls are clean and whitewashed, and long, rectangular skylights cross the ceiling, pulling in the light, casting away anything strange or mysterious I may have felt towards the place. After my previous experiences here, in fact, it all seems a little dull.

I cross over the room to inspect the first of the

displays. It's a collection of paintings, all of a single human eye. Effectively, it appears to be the same painting done over and over again, only using different colours. I stand there for a while, pondering over what it might mean. Something to do with me being studied at the same time as I study the paintings, I guess. Or maybe the artist is just particularly good at doing eyes. Probably wouldn't be such a smart-arse if he was given twenty horses to paint.

I move on to the next display: a collection of electronic screenshots of various computer command prompts. Representing our slavishness to the digital age, perhaps. Or maybe the coldness of artificial intelligence. Either way, I can't escape the feeling this person hasn't really done anything. At least the last guy actually painted something; this one has just printed off screenshots from his computer. Christ, even I could have done that.

I leave the displays and walk across to the adjoining gallery. It's a much smaller room, and I notice with a pang of annoyance that Marla's display seems to be tucked away into the corner. An elderly couple is admiring her paintings, and Marla is explaining something to them.

I set off across the room, waiting patiently for her to finish with the visitors.

"Hey, Eddie," Marla says cheerily once she's free.

"Hi."

She comes over quickly and kisses me warmly on the lips. It seems such a natural thing to do, and I can tell she's in a buoyant mood.

"How's it all going, then?" I ask.

"Brilliant," she says. "I've already had a sale and it's only, what, half-twelve?"

"Really? Well, I'd better get in there quick then, hadn't I? Otherwise I'll be left with the rubbish at the end."

Marla playfully slaps me on the arm.

I walk across to get a better look at the display. The theme here seems to be shoes. The early paintings are realistic depictions of Victorian working life: an old man bent over a wooden last, dozens of factory women in white aprons sewing at their stations. The detail within them is really quite staggering. The display then moves on to more progressively contemporary styles (some abstract art based around the design of the shoe itself) and finishes on a painting of one solitary shoe left discarded on a cobble-stoned street.

"It's supposed to represent the rise and fall of the shoe industry," she says, almost apologetically. "Of industrialisation itself, I suppose. I think that's why they accepted my application so quickly. Because of the local interest."

"And because it's bloody good," I say. "Really. Much better than some of the other crap round there."

"Eddie," Marla scorns.

"What? Some of them aren't even proper paintings."

"Shh."

I study the paintings once again. I like the one of the shoe on the street, but decide it might be a bit too morose. I finally settle on a pop-art painting: four men in flat-caps and work clothes, walking barefoot across a zebra crossing, parodying the *Abbey Road* album cover. "This one, I think. Yeah, this'd look great in my flat. Put me down for it."

Marla walks over to her little table and pens something into her notebook. There's no mention of price, but I decide not to sweat it. I need to be casual about these things, after all, if I'm to compete with her former boyfriends.

Marla comes back over to me, resting her hands on my shoulder and kissing me again. "Well, thank you, Eddie," she says. "That's sweet. Two sales!"

"Steady on, now," I say. "Don't want to be putting Southeby's out of business."

She laughs generously. "So, how did the stag night go?"

"Oh, you know. Pretty quiet."

She looks to me disbelievingly. "Yeah, I'm sure. Is that a love-bite on your neck?"

"It's a whelk," I explain. "From the paintballs." I'm suddenly overcome with fear that she won't believe me. "Look, I've got loads of them," I say, unbuttoning my shirt to prove it.

"Err, it's okay, Eddie," she says quickly, holding out a hand to stop me, glancing nervously around the gallery. "I believe you."

"Oh, right," I say. "Probably not the place for it, eh?"

"Not really, no. So Dave had a good time, then?"

"Yeah, great. And Bri even met a girl. She really likes him!"

Marla narrows her eyes. "Where was this stag night, the local mental hospital?"

I laugh. "Ah, he's not so bad once you get to know him. He can actually be quite sweet behind that arsehole exterior he puts up."

"Well, good. I'm glad you had fun. And you're all ready for Saturday?"

Saturday. The day after tomorrow. Like the disaster movie. I can almost hear the tidal waves rumbling towards me.

"Ready as I'll ever be," I say.

"Ah, you'll be fine," she says, rubbing my arm. "Just remember all the stuff we went through. And what you read in the book. You'll be great."

"Well, I hope so," I say. "I really wouldn't want to let Dave down now."

"You won't let him down. You're his best friend. You couldn't do anything to let him down."

We share a moment looking into one another's eyes, questioning the validity of that statement.

A small group of visitors descend on the display, cooing with approval. Marla is positively bubbling with excitement, and I can tell she's itching to approach them.

"Hey, why don't I let you get on?" I say.

She opens her mouth to protest.

"No, it's fine," I insist. "I need to get back to work, anyway. I'll pop back later."

"Are you sure?"

"Absolutely," I say, kissing her on the forehead. "Just remember." I point at the Abbey Road painting and then cock a thumb towards my chest, mouthing the word *mine*.

She smiles and heads over to the visitors, and I leave the exhibition room to the sounds of her easy patter running them through the paintings, aglow with a sense of pride in her.

Once outside the gallery, my phone rings. Dave.

"Dave," I say into the receiver.

"And how's my best man doing?" he asks.

"He's doing pretty good, as it happens. What's up?"

"I'm just phoning about Saturday," he says. "Making sure everything's in place. I don't want any fuck-ups."

"Don't worry, I know the drill. Round your place for eight, right?"

"Yeah, and then we'll go up in the van. You'll have to drive. I'll be a mess. Just try not to bloody crash it this time, alright?"

"I didn't crash it the first time," I say.

"Then we'll check into the rooms," Dave says, ignoring my protests, "meet up with the boys, and walk to the church from there."

"Roger," I say. "Loud and clear." I look up to the hard blue sky, slipping on a pair of sunglasses. "Looks like we might have the weather for it, anyway."

"God, I hope so," Dave sighs. "Allie wants a lot of the photos done outside."

"Don't worry. It'll be fine."

"You just make sure you're here on time, Eddie."

"Eight o'clock. I'll be there."

"Christ, mate, my ring-piece is going ten-to-the-dozen right now."

"Well, thanks for that image, Dave. I'll go and have my lunch now. Look, just try to relax. Everything'll be fine. And I'll see you on Saturday."

"Eight o'clock," he says.

"On the dot," I say, hanging up the phone.

♂

I pull up outside The Fishmarket some four hours later, miraculously into exactly the same spot.

I take my phone out of the glove box and key in Kate's name. It rings for such a long time I think she's not going to answer, but just as I'm about to hang up her voice comes at the line.

"Hello," she says breathlessly.

I start to worry that I've interrupted some sort of sexual dalliance. Who has sex at four o'clock on a Thursday evening? Lesbians possibly, I suppose. Having said that, I'd bet Marla's the sort for having sex at four o'clock on a Thursday evening. Just the thought of it sends a stir of arousal through me. She's probably in there now, all hot and pent-up from all those creative juices sloshing about.

I shake the thought from me, determined to get this conversation over and done with as quickly as possible now. "Hi, Kate," I say. "It's me."

"Hi, Eddie. Hang on a sec. You've caught me getting out of the shower."

I have a little mental sigh of relief while I wait for Kate to do whatever it is she needs to do.

"I'm back," she says, after a while.

"Great," I say. "I'm just calling about the wedding. You know, checking you know the plan."

"I think we do, yes."

"The wedding's at half-one. So you need to be in Felston for twelve, ideally."

"We did get the invite, Eddie."

"I know, I know. But I just want to make sure everything's in place. It *is* kind of my job, after all."

"Wow. Is my little bro becoming a man?"

"Kate, I'm serious. Remember it'll take you a little longer to get out of London. So make allowances for that."

"I *have* lived here for six years, you know?"

"And it's the M40, then the A40 at Oxford. Don't just stick on the M40; you'll end up Christ-knows-where."

"And you're presuming I can't read a map because I'm a woman or a lesbian?"

"Both. Double whammy."

"Cheeky bastard," she laughs. "Don't worry, we've got the sat-nav. We're a little more technologically advanced than you bumpkins up there."

"Yeah, well, a wise man once told me not to trust those things, so make sure you watch where you're going as well."

"You really are taking this thing seriously, aren't you?"

"No point in doing things by halves," I reply, shrugging to myself in the car.

"Well, good. I think this might be good for you."

She pauses. "Decided when you're moving to London yet?"

I sigh. "I was actually thinking about it. Seriously, I was. Although I've had a slight change of circumstance down here, so things might have to be put on hold for a while."

"Change of circumstance? Well, this sounds juicy."

"You'll find out at the wedding," I say.

"Well, you know I'm going to keep nagging you about moving down here until you finally do it, don't you?"

"Oh, I know it."

"Like I say, you're always welcome to stay at our place until you've settled in somewhere."

"Jess wouldn't mind?" I tease.

"Jess loves you. You'll just have hold back on the Scottish jokes for a while."

"But they're my best ones!" I groan. "No, I appreciate the offer. Really. I'll bear it in mind. How's the adoption thing going?"

"Sloooowly," she says with exaggerated exasperation. "I'll tell you about it on Saturday."

"Okay. Well, I see you then, shit-for-brains."

"Bye, spanner," she says quickly, hanging up.

I curse to the empty car and laugh.

Pocketing the phone, I reach behind to the back seat and grab the flowers. A nice touch, I thought. A little water remains in the wrapping and it dribbles out onto my lap. I curse again and quickly climb out of the driver's seat, patting myself down. For all intents and purposes, it looks as though I've peed myself, so I stand in the sun for a minute or two, scrubbing at the incriminating patches with my fist. When I'm satisfied the patches are no longer immediately obvious, I head inside the gallery, past all the displays (which I now think, with a sniffy air of art-critic disdain, are nowhere near as good as Marla's).

As I enter the exhibition room housing Marla's display, something stops me dead in my tracks. Joe is standing there, his hands defiantly on his hips. Marla is clearly trying to plead with him to leave, but he's showing no signs of relenting. He's shaking his head, standing firm. At one point he even reaches out and grabs Marla by the arm. This sends a jolt of rage through me, and I quickly hurry across the room.

"Oh great," Joe sneers. "Here comes fucking Superman. And, look, he's brought flowers."

"Joe, what are you doing here?" I ask.

"What? No, don't call me by my name. You don't even fucking know me, so don't call me Joe."

"Okay, then." I say, more slowly this time, as though talking to an idiot. "What are you doing here?"

"It's public property, isn't it? I can be here if I like. I go where I want, not where people tell me. Especially not wankers like you."

"You're upsetting Marla," I say.

"You're upsetting me," he retorts. "With your face."

"Why don't you just leave?" I ask, the anger bubbling up inside me now.

"Why don't *you* just leave? And not come back? Who the hell are you, anyway? *What* the hell are you, even? You're nothing. You're Marla's little plaything. A rebound boy. Nothing more."

I'm positively boiling now. I think back to the stag-night, and to Pete courageousness. I think of how sometimes a man has to make a stand against things if he wants to change them. I think of how Clint Eastwood wouldn't take shit like this, not for a second, or John Wayne in one of Dad's old cowboys. I think of Buzz Aldrin and how he lamped that conspiracy theorist square in the chops, and how that guy deserved every bit of it because he was being a right prick to Buzz.

And I lever back my fist to take a swing, almost without knowing I'm doing it.

I've never punched anyone before – not as an adult, at least – at it seems my aim is a little rusty. My fist arcs too early, missing Joe's face and slamming plum into his Adam's apple.

Joe staggers back, emitting a horrible rasping sound, his eyes bulging in their sockets. Then his legs give way as he fights for breath, and he falls down onto his backside.

"Eddie, what the hell are you doing?" Marla gasps.

She immediately crouches down to tend to Joe. I'm a little ashamed to admit this irks me even further.

"Well, he was asking for it," I say stupidly.

"He was *asking for it*? Christ, what are you, ten years old?"

"He was causing you problems."

"Eddie, you don't resolve problems by going around *punching people*. And I don't need protection, thanks, or whatever the hell it is you think you're doing. Now, please, get the hell out of here. You've ruined everything." She's getting a little teary, trying to tend to Joe while looking around at the shocked visitors, mouthing apologies to them.

"I bought you some flowers," I say, holding up the bouquet, wishing to Christ I could re-do this whole thing, that I could just walk in and give her the flowers and keep out of everything else.

Marla looks to me through incredulous, watery eyes.

"I'm sorry," I say weakly.

"Yeah, you will be, mate," Joe rasps.

"I wasn't talking to you, dickhead."

"Eddie, for God's sake, leave!" Marla yells venomously.

The anger in her voice jolts me into action, and I turn to make my way out. As I storm across the room, a tubby, balding, bespectacled man comes walking the other way, dressed in loose chinos and a flannel shirt, looking like he just stepped off the last hippy-train out of Goa. The curator, no doubt.

"Just what the hell is going on here?" he demands.

"Oh, piss off," I bark, as a thunder past him.

Once out into the street, I throw the flowers down hard on the pavement, scattering them in a circular fashion. The flicker of an old memory returns to me, but I disallow it from fully forming in my mind.

I storm back towards the car, looking up to the sky and bemoaning any god up there with half an ear to listen. No god on the side of Team Eddie, anyway.

I climb into the car and, after four of five angry and abortive attempts, finally manage to start the engine. As I pull out of the parking space, I get to thinking about how everything I touch seems to turn to shit in the end, how anything pure or good in my life will always end up nothing but a mound of dust in my hands. I should have known it. I should never have got involved with Marla at all. I should have just walked out of her house that morning. I should have left her to her trail of fucked-up exes – of which, I suppose, I'm now one – and just carried on with my own life: a mildly unhappy life, perhaps, but one that was ultimately pain-free if only through its lack of eventfulness.

All this thinking about what I *should* have done starts to feel a little pointless after a while, so I turn my mind to thinking about what I'm going to do next instead. A plan forms in my head, and I begin to feel better about things, a little calmer and more clear-minded. I can see it all before me now, the fog of anger drifting away to reveal a twinkling, inviting cityscape in my mind.

And it's then I resolve that, after handing in my notice at work tomorrow, I'm going to call Kate to let her know I will be coming to London after all.

17. Getting There

"Okay," I begin. "Suits?"

"Check."

"Shoes?"

"Check."

"Rings?"

Dave unzips the front compartment of his suitcase and peeks inside. "Check."

"Then I reckon we're all set."

We're standing in Dave's living room. Our suits are hanging in their carriers on the door handle. Our cases are lying on the floor with a load of other miscellaneous items: flowers for the parents, boxes of buttonholes from the florist, crates of champagne bottles and toasting flutes.

We've got the place to ourselves. Alison spent last night at Marla's and they're travelling to Felston directly from there, in Robin and Jean's car. Robin apparently has a Mercedes he rarely gets to use, and is relishing the idea of driving it up there with ribbons and bows attached.

Dave takes a final look around. "Right," he says, "I suppose that's it, then."

"Yep. That's it."

We share a strange and awkward moment just looking at one another, and then we get to work, taking the things out to the van in staggered shifts, being careful to lay the flowers on top of everything else so not to squash them.

Once we've loaded everything up, Dave hands

me the van keys with a slow reluctance. "Right," he says. "I'll go and lock up."

While Dave goes back into the house, I get into the driver's seat and phone Dad.

"Hello?"

"Dad, it's me."

"Hello?"

"It's me, Dad. Put your ear to the receiver."

"Hello?"

"The receiver, Dad. At the top."

"Eddie?"

"Yeah, it's me. Just checking everything's still okay for today."

"Everything's fine, son."

"Because it's not too late to go down with Pete and Brian if you want," I suggest.

"Those two don't want us hanging around. We'll be fine making our own way."

Secretly, I'm rather pleased. I'm still yet to meet Barbara myself, and it feels a little early to be unleashing Brian on her just yet. Besides from this, Brian has been making noises about inviting Jo to the wedding, so it could be quite a squeeze with the five of them and their luggage all packed into Pete's *Mondeo*.

"And you're sure you know the way?" I ask.

"Son, I was driving all over the country before you were even born," he says.

"Okay, okay, I get the message," I say, willingly accepting my admonishment. It's good to hear Dad talking like this again, like he did when we were kids and he was a man full of drive and purpose.

"Dave alright?" he asks.

I look over to the house, where Dave's trying to lock the front door. He fumbles clumsily with the keys, dropping them onto the pavement, cursing.

"Well, he seems to be just about holding it together," I say. "Did you go and see the vet?"

"Yeah, they're doing well, son. He said we can take them now. I asked him to hang on to them until we've got today over with. He's charging me extra for it, of course."

"Well, I'll help you out with that," I say. I look to Dave, heading back towards the van now. "Look, I better go Dad. Give me a call once you get into Felston, okay?"

"Will do. See you there, son."

"Bye, Dad."

The passenger-side door opens and Dave bundles himself into the van. "Who you talking to?" he asks.

"Dad."

"He alright?"

"Yeah, he's good," I reply. "This Barbara seems to be doing wonders for him."

"Well, that's what a good woman does to a man, Ed. I mean, look at me." He holds up his hands, as though advertising himself as the perfect model of manhood. "What about you?" he asks. "You seem a bit quiet this morning."

"I'm fine," I say, a little too defensively. "Just got a lot on my mind with all of this, I suppose."

Dave laughs throatily and slaps his hand on my shoulder. "Hey, I'm the one getting married, not you."

"Yeah, I know," I say, starting up the engine and pulling out of the space.

"Got your speech?" Dave asks, before we've even reached the end of the road.

Well, I've got *a* speech. So much of it is plagiarised, I'm not sure what percentage could be declared mine at all. It was more an exercise in filling in the blanks than anything else.

"Yeah," I reply.

"Want me to have a quick look through it?"

"No! You can't do that!"

"Just to make sure it's okay," he says.

"Just to make sure there's nothing incriminating in there, more like."

"Look, Ed, we got to be sure about this. These people aren't like us. They've had educations that were paid for."

"*I've* had an education that was paid for," I say, baulking.

"What, some shitty polytechnic in Rotherham? Do me a favour. I'm talking about *schools* that were paid for."

"It wasn't a polytechnic!" I say. "It was a proper university. In Sheffield."

"Look, whatever. These people are a slightly different breed, is all I'm saying. They're used to different things."

I sigh. "They're just people, Dave. Like anybody else."

"Well, that may be the case. But the point is, they don't want to be hearing about me getting bollock-naked at Huddersfield away, or about that time I slept in a Tesco car park. So keep it on the straight and narrow, alright? And don't go mentioning us getting arrested!"

"God, give me some credit," I plead. "As if I'm going to mention that. Anyway, it was only a caution – and a *wrongful* one, at that."

We drive for some time in an edgy kind of silence, until we're a good way down the A43 and Dave decides to switch on the radio.

"And this week's highest faller at twenty-nine: it's Eddie Corrigan."

"I used to love this track, Reggie."

"Well, it was flying high last week, Edith, but really seems to have taken a nosedive lately. Anyway, here it is – take it away, Eddie."

"Load of old bollocks," Dave sighs, skipping to the next station.

"In other news today, Eddie Corrigan is well on his way to Dave's wedding. If you recall, Eddie has been at crisis-point since punching Marla's ex-boyfriend, Joe, in the throat earlier in the week. Many had been doubtful that Eddie would take part in the wedding at all, but he appears to have defied-"

Dave turns off the radio. "Hate it when the football season's over," he sighs. "Got a smoke on you?"

"Thought you'd given up," I say.

"I'm not married yet."

I reach into my pockets and pass across my cigarettes. He winds down the window, letting the air bluster into the car, and lights one.

"Tell you what, mate," he announces. "My guts still aren't right. Must be the nerves. Might have to make a pit-stop along the way."

"We'll stop off at some services," I say. "Probably should get something to eat, anyway. You had any breakfast?"

"Couldn't stomach it."

"Well, you should have something. It'll be a long time before we get the chance again. Maybe just a couple of sarnies."

Dave groans with uncertainty, rubbing his belly.

A silence falls over us again, and I turn my mind to horrors ahead. I haven't spoken to Marla since the incident at the gallery, since she shouted at me with such venom that it seems impossible to imagine her being able to talk to me in a civilised manner ever again. I can't help but wonder what happened after I left. She seemed so concerned for Joe, and he no doubt played the sympathy card for all it was worth. In a film, they would have rushed off home without passing Go for a spot of reconciliatory sex.

I shake the image from my mind, concentrating on the task at hand. My thoughts become a tangled mess when I think of the challenges I face. As if I don't have enough to worry about just performing the best man duties, now I have to consider steering clear of Marla – a task so difficult it barely warrants thinking about – while at the same time trying not give anything away to Robin and Jean. I know by now I should hardly care about that, but I still do. I want to do this one thing for Robin. Even if I'm escaping to London under the cloak of nightfall, never to see any of them again, I want to at least ensure Jean has a nice day, free from any drama. I feel I somehow owe that to them before disappearing for good.

And then a sudden thought hits me: the marriage won't be the end of this, but rather the beginning. There'll be parties, summer barbecues, christenings – all of which Marla will be attending. A lifetime of ducking out of things and making excuses. Perhaps I should make a clean cut, just leave and forget about this place entirely. There'll be new friends in London, I'm sure: a fresh, sophisticated batch of friends, pre-cultured and ready for immediate use. I imagine sitting around a table with the kind of people who wear suit jackets with their jeans. We're drinking red wine and talking about some play we've all just seen. Fuck no, I'd drive myself insane with my own bullshit. I need Dave and the boys to save me from myself half the time.

"In four hours' time," Dave says, drawing on his cigarette, "I'll be a married man." He's looking out of the window at the mustard fields, deep in thought.

The car now smells of cigarette smoke and rapeseed. I'm not sure if the cigarette is the same one, or whether he's lit another. I was so lost in my own thoughts that I have no real idea how much time has passed.

"Well, that's a good thing, isn't it?" I ask, scanning the roadside for signs of how far we've come.

"Is it?" He takes another long draw on the cigarette, blowing the smoke forward so that it blossoms against the dashboard before rushing out of the window.

"Well," I say uncertainly, "yeah."

"I'm not so sure to be honest, Ed."

I look across to him for as long as I safely can. "Are you serious?" I ask.

"That's the question, isn't it? Am I serious? Am I serious *enough*?"

"You've never mentioned any of this before."

"I suppose I've just been kind of denying it. But now the day's finally here – I don't know – there's just something so *final* about it all."

"Look," I suggest, "maybe this isn't the best time to be considering this sort of thing. I mean, you said yourself you'd be a mess."

"Ed, this is the *only* time I have to consider it. Three hours and forty-five minutes, to be precise."

"But you love each other, don't you? You're always banging on about her. And you've never mentioned being unhappy before. I mean, I just don't see where this is com-"

I look across to Dave, who is grinning manically.

"You're a right soft prick, Eddie. You know that, don't you?"

"Oh, you twat!" I gasp.

Dave bursts into uproarious laughter. "That was brilliant! Your face! Course I want to marry her, you plank. God, look under *gullible* in the dictionary and there'd be a picture of your ugly mug right there."

I'm actually pretty annoyed. "You've got a pretty sick sense of humour sometimes, Dave. I mean, *Jesus*. Do you *want* me to crash this van or something?"

Dave's still laughing, his big shoulders bouncing up and down. "Aw, I'm sorry, mate. Just thought we could do with a laugh. You know, break up a bit of the tension."

"Do you see me laughing?"

"I thought you didn't want to be my best man, anyway," he says, winking.

"Yeah, well, I don't. Not now."

And in that moment, I realise something. For at least twenty seconds there, I thought the wedding might not be going ahead. I thought I might be absolved of my duties. A few weeks ago, that may have been a cause for celebration, but it didn't feel good, not even for one of those twenty seconds. It felt pretty horrible, which can only mean one thing – that I was thinking of Dave for once rather than myself.

It's with this pleasing thought in mind that I spot a sign up ahead, letting me know that it's half a mile to the next services.

♂

It's quite astonishing to learn just how many over-the-counter medicines there are for diarrhoea: dissolvable tablets, syrups, chews. The pharmacy has half a section of shelving dedicated solely to this predicament. I pick up a box of Imodium AD and turn it over in my hand. Suitably impressed with its promises of *multi-system relief*, I take the box over to counter.

The young girl at the till is annoyingly pretty. I want to explain that it's not me who needs the medicine, that my bowels are in the best of working order, but rather my friend, who only really needs it for his pre-marital nerves, which when you think about it is actually quite sweet, possibly even noble. But, of course, I don't say anything of these things. I just pay for the tablets and leave the pharmacy.

Out in the shopping complex, I have a quick scout around for Dave. After a minute or two of searching, I head back to the van. He's not there either, so I sit down one of the low car-park walls, basking in the sun and eating one of the sandwiches I bought from the pretentious delicatessen, the kind of place where they call salt and vinegar crisps 'sea-salt and balsamic' just so they can charge fifty pence more for them.

Dave emerges from the service station a couple of minutes later. "That should settle me down for a bit," he announces, rubbing his stomach.

I reach into my plastic carrier bag. "Got you these," I say, throwing the box of tablets across.

He catches them and studies the box, as an Egyptologist might study The Rosetta Stone. "Thanks, mate," he says after a time, popping a couple onto his tongue.

I reach into the bag again and pass a bottle of water to him before getting into the van.

"Did you fill her up?" Dave asks, sinking into the passenger seat beside me.

"Yep. Got this as well." I reach into the bag for a third time, producing a Bruce Springsteen CD.

Dave loves Bruce. As a carpenter, and therefore to some degree a working man, I think he believes Bruce represents him in one way or another, although quite how an Italian-American multi-millionaire from New Jersey represents Dave from Northampton is anybody's guess. Still, it's music we both agree on, so it seemed a wise choice.

"The Boss!" Dave cheers, taking the CD from me and tearing off the packaging.

I paid a ludicrous price for the CD in the service station's record shop. Still, it was the only one that would do, and I don't mind if it means making Dave happy. Since my revelation back on the A43, I've been overcome with a determination to make the day as enjoyable and stress-free as possible for him, hence why I've medicated him, watered him, and treated him to some of his favourite music.

We pull out of the car park to the opening strains of *The River*, Dave accompanying the music with a little air guitar. Lyrically, it's probably not altogether appropriate for the day: a maudlin ballad about a man who knocks up his girlfriend, marries her in haste, and spends the rest of his days working a life of drudgery thanks to the flailing economy. But musically it's perfect, and we break out into an uplifting sing-along as we continue on our way.

The miles roll by as easily as the songs – *Thunder Road*, *Racing in the Street*, *Bobby Jean* – and it's only when we're a good way down the A40 and into the third chorus of *Badlands* that things take a turn for the worse.

Without warning, the engine begins to splutter

and lose power. At first, I'm convinced it's something I'm doing wrong, pumping my foot on the accelerator with a confused kind of curiosity, but as the vehicle continues to lose momentum I start to come round to the idea it might be something mechanical.

Dave looks at me in horror.

We're approaching the entrance to a farm, so instinctively I indicate and pull over. As the vehicle slows to a near halt, the engine cuts out completely and Bruce stops singing.

"What is it?" Dave asks urgently.

"I don't know," I reply. "She just lost power on me."

"What did you do?"

"I didn't *do* anything, Dave."

I turn the key in the ignition. The engine rasps and chokes and splutters like a forty-a-day smoker, but refuses to start. I try again, to an equally unsuccessful end.

"You must have done something," Dave says.

"I told you, I didn't do anything," I say angrily. "All I did was-"

And then it hits me. I groan and slump back against the headrest. "It's diesel, isn't it?" I ask.

"Of course it's diesel. Why, what does that...oh, fuck! You put petrol in it?"

I nod slowly.

"Why did you put petrol in it?" he asks.

I'm incensed. "Well, I thought to myself: *do you know what would really fuck Dave's wedding day right up, Ed? Putting petrol in his diesel van. That'll be a laugh, won't it?*"

"Don't even joke about this, Eddie."

"Well, stop asking stupid questions. You think I did it on purpose? You know, most vehicles are petrol, Dave. In most cases, the owner of the vehicle should probably mention first if they want anything other than petrol putting in."

"The thing makes a noise like a fucking Sherman tank, Ed. Didn't that give you some kind of clue? I mean, Christ!"

We both slump back in our seats, all argued out. After a while, I try the ignition once more.

"It's no good doing that now, is it?" Dave sighs. "Just leave it."

"If you've got a hosepipe in the boot, I could try sucking it out," I joke.

"Ed, if I had a hosepipe in the boot, I'd tie one end to the exhaust and stick the other end in your gob."

"You'd have to figure out how to start the engine first," I remind him.

Through the absurdity of it all, we both start laughing, that sad and quiet kind of laughter bordering on despair.

"No," Dave says. "This isn't funny. Not one bit. What are we going to do?"

"Are you with the AA?" I ask.

"Never needed to be," Dave replies. "I know a few blokes with vans and Simon usually sorts out any problems for me."

"Bet you wished you asked Simon to be your best man now," I say.

"Hell yeah."

We spend the next few minutes trying to work

out the logistics of the thing. To call anyone from Northampton is off the cards, we agree. It would take them well over an hour to just get here. We debate the pros and cons of calling another wedding guest – Dad or Kate, perhaps – and hitching a ride into Felston with them. Most of them will be travelling through this way as it is, only Dave doesn't seem too happy about leaving the van here. He also seems to think that a man shouldn't be getting married at all if he can't even make it to the wedding ceremony on his own initiative, and I suspect cadging a lift would be something of a humiliation for him.

Just as we seem to be running out of options, we hear a voice calling out to us. Looking out of the passenger-side window, we see a farmer standing at the fence, rambling incomprehensibly. We soon get the idea he's not too happy about us making an impromptu stop outside his farm.

Dave smiles at me wickedly.

"No way," I say.

"We're only about twenty miles away now."

"I don't care."

Ignoring my protests, Dave winds his window down fully, leaning out with his arm. "Excuse me, mate," he shouts, nodding over the farmer's head and into the field behind him. "Is that your tractor?"

♂

"This is kind of fun, right?" Dave asks, as we

bounce up and down uncomfortably on the suspension seat.

"Yeah," I reply dryly. "Fun."

"I've always wanted to ride in one of these things."

"Well, looks like your dream has finally come true."

"Oh, cheer up, Ed. It's my wedding day!"

Dave is alight with boyish excitement, looking around at his surroundings gleefully, amazed at being *so high up*. We're sharing the passenger seat of the cabin. Dave's in the middle so that I'm squashed up against the window, trying to prevent my head from sporadically bashing against the roof. At our feet sits a black-and-white border collie, who seems almost as excited as Dave about the excursion. She's panting away frantically, steaming up the bottom of the windscreen and fast removing any oxygen left inside the cabin. Every thirty second or so, I find myself checking the wing-mirror to ensure the van is still there behind us and hasn't come away from the tow-bar, leaving all our wedding gear stranded in the middle of the A40.

"So, where you boys come from, then?" the farmer asks.

The farmer himself seems in high spirits, although I suppose he would be seeing as he's just made two hundred quid for a couple of hours' work. He's dressed in a thick lumberjack shirt despite the heat, with a pair of corduroy trousers and Wellington boots. An interesting amount of grey, wiry hair is sprouting from the sides of his face and ears. In fact, he looks so typically like a farmer that it's hard to believe he actually is one, and not just some television actor dressed up for the part.

"Northampton," Dave replies.

"Oh, aye," the farmer says. "I get down to market that way every now and again."

Christ. Now we're making small talk with the farmer.

"Excuse me," I say, leaning across so that he can hear me over the roaring engine, "but can't this thing go any faster?"

The farmer frowns. "It's a tractor, lad, not a Lamborghini. I'm already going full pelt." Full pelt is approximately thirty miles-per-hour. "Don't worry," he adds. "She'll get us there on time."

It's not so much the time constraints I'm worried about. I'm dreading Marla, Robin and Jean passing by in their tarted-up Mercedes. They'd recognise Dave's van in an instant, and I'd hate for them to witness me ballsing up the most rudimentary part of the day in such spectacular fashion.

We pass a sign telling us it's another fifteen miles to Felston.

"I remember my wedding day," the farmer pipes up. "Thirty-five year ago now."

"Yeah?" Dave says.

"Aye."

We wait for him to elaborate, but clearly this is all he has to say on the subject.

"And?" Dave prompts.

The farmer turns to him. "And what?"

"Well, was is a good day?"

"Oh, aye. Lovely day." He fixes his eyes back on the road.

Dave looks to me, grinning a little and raising his eyebrows.

"Course, she left me a few years later," he goes on.

Dave stops smiling, becoming serious all of a sudden. "Oh, sorry to hear that," he says.

"Aye, some fella with over a hundred acres up in Gloucestershire. Worst thing I ever did, looking back on it." He coughs and wipes the sleeve of his shirt across his mouth.

"You never remarried?" Dave asks hopefully.

The farmer sucks the air in through his teeth, shaking his head. "Once bitten, twice shy," he says. "Fool's game, if you ask me. Nah, it's jus' me and Sal now. Ain't that right, ol' girl?"

Sal tilts her head up in the farmer's direction, her tongue lolling stupidly from her mouth.

The farmer frowns. "Not that you should let that put you off, lad," he says. "I'm sure you got yourself a good 'un."

"Yeah, I have," Dave says, reaching down and ruffling the fur on Sal's head.

"Not like that whore o' mine," the farmer goes on, fighting angrily with the gear-stick. "Some days I wish I'd taken the rifle to her. Would've been a damn sight cheaper, too." He laughs mirthlessly. "Plus, I suppose I'd be a free man again by now."

Dave and I exchange a worried glance.

"Still, time heals, eh?" Dave says hopefully.

"Better to have loved and lost," I chip in.

"Eh?" the farmer grunts, still battling with the troublesome gear-stick.

"Than never to have loved at all," I elaborate, wishing I'd kept my mouth shut.

"Says who?" the farmer demands.

"Lord Tennyson, I think."

"Oh, right," he sniffs. "Well, *Lord* Tennyson probably never had his missus piss off for the first swingin' dick with a hundred acres that came her way. Probably would've had a different stance on the matter, elsewise."

I'm really in no mood to argue. "No, you're probably right," I say.

"You married, then?" he asks.

I shake my head.

"Not a queer, are yer?"

I wonder what might happen if I told him I was. Would he stop the tractor and throw me out right here, in Arse-End Of Nowhere, Oxfordshire? Or, worse still, nip back to the farm for his trusty blunderbuss? Probably best not to find out.

"No," I reply.

"What's wrong with yer, then? Got a girlfriend?"

"Not exactly," I reply.

"Well, what does that mean?" the farmer asks. "You've either got one or you ain't. Ain't no in-between about it."

Clearly this is a man who hasn't dated since the Nineteen Fifties.

"Well, then I suppose I haven't," I say.

Dave laughs. "Eddie's not so good with the

ladies," he says.

I look to him in disgust, the treacherous toe-rag.

I fold my arms and look out the window, resolving not to talk to either of them for the rest of the journey.

We arrive at Felston half an hour or so later, spluttering noisily into the place like a loud, drunken cousin who hasn't been invited to the party. Perhaps it's just my imagination, but I swear I see a good deal of the curtains twitching in the cottages as we pass.

"There's a garage just up the road here," the farmer announces. "Want me to drop the van off there so you can pick it up tomorrow?"

Agreeing this would be a good idea, we thank the farmer and climb down from the cabin. We walk back to the van and unload our belongings out onto the pavement. When we have everything we need, Dave pats the side of the tractor and we wave the farmer off. As he putters on loudly up the road, I count my blessings that we appear to have made it into the village unnoticed, at least by any of our own party.

I check my watch, noting we're still doing okay for time and that, in all probability, most of the guests won't have arrived yet. Taking a deep breath of fresh country air, I think about how we're finally here, how this is it, how there really is no going back now.

"Right, then," Dave says, picking up his case and suit-carrier. "Let's get ourselves checked in, shall we?"

18. Faint Shadows

I straighten my bow tie in the mirror. "There," I say to Dave, standing beside me. "I reckon I've got it."

In all honesty, I've been practicing with it since picking up the suit from Handley's on Thursday, after my disastrous meeting with Marla at the gallery. Just the expression on the proprietor's face as he handed the suit over was enough to make me determined beat the damn thing into submission.

I stand back from the mirror and tweak the tie one last time. Perfect.

Dave gives me a quick up-and-down inspection. "Looks good," he says.

I turn back to the mirror. He's right; it does look good. It's amazing how the right clothes can have such an empowering effect, how they can make a man walk a few inches taller and feel altogether different about himself.

We're standing in my guestroom above The Bull. The room is a good-sized double, full of character and olde-worlde charm. A thick, knitted throw is draped across the bed. On the cabinet beside it stands an old-fashioned bedside lamp with a floral shade. I haven't looked in the drawer yet, but I'm willing to bet there a Gideon's Bible tucked away in there. Over by the window, which looks out across the rolling Oxfordshire countryside, is an antiquated chez lounge.

"How do I look?" Dave asks, thumbing the

buttons of his waistcoat into place.

He looks like the slightly fancier-dressed version of me. We're both in matching mauve waistcoats and bow ties only he's wearing a longer, pinstriped jacket and grey trousers, as if to distinguish himself as the man of the hour. I notice the waistcoat seems pretty snug around his thickening midriff, and I'm a little worried for the buttons there, but overall he looks great. I'm just about to tell him so when a knock comes at the door.

I answer it, and Brian and Pete step into the room, both of them dressed in smart suits. I'm particularly pleased to see Brian has made the effort.

"Thought we'd come and see how you were getting on," Pete says.

"Pretty much done now," I tell him. "Grab a buttonhole, lads."

I point to the open box on the bed and they make their way over, each pinning a white carnation to their lapel. It's a fiddly job, as Dave and I found earlier, so we spend quite a few minutes trying to get them properly secured.

With this done, I hand the box over to Pete. "Hold on to this," I tell him. "All the men should already have one, but there's a couple of spares in there, just in case."

Pete nods, seemingly happy to be given something to do.

"Got the rings?" Dave asks.

I tap at my inside jacket pocket. "Yep."

"I reckon that's it, then."

We stand around for a moment or two, just looking at one another.

"Good luck, mate," Brian says after a while.

I'm about to thank him when I realise he's talking to Dave. "Yeah, good luck, Dave," I say instead.

"Cheers, boys."

We perform a mildly embarrassing group hug and then make our way from the room.

As I lock the door, Dave checks his watch. "Probably got time for a swift one downstairs, I reckon," he says.

I check my own watch. We do have a fair bit of time to kill, and at least being here means there's no danger of bumping into Alison (or Marla, for that matter) too early, with the bride's side of the family preparing at the guesthouse down the road to avoid just such a disaster.

"Why not?" I agree.

We make our way down the musty-scented corridor, descending the old, creaky staircase.

"Where's Jo?" I ask Brian.

"She went off with the girls," he replies. "Thought she'd enjoy it more than hanging around with us."

"Good idea," I say. "Let them get to know each other a bit."

"Did you see Allie?" Dave asks Brian urgently.

"Yeah."

"How did she seem?"

"Yeah, she seemed fine, mate. Dunno why. I'd be suicidal if I was about to marry you."

We enter the front barroom of pub. A couple of

middle-aged local men are sitting at the bar, and they raise their glasses with a little cheer as we walk in, all suited and booted. They seem like typical village types, wearing an alarming amount of tweed and sipping real ale.

Behind the bar stands the young girl who caught my interest the last time I was here. She's dressed in a tight-fitting top, showing her breasts off a little too well. Her face is pretty – a little angelic, even – only she's wearing a heavy eyeliner and a stud through her bottom lip, giving off just a whiff of rebellion and corruptibility.

She smiles at us as we walk up to the bar. My guess is she doesn't usually see a lot of young men around here, and our presence is something of a novelty for her.

Brian orders two lagers and two pints of Guinness, and we pull our stools up.

"You all set for today?" the bargirl asks, pouring the drinks.

"I will be after this," Dave replies happily, taking the first pint of lager and drawing it to his lips.

"I'm Emily, by the way," she says, looking directly at me.

"Eddie," I say, floundering a little under her glare. "This is Dave, Brian and Pete."

"Are you the best man?" she asks, passing me a Guinness.

"I am out of this lot," I reply, taking it, our fingertips touching for a millisecond.

The boys laugh, and I bask for a few seconds in the glory of my incredibly witty comeback. Is this flirting? Am I actually flirting? It's been so long since I've engaged in a bit of it that it's hard to tell. Perhaps I'm just confusing it with general niceness.

"I don't doubt it," Emily says, smiling a sweet smile that doesn't match the wickedness in her eyes.

Oh yes, definitely flirting. Is this wrong? What about Marla? She's probably back with Joe by now anyway, spending all his money on Christ-knows-what. I imagine them in a sprawling bathroom – the biggest bathroom ever seen – sharing a Jacuzzi, a fat Cuban cigar lolling from Joe's mouth as he watches her perform some kind of soapy and seductive dance.

Fuck it. She hasn't called me, anyway. Not even to see how I am.

"How long have you been working here, then?" I ask. Not the best opening gambit, admittedly.

Emily shrugs her shoulders. I notice how smooth-skinned and supple her shoulders are, like two forbidden apples.

"About a year or so now," she replies.

Great. A year or so. Which means that unless the landlord here is flagrantly disregarding all manner of licensing laws, she must be nineteen years of age at the very least. Nothing wrong with that, surely. Although I might need to consult the boys on it later, just to be certain. Ten years' difference. It seems a long time when said like that. When I was her age, she was nine! But, I'm not her age and she's not nine, so why don't I just relax and enjoy something for once in my fucking life? Have a bit of fun with it?

My mind scrambles for something to say, something devastatingly, earth-shatteringly suave.

"I think my pint's a bit flat," Brian murmurs, just as I open my mouth.

"Really?" Emily reaches over the bar and unabashedly grabs his pint, taking a large sip from it herself. "Hmm. Might be a problem with the gas. Give me a sec."

She disappears through the back door and the boys look to me, smiling deviously.

"Reckon you might be in with her," Dave says, nodding.

"You reckon?"

"Yep."

"Emily," Brian says thoughtfully. "I've always wanted to shag a girl called Emily."

"Or Amelia," Pete chips in.

"Bryony," Dave offers. "No, Felicity."

"Penelope," I say.

"Beatrice," Brian says.

We all burst out laughing, Pete almost spraying a mouthful of lager across the bar.

"*Beatrice?*" Dave repeats indignantly. "It's supposed to be posh girls, Bri, not your gran."

My phone starts ringing over the laughter. I take it out of my pocket, seeing Marla's name screaming up at me from the display screen, emboldened as if to highlight my shame. For a crazed moment, I consider ignoring it. Thinking again, I step away from the bar and push the call-receive button.

"Eddie?"

"Hi," I say.

"Hey. Where are you?"

Her voice sounds like music to my ears. Just two days without her and I'm already reduced to missing the sound of her voice. What a sap.

"We're in The Bull," I say.

"Well, you better get going. We'll be leaving soon, and Alison needs to arrive last."

"Okay," I say. "Everything alright?"

There's a pause whilst Marla seems to consider the meaning of this. "Yeah, everything's fine," she says.

"Good. We'll see you there, then."

I hang up the phone just as Emily returns to the bar.

"Might have to put a rain-cheque on that pint," I say. "We need to leave."

"So, I'll see you later," she says, almost making it a question. "For the party."

"Yeah," I say tentatively. "For the party."

Dave quickly downs the last of his pint, stands from his stool and belches loudly. "Right, then," he announces. "Let's get fucking married."

♂

Felston is looking typically glorious this afternoon. The sun is out in celebratory fashion, and the few clouds drifting lazily across the sky are pure white and benevolent, as though only up there in decoration as opposed to signalling any threat of rain. Our short walk to the church is downhill, providing us with a magnificent view across the countryside: the undulating fields of brown and green, peppered with the odd white specks of sheep grazing in the distance. We pass ancient, thatched-roofed cottages, each built from the same locally sourced limestone, each fronted by small, immaculately kept gardens. It's hard to believe that this place actually exists, here in the real world, and that we haven't just entered some theme-park entitled 'English Chocolate-Box Village Land'.

We're all walking alongside one another, the four of us, until Brian decides to hurry a few paces ahead, swinging his fist to and fro as though ringing an imaginary hand-bell. "Dead man walking here!" he hollers, in a pretty terrible Southern American drawl. "We got a dead man walking here, people!"

"Leave it out, Bri," Dave sighs, although he's smiling.

"Sorry," he says, falling back in line with the rest of us.

"Hey, who's going to keep Bri in check when you're gone?" Pete asks.

"I won't be *gone*. Why's everyone talking like I've got some sort of terminal illness? I'll still be around. Besides, looks like Jo's doing a pretty good job on him, anyway."

"No woman's gonna change me," Brian says, proudly raising his chin.

"Really?" Pete asks. "I don't think I've even heard you call anyone a cunt all day."

"*You're* a cunt," he huffs.

"And what the deal with the hair, Bri?" I ask.

Brian's hair is neatly trimmed and styled, as though he paid the barber a visit for the first time in fifteen years.

"It's a wedding, isn't it? I'm entitled to have my hair cut, aren't I?"

"Hey, I'm not knocking it," I say, holding up my hands. "You look good."

Brian pokes his fingers at his hair awkwardly, unsure of how to take this compliment.

"You remember everything Reverend Hall told you?" Dave asks me.

I think back to my last visit to the church, a sweaty, hallucinatory experience I'd rather forget. In all honesty, I can't remember anything that was said. Not a word.

"Ah, don't worry," says Dave, clearly noting my perturbed expression. "Just follow the instructions and you'll be fine."

We're the first people to arrive at the church, and things seem oddly quiet. A sandwich board has been propped up on the pavement, stating 'NO PARKING – WEDDING IN PROGRESS', but apart from this there's no real indication that anything momentous is about to take place. I suppose that's the thing with weddings; they're really only momentous if you're taking part in one yourself. To anybody else, it's just a bunch of people dressed up nice.

As we cross through the churchyard, I feel none of the trepidation I did before. The gravestones to either side of me now feel like nothing more than signifiers of old dead people, people who have had their turn on the wheel and bought their ticket for whatever come next, fair and square. The yew trees are just that: trees, and quite pretty ones at that when studied properly. No longer do they seem like the clawed, arthritic hands of giants bearing down on me. Just trees. A part of life and a part of death. Nothing more, nothing less.

We enter the church, and the air immediately becomes cooler, although not in an unpleasant way (it's actually quite refreshing to step out of the midday heat for a while). There's nobody to be seen inside.

"Hello?" Dave calls, no doubt feeling a little silly about having to announce his arrival at his own wedding.

After a time, we hear the sound of a door unlatching and Reverend Hall appears by the altar.

"Ah, hello," he calls cheerily, hurrying down towards us.

He's in full regalia today, in a long black cassock with a large crucifix pendant hanging around his neck. His round, adolescent face lights up as he approaches, his soft cheeks blushing.

"Good to see you," he says, chuckling. Reverend Hall seems to have a habit of chuckling just to fill the silence. He shakes each of us by the hand. "So, all ready for the big push?" he asks, bobbing up and down on the balls of his feet.

"I think so," Dave replies.

"Good. Now, I'll just need David and Edward to follow me through to my office back here. Just need to run through a couple of questions for the records – nothing to worry about. Perhaps you two gentlemen would like to wait outside for the others to arrive."

Reverend Hall makes his way back up the aisle, humming a little ditty.

"Come along, Edward," Dave says, smiling. "I'll see you two gentlemen on the other side."

"Lead the way, David," I say, extending my arm.

We follow Reverend Hall up the aisle and into a small office at the back of the church. The room is tiny and cluttered. A wooden table is pushed up against the wall and a battered-looking filing cabinet leans drunkenly in the corner. Everything is piled high with lever-arch files and boxes. It surprises me; I would have had Reverend Hall down for a particularly organised man.

"I'll just grab the register," Reverend Hall says. "Please, take a seat."

Dave takes one of the two chairs at the table. I realise there isn't actually anywhere for me to sit, so I stay where I am.

"Edward, you'll be witnessing today," the reverend says, laying the register on the table and taking the seat next to him.

I nod and alter my footing, folding my hands neatly in front of me, adopting my best and most serious *witnessing* stance.

"Now, just a couple of standard questions: firstly, can you confirm your full name?"

Dave clears his throat. "David Barry Atkinson," he says.

A little bubble of laughter tries to escape my

lungs, but I manage to suppress it.

"Occupation?"

"Chippie. Carpenter." He thinks for a while and raises a finger in the air. "Like Jesus," he adds, grinning wildly.

Reverend Hall smiles warmly. "Actually, that's something of a myth."

"Really?" Dave asks, his finger still hovering expectantly in the air. He looks genuinely devastated.

"Possibly," Reverend Hall says, trying to be conciliatory about it. "There are various interpretations. Date of birth?"

Dave momentarily looks a little too stunned by the Jesus revelation to continue, but then seems to pull himself together enough to give his date of birth. He goes on to confirm he absolutely, definitely has no other wives tucked away anywhere, here or abroad, and that there's no legal reason why he can't marry today.

After asking Dave a few more basic questions, Reverend Hall picks up the register and leads us out of the office, laying it on another table just off to the side of the altar.

"The signing will be done here," he explains. "After the ceremony. Take a seat on one of the front pews for a while. I need to be outside to welcome the guests on their arrival. I'll pop my head in the door and give you a thumbs-up when we're about to get started."

It seems a little strange for a man of the cloth to be giving anyone a *thumbs-up*, but we thank him nonetheless and he makes his way outside.

Dave sits down on the pew and exhales heavily, looking up to the rafters of the church. I take a seat next to him.

"How are you feeling, Ed?" he asks.

How am *I* feeling? It seems absurd for him to even ask such a thing. It hammers home just what a selfish bastard I must have been these past few months, if he has to think about me at a time like this.

"Good," I reply, looking around the church as if to demonstrate how carefree I am about it all. "I feel good."

"Talk to me about something, will you? Anything. Just to take my mind off the nerves."

I think it over. Our lives have been so consumed by the wedding lately that it's hard to think of anything non-wedding related. I couldn't talk about Marla, of course. That'd be a bloody disaster, like lighting the fuse and walking off. "Well, I'm moving to London," I eventually say.

Dave looks to me in surprise. This seems to have done the trick. "Why?" he asks.

"I don't know. Just feels like things have gotten a little stale for me around here, like I'm not really going anywhere. I think a change of scenery could be good for me."

Dave nods. Good old, understanding Dave. "What about your job?" he asks.

"I quit."

"What'll you do for money?"

"I don't know. Get another job at some point, I suppose. I've got a bit to tide me over. And Kate's offered to put me up for a while – until I'm back on my feet, like."

"Well, that's good," he says. "Sounds like you're doing the right thing."

"Really?"

"Yeah."

"To be honest, I thought you'd call me a ponce."

"You'll always be a ponce, Ed. You may as well go and be one in London. In fact, you'll probably fit in well down there."

I laugh. "It just feels like for the first time things are finally settled around here, you know. There's always been one thing or another holding me back, but now everything seems sorted. You're getting married. Dad's doing well. I mean, bloody hell, even Bri seems to be getting his shit together. I just don't see what's keeping me here anymore." Images of Marla drift into my mind, and I shake them away as quickly as they arrive.

"Well, make sure you come back and see us every once in a while, alright?"

"It's only an hour away," I remind him. "And you can visit me, too."

"Christ, don't. Allie'll be wanting a place down there if I'm not careful. And I've seen the prices. But I'm pleased for you, Ed. Really. Put it there."

He holds out his hand and I shake it. We smile at one another a little awkwardly.

A cough comes from the back of the church, and we look back over the pews to see Reverend Hall nodding his head enthusiastically, holding his thumbs aloft.

"Looks like we're good to go," Dave says.

We stand and assume our positions, Dave at the

altar with me standing at the right-side front pew, closest to the aisle.

The congregation begins to trickle into the church, with Alison's mum and Dave's parents at the forefront. Following closely behind them come other family members, and then after this Robin and Jean. They wave excitedly at me as they take their seats, and I raise a hand to wave back weakly.

Over the course of the next few minutes, the rest of the congregation come in to take their places. Reverend Hall makes his way back up the aisle to stand in front of Dave. There's a short, whispered conversation between the two of them, with Dave nodding his head extravagantly to signal he understands, and then comes a sudden blast from the church organ. It startles a good few of the guests, and they jump in surprise, looking to one another afterwards and laughing a little with embarrassment. The tittering soon dies away as everyone stands and all eyes are averted to the aisle, where Alison is walking, arm in arm with her father.

She looks like everything you'd want a bride to look: elegant, regal, beautiful. Her dress is traditional white, with a long train tailing behind it. Her face is masked behind a veil.

I look over to Dave to see him beaming with happiness and pride, his smile taking up most of his face. It looks as though his head's about to burst.

Looking back down the aisle, I spot Marla walking behind Alison. She looks stunning in a strapless, satin dress, closely matching the colour of my waistcoat, folded elegantly into waves at its front. Her hair is styled in a pretty bob, tucked back on one side to reveal a sparkling chandelier earring. I hardly want to look at her, but find it impossible not to.

Marla looks to Dave and smiles, opening her mouth generously as if to mime: *oh-my-gosh-isn't-this-exciting?* And something inside me just crumples.

She looks across the pews at all the faces, her eyes meeting mine for a millisecond before glancing downwards as if to tend to Alison's train.

The organ drones on while Alison nears, drawing a fresh batch of *oohs* and *ahhs* from each row of the congregation she passes.

She stands alongside Dave, who reaches out his hands to take hers, and Alison's father withdraws to his position at the pews. Marla takes a step back, holding onto the bouquet. Reverend Hall gives a quick raise of his eyebrows while looking to me, and I step towards to the altar, standing alongside Marla. He then asks for everyone else to be seated and church is filled with a collective *whomph*, the sound of a hundred people all sitting at once. He waits for the coughs and creaks to subside as people make themselves comfortable, and then opens his mouth.

"We are gathered here today…" he begins, and already my mind is drifting.

I briefly glance across to Marla. God, she looks beautiful. Fucking horribly, devastatingly beautiful. Why can't I be free from this woman? What devious and manipulative higher power continuously sees fit to draw us together like this? Whoever it is must have a pretty sadistic sense of humour, anyway. Or maybe there is no higher power. Maybe we're just two bits of flotsam caught up in the same current, forever encircling one another in this demented kind of dance. Yeah, this is what I need to do – forget about all that faith and love and destiny mumbo-jumbo. Concentrate on the facts, apply the science. What could be more British? The only reason I'm finding Marla so attractive now is simply because my DNA, somewhere many fathoms down in my subconscious, is telling me I need to plant my seed inside her, that she'll make a good and healthy mother to my younglings, protect them from the harsh world until they're old enough to repeat the cycle. That's all. We've buried this under thousands of years of civilisation and art and culture and romance, but when it's all boiled down to the cold, hard crux of the matter, all you're left with is this one core truth. It's like the dirty little secret of mankind, perpetually being papered over with our own self-importance but always lurking somewhere beneath the surface. So, in these terms, Marla is nothing more than an attractive carrier pod to ensure my genetic sustainability on this planet. And probability dictates there'll be plenty of other carrier pods out there – London must be teeming with them! So my genes can rest easy and stop leading my emotions astray. I can forget about her and get on with my new, exciting, cosmopolitan life.

But, fuck me, she does look pretty.

"...and if Edward could just present us with the rings," Reverend Hall announces, jerking me from my thoughts.

I hear the crackle of static, intermittent electronic bleeps, so clearly it makes me look around to see if anyone is hearing it.

1201 alarm...

Roger, 1201. We're go...same type...we're go.

I move slowly forwards. My legs appear to be doing all the work for me, without any assistance from my brain at all. I seem to be moving incredibly slowly, as though trudging through syrup.

Altitude/velocity light. Three and a half down. Two-twenty feet. Fifteen forward.

Feeling the eyes of the room upon me, I reach into my right jacket pocket, taking out the box and opening it. Dave removes the ring from its holder with a shaky hand and, taking Alison by the wrist, slips it onto her finger.

Eleven forward. Coming down nicely. Two hundred feet.

I dig into my right pocket and retrieve the other ring, opening the box for Alison to do the same.

Four and a half down. Five and a half down.

Alison takes the ring. She smiles at me through the veil. It's a warm smile, and I'm suddenly overcome with a great feeling of affection towards her. In that moment, I know Dave's doing the right thing. I know Alison will always be there for him.

Forty feet down, two and a half. Kicking up some dust. Faint shadow.

Alison takes Dave's wrist and slides the ring

onto his finger, pushing a little harder to jolt it over the knuckle.

Contact light. Okay, engine stop. Mode control – both auto. Descent engine command override, off. Engine arm, off. Four-thirteen is in.

We copy you down, Eagle.

I stand watching Dave and Alison, watching them gazing lovingly into one another's eyes. It's a thing of wonder to see two people looking at each other this way.

Houston, Tranquility Base here. The Eagle had landed.

Roger, Tranquility. We copy you on the ground. You got a bunch of guys here about to turn blue. We're breathing again. Thanks a lot.

My role seems to be over so swiftly that I'm rendered into a state of numbed surprise. I'm rooted to the spot, wondering if there's anything else required of me.

"Thank you, Edward," Reverend Hall says, nodding eagerly and clearly wishing me away.

I retreat back to my position, smiling broadly. No fuck-ups thus far. I didn't trip over or drop the ring or accidentally head-butt Alison on the nose. I didn't get the rings muddled or clam up with stage fright. I didn't do anything wrong. In fact, I'm pretty sure I did alright.

I look across to Marla, who is watching Dave and Alison run through their vows, smiling happily. She carefully brushes a rogue tear away from her cheek with her fingertip, no doubt worried for her makeup. I'm yearning for her to look over to me, but I know through her stubbornness she won't.

When the vows are complete, Reverend Hall reads a couple of short passages from the Bible and then announces that, by the power vested in him, he now declares them man and wife and Dave may kiss the bride. Of course, Dave accepts this offer with reckless abandon, swinging Alison back a full ninety degrees and planting the biggest smacker of all time on her. The congregation whoops and cheers, and Dave arises with heroic panache, pumping his fist in the air. Everyone's laughing at Dave now, glad for a bit of comic relief after the seriousness of the ceremony.

And that's that. Done deal. Dave's a married man and nothing seems to have changed. So far as I can tell, the world is still as it was, and I suppose now everything will just carry on as it did before, as it always has done.

I'm not exactly sure what I was expecting might happen, but it does all seem a little anti-climatic. I mean, I wasn't expecting a thunderstorm or a plague of locusts, but I did think things might feel a little different. But I suppose it's just the same old world, still belligerently turning round no matter who gets married, who gets heartbroken, or who dies.

Dave and Alison are ushered over to the register for the official signing. Marla and I follow after them, and Revered Hall calls the Atkinsons and the Gardeners forward too. The organ fires up once again whilst Dave and Alison sign, and then Marla and I step forward to countersign, standing awkwardly close to one another. While we seek out the correct dotted lines, our hands even touch for one excruciating moment.

Once this is done, we step away and lastly the Atkinsons and the Gardeners move forward to seal the deal.

After this, we're all recalled back to the altar and, with the organ music still playing, Dave and Alison are instructed to make their way from the church. Off they go, hand-in-hand, and Marla and I follow suit, with the parents behind.

"Nice, huh?" I whisper to Marla.

She doesn't respond, staring fixedly ahead at the newlyweds instead. Maybe it's just that my voice was drowned out by the blaring organ pipes. Maybe not.

I spot Jean in the pews, and force myself to smile as we pass. She's dabbing at her eyes with a handkerchief. Next to her, Robin nods and gives me a little wink.

As I pass Brian, seated towards the back, he holds up his hand in expectation of a high-five. Needless to say, I leave him hanging, and Pete, in the pew behind, leans forward to bat his arm back down.

We reach the church doors, and as we wait for Dave and Alison to negotiate the steps, I turn back to the congregation. Many of them are now foraging around for boxes of the secretly stockpiled confetti.

Marla hurries forward to help Alison with her train, and I watch as they go down the steps together out into the churchyard.

Taking a deep breath, I follow them out into the

light.

♂

I'm sitting a way off from the church, watching the congregation trickling slowly back towards The Bull. It's nice just to be up here alone, on a hill that offers panoramic views across Felston and its surrounding countryside. Seeing the people trickle away from the church is rather like watching the end credits of a film, only with the people of my life in place of the cast members.

Dave and Alison lead the way, walking happily arm-in-arm with dramatic aplomb. Alison is holding her veil down in the breeze and Marla is walking behind, holding the train of her dress off the ground. I know I should probably be down there behind Dave, but I needed the time alone. Once the ceremony had finished there was a lot of faffing about outside, with the photographer gathering various people together and running through his extensive shot-list in painstaking detail. Somewhere amidst it all, I managed to sneak away for a bit of peace and quiet. It hardly matters; the world won't come to an end just because I arrive at The Bull ten minutes behind everyone else. In fact, I daresay with all the excitement, my absence might not be noticed at all.

I take out a packet of cigarettes from my jacket pocket and light one up.

The parents are following behind Marla. Dave's mum, Denise, is flitting insect-like from one person to the next, touching the arms of Alison's parents affectionately, excitedly recalling the events of the ceremony and throwing back her head to let loose that wonderfully dirty laugh of hers. The Gardeners seem a little overwhelmed and awkward, but are nodding along enthusiastically. It's okay; I've no doubt they'll come to love her enormously over time (I've never met anyone with half a heart who doesn't in the end).

Robin and Jean are there too, both laughing along with it all. I can see thirty Christmas Days to come in this one scene, decades spanning ahead in which these people will grow together like old trees sharing the same soil, until it becomes impossible to remember a time when they were not in one others' lives. And it all begins here, in this moment, on the great leveller of the wedding day – days that remind us how we're all just people in the end, trying to get along as best we can.

I see Brian and Pete leave the churchyard. Brian is walking alongside Jo, and he reaches out uncertainly to touch her back, still at that wonderfully jittery point of a relationship where neither party is entirely sure what to do with their hands.

Kate and Jess emerge next, at the complete opposite end of the relationship spectrum, so comfortable in one another's company that it must even seem possible to predict what the other is thinking. I feel an overwhelming sense of affection for Jess, walking happily alongside Kate. She's been looking after my sister for such a long time now. Whatever it was Kate needed when she headed off for London, Jess has provided in abundance. She was there for Kate when, in all honesty, I couldn't be, and I've never even thanked her for this – at least, not properly. Perhaps I'll tell her at the party. Or perhaps I'll just take the piss out of her – which, as I think we both understand, is just another way of saying it, after all.

Towards the end of the procession, I spot Dad and Barbara. They're perhaps at the stages of their lives where they're beyond the early relationship jitters: too familiar with the world, too wise to it all. But they seem incredibly happy in each other's company, strolling along with a quiet kind of contentment that seems to transcend the excitement of the day. I feel a great sense of liberation, tinged with a little sadness. Dad doesn't need me anymore – at least, not in the way he did before. But happiness, too, because I know Dad's going to be alright.

As if following the trail of my thoughts, Dad stops walking and looks up the hill, directly at me. It catches me cold. Perhaps a hundred people have walked this way, and not one of them spotted me up here. It's as though some secret genetic bond within the Corrigan Y-chromosome has allowed this to happen, something shared between us and nobody else.

Dad kisses Barbara on the cheek, sending her on with the rest of the party, before making his way up towards me. It takes him a while to get up the hill. He's still strong and powerful from thirty-odd years of digging, but I guess old age is finally catching up with him in the fitness stakes.

"How's the form there, Eddie?" he asks, reaching the top of the hill a little breathless.

I nod and smile. "Fine. Just taking a minute out."

"Bit of time to think, eh? Mind if I join you?"

I nod my head towards the space on the bench beside me. Dad's sits, exhaling heavily.

"Kate told me you're thinking of moving down to London," he says, once he has caught his breath.

I nod. "Yeah, thinking about it," I say.

"You set on it?"

I consider this and nod again. "Pretty much."

"Well, good for you. Kate's done alright out of it – don't see why you shouldn't either. You're a smart lad." He pats me on the shoulder. "Good for you."

"Cheers, Dad."

"Nice wedding, eh?"

"Yeah."

"Good day for it, an' all."

"Yeah."

Dad looks around, taking in the full scope of the view. "Nice spot up here, eh?"

"Yeah," I agree, "it is."

Dad glances across to me, frowning a little. "Thought you'd be happier about it all, son," he says.

"I am. Just a bit nervous, I suppose," I sigh. "I seem to fuck everything up in the end, after all."

His frown deepens. "What do you mean by that?"

"Well, there's Marla for one. I fucked that one

up pretty royally."

"What happened?"

I take a last draw on the cigarette, dropping the butt and crushing it under my heel in frustration. "Just got the wrong end of the stick, didn't I? Thought it was a bit more than it was."

"Eddie, she let you bury a dog in her garden. There must've been something to it."

"I don't think so," I say. "Think I was reading too much into it, that's all."

"Well, have you asked her about it?" Dad asks.

"Not in so many words."

"So no, then."

"Anyway, it's not just Marla. There are other things."

"Like?"

"Well, work is another one. I mean, I'm terrible at that. Really, you should see me. I can't stand it."

"Lot of people don't like their job, son."

"And Mum."

Dad turns his attention away from the view, swivelling on the bench so he's facing me fully. "Well, what's that got to do with you?" he asks, a little angrily.

"Well, I sent her out there, didn't I? To the shops. I mean, even at nine years old I was a little fuck-up. If I hadn't thrown that little hissy-fit she never would have gone out for ice cream. She'd still be here now, wouldn't she? Being a part of all this. Fuck, Mum would have loved today."

Dad straightens himself out again, looking back out across the fields. "Ah, Eddie." He puffs his cheeks, blowing the air out. "Eddie. Is that what you've been thinking?"

"It's not what I've been *thinking*. It's what bloody happened."

"Son, she was always going to the shops. We discussed it before I even got in the bath that day. She was going to finish the washing up, and then she was going to the shops. That was the plan. We needed milk. And bread for tomorrow's sandwiches. Your stupid bloody ice cream had nothing to do with it."

I look across to Dad.

"I mean, I suppose she just decided to pick that up while she was there," he goes on. "Just to keep you quiet, like."

"She was always going?"

"Yeah."

"She told you that?"

"Yeah!"

I try to speak, but only splutter out a cough instead. It feels like hot pins have been pushed into the backs of my eyes. "Well, why didn't you ever tell me that?" I finally manage to ask.

"You never bloody asked, did you? I didn't know about any of this."

I feel the warm splash of tears on my cheeks. "Oh, shit," I gasp.

Dad looks to me, clearly uncertain how to handle a crying twenty-nine-year-old son. "Well, you're in a right old state over it, aren't you? There there, son." He pats me a little on the back. "There there. It's alright."

I wipe my hands down my wet cheeks. "God, all these years," I gasp. "All these years I thought

I'd killed her."

Dad laughs a little, but quickly straightens out his expression when I turn my sorrowful face to his. "Listen, son. There's only one prick out there that did that, and it isn't you. God knows where he is – probably somewhere out there living the life of Riley, not even giving a second thought about what he did. But you can't let those things eat you up too much. You start doing that and you might as well be dead yourself. You think Mum would want to be seeing you like this?"

I bury my face in my hands, sobbing properly now, sobbing like I probably should have done the day we buried her. Crying the tears of twenty years ago.

"No," Dad goes on. "She'd want to see you as a proud man now. With your head held high. And she'd be pleased as punch with all this moving to London business. I just know she would. She'd have said it's a good thing – it's a good thing for Eddie to get out there and start living properly."

I withdraw my head from my hands.

"She'd also have said be careful not to let things pass you by, either – things that are staring you right in the face. You shouldn't be afraid of doing things, son. Because you had nothing to do with what happened that day. Nothing at all. But the worst thing you could do on her account is stop living. Stop taking the odd risk or two. Because that's what makes life what it is, you know. And that'd be the real insult to her, like – to not live life to the full."

I nod and dry my cheeks off for a final time,

determined not to cry any more. I blow out a big ball of air and reach back into my pockets for my cigarettes, lighting one up.

"Oh, and she might have had a thing or two to say about that smoking, too," he adds, frowning.

I laugh hollowly, emptily. "Thanks, Dad," I say.

"Aye. Now, come on, you soppy eejit," he says, standing from the bench. "Let's get back to celebrating with your man there, eh? I'll even buy you a pint."

19. Once More, With Feeling

"You're getting too heavy for this," she sighs into my ear.

"No, I'm not," I protest. "One more time."

But I'm not kidding anybody; I am *getting too heavy for this – too long in the arms and legs. I'm getting too old for The Moon Walk.*

Mum's carrying me in her arms, my face nuzzled into her neck, which smells of soap and this morning's shampoo. I'm wearing my favourite NASA pyjamas, and she's jigging me up and down, humming the tune of a song playing on the stereo: the Pogues' A Rainy Night in Soho.

Mum's twirling us slowly around, so that we're melded in a strange, lopsided kind of dance.

"Okay," Mum agrees. "One more time."

I cheer and lean back, extending both arms in anticipation. Mum takes hold of each of my wrists.

Now for the tricky part.

Carefully, I unravel one leg from around her waist, placing my foot against the outside of her thigh. Next, I follow suit with the other leg, so that both of my feet are pressed against her, my knees crooked. Then, slowly, I begin to straighten out my body. Mum bends to the side a little so I'm able to stretch out fully. Leaning back as far as I can, my pyjama top slides down my body and bunches around my underarms. I hang my head back, enjoying the view of a world upside-down, knowing this could be our final voyage, our Apollo 17, and so determined to savour every moment of it.

"The Moon Walk!" I cry triumphantly, beginning to ascend her leg, one small step at a time.

The higher I climb, the more my body rotates, bringing my head closer and closer to the ground. I imagine the grey carpet below as a lunar surface. I'll have to remember the qualities of this carpet; the people back home will want to know about it.

I think of Gene Cernan, the last man on the Moon. Just before leaving, he etched his daughter's initials in the dust, where they will remain for as long as the Moon itself. It's difficult for a person to comprehend such permanence.

Freeing one hand from Mum's clasp, I reach down, my fingertip hovering just millimetres above the carpet.

"Aliens!" Mum cries suddenly, leaning forward to blow a raspberry against my bare, bulbous stomach.

This tickles me into a spasm, and I roar with laughter, wriggling desperately in an attempt to free myself. Mum scoops her arm under my knees and tosses me high into the air towards the settee.

I enjoy the descent, down through the thermosphere, the mesosphere, into the stratosphere. Temperature: five thousand degrees Fahrenheit. Speed: twenty-five thousand miles-per-hour – the fastest anyone has ever been before. Into the troposphere, freefalling now, parachutes opening, coming back down to Earth.

As I hit the cushions, I imagine a heroic splashdown in the Pacific Ocean, ready to be received by a Navy warship and an adorning public.

Edward James Corrigan: the thirteenth man on the Moon.

♂

Knifes are being clinked against champagne flutes. I'm standing on the stage of The Bull's function room, a bright light hammering down directly into my eyes and turning the audience into a sea of barely visible silhouettes. I'm squinting out at them as the sound of cutlery on glass diminishes and a hushed silence takes over.

I cough dryly.

My heart is pounding in my chest, so violently I imagine the crowd must be able to hear it through the microphone clutched in my clammy palm.

"Hello," I say weakly into the receiver.

A nervous titter of laughter goes around the room.

I clear my throat again. "Hello. I must say…"

The darkness seems to deepen and swell, growing all around me. I imagine myself a voyager, suspended in the darkest reaches of Space, floating in an impossible infinity, the spotlight a distant Earth to which I must set my coordinates.

"I must say, it's a great honour that Dave has asked me to do this for him today. It's wonderful to know that after all these years, he's finally agreed who the best man really is."

Half-hearted laughter rises from the audience, the laughter of politeness, of relief that I've managed to get going at all.

I bend down to pick up my champagne flute from the stage floor, taking a huge gulp from it that does nothing to quench my bone-dry throat. Placing it back down, I look to the crumpled sheet of paper in my hand. The words seem to ripple like water, and I blink furiously to steady them.

"For those of you that don't know me, I am the best man, and my name is Eddie What-Would-You-Like-To-Drink. Please feel free to come and talk to me at the bar later, only I do insist you use my full name when addressing me."

More gentle laughter comes drifting out of the blackness.

I cough again.

"And...err...and..."

I lower the sheet of paper, looking out into the abyss. Somewhere out there, a hundred or so well-fed diners are pleading with me to get on with it, to just tell a few more gags and say something sweet about Alison so they can carry on with the act of getting anarchically pissed. They probably hardly care what I say at all, so long as I do it in a reasonable timeframe.

I can hear their impatience growing before me, like the rumbling belly of a beast, like the growling of engine boosters.

I sigh and stuff the piece of paper into my pocket. My brain is screaming orders to my body, but my body is refusing to obey – my body has just booked two weeks on the Costa Brava, half-board, and is making its own plans for the evening.

I walk to centre-stage. Some of the audience members are muttering amongst themselves now.

"I did have something written down," I say a little too loudly into the mic, reclaiming the silence. "I had something written down but it wasn't very good – just more of the same really. To be honest,

I got pretty much all of it from the Internet."

Another bout of laughter comes, this time more hearty and genuine.

I cough once again.

"It's been a strange time for me, these past few months," I say. "I suppose I've not really been myself. When Dave asked me to do this, he said something interesting – he said I'm his best mate, so it makes sense that I'm his best man, too. Well, I don't think I've been a very good best mate lately. To be honest, I don't think I've been a very good best mate for a long time."

The crowd begins to rumble with curiosity again.

I breathe deeply and steady myself, taking a psychological run-up to the words.

"My mum died some years ago," I continue. "She was run over by a car. They never found out who did it. I know this might not seem like an appropriate subject for today, but I just wanted to tell you a little bit about what Dave did for me back then. Dave came round to my house every single day. In fact, I got pretty sick of him being there in the end. At the time, I assumed it was because he fancied my sister – which he did, by the way."

The audience laughs, a big laugh like they've been holding their breath for some time.

"He came round every day, and he'd always bring something with him – a toy or something new, just something I wouldn't have seen before. I was never really interested in the things he brought. I was never really interested in anything, I suppose. I didn't talk very much. Dave kind of did the talking for both of us. Looking back on it, I don't suppose I was particularly good company back then. But he kept on coming regardless. He'd stay over a lot of nights, too. He'd just bring his sleeping bag and make himself at home and that was it. Sometimes he'd stay for days on end, until eventually he had to go home so Denise could wash his clothes."

Another knowing bout of laughter comes from the audience.

"Anyway, I don't really know why I'm telling you this. I suppose I just wanted you all to know that he did that."

I take another swig of champagne. The spotlight appears larger now, like I'm making an approach.

"I found something out today," I go on. "I found out that you can't put your life on hold – not for anything. The world doesn't wait around for anyone. If you're not on the train, you just sort of get left at the station. Well, I was at the station for a long time – for a lot of years. I was afraid of things. I can see that now. Afraid of changing jobs, afraid of getting close to anything – afraid of churches, for God's sake. It's no way to live, being afraid like that. You might as well be dead. But once you let go of that fear, you start seeing things in a different light. It's like opening the curtains, you know. And that's how Dave has always been – living without fear, always jumping in at the deep end. Living with the curtains open."

I smile.

"A lot of people would have said it's too soon for Dave and Alison to be getting married today.

God, *I* said that. I thought he was rushing in. But there's nothing wrong with rushing in. You rush in and you see what happens. And if it doesn't work out, you go and do something else. Because life's too short not to. And Alison, wherever you are out there, I know you'll be great for him – I really do. You're funny and honest and good – and you're hot, too. I mean, like black-and-white-movie-star hot. Really, you looked amazing today."

The audience is laughing in shrill disbelief now, some of them clapping their hands. I realise I'm toeing a fine line, but it feels wonderful to be toeing any line at all. It doesn't matter if I fall. There's nothing wrong with falling. It's just a part of being human.

The spotlight seems huge now. It seems to take up most of the room: a great, warm, welcoming light.

"But good luck with it – both of you. I know you'll be happy, and happiness is probably the only thing you need in life after food and water. If you're happy, then you don't need much else."

I take the piece of paper out of my pocket again.

"Now, the good folks at Google inform me that it's my duty to thank a few people here today on Dave's behalf. So first let me thank Alison's parents, Charles and Helen. Today could never have happened without you – or your chequebook. You know, watching the ceremony today, I was struck with the idea of just how funny it is that history seems to repeat itself. It wasn't so many years ago that the Gardeners were sending little

Alison off to bed with a dummy...and here they are again today."

The audience laughs loudly.

"And thanks also to Dave's folks, Clive and Denise. You really have raised a fine son – so a round of applause for Dave's brother, Chris, ladies and gentlemen."

More laughter.

I hesitate.

The light is all I can see now. I'm in its gravitational pull.

"And finally, thanks to the maid of honour, Marla. She's done a great job of looking after Alison today." I pause, the thousand and one things I really want to say flicking through my mind in a nanosecond. "So, thank you, Marla. Now, this just leaves me with one thing left to do. So if you'd all like to raise your glasses, I'll just say drink up and be merry. Live long and prosper. Go forth and multiply."

More laughter.

"To Dave and Allie!" I cheer, raising my glass.

"To Dave and Allie!" the audience booms, reminding me just how many people are out there.

The lights go up and the room bursts into applause. I'm standing there on the stage, blinking at my new surroundings, acclimatising. It feels like I'm seeing everything afresh, like I'm breathing new air and hearing everything more acutely.

It feels like coming back home.

♂

I splash my face in the sink and look at myself in the mirror, enjoying the feeling of water trickling down my cheeks and neck. I smile openly at my reflection. It's strange to see a smile of mine that isn't forced or made up for the cameras. A feeling of warmth radiates inside my belly; a feeling that goes beyond the smoked chicken I ate earlier.

It's over. I've done it. And everyone seemed to like it. On my hurried journey from the stage to the toilet, it was all backslaps and congratulations. *Well done, Eddie. Good job, Eddie. Great speech, Eddie.* Their voices are still ringing in my ears.

As I'm drying my face off with a handful of paper towels, I hear the toilet door open and close. I hear the click of a lock. Lowering the towels from my face, I see Emily from the bar standing with her back pressed against the door, watching me closely.

"Err, this is the gents'," I tell her.

"I know," she says, smiling.

"What are you doing?" I ask.

"That depends," she says, biting her lower lip. "What do you want me to do?"

"Excuse me?"

Emily pushes herself away from the door and comes over to where I'm standing. She hoists herself up into a seated position on the marble-effect surround of the sinks. "I've seen the way you've been looking at me," she says.

She's changed out of her work clothes and into a short, frilly gypsy top, which she has seductively

– and deliberately, no doubt – pushed down at the shoulders. Her impossibly toned midriff is on display, and she's squeezed herself into a pair of achingly tight-fitting jeans.

"Shouldn't you be at the bar?" I ask.

"Just finished my shift," she explains, leaning forward and straightening my tie, which I'm pretty sure didn't requiring any straightening in the first place. "I liked your speech, by the way."

"Thanks."

"All that stuff about living for the moment, not being afraid to take risks. It really struck a chord with me. I mean, sometimes living in a place like this can just be so fucking *boring*, you know?"

She takes a compact mirror from her pocket and opens it, dipping her fingers into the powder inside and sprinkling it across the reverse of the lid.

"Is that *coke*?" I ask.

"Uh-huh. You want some?"

"No, no. I'm good, thanks."

She shrugs. "Suit yourself. But could you hold this for me a sec?"

"Okay."

She places the open case onto my upturned palms and proceeds to roll a ten-pound note into a thin, makeshift funnel. Once satisfied with her handiwork, she bends down and snorts the line off the mirror. Just holding the case whilst she does this gives me a disproportionate sense of criminality, as though I've been forcibly shanghaied into abetting an international drugs syndicate.

I look warily over to the door, hoping it's properly locked.

Emily rises with a quick shake of her head, dabbing at her nose.

"You know, that's probably not very good for you," I say.

"Oh, really. Do you think you know what would be *good* for me, Eddie?" She's holding my gaze, smiling devilishly.

"Err…I'm not sure…wait, is that a sexual reference?"

Emily bursts out into a brazen, intoxicated bout of laughter. "Wow! Way to take the passion out of a room, mister."

It's a toilet. How much passion could there have been in it in the first place?

"So, what do you say?" Emily asks. "Fancy taking a *risk* with me right now?" She bites her lip again, bringing one leg forward and pressing it against my crotch.

"This really isn't what I was talking about," I say, trying unsuccessfully to keep my voice steady.

She reaches out suddenly and grabs me by the lapels, pulling me between her legs. She kisses me hungrily, whimpering. I'm pretty sure I've had dreams that run vaguely along these lines – bloody dirty, great, erotic dreams – only somehow in the realms of unconsciousness it all seemed a little less bewildering.

"Wait!" I say, pulling away from her. "This really isn't what I meant."

She frowns in confusion, and then her expression changes to something more like one of anger. "So, what? You don't want to fuck me now?"

She would have let me fuck her. There's just something so overwhelmingly disappointing about this entire situation.

"No," I say. "I mean, yes. I mean, it'd be great, I'm sure. Hypothetically."

"Hypothetically?" she gasps. "I was practically giving you a footjob, Eddie."

"I know. And it's all very nice, very flattering. It's just…I can't."

Suddenly, inexplicably, Emily crumples into great, heaving sobs. "You don't fancy me," she wails, possibly experiencing the quickest comedown in drugs history.

"No, no," I insist. "I do fancy you. You're very nice. You're lovely." Even with my limited experience of women, I realise I'm opting for a bad selection of adjectives. "I mean, you're really hot. Really. And any bloke would be lucky to…you know. Just not me."

"Why the hell not?" she demands.

"Because…"

And it really only occurs to me for the first time now.

"Because I'm in love with someone else," I say quietly, speaking the words slowly, like a mathematician unravelling the mystery of his life's work. "And I'm pretty sure I've fucked everything up enough already. I don't think having sex with you here in this toilet is going to help anything."

Emily's tears are easing off now. She wipes at her cheeks with her hands. "God, I feel like such a fucking idiot," she sighs.

I walk over to the paper-towel dispenser, returning with a good handful. "Don't," I say, handing them to her. "Please. You've helped me realise something. Look, why don't you stay with us? Enjoy the rest of the party?"

She's nodding and dabbing her eyes with the paper towels. "I got a lot of drinks on my tab tonight," she says, jumping down from the sinks, all of a sudden seeming much happier.

"Good," I say. "Stay and have a good time."

"Okay," she agrees.

Emily heads over to the door and unlocks it. As we walk out into the hallway, she stops, turning back to me. "Thanks for not shagging me, Eddie," she says. "I think it probably was for the best, after all."

I shrug a little uncertainly. "Hey, anytime," I say. Never in my life did I imagine being part of such a conversation.

She leans forward and hugs me tightly, bringing her lips close to my ear. "I think you're a great person," she whispers. "You've got a really nice aura."

"Great, thanks," I say.

"Eddie!" a voice calls. "There you are!"

I look over Emily's shoulder and down the hallway, to where Jean is standing, her head cocked slightly in curiosity. I try to free myself of Emily's clutches, but she's suckered onto me like a coked-up limpet.

"Hey, why don't you go and get that drink?" I suggest.

This seems to do the trick, and she releases me. "Okay," she replies happily, tip-toeing up to kiss me on the cheek before heading off for the bar.

Jean politely nods to Emily as she passes her, and then she makes her way towards me. She's dressed in a knee-length white evening dress, with matching stilettos. I notice how she's tottering a little unsteadily on them, champagne flute in hand.

"I realise that didn't look too good," I say as she approaches

"Who was that?" she asks.

"That's Emily. The speech just got her a bit emotional. Turns out she lost her mum too." At some point in time I'm going to stop lying to this woman. Just not today.

"Oh, I see," Jean says. "Poor dear. Anyway, I've come to see if everything is alright between you and Marla. Don't think I haven't noticed you've not said two words to each other all night. And Marla's being her usual stubborn self about it, of course. Honestly, sometimes I think she's part-mule."

"Robin's side, no doubt."

"Oh, Eddie," she titters, patting me on the forearm.

"No, everything's fine, Jean," I say. "We just had a bit of a falling out. Nothing serious. It'll blow over."

"Well, for goodness' sake, make it up, dear. I'm not sure I can take much more of her like this."

"She's been upset?" I ask.

"Oh, yes – for days now. Just moping around like a cat with a sore tooth. I've no time for such self-pity. It's quite clear to me and to anyone else with an iota of sense how she feels about you. So what's the use in all these dramatics?"

"It is?" I ask.

"Oh, abundantly. Of course, I blame all these silly American television shows. People never used to make such a fuss over things before-"

"Wait, Jean," I interrupt. "What exactly are you saying?"

She takes a large sip of champagne. "Oh my goodness. You men. Of course, I shouldn't be surprised – I practically had to strong-arm Robin into the jeweller's before he would propose to me. Honestly, it's as though you're all born with a pair of blinkers attached. Marla is – how do you say it these days? – *crazy about you*, my dear."

I draw in a large breath and hold it. "What makes you say that?" I ask.

"Well, she hardly went a day without mentioning you, for one. Particularly lately – it's all been Eddie this and Eddie that."

"She *talks* about me?"

Jean frowns, appearing confused. "Why yes, of course she does, dear. Apart from the past couple of days, I suppose. Naturally, I knew something was wrong immediately. Mother's instinct, you might call it. Anyway, what-"

"I'm sorry, Jean," I say, reaching out and taking hold of her by the arms. "Could you excuse me for a moment? I think I need to talk to her."

"Oh, goodness me, please do. You'll be doing us all a good turn. That's why I was coming to find you."

"We'll talk later, okay?" I say. "And thank you, Jean." I lean forward and kiss her forehead, prompting a surprised little *oh* out of her. "Thank you."

I break away from her and hurry down the corridor, spurned on with fresh impetus now.

In the reception room, the party is in full swing. The dinner plates have been cleared from the tables. Many of the guests are standing and intermingling.

I spot Marla talking to Kate and Jess, Robin standing alongside her. Kate is looking classically pretty in a lavender cocktail dress with a cotton cardigan; Jess has opted for a typically eye-catching electric blue number. I notice the conversation doesn't seem quite as congenial as I might have expected. Kate appears thrown, looking from Marla to Robin in silent confusion. Marla has her hand to her mouth, as if in shock or on the precipice of tears.

Marla spots me and quickly excuses herself from the group with a panicked wave of her hand, heading for the French doors on the far side of the room.

I hurry over to Kate. "What's wrong?" I ask.

Kate looks to me, still maintaining that bemused expression. "Eddie," she says.

"What happened?"

"I don't know. We were just talking – about you, actually. I told her about you moving to London and she just seemed to...I don't know."

I sigh and look down to the floor.

"What's going on, Eddie?" Kate asks.

"Never mind," I reply. "I'll explain later."

"I think you should probably go after her, Eddie," Robin suggests.

"You think it'll do any good?" I ask.

"Well, I'm certainly not doing it. I gave up those duties a long time ago. Go on," he says, winking.

I smile and lay a hand on his shoulder. "Thanks, Robin."

"Go, go," he urges.

I leave them and make my way across the room after Marla. Brian spots me and moves to intercept my path. He's standing alongside Jo, one arm around her waist and looking mightily pleased about it.

"Hey, nice speech, Eddie," he says. "Really, I mean it."

"Later, Bri," I say, taking him by the shoulders and gently ushering him aside. "We'll talk later."

I continue on, through the French doors and out on to the expansive veranda. A few tables and chairs have been set out here, but for now it's empty. I look across the veranda and out over the railings, into the garden. No sign of her. Then I hear a quiet sniffling sound, and I follow the noise until I find her, sitting on the wooden steps leading down to the garden.

"So, you thought you'd just piss off to London without so much as a goodbye?" she asks, not turning her head to me.

I sigh and move slowly towards her, sitting down on a higher step, a safe arm's distance away. The sun is low now, the horizon reddening with the promise of another fine day to come. Out in the garden, the trees are turning to silhouettes; the children's play-area lies empty.

"I don't know what I thought," I say. "I rarely do."

I look down to Marla. Her shoulders are still heaving a little, as though she's stifling the last of her tears. She still looks beautiful, though: her exposed back and shoulders, her skin in the half-light. I want to reach down to her. More than anything in the world, I want to do that.

"Nice wedding, eh?" I say.

Marla doesn't reply.

I rest my forearms on my knees. "You know, this is the first wedding I've ever been to. I must be the only person to have almost reached thirty without having been to a single wedding."

Again, Marla doesn't respond, but she turns her face slightly towards me so I know she's listening.

"I suppose it comes from having a small family," I add.

"This is my second one this year," Marla says, a little croakily.

"Lucky you," I say. "I think one every three decades might just about be enough for me. You looked beautiful today, by the way. I thought you did a really good job."

She nods her head. "You too."

"I think that book you gave me actually helped."

"You read it?"

"Every word. You helped, too. I never really got the chance to thank you properly."

"Well, you did okay," she says. "Didn't even

punch anyone in the throat."

I snort a little with laughter. "I wasn't aiming for his throat. I've never really punched anyone before."

"Who'd have guessed?"

"It's much more difficult than they make it look on the telly."

Marla chuckles now, a little begrudgingly.

"Honestly," I go on, "you've got all these guys that have grown up on a diet of *The A-Team* and *The Fall Guy* – they probably don't realise how difficult it is to punch someone in real life. I mean, it's *really* hard."

Marla's laughing harder now, until she forces herself to stop. "No, it's not funny. That was a bad thing you did."

I smile a little. "Yeah, I know. Was he okay?"

"Well, he won't be singing karaoke for a while, let's put it like that. But he's alright – I think you wounded his pride more than anything else."

"How did the rest of the exhibition go?"

"I sold everything," she says, still sniffling a little. "They've asked me back."

"You sold *everything*. That's great."

She turns her head back towards me. "Apart from the one you wanted. If you still want it, of course."

"A Marla Dimitri original? Are you kidding me? I'll be able to flog that for a fortune in a few years' time."

She laughs quietly, and I realise how much I've missed the sound of it.

"Is he still bothering you?" I ask. Of course, *have*

you gone back to him? is my real question.

Marla shakes her head. "No. No, I think perhaps he needed something like that to make him realise it was really over."

I feel like jumping for joy. I feel like tap-dancing across this veranda. But I don't, of course. Instead, I simply move down and couple of steps so I'm sitting close beside her, close enough for our hips to be touching. She turns her face away, perhaps through anger or embarrassment, or both. I raise my hand to her chin to disallow it, turning her face towards me.

"I'm sorry," I say. "Really."

"Yeah, well, so you bloody should be. I mean, what do you think this is, Eddie? Us?"

I shrug. "To be honest, I thought you might have gone back to him."

She sighs and rolls her eyes. "Eddie," she whispers.

I lean forward to kiss her. To my eternal gratitude, she doesn't entirely fight it.

The sound of cheering comes from inside, somebody warbling something into a microphone, and we break the kiss.

"Sounds like they're getting ready for the first dance," I say. "You realise they'll expect us to join in first?"

"God help us," Marla sighs. "It's not salsa, is it?"

I laugh. "We could always hide on the swings," I joke. "It's pretty dark out there now. They'd never find us."

"Good plan," she says suddenly, grabbing me by the hand and hurrying us down the garden.

I'm surprised she's taken my suggestion seriously, but to hell with it. It feels good, hurrying off into the dark like two rebellious children. The light has dropped to such a degree now that it's hard to see where we're treading, but on we blindly go, stumbling over the grass, giggling hand-in-hand.

We arrive at the swings and each take one.

"I haven't done this for years," Marla says happily, kicking her feet off the ground to swing back and forth.

I kick away myself, setting into a gentle rhythm alongside her.

Just as we begin to swing, two figures appear under the light of the veranda: Dave and Alison.

"Stop," I hiss, setting the soles of my shoes down and reaching out sideways to halt Marla's momentum.

I point across to the veranda to alert her.

"Eddie!" Dave yells. "You out here?"

"Marla!" Alison calls.

Marla puts her fingers to her lips. We're snorting childishly, barely able to conceal our glee.

Dave walks across the veranda, stops, and looks out into the garden. He stands there for some time, hands on hips, and I begin to think that perhaps he's spotted us.

"Never mind," I hear him mutter to Alison, before they both turn away and head back inside.

"We're bad, Eddie," Marla whispers. "We're bad people."

"Yep," I agree, pushing the seat of her swing and setting her back in motion.

I start to swing my own legs again. "Bet you I can go higher," I say.

"Eddie," Marla sighs. "How old are you?"

"Am I to take that as an admission of defeat?"

Marla begins to kick her own legs harder. We're both going at a good speed now, swinging into the darkness ahead of us, the air rushing into our ears.

"You realise I'm coming with you, don't you?" she asks, having to raise her voice a little. "To London?"

I look across, noting I've fallen out of sync with her and so slowing my own pace until we're harmonized once again. "You seem to be working under the assumption I want you there," I say.

"You want me there."

"Do I now?"

"Yeah."

The music has started up inside now: the first dance. We're swinging to the rhythm of the song, an old Dean Martin number.

"No shagging any Welshmen," I say. "In fact, no shagging *any* men. I'm going to be quite particular about that, I'm afraid."

Marla shrugs. "Seems fair. No punching anyone. Even if you think I've shagged them. Ask me first."

"I can work with that. No throwing paint over my car."

"Pfft. I'd be doing you a favour. No puking in my bin."

"No reading my texts."

"No not calling me."

"No not calling *me*!"

"Fine."
"Good."
"Agreed."
"Agreed."

♂

I'm standing at the front bar of The Bull when Dave asks me about Marla.

It's two-thirty in the morning, and most of the revellers have trickled back to the guesthouse down the road now, suitably drunk and suitably happy. Now the front barroom is empty but for us and the weary-looking barman.

"I don't know," I say. "We just click on some weird level, I suppose."

The barman approaches us. "Last orders, chaps," he says, yawning. "Been a long shift."

"I was just after a bottle of champagne," Dave explains. "For the room."

The barman nods and makes his way over to the fridge.

Dave reaches across to me, laying his arm across my shoulders. "Been a good day all round, eh?" he says.

"Yeah," I agree.

"Where is she?" he asks.

"She's gone up. I told her I'd be up in a sec."

"Oh, right," Dave says, raising his eyebrows. "Looks like I could've saved money on that extra room."

"Hey, you're married now," I remind him.

"You've got no say over it."

Dave laughs. "Yeah, I'm sorry about that, mate. I was just panicking a bit. I think you'll be good for each other."

"Really?" I ask.

"Abso-fucking-lutely," he says, grinning. "You're both equally as bonkers."

I smile. "And I meant what I said in the speech. Something just changed today. I don't know, I just had my eyes open properly for the first time. You and Allie are going to be great together."

"Didn't she just look the best today?" he asks.

"Yeah, she did."

Dave's grin widens. "My wife," he says, almost in disbelief.

The barman returns with a bottle of champagne.

"Actually, make that two," Dave says. "We've got a double celebration tonight." He winks at me.

The barman nods wearily and heads back to the fridge.

Dave picks up the bottle. "Well, it's been a funny old ride, Ed," he says.

"Yeah, you could say that."

"But all's well that ends well, eh? And that's Shakespeare, motherfucker. He knew his stuff alright."

I nod. "So they say."

The barman returns with a second bottle. I take it and thank him and we make our way from the bar, each grabbing a couple of empty flutes on the way out.

We ascend the first flight of stairs up to the rooms, a little unsteady on our feet.

"Well, this is me," I say, once we're on the first-floor landing.

"I'm up in the bridal suite," Dave says, pointing at the ceiling.

"Yeah, I know."

"Well," he says, chinking his bottle against mine, "happy fornicating, Ed. I'll catch you tomorrow." And with this he goes bounding on up the stairs.

I can't help but smile. I'll miss him in London, that's for sure.

I turn to head down the corridor, catching a glimpse of myself in the mirror on the landing, bow tie hanging loosely around my neck, champagne bottle in hand. It almost seems as though it's not me – or rather, it's the new me, the me that's been lurking away for all these years, the me that was probably there all along if I'd have just reached out and bothered to find it.

I laugh at my own sappiness and head from the landing, walking down the corridor, walking towards Marla.

20. Past & Presents

Buzz rears up on his hind legs, resting his paws against the seat of the bench. I stroke his black-and-white-spotted head, and he drops back down onto all fours, sniffing curiously around my ankles. Being outside is still a novelty for him, and the world is full of wonder. He's getting bigger now, stronger every day. Soon he'll have outgrown Badger, a sure sign that a larger breed must have mated with her.

"We're just going to put everything on hold for a while, Kate," I say into the phone pressed against my ear.

"But you're still coming down?" she asks.

"Yeah, both of us. Marla thinks it'll be good for her painting, being in the city. Just need to get things settled here. I've got a buyer looking at the flat tonight, and Marla's thinking about renting her place out."

"You'll move in together?"

"I guess so," I reply. "It'd be cheaper."

"Wow. And who said romance is dead?"

I laugh. "I just get the feeling money will be kind of tight for a while. Until I get a job, at least."

"Remember what I said about getting you in at my place. It'll be low level at first, but it'll be money."

"And have you for a boss? I get enough of that already, thanks."

"It'd be in a different department," Kate sighs.

"Yeah, well, I'll let you know if I'm starving."

I feel a pair of hands on my face, covering my eyes.

"I better go now, Kate," I say, "Marla's here."

"Hey, how did you know it was me?" Marla whines behind me.

I say goodbye to Kate, hanging up the phone. "Because you're the only douchebag I know," I reply.

Marla draws in a breath of feigned offence and climbs over the bench, sitting sideways on my lap, her arms draped over my shoulders. "Now, come on, we both know that's not true," she says. "All of your friends are douchebags."

I laugh again and kiss her.

"Nobody here yet?" she asks.

"No. Late as usual. You've got paint on you." I brush at the flecks on her cheek.

"Occupational hazard," she delights in saying. "Shall we take a walk over?"

I look across the park to the bandstand, freshly painted, looking like new. "Yeah," I reply.

"Let me walk Buzz."

I hand her the lead and we head off. It's a fine day, the sky deep blue and expansive, with the sun beating down on us. The seasonable weather has brought people out in numbers: sunbathers, footballers, Frisbee players, book readers, ice-cream sellers, OAPs on deckchairs, skinny young men stripped to the waist, displaying their tattoos and pigeon-chests to the girls. Life in all its forms.

"He's getting bigger," Marla observes, watching Buzz scurrying off ahead, intrepid and unafraid.

"You should see what he eats," I say.

We reach the bandstand and walk up to its stage. The paint on its railings appears so glossy and freshly applied I hardly dare lean on them. It pleases me to see it this way. Only a matter of weeks ago it was an old and haggard-looking thing; now, with the arrival of summer, new life has been breathed into it. Like the park itself, it has endured the cold, winter months and emerged stronger and prouder into the light. The trees all around us have fattened themselves out, feasting greedily on the sun. The grass has thickened and blushes a deeper green. And after this have come the birds and the insects, remembering how to sing and how to live again. And after this still, the people, all around us now, shouting and laughing, singing their own kinds of songs. The great fast of the world is over for another year, and everyone will eat a little more gratefully for a time.

Marla picks up Buzz holds him close to her, gently biting him on the neck. Buzz attempts to return the favour, trying to nibble Marla but unable to crane his head far enough back, his mouth agape, a low and playful growl sounding from his throat. She returns him to the ground and unclips his lead, spitting out a few hairs. Buzz goes tottering around the bandstand, head down, sniffing at every square-inch of the ground.

Marla sits up on the railings and I cross over to her, supporting her so she doesn't fall backwards.

"So, you're still sure?" I ask, kissing her. "About London?"

She nods. "I'm sure."

"I seem to recall you saying something about not being able to handle being with *someone like me*."

"Well, I suppose I'll have to get used to it, won't I?"

"I suppose you will," I agree, gently pushing her backwards a little, forcing a joyful squeal out of her.

"Play nicely children," I hear a voice say behind us.

I turn to see Dave and Alison. Both appear to still be in full holiday mode, Dave in a loose, crumpled shirt with shorts and flip-flops, Alison in an airy beach dress. And both are still boasting impressive tans from their fortnight in the Maldives. At their feet is Bruce, another black-and-white terrier puppy, straining at his lead to greet Buzz.

Dave opens his arms out wide. "Happy birthday, Eddie!" he cheers, bounding forward and enveloping me in a giant bear hug.

"Thanks, Dave," I say, my voice muffled against his chest.

He releases me and goes over to kiss Marla on the cheek. I do the same to Alison. Over in the corner, Buzz and Bruce are playfully trying to bite one another on the snout, presumably the canine equivalent of brotherly affection.

"Heads up, you Paddy bastard," Dave says. "I got you something." He tosses a present across to me and jumps up onto the railings alongside Marla, putting his arm over her shoulders. "Well, go on, then," he urges. "Open it."

I tear off the wrapping paper.

"A London guidebook," I say, a little anti-climatically.

"This is a man who gets lost in the vegetable section of Morrisons," Dave says to Marla. "He's gonna need that where you're going – trust me."

"Hey, I got you to the Cotswolds alright, didn't I?" I protest.

"Farmer bloody Giles did, more like. Anyway, the real present's inside."

I open up the cover. Wedged between the pages are four concert tickets: Bruce Springsteen in Hyde Park.

"We're seeing The Boss!" Dave cheers. "All of us!"

"Marla and I are delighted," Alison adds, with more than a little hint of sarcasm. "We wanted West End tickets."

"What, a bunch of fellas prancing around in tights?" Dave asks. "I don't think so. This is the real deal." He jumps down from the railings, walking over to punch me gently on the arm. "Isn't this great, Eddie?"

"Yeah, this is great, guys," I reply. "Thanks a lot."

"It's not for a while yet, so make sure you get a place sorted first," Dave says. "Then we can crash at yours."

Pete comes up to join us on the bandstand, with Atari following behind him, struggling a little with the distance between each step. Atari is smaller than Buzz and Bruce, her spots browner, more like Badger's before she turned grey. Her two brothers make a dash for her, boisterously nuzzling at her ears.

"Not proving too much for you, is she?" I ask Pete, nodding down to Atari. "Because it's not too late to change your mind."

"Are you kidding me?" Pete asks. "Do you realise how many women have spoken to me this morning?"

Dave shrugs. "Chicks dig a guy with a dog. It's all psychology. They see you caring for a dog and suppose you couldn't stink too much at being a dad."

Alison folds her arms, looking at Dave in mock reproach. "Is that so?" she asks.

Dave shrugs again. "Human nature, baby."

"Remind me again why I married you?" she asks, arching her eyebrows.

"Err, I believe it was because I'm awesome," he replies flatly.

"You realise you've signed up for a lifetime of this?" I ask Alison.

"Yeah," she replies. "More fool me."

"Hello, hello," Dave says, nodding over the railings. "Here come the lovebirds."

I look out from the bandstand to see Brian and Jo making their way towards us. Brian's looking conspicuously normal these days. Gone are the faded denims and the greaser hairdo, in have come new jeans and fashionable checked shirts rolled up at the sleeves. Luckily for Brian, check is back in again for the first time since Cobain bit the bullet, so it's a compromise he's prepared to make under the guise of revisiting his grunge years. Scurrying along with them is yet another terrier-cross, smaller and lighter like Atari, but sporting a distinctly unfeminine studded collar. Brian wanted to call his dog 'Black' (after Led Zeppelin's *Black Dog*), but I vetoed this and told him he couldn't have her unless he decided on a more sensible name. After much back and forth over it, he eventually defected to The Rolling Stones and settled on 'Angie'.

The three of them come up to the bandstand to join us, Angie receiving the obligatory mauling treatment from Bruce and Buzz.

"Happy birthday, Ed," Brian says.

"Cheers, Bri."

"Thirty, eh? What a pisser."

"Oh, I don't know," I say. "I've got a feeling my thirties are going to be good."

"Yeah? Me too, actually. Reckon this could be the band's breakthrough year, you know." Brian looks around and seems to realise where he's standing. "Hey, remember when we used to come here and get pissed?" he asks. "We were only about fifteen."

Dave leans over to Alison. "I'd just like to point out I never did that," he lies.

"I suppose today they'd give us an ASBO," Brian says.

"Perhaps somebody should've given you an ASBO, Bri," Dave suggests. "It might have done you some good."

Everyone laughs and Brian looks as though he's about to swear at Dave. Then he seems to remember he's standing next to Jo, so he holds his tongue, instead handing a present across to me.

It's an 'Acre of Moon' kit, unwrapped.

"Means you own a piece of the Moon now," Brian says. "Land deeds, mineral rights – everything."

"That's great, Bri," I say. "Thanks a lot."

"And there's even a map in there," he adds. "In case you ever need to find it."

"Great," I say. "Don't want anyone building on my land, eh?"

"Second best thing to going there yourself, right?"

"Right," I agree.

We all chat idly for a few more minutes until we spot Dad and Barbara making their way towards us. Walking along with them is the fifth and final puppy, again fair-tanned like Badger: Moose.

When they reach the bandstand and try to come up the steps, Moose stops and holds firm, refusing to budge.

"Just like her mum, eh?" I call down to Dad, laughing.

"Aye, son," he agrees. "Just like her mum. Looks like you'll have to come down to us instead."

"You ready then, Ed?" Dave asks.

We're all going off to Mum's grave – a little birthday ritual I've fallen into over the years – followed by a meal at Giacomo's, then on to The Awl for Ted's pub quiz. Most years it feels like a glum and obligatory affair (the grave visit, that is, not Ted's quiz), but this time it feels different, all of us going together, more like a celebration.

I reach over to Marla, slipping a hand into her back pocket. "Ready," I say.

We begin to filter down from the bandstand, two at a time, with our litter of puppies in tow.

"This is fun, right?" Marla asks.

As we set out across the park, the dogs appear to become overwhelmed by the sense of freedom on offer, bounding ahead as far as their leads will allow, hungry for the new world ahead of them.

"Yeah," I agree, reaching over her shoulder and pulling her towards me, "this is fun."

Printed in Great Britain
by Amazon